SINS OF THE YOUNGER SONS

ALSO BY JAN REID

The Improbable Rise of Redneck Rock

Deerinwater (novel)

Vain Glory

Close Calls

The Bullet Meant for Me

Rio Grande

The Hammer: Tom DeLay, with Lou Dubose

Layla and Other Assorted Love Songs

Texas Tornado: Doug Sahm, with Shawn Sahm

Comanche Sundown (novel)

Let the People In: The Life and Times of Ann Richards

SINS
OF THE
YOUNGER
SONS

A NOVEL

JAN REID

TCU Press

FORT WORTH, TEXAS

Library of Congress Cataloging-in-Publication Data

Names: Reid, Jan, author.
Title: Sins of the younger sons : a novel / Jan Reid.
Description: Fort Worth, Texas : TCU Press, [2017]
Identifiers: LCCN 2016045831 (print) | LCCN 2016047167 (ebook) |
    ISBN 9780875654287 (hardcover) | ISBN 9780875656632 (ebook)
Subjects: LCSH: ETA (Organization)--Fiction | Moles (Spies)--Fiction. | Basques—Political
    activity—Fiction. | País Vasco
    (Spain)—History--Autonomy and independence movements--Fiction. | LCGFT:
    Spy fiction. | Romance fiction.
Classification: LCC PS3568.E47655 S56 2017 (print) | LCC PS3568.E47655 (ebook) |
    DDC 813/.54--dc23
LC record available at https://lccn.loc.gov/2016045831

TCU Press
TCU Box 298300
Fort Worth, Texas 76129
817.257.7822
www.prs.tcu.edu
To order books: 1.800.826.8911

Cover and Text Design by Preston Thomas, Cadence Design Studio

FOR

RICK PRATT

DAVID WILKINSON

CHRISTOPHER COOK

For seven years I kept a dead man in my room
By day on the cold floor, and at night enfolded in my arms
I washed him with lemon water one day in every week
One day in every week, and that was a Friday morning

BASQUE SONG

ETA

BASQUE COUNTRY AND LIBERTY

Euskadi ta Askatasuna

Basque Country

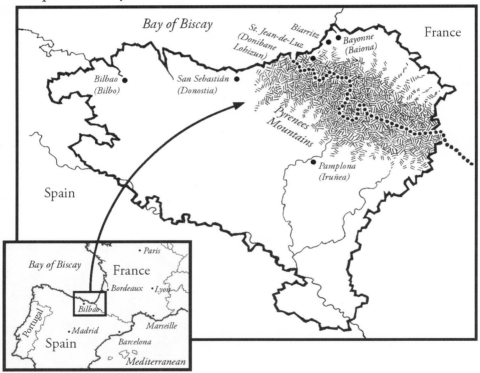

CONTENTS

MANDAZAINA

THE MULETEER

ONE

SEPTEMBER 1993

Black of head and mane, the French bay horse was good-natured and lazy. He tried to get along, and Luke Burgoa's strange Texas saddle no longer bothered him. Luke was leading two pack mules hitched head to tail over a rise. The first mule was big, stout, and black, the other a plump strawberry roan. Luke rode with his hip twisted in the saddle, keeping a gloved hand firm on the lead rope clipped to the black one's halter. He liked the personality of mules but for the same reason didn't trust them.

The trail ride through the western Pyrenees grew out of an old tradition of grazing. In mountainous country you pasture livestock high in the summer, low in the winter. These horses belonged to a co-op of landowners who provided the drovers' labor and entrusted their direction to a man named André Roumanille. For a stiff price the guest riders played at being wranglers, cowboys. André's hired wranglers wore stained shirts, farm hats, and sideburns, looks of day wages and weary patience. They had to try to keep the amateurs from getting hurt. Most of the guests laughed and carried on in French. Between young men and women, looks shot like arrows.

Early that morning, Luke's red mule had nailed a horse with both hooves for nosing too close to its tail. The disorder sent a regal-nosed woman in jodhpurs wailing down the slope on a runaway mare. A wrangler scooped her off the horse before real hurt was added to her fear and indignation, but among hoots of excitement there had been some dark probing stares. It was no way for Luke to get started as an unobtrusive Yankee trader.

He rode bareheaded and wore a chamois cotton shirt, Levis, scuffed elkskin boots, and a pair of tight fitting trim-line chaps that Montana

3

cowboys called chinks. He had blue eyes, a pointed chin, dark curly hair going gray, and a bent nose that was not genetic. His helper on the trail ride didn't look like he wasn't going to be much help. Guido de Marentes was a Spaniard, an Asturian. Luke had found him out of money in a bar in Soumoulou, a French hamlet where Luke came shopping for mules. He started to call him up then looked again, closer. Guido's horse, a big plodding dun, looked like it was bred to hold up under suits of armor. Guido used an odd French saddle with stirrups that cupped his boots like bicycle pedals. All day he had been riding through a murk of hangover. Luke heard a rasp of snoring.

"Guido," Luke said. The boy opened his eyes and batted them with interest. "Take the mules for a while. Just hang on the rope. They're doing fine."

As Guido moved the dun around, the black mule bared his teeth and nipped at the horse's withers. Luke gave the lead rope a punitive snap, then handed it over. "I've got some whiskey," he offered. "Would that help?"

"I don't think so."

Bobby Czyz, a handsome Pole from New Jersey, had broken and rearranged Luke's nose in the 1980 Olympic trials. Luke knocked the future professional world champ on the seat of his trunks in the second round with a straight right behind a feinted left jab. Czyz came back in a fury, but Luke never went down or had to take a standing eight-count. The thought that the referee might have raised Luke's glove haunted him still. Jimmy Carter had vetoed US participation in the Moscow games over the Soviet invasion of Afghanistan, and in a swing of European tourneys arranged as a consolation prize, fourteen US fighters and eight trainers were among the eighty-seven people killed in a Polish Airlines crash outside Warsaw that spring. Bobby Czyz hadn't made the trip to his family's old country because he'd been hurt in a car wreck. After the Olympic trials Don King had called Luke once about turning pro, but the plane crash spooked him right out of that game. Every time Luke got on a plane he knew he was pushing his luck.

Luke was now an agent for a US intelligence agency he called the Outfit. He was working non-official cover, which meant that if anything went wrong on this operation, he had no diplomatic immunity. The Outfit might try to help behind the scenes, but its officials would deny all knowledge of his activities. Police in three countries might charge him with violations of international law. Yet the Outfit thought it best to send him traveling under his own name and using his own passport. For coded messages they had assigned him a cryptonym, LIONHRT. He wondered if that was supposed to mean "lion heart" or "lion *hurt.*"

Gaunt and sobered by the long day's climb, the riders and animals passed through a cool shaded grove, with Luke and his mules bringing up the rear of the column. Out ahead, the beeches parted for a broad slant of open ground. As Luke's horse came into the sun, yellow hummocks of gorse set the terrain aglow. The mountain valleys below were some of the richest country Luke had ever seen.

He prodded the bay up another rise with a stone cross on the summit. He couldn't read the etchings on the cross; moss and lichens had covered them up. Laid around the marker were smaller crosses made from twigs, tinfoil, rubber bands, ice-cream sticks. Luke raised a pair of binoculars and searched the line of riders. They were strung out over a quarter of a mile. The horse moved under him, pawing at rocks to uncover tufts of grass. "Whoa," he said.

He trained the glasses on a man who wore dungarees and a khaki shirt, with sleeves of a sweater tied around his throat. His carriage in the saddle was awkward and anxious. He had little business on a horse in rough country and knew it, but his posture conveyed something more—he was on the lookout for ridges and silhouettes. He had seen Luke and the binoculars. Luke moved the glasses on toward the valleys below. No cause for alarm. *I'm just a sightseer on a hill.*

The man's name was Andoni Peru Madariaga. Nom de guerre "Aitzgorri." He took it from a red rock massif in Cantabria. According to intelligence accumulated by Spanish security agencies and the Outfit, Madariaga was *máximo dirigente,* the leader, of the separatist and terrorist organization ETA. The acronym was pronounced *ehtah,* for Euskadi ta Askatasuna, Basque Country and Freedom in Euskera, the language of the Basques. About forty men were thought to be members of the *zuzendariak,* ETA's executive committee, but Madariaga controlled the weapons and the money. He was wanted in Spain for everything from assassinations to sabotage of a nuclear power plant. He had once studied to be a priest.

A fugitive in Spain and underground refugee in France, Madariaga had joined his wife for the moving of the horses. Maybe the risk he took spoke well of the man. The book on his wife was thinner. For a decade there had been an outstanding Spanish warrant for her arrest, and she also had an alleged ETA alias—"Nafar," Basque for Navarrese. The Spaniards claimed Ysolina Madariaga was a propagandist and tactician in ETA's political office. But the Outfit's file indicated she had been no more than an environmental activist, and the French apparently had no problem with her. She was a legal resident alien in France, a doctoral candidate in history at the Sorbonne. The image in the binoculars piqued Luke's interest more. She turned her head talking to her husband and Luke got a pretty good look at her. Cut to her collar, her hair was a blend of brown and blond, aglow in the sun. Long blue-jeaned legs, and her bottom made a nice fit in that saddle. If he had been writing the Outfit's brief he would have worked more of that into the file.

She rode a small pretty horse, coal black except for two white socks. Like her husband, she used a saddle that looked English except it was bulkier and more padded. On the ground beside her was a collie. The dog padded along and looked up at her; the white skirts of its broad rump sashayed in tempo with hers.

Luke clicked his tongue at the bay and at a slow jog trot angled toward the head of the column. He brought the gelding to a walk as he came upon Madariaga. The woman glanced at Luke and spoke to the dog. It turned about and smelled the new horse, watching not to get stepped on. "How are you, *ezkoziar artzainzakur?*" said Luke, using the Basque name for collies, Scotch sheepdogs.

Luke's use of Basque drew from her a look of suspicion and a glare from Madariaga. The separatist had a cleft chin and a sturdy set of jaws. "We had them when I was a boy," Luke explained. "Does yours have a name?"

Madariaga's wife squinted at the sun and let her horse amble sideways. "His name is Barkilu," she answered. Her eyes were as dark and swimming as a doe's. Cheeks of pearl and smoke. "An obscure play on words. It means 'sweet biscuit' in Basque."

"Nice mare," said Luke. "Is she Arab?"

"Seven-eighths," she replied.

"They're pretty. Faces and necks like movie stars."

"Horses age better than humans," she said with a smile that to him was like the sun coming up. She looked his gelding over. "And yours?"

"Just an average horse. Keeps me off the ground."

She eyed his tack. "And the saddle. Where's it from?"

"The southwest part of the United States."

"Ah. Now I place your Spanish. It's nice."

Luke crossed his hands on the horn and said, "I'm Luken Burgoa."

"*Enchanté*," Madariaga rebuffed him in French.

Neither of them introduced themselves, but she said, "I like your chaps."

"That's an interesting word, chaps," said Luke. "It comes from the scrub oak forests in this country. '*Txapar*' in Basque, '*chaparro*' in Spanish. Where I grew up, low thickets are heavily thorned. Vaqueros started calling the brush '*chaparral*.' To keep the thorns out of their legs they invented cowhide leggings and called them '*chaparreras.*' Shortened in English to '*chaps.*'"

"What did you see up there?" asked Madariaga. "With the binoculars."

"I don't know. I was just admiring the scenery. There's an old stone cross. And handmade smaller crosses."

"They're grave markers of pilgrims," the wife said.

"Pilgrims?" said Luke.

"Yes," she said. "They cross the mountains here and then go west to Galicia and Santiago de Compostela, the alleged tomb of Saint James. In the Middle Ages they died by the thousands in the Pyrenees. They believed a story that disciples hauled the corpse of the saint all the way from Jerusalem to Galicia. People still make the pilgrimage; some believe the myth but most hike just for the scenery and fun of it. They can get lost and die up here, if they get bad weather and are unlucky."

"When the pilgrims first came, Basques despised them," Madariaga said. "They'd rob them of their food. Get on their backs and ride them. Buggered them like sheep."

Luke grinned and moved the bay around them. "But in time the Basques sought the way of the Lord. Seems like twice the heartache and half the pleasure."

The riders pitched camp beside some corrals and a creek. After tying up their horses, Luke and Guido moved fast to unload the mules. "Hyah, quit," said Luke, giving the black's rope a hard yank when he saw the knees buckle. They tossed bedrolls and tote bags clear then lifted the orange panniers off the packsaddle trees. They set them on the ground out of the way fast and then jerked and unbuckled the cinches. "Now," said Luke—and in tandem they removed the packsaddles and pads. The mules went to their knees, then wrenched over on their backs, squirming and digging the dirt like poodles with a find of rotted fish.

Leading her horse to the creek, Madariaga's wife stopped and watched. "Have to let them do it," Luke told her. "They'll wreck the riggings, tear down the barn." The red mule noticed the Arab mare and clambered to his feet.

"An American *mulero*," she said. "In all the Pyrenees, there used to be no more than three or four roads that wagons could cross. All the freight came across on mule trains. You still find maps that mark the trails. Now you don't see so many mules. Are there lots of mules in America?"

"Not any more. We have a labor union called the Teamsters—a reference to mules moving freight. Now even the origin of the word is forgotten. Teamsters drive trucks. If you take away plows and freight, it's so long, mules. Breeding them's not easy. Your mare, for example. Can you see her standing still for a burro?"

"Please. She's already had two foals and didn't like the job."

"Maybe she'd enjoy a little variety. I'd like to see an Arab mule."

Her green eyes were flecked with gold. They hadn't wavered, and Luke wasn't about to break it off. She said, "Some people like saddle mules. Why?"

"They have more stamina. They recover from a hard day faster. And they're very sure-footed. Good in the mountains. They'll take on cliffs that scare horses." He gripped the halter rope under the mule's chin and scraped its nose with his knuckles. The mule moved his face aside. Human caresses interested him far less than the Arab mare. "Mostly I just like the fool things."

Guido handed him the black mule's rope and started unsaddling the horses. Luke let her move the mare ahead and followed with the two mules.

"I'm sorry my husband was rude to you," she said.

"Was he? I'd just say he wasn't being friendly. I'm not his friend."

She cocked her head and considered him. "Your name again?"

"Luken Burgoa. I prefer the English, Luke."

"Your name is Basque."

"Yes. My grandmother says it means 'of the hill.'"

"In America you were raised a Basque?"

8

"Inside the fences of a ranch. To the neighbors I'm just another South Texas Mexican. You still haven't told me your name."

"Ysolina."

"Pleased to meet you," he said. "And your husband's name is Peru? A man who's named for a country?"

Her eyes went cold. "It's a common name. If we were English, I'd call him Peter."

Luke had pushed too hard and fast. He saw the crowd of people and horses beside the stream. "Mine had better wait," he told her. "Maybe we'll talk again."

"About dogs and mules?"

"It's a start."

By dark the crowd had nearly doubled. In folding chairs, riders and campers sat around a large snapping fire. They handed around bottles of wine and on tablecloths laid out dinners that friends had driven in. Three or four of them brought out guitars and sang. Luke had laid out his merchandise on yellow ponchos and hung a Coleman lantern on a tree limb. He framed the exhibit with his saddle and the packsaddle trees. Step right up. We got sixty-foot coils of maguey and braided cotton ropes. Navajo saddle blankets and mohair pads, aren't they nice, trimmed in leather. Fish cord cinches, brass cinch rings, slickers and dusters. We got rinky-dink gadgets—rattlesnake hatbands, a bridle bit with cheek pieces molded like six-shooters, cheap belt buckles from the Fort Worth Fat Stock Show. The wranglers looked right past the junk. Rawhide hobbles, quirts, and chaps were going fast.

Several weeks of staging had improved Luke's French, and Guido was on hand to interpret when the synapses fired blanks. Luke declined to bargain on the chaps—eighteen hundred francs, three hundred dollars. He sold one pair to a slim girl in jeans who had a long comely neck. She had put her hair up under a short-billed cap and wore cowboy boots with tops of peacock blue. They were made for the street, not the saddle, but Luke praised them anyway. During the transaction her eyes kept finding Luke's young helper.

When she rejoined her friend around the fire, Luke said, "What do you think, Guido? Didn't I say there'd be more to this job than wages?"

He shrugged. "She's French."

"Are you prejudiced? Where do you think we are?"

Guido smiled. "They have an attitude, señor. 'Africa,' they say, 'begins at the Pyrenees.' If you happen to be a Spaniard that makes them very hard to predict."

"Just the same, youngster. I saw what I saw. There was enough interest there it almost spilled on me."

Guido yawned. "Tomorrow. Tonight I need some sleep."

Luke repacked carefully. He tested the panniers first by hand, then on a set of scales hung in the tree. If the packs weren't balanced the saddle frames would gall the mules. André Roumanille came up behind him, smoking a pipe. André's sheep ranch was in the old province of Béarn, just east of the French Basque Country. He spoke English well. André claimed to have been a member of the French Resistance during the war. He was thick in the shoulders and thicker of waist, a man at ease with the quality of his daybreaks, if not the number left to him. In granting Luke the tack sales, he demanded 35 percent.

"So, American," he said. "How did we do?"

"We made money," Luke said.

"Excellent," André replied. He offered a flask of brandy.

Luke made a toasting gesture and turned it up with caution. "To the franc," he proposed. "You French put philosophers and composers on your currency. American dollars just have politicians."

"When we are rich, then you will sell me your saddle."

They turned and considered the saddle. "Guido, you're my witness. If I'm killed, I will my saddle to André Roumanille."

Around the fire, as the guitar playing, singing, and storytelling went on, the collie nosed among the tourists, getting his ruff tousled. Seated on the ground, Ysolina leaned back in the crook of her husband's legs and pulled his arms around her. Luke felt a sure bite of envy.

André went on toward the fire of the drovers and Luke walked out from under the trees and admired a fine quarter moon. He flinched at something he didn't recognize, then saw white mist that flattened out through the valley, dimming and losing a village and farmhouse lights. The mist moved quickly, piling and coiling when it came again to trees. It blurred the moon and laced through the foliage, so fine he could barely feel it on his face.

The next morning sunshine gleamed on the high rock cliffs but had not yet reached the horses and riders. The dominant male was a *camarguais,* a grayish-white horse bred in the delta marshes of the Rhone. Two days of pressure from the wranglers had left him in a wild-eyed dither. Adding to his state were defiant younger males the men had driven among his mares. He bit snatches of hair and hide from rumps that didn't move fast enough to suit him. He ran up the slope to an overlook shelf and angled back down with hardly a pause. Ears were laid back, and crowded necks scissored. He patrolled out front, snorting at the men and at his rivals.

Seated on his paint, André Roumanille called the riders close around. He spoke French slowly, with a few murmuring interpreters, one of whom was Guido. "Today we start them down the steepest part. Also the most dangerous. What we do is keep them bunched up and moving. After today it will be easier. The valleys will broaden out. The passes won't be so narrow. Villagers will come drink with us at night. There'll be dances. A grand time."

He gestured toward apprentice wranglers. "If you get tired or uncertain, drop back and ride with the boys. Enjoy the view. They'll bring you down slowly. Consider your horses; watch them closely. You may think yours are up to it. Maybe yes, maybe no. If your horse gets its head down, or starts to shake, get off and get the saddle off. There's no excuse for riding a horse to death."

"And if you do it to us?" someone said.

André had a grin like Burt Lancaster's. "I have your signed release."

Some laughed. Luke pulled the bay's head around and walked him back to Guido and the mules. He swung off, handed the reins to Guido, and again checked the packsaddles and carriage of the panniers. As usual, the mules had blown up, holding their breath, when he strapped the dual cinches across their bellies. He yanked the girths through the rings until he could just slip two fingers between the hide and webbing. The red mule sighed as he did this and raised a rear hoof. The roan wasn't as strong as the black one, but he was more reliable; Luke had rewarded him with less weight and positioned him at the rear. Luke tightened his horse's cinch and climbed back on. "Everything all right?" he asked Guido.

"Try not to worry," the youngster quipped. He raised the lead rope and wrapped it around his neck.

Tied behind Luke's cantle was his rain slicker. In his saddlebags were canteens, hard cheese, canned and dried fruit, and a stash of hydrocodone. Another day would transpire at a bone-jarring trot. He slipped on a pair of soiled leather gloves and as he pulled them tight with his teeth the black Arab appeared beside him. "Good morning," he said to its rider.

Ysolina nodded and responded in kind. Khaki britches were stuffed in her boots. She had taken her blue cotton shirt off and tied it around her midriff, leaving the molded form of a brown leotard. Small breasts, freckled shoulders. "Ysolina," he said. "Is that a Basque name?"

"No, my blood's impure." She said it in a dry way and parried his glance. "I'm named for a grandmother who was Galician."

He examined her saddle, and with it, the contents of her khakis. Built into the pommel were two sturdy outward wings wedged between her thighs. "Where'd you get the saddle?"

"Bought in Italy. It's an Australian stock saddle."

"Oh. Never seen one before. They're all the rage in some parts of my country. Place called Hollywood."

She smiled. "Australian saddles were designed by working vaqueros. Just like your own."

"They must not rope."

"The hardest thing for me," she said, "is when the horses cross a gully or creek. They start down running and braking at once, so you're leaning back; but the second they hit the bottom they lunge and are up and running harder. How do you stay on? With that thing between your legs?"

He stared at the saddle horn and said, "Why, yes. It doesn't always work but I'd sure be lost without it." He rubbed the twenty dollar gold piece set in the horn with his thumb and then caressed its neck and head with his fingers. "You kind of have to stroke it, keep it perked and handy. But when the time comes you just grab hold and hope it never goes away."

She laughed and kicked the Arab into a jog.

Madariaga had put the collie on a leash and was staying behind. Luke raised his hand in passing and drew a frown. Ahead, the camarguais stallion gave a whistling snort and took off, the herd jostling and running after him. Everybody was yelling then, hurrahs from the camp behind them, a long blast of a Jeep horn. The excitement had Luke's bay horse snorting and stamping. Luke tightened the reins for a moment, and then let him go. The camarguais was no racehorse, but he could cover the ground. Close behind him, at a lumbering gallop, was a brown mule. The mule's mane was cropped, and the shaved tail resembled a broom. A donkey stripe ran the length of his spine.

For an hour the drovers ran them hard through cool wind and flowers, scents of tall grass and pine. A towering rock-wall canyon endangered the riders but bottlenecked the herd and slowed it down. The quirts that Luke had sold them were getting thoroughly broken in. When horses ignored the shouts and made a run for higher ridges and trees, the wranglers cut them off, whipping their necks and noses.

Sure and reckless in the saddle, Madariaga's wife worked the Arab hard, too hard, Luke thought. Then she'd stop, wait for the herd to pass, and lope her horse along the other flank. It took nearly an hour to push the horses down the steep ravine with its margins of loose rock and dry pans of streambed that hooves skidded on like glass. The horses were given time to drink, and when the cliffs and afternoon shadows released them, they hit the next stretch of grassland running. Ysolina had buttoned the shirt over her leotard and piled her hair away from her neck. Luke kicked the bay and smooched and got him running. Beyond her were villages, hilltop churches, green farms and linen plains. A storm colored the horizon; there was a fragment of a rainbow. In the canyon they kept hearing a loud propeller-driven plane. She looked at Luke and pointed—the sky sprouted perfect tops of mushrooms.

Parachutes, he realized. French paratroops on maneuver.

She slowed the Arab and let his horse come alongside. She pulled the mare's head in and turned back to him. "There's been an abdication. The new stallion is a mule."

The camarguais had tired and no longer led the herd. Now the brown mule trotted out front. The drovers liked this arrangement at first, for it slowed the herd. When they booted their horses close, the mule threw back its head and attained its crude gallop. As they neared the end of a valley one of the saddle horses went down. The men cooled off the horse and got it back on its feet, but the episode was scary.

André rode back through them, ordering some of the pleasure riders to call it a day. "One more canyon," he called, "and we're done for the day." His shirt was soaked, and the paint looked like it had dropped three hundred pounds. Though the ravine curved out of sight with the river, the slope was gradual, and the mouth was broad. But the mule balked; he wheeled about and ran back toward the other end of the valley. The unsaddled horses dipped their heads and followed. The wranglers got them turned and tried again. Three more times, the brown mule trotted to the canyon entrance, and then as horses whinnied and humans cursed, the mule headed back the way he had come. Wranglers leaned far out of their saddles and lashed at him with their quirts, while horses escaped into the trees. Chaos.

André loped his paint toward him. "Mule man!" he yelled. "What's wrong with that thing?"

The haste of André's arrival upset the bay. "Is this the low end of the summer pasture?" said Luke when he regained control.

"Yes, it is."

"The herd's been loose too long. They're acting like wild horses. Part of the brain remembers last winter; the other thinks they're at the end of their range. And that mule doesn't know anything about your place. As long as he won't go, you've got trouble."

Luke liked the old man and feared for his health. André mopped his face with his hand. "We're almost there."

"Stop them and rest, like you did last night. Make it up tomorrow. Somebody's going to get hurt."

"No," he said. He yanked at the straps of a saddlebag and pulled out an old military .45. He meant to get rid of the headstrong mule. Luke and Ysolina rode beside him. "André, wait," Luke argued. "If you kill the mule, you'll get young stallions spoiling for a fight. Let me try to lead that mule, and the herd will follow."

André put the gun back in the bag. "All right, you catch him."

While Luke stood on the ground, tightening the tired bay's cinch, André shouted the plan to the others. Grinning wranglers surrounded him, offering coils of lariat he had sold them at a most inflated price. He couldn't use them—they were too new and stiff. One tossed him a coil of plaited horsehair rope. It felt too light to throw with any distance and accuracy, and Luke hadn't tried to rope anything in years. Whistles of admiration arose when he shook out a loop and measured the length. "I'm not very good at this," he labored in French. "Two tries. No more."

A cordon of hands showed him the way.

He stopped beside Ysolina and her mare. "You ride better than I do," he said. "Can you help me?"

She considered the state of her horse and nodded. Her face was filthy, but a grin cut through it. "We'll drive him up to where he turns," Luke told her. "You'll be on the right; I'll stop mine. If the mule decides to go on in the canyon, that's good, let him go, but get off to the side; the rest will be coming. He'll probably balk again. If he does, try to keep him from making a wide turn. Bring him back directly at me. Don't let him run you into the rocks. I need him coming at me on my right. I can't make a hard throw. You understand?"

"Let's go."

They picked up the mule and harassed him at an easy lope. He clattered and swerved, shooting glances at them. Luke stopped the bay, tightened the reins, gripped them with his left hand, and measured the loop by the horse's knee. A busy rope would catch the mule's eye and alter his course.

The mule bucked to a halt on the same fringe of grass, but instead of veering left, he lurched back to the right, in front of Ysolina's mare. The surprise and near collision almost threw her. But she drove the mare out of the pivot and crossed behind the mule; the Arab's neck arched and her jaws bulged—a pretty thing to watch. "*Et, et, et,*" Ysolina called. For a second that froze Luke. He had often heard that clucking reproof from his grandmother. Be careful, in Basque.

Ysolina was feeding him a throw if he judged it right. He backed the horse up, preparing an underhand lob. He slipped his right boot out of the stirrup, in case he needed to bail. They were coming awfully fast.

The loop hit the mule's mouth and almost slipped over him, but the head's backward flinch secured it. Then came a humming pop of rope,

15

violent creaks and groans of leather, and pain like fire across Luke's hip. The impact spun the mule around and left him splayfoot and staring. Luke's horse grunted and reared up. Hanging on by the horn, with the saddle jerked off-center, Luke feared the bay was coming over on him, but the gelding got his front hooves down. Luke hauled himself higher and shifted enough weight to stand down in the stirrup and correct the saddle's angle. The mule moved about wide-eyed and snorting. Luke let him do that that but pulled in slack; the mule gave up. "Come on, baby. Let's go home."

The French sons of bitches didn't even cheer.

André and Ysolina rode nearby. "He'll go now, you think?" André called.

"Yeah. Where do I take him?"

"Follow the river. You'll see."

Ysolina yelled at him in Spanish. "That was fun. Are you all right?"

"Yeah," he yelled back, though the rope burn stung, and once you get one it's going to smart for a while. "Good riding back there. Rest that horse. She's a fine one."

The mule stiffened as they neared its range's barricade but trotted on through. Another set of chiseled white cliffs grew up along the river. Luke looked back and saw the horses coming. The cliffs were bearded with ferns and dark stains of seeping water. The end of the ravine was abrupt; the cliffs became a jumble of house-sized rocks. Talking all the way, Luke came into André's system of corrals before he knew it was there.

At the bright opening of the next valley, two rows of wood posts angled inward from the river and the boulders on the right. On the way up, Luke had seen the posts and thought them curious. Now they were connected with single strands of wire. Hung from the wire were fluttering cloth rags and a tinkling assortment of soup cans, lightweight wind chimes, anchovy tins. Luke led the mule inside the catch corral, circling the perimeter at a trot. Lengths of fire hose were filling portable troughs with water siphoned from the creek. Pushed in by shouting wranglers, the tired horses circled after the mule. They were imprisoned, in the dimness of their brains, by anything they couldn't jump.

THREE

Overnight a front had blown in off the Atlantic. The sky at first light was bluish gray and chilly, and bands of cloud enclosed the mountains. A television crew from Toulouse had arrived during the night. The portly cameraman roved the breakfast fires with an interviewer who was part Asian, pretty, and enamored of her long black hair. She touched it often. André granted his interview with the mountains behind him, one boot on a rock.

Luke had tied his animals' halter ropes and rubber feed buckets to the trunk of a fir. He brushed them as they crunched the grain, then saddled the horse and loaded the mules with help from Guido. He was a good hand after all. Luke cursed on finding that the roan's nylon halter was badly worn; the others were buried far down in the panniers. Instead of digging out a new one, he looped a rope around the red mule's throat, snug behind the jaw, then twice around the nose, back again over its ears, and down the jaw. He tied the other end with a bowline to the black's saddle frame. He put on his rain slicker and winced from yesterday's rope burn as he mounted the bay.

Luke led the mules around the rim of the camp and past the Madariagas' campsite. The tent was struck, the Arab mare saddled. The collie paced and fretted. Madariaga jerked a bag free of his tack and slung it over his shoulder. "You're right," Ysolina's voice carried. "You should never have come. I never should have asked you. Never is all we know!"

"Excuse me," Luke interrupted. "I've also got a problem with photographers. But André says they're only going to shoot one day." He looked at the foggy ridges. "I have a compass and maps. Can't we make our way up there? By nightfall they'll be gone."

Madariaga sat down and started taking off his riding boots. "The American wants to lead me through the mountains. The American wants to help." He pulled a pair of hiking boots out of his bag and laced them on with yanks of contempt. He put on a green wool sweater and shoved a poncho, a canteen, some packaged food, and a canvas-holstered pistol inside a shoulder pack. He didn't bother to conceal it.

"I'll see you tonight," he told Ysolina. The cheer in her eyes was gone, replaced by anger and hurt. Madariaga pulled out an apple and took a bite as he started up the slope. He turned and peered at Luke. "Well? Are you coming? Don't be afraid. The trails were cut by mules."

He devoured a quarter-mile incline with bowlegged thrusts, leaning into it, letting his fingers graze the ground. When the terrain leveled he squared his shoulders and extended his stride, scarcely winded. On foot the man was brazenly superior.

Thickening clouds cut off the campsite and horses below. "Who are you, Burgoa?" Madariaga said.

"I grew up on a sheep and goat ranch in the United States. My ancestors are Basques who came over with the Spaniards and wound up in Mexico. I went to a university called Texas Tech. Officer in the American military, undistinguished career. That's about it."

Madariaga shrugged into his poncho. "Lure of the old country? An adventurer on a lark?"

"No, just a simple smuggler. *Gaulan*, night work, right? It's an old and honored profession."

"You're peddling contraband bridles?"

"I want to sell you guns."

Madariaga gave him a more thorough look and plunged into thick beech woods. There was no trail that Luke could read. In winter, the winds up here could reach hurricane force. Trees were snapped off and uprooted whole from the soft rotting earth. Madariaga picked his way without consideration of Luke or his animals. With both hands occupied, Luke could only duck and shoulder at the slap and claw of branches and foliage. The slicker helped, but he was soaked.

Moving strands of mist brightened stands of emerald ferns. The forest echoed the tocks of a woodpecker. Working through a jumble of fallen trees, Madariaga stopped, raised one hand, and dug in his pack with the other. The horse fluttered his mouth, and the pack mules stopped. One of the apparent tree trunks grunted and heaved upward from the soil—a startled boar. They were so close upon it Luke saw the blood streaks in its eyes. The boar faced them, popping its tusks with cracks like pistol shots. The mules backed up with bangs of the packs and honking, rasping wheezes, and his horse started pitching. Luke hit the ground but managed to hang on the mules' lead rope. They dragged him into a tree.

He got to his feet and walked with them, talking them down, tasting blood in his mouth. When he turned, Madariaga held the bay's reins and the gun. "Thanks for catching the horse," Luke said. He bent over, winded, a hand on his knee.

"I don't believe your story," Madariaga said.

"That right? What's your version?"

"You're CIA or one of the other secret polices in your country."

Luke tended his busted lip. "If that's true why would I be using my own passport? You'll find me easy to check out; I used to be an athlete in international competition. The people who helped me find you are your sympathizers, not your enemies."

"What kind of athlete?"

"Boxing. A middleweight fighter."

"You should have kept on doing it, *ukabilikari*. We have guns and suppliers we know and trust. Tell me why I shouldn't kill you."

"Because you've got that good-looking wife back there, and there's a television crew with them today. I can't just disappear. You've got enough problems with the French."

Madariaga turned away and resumed climbing. The rain whirled through the trees in squalls, and then receded back to mist. The horse and mules were still jumpy with fright. They came out of the beeches into a long meadow that blurred into the fog.

Madariaga said, "So, *kontrabandista*. What have you got?"

"AK-47s. Dragunov SVDs—"

"Russian sniper rifles," Madariaga said of Dragunovs.

"Among the best, they say."

"Are you entertained by assassinations?"

"No. I'm just a guy with some goods. My sympathy's for sale."

Madariaga grinned with scorn and struck out again. They arrived on a shelf of jade-green rock. The wind sounded like something large breathing. *"Lainaze,"* he said, with a nod at the cold and foggy wind. Luke looked over the edge and far below saw the tops of very tall trees.

"Give me some prices," Madariaga called.

"Not now," Luke said. He loosened the reins and made himself trust a creature's judgment. The horse and mules stabbed at the rocks and lowered themselves, hooves clacking, with extreme consideration. A bright yellow dome materialized in the gray murk ahead. Some hiker had pitched a tent just above the narrow trail. Madariaga barked a loud summons. In a moment the tent flap parted, and a bearded face peered out. With a red shirtsleeve, the hiker waved them past. As they approached the tent Luke's eyes were on the mules.

"Easy," he crooned. A wind snapped the tent flap loose and it stung the bay's face with a loose nylon rope; the horse snorted and backed up, colliding with the black mule. The black staggered, then gathered its shoulders and lunged, eyes wild, pulling with all his strength. The bowline tied to its saddle frame was no slipknot. The roan mule floundered on his belly, trying to roll to safety but blocked by the saddle and packs. Both hind legs were over the side.

"Jesus," cried Luke, trying to hang on. The horse strained to escape the tent flap, and the saddle was wet.

"What can I do?" yelled Madariaga.

"Come get the reins!"

When Madariaga had them Luke jumped off. He slipped on the rocks and almost went boots first into that cold and foggy wind. He caught himself by yanking the black mule's lead rope. The roan mule groaned and scraped at the stone ledge like a clawing cat. A string of green slobber hung from his mouth. The red mule was hanging dead weight against the lariat and bowline knot. Luke heard the fiberglass packs bang against the rock and saw the mule staring at him in terror.

"Get out of there!" yelled Madariaga. "They'll take you with them!" Luke got a hunting knife out of his saddlebags. He reached the black and threw his left arm around the pannier. As he sawed at the lariat tied to the frame, he kept slipping on the wet rocks. At last the rope broke, and the black bowled him over, getting away. The roan mule honked and screamed until there was a hundred-yard landslide, broken saplings, shattered packs. No need to look.

Luke lay on his back, gasping. The hiker stood at a wary distance. "What happened?" he said in English, a German or Dutch accent.

Luke spoke English for the first time in several days. "You just killed my goddamn mule."

"But there was no other place for the tent— "

"Get away from me."

Madariaga had managed to stop the black mule while holding on the horse's reins, but mules are fond of their kind, and the one left standing was sore upset. Luke hobbled to them and grabbed the mule's rope, then led him to a safer and broader spot. He tied the rope to a tree, lifted off each of the panniers, put them on the ground, then set about cutting the mule's breast strap, breeching, and cinches.

When that was done, he threw it all over the cliff. Madariaga watched him intently. He raised the reins of the horse. "This one, too?"

"Shit, no. I'm not going to hike out of here." He tied the reins to the saddle horn to keep the bay from stepping on them. The disconsolate mule stared at the fog for a long time. Finally he dropped to his knees and rolled on his back, digging the mud with his neck before he stood again. A social creature, he would follow them down. Luke sat cross-legged and shoved the knife blade in the ground.

"How much Basque do you know?" Madariaga said.

"Not much. I pick out words but can't begin to follow it."

"Do you know the expression *ameriketak agin*?"

"Soup or salad?"

"It means to make a fortune."

"Yeah, well, then you get into luck."

"Every village—almost every family—has people over there, on both continents. Your country is much admired. But this is none of your business. Go home, man. You're not wanted here. We don't need you."

"What do I call you, Madariaga? Do you have a title? A rank?"

"Whatever you want. Call me Peru."

"Thank you, I'm honored. You've been on the Spaniards' most-wanted list for two decades. Ever since Franco died, ETA hasn't made sense. Spain's given you regional autonomy, seats in their parliament, and a Basque police force. Last summer the Tour de France started in San Sebastián, a big deal for that city. One of your guys roasted his hand throwing Molotov cocktails in a parking garage. One burned up the truck of a French TV network and another one loaded with bicycles. That's the best you can do? If this is a war of liberation you'd better get busy."

Madariaga walked to the precipice and stared at the dead mule.

"What brings you here, Burgoa? Is it just the money?"

Luke wiped the dirt off the blade with his gloved hand, closed the knife, and put it back in his jeans. "Oh, I think about the lack of it, day and night. But who's to say? For all I know, you're Thomas Jefferson."

LAKIOLARIAK

TRAPPERS

FOUR

DECEMBER 1973

ETA's commandos called themselves *gudariak*, freedom fighters. They did not go after Francisco Franco because they doubted they could get to the Caudillo, and he was dying anyway. So they went after his hatchet man and heir apparent, Admiral Luis Carrero Blanco. The admiral was a titled duke and grandee of Spain. He rarely left Madrid anymore, though he was chief of naval operations. As Franco's health failed, he had redefined his own role as Chief of State for Life and made his friend Carrero Blanco President of the Government. Because of his dark bushy eyebrows they called Carrero Blanco *Mozolo,* the Owl.

They thought they could kill him because of his faith and routine. Carrero Blanco lived in an apartment on a small triangular block across the street from the United States embassy. Every morning except Saturday, at nine o'clock a chauffeured black Dodge would halt beside the curb and carry him to mass. The bodyguard rode in the backseat, too. The Owl wore crumpled suits and had a hat he almost never put on his head. He carried it and fiddled with the brim.

The night before the attempt, the nine commandos granted themselves an indulgence. It was very cold. The stores and streets were full of Christmas decorations, and newsstands trumpeted the just-concluded visit to Madrid of Henry Kissinger, the American secretary of state. The nine went to La Latina quarter and into a back room of a cafe called Los Bilbaínos, which they entered from an alley. They were served a Basque delicacy, baby eels in garlic sauce. Peru Madariaga cut the cross of grace in each of the hard rolls' crusts. They grinned at each other, sipped wine and beer, and poked forks at the tiny eels sizzling in ramkins with oil, garlic, and chilis.

The oldest one was thirty. Peru was the youngest, at eighteen. Basques accounted for nine out of ten arrests in Spain in those days, and Madrid's streets swarmed with undercover cops and informants. The commandos' false documents claimed they were from places like Zaragoza and Toledo, but their papers were belied by their drawls and the way their *ssss* came out *ssst*. One snatch of overheard conversation could have brought down the operation. But their insides felt close to rupture from the tension and anticipation, and they knew it might be their last night of freedom. It might be the last night they lived.

Peru and most of the nine feared two strangers who had been allowed to go in their tunnel. They wore black clothes and gloves and winter caps, carried something heavy in an athletic bag, and spoke Spanish in unusual accents to the lead commandos, Oier and Iñaki. Afterward their leaders snapped at them to ask no questions. Iñaki said only that the men were experts and were providing insurance of the action's success. But who were they? Americans? Peru thought that letting them in the flat had put all their lives in danger.

The commandos had been such rubes when they hit town. Only Oier and Iñaki had ever set foot in Madrid. The ones who'd never left Euskadi were unused to seeing men with mustaches or countryside so feature-less and ugly. Some carried pistols in their coats and boots on arriving, the dumbest thing they could do. The range of consumer goods daz-zled them. One bought twenty pairs of handcuffs from a police supply store near Puerta del Sol because they couldn't be obtained in the Basque Country; his expression crumpled under the leaders' rebuke. Gypsies burglarized their first two apartments. But after a year they jumped on the Metro and zoomed all over the place. They got drunk and laid and told their women nothing. The ETA commandos grew streetwise, cocky.

Peru had grown up in Oñate, a pretty town in the lush Cantabrian cordillera. His father was a Jesuit school principal and devout member of the Catholic laiety. They were *euskaldunak,* speakers of Basque, but they risked speaking it only in their home, for Franco had made uttering their language a penitentiary crime.

Peru's father sneered inside their home that Franco had announced to the nation on New Year's Eve, 1939, that a giant deposit of gold had been discovered in Spain. Some hustler told him that. Another hustler, an Austrian, convinced him he could make gasoline out of water and a secret weed prolific on the peninsula. He claimed Franco kept a mummified right arm of St. Teresa of Avila with him at all times. These rants gave Peru's mother fits of nerves; she feared one of their children would repeat them. Her only pleasure anymore was smoking cigarettes. The regime even controlled that, authorizing only the sale of foul Tabacleras, the oldest tobacco company in the world. The house reeked of them.

Peru always wanted to be outdoors. He excelled in the rough game of rugby. His resentment grew into revolt in annual treks to the Franciscan Sanctuary of Arantzazu the last Sunday night in August. It was six kilometers from the center of Oñate, but a strenuous up-and-down hike was required to reach it. As legend had it, there in 1468 a goatherd came upon the Virgin Mary entangled in a bramble of hawthorns. In astonishment the goatherd cried out, *"Arantzan zu?"* Thou, among the thorns? On beyond the sanctuary lay trails to the red rock massif called Aitzgorri, the name Peru took as his nom de guerre. Hundreds of boys climbed those mountains, singing songs in Euskera and joined by radical priests.

Aberri Eguna, the Basque national holiday, always falls on Easter, which in 1968 was April 14th. In San Sebastián, the cultural capital on the coast that *euskaldunak* call Donostia, parents pushed babies in strollers toward an afternoon of dance, food, and music, while older children played tag out in front of their families. The Spaniards attacked with helicopters and rubber bullets, decking them with winds of the rotors and spraying tear gas while squadrons of mounted police rode horses right over those that fell. Hundreds of people were arrested and tortured for information, for names. The scale of injury and destruction was hardly the same, but in the minds of rebellious young Basques, history had repeated itself. The regime's assault on Aberri Aguna and Easter was an encore of Franco's Nazi masters firebombing of Guernica thirty-one years earlier.

ETA's firebrands had already robbed banks, a reason the regime attacked the Easter celebrants. Weeks later ETA avenged the killing of a member by murdering a Spanish provincial chief of police. The ETA revolt ensued with bank robberies and kidnappings and shootouts with Guardia Civil. Four years later there were five hundred of them, and as they squabbled and split into factions, the Spanish Basque provinces came under martial law. Peru was a student at the Jesuits' Universidad de Deusto in Bilbao when the senior *gudari* Iñaki pulled him aside on campus and told him to pack two small bags—they were going to Madrid. He had been chosen because of his role in the kidnapping of a Pamplona industrialist whose ransom netted ETA fifty million pesetas, about $800,000, and days after that man's release he was on a team that got off with 3,000 kilos of Goma-2 explosives from an industrial munitions dump near San Sebastián.

The nine resided in a basement flat with one toilet and shower stall and enough room for five military-style double-stack bunks. Peru had to take the high bunk over one who called him Altar Boy. A year older than Peru, Deunoro Berroscoberro was big and had a vile temper. The others called him by his alias Jale, big eater, pronounced the way the English say *holly*.

The backgrounds of Peru and Jale could not have been more different. Jale could barely read and write and do arithmetic because his pop told him to quit school at fourteen and bring his muscle to a work gang in a Bilbao brickworks on a riverfront of the Nervión. His pop, the molder, all day slung and packed wet clay into molds lined with sand to keep the clay from sticking. He bossed the crew and yelled at them to work faster, harder, for they were paid by the number of green bricks they produced. Jale wheeled the wet bricks to wooden planks and stacked them to dry for the kilns. They got paid when they produced a thousand bricks, as counted by a company hack.

Jale had grown up knowing a Bilbao cloaked gray and black from the coal smoke of the chimneys, its sky filled with the cranes of shipyards, steel mills ablaze at night. But the riverfront had turned into a ghost town that reeked of shit and urine. Though drowned corpses abounded, the last thing you expected to pull out of the Río Nervión was a fish. Basques in other parts of Euskadi nicknamed the city Botxo, the Hole.

Foreign and mechanized competition had priced the brickworks on the Río Nervión out of existence. With no other jobs available and doles forbidden to Basques, Jale's pop drank himself to death, and the boy with the strength of a man took to the streets. He burgled rich folks' mansions and mugged strangers, and when he had money he got drunk on a mixture of Coca-Cola and rotgut wine. In a former tool room of the deserted brickworks he made a home for himself and a mongrel bulldog he named Piztia, or beast. From his pop's tools Jale scavenged a bow-shaped knife called a cuckle. An old wino on the ruined docks told him that thing in his belt looked like a scimitar of Franco's shock troops, the Moors.

Peru doubted Jale ever had much use for a toothbrush, and he seldom laundered his socks. But they were thrown together and assigned to share the same wobbly bunk because they were the youngest. There was a large park nearby, and on warm days they sometimes divided up in games of soccer. Jale was quicker of feet than he looked like he would be, and one day when he and Peru were sprinting after a ball, Jale tripped him and took him down hard, and then laughed at him.

Peru trotted to the ball, scooped it up, lowered his shoulder, and ran over Jale, rugby style. Jale came up yelling in Basque and wanting to fight, but the others got between them. Later their leaders swore they'd leave them floating dead in the river if they ever lost their cool again like that. That burst of cursing in Basque could have brought them all down. Beside the bunks that night Jale was subdued and apologetic. "Just playing around," he said, lowering his voice. "I mean, look around at these guys here. Me and you, we've got each other's backs. We'd better."

Twenty years later three of the nine commandos at that last supper were dead, one had vanished, and three were in prison, unlikely to ever get out. Only two would still be in ETA's fight: Peru and Jale. Events had joined them at the hip.

Barrio Salamanca in Madrid was an upper-middle-class neighborhood of buildings of up to a dozen stories. The Owl's driver would make a short loop through the maze of one-way streets and come back around beside the embassy and the massive Jesuit church across Calle Serrano. The Owl would walk up the steps with the bodyguard. Inside he'd dip his fingers in the font and cross himself. He then walked down the broad center aisle to his accustomed place in the third pew on the left. The bodyguard sat directly behind him, twelve rows back. The forward pews were reserved for those of the elect, so the *gudariak* couldn't sit near him. Sometimes they would go down for communion to sneak a look. The stone floors and vaulted ceilings were an echo chamber—especially of high-heeled shoes. When the Owl heard a promising pair coming his head would twitch slightly, and when his glance was rewarded, the bushy eyebrows shot up.

One day Peru saw the Owl come down the steps in conversation with two priests, who rode away in an olive-green Fiat with doors that bore the words Army Landed Forces. An old man showed up at the church some days. He approached the Owl with a deferential nod, and they shook hands and stood for a few minutes talking. The old man was a favorite bodyguard, long retired to his pension. They laughed and touched each other's shoulders. They were friends.

Peru's assignment that day of December 20,1973, was to create a diversion. The Barrio Salamanca was mostly a tight cluster of buildings erected right up to the sidewalks and streets, but across the six-lane Paseo de la Castellana was the Plaza de Emilio Castelar, and beyond that were private mansions, grounds, gardens. One day through steel gates Peru had looked across a pond and blinked; in a well-fenced exercise yard he saw a black fighting bull. There were corrals and a barn. A rich man's keepsake, he supposed, or breeding stock. Some days the bull stood and looked out at the traffic serenely. Others, it trotted the fences like a predator trapped in a zoo. The feeders and pen cleaners were wary. They fed it early in the morning. The bull was always there.

The morning dawned slow and gray and colder still. Intermittent light rain fell, and in the Barrio Salamanca there were two brief, localized power failures. The first one enabled Peru to walk up in a plumber's uniform and cap and spring the mansion gates open wide nearest the pen, which was shielded from the house by the barn and a stand of trees. By the time the security system sorted through the loss of electricity and turned on a generator, he had to be finished with what he had to do. He put on gloves, walked around the pond, and with wire-cutters brought down one section of the pen. The bull heard the snipping clicks and walked out of the barn. He watched, flicking ears that were as long as Peru's forearm. The bull snorted once and dug the dirt with a hoof, but it seemed more like a nervous shifting of weight than a threat.

Many blocks away, Jale sat in a stolen Austin 1300 at the corner of Diego Leon and Claudio Coello. He watched plainclothesmen pull up an unmarked jeep beside the US embassy. Marines in dress blues and white gloves came out of the embassy gates and stood around the jeep, talking to the men. They had a direct view of Jale and the Austin 1300. He almost panicked and got the hell out of there. When Jale got a hand signal from a commando he lurched the Austin into traffic with haste that made a traffic cop give him a hard look.

By then Carrero Blanco had emerged from his home and gotten into the back seat of the Dodge. A commando on foot watched the Owl and his bodyguard as they walked up the cathedral steps. Two *gudariak* wearing shirts and caps of an electrician's company watched Jale drive past them in the Austin. One smiled and touched his eyebrow in a signal that the action was a go. Jale double-parked the car, locked it, and walked away. The bogus electricians hustled down into the flat and set the battery to be tripped by the next power failure.

"*Barkazio este natorkizu,*" Peru apologized in Basque to the bull. I come to you asking for forgiveness.

He walked around a section of fence that was still intact, dropped the pliers in a pocket of his jacket, and from the other pulled a Luger Mauser with a silencer. With quiet pops he put three rounds in the bull's shoulder mass, then danced back. Peru was scared, for he had no experience with bulls. It made a slight sound but otherwise reacted only with a rippling shiver of hide. Peru shot him twice more in his chest and neck. The bull was breathing hard and walking now and bleeding, but he didn't seem to attribute any of these bee stings to the man. Peru went to both knees, took careful aim, and shot the animal in the balls.

In no time both of them were out on the grounds, running.

Peru had no idea where the bull might go. If it crashed in the mansion or splashed in a swimming pool that was fine with the commandos. But the bull galloped straight up the cobblestones toward Peru, who jumped around to face it, his heart pounding. The bull gave him a look and surly sling of his horns but ran on past him. Peru threw the pliers and gun in the pond and followed the bull. There were horns honking, a screech of tires, and a smash of glass and metal.

Peru was young and awed enough that he ignored his orders to move on quickly from whatever havoc he created. The bull had halted four lanes of traffic and assaulted a small car. The driver was slumped away from the door, holding his shoulder in pain and wonder. All the honking horns agitated the bull more. On the sidewalk women in furs screamed and took off their shoes to run. The bull gave chase, hooked a newsstand, and flung the wreckage high in the air, newspapers aflutter. Already sirens wailed.

Peru stuffed his plumber's cap and jacket in a trash barrel and walked faster. Municipal police skidded up with their lights flashing, and behind the safety of their cars they took potshots at the bull. The battle of the bull raged over many blocks and a good fifteen minutes. It left a trail of smashed flowerpots and Christmas decorations, splatters of blood on walls and windows, yapping dogs trailing leashes. A man walked out of a café with his nose in the morning stock reports and was gored in the back.

The commandos had stolen three police radios.

One cop said: "A *bull*? What do you mean, a bull?"

"A bull. Come see for yourself."

"H-20, Z-40, we need some backup! Over."

"My god. I see it coming this way. Over."

"Where are you?"

The cop muttered the intersection and added, "I'm backing up."

Some cop laughed.

A few blocks away Carrero Blanco and the bodyguard came out from the mass. The bodyguard opened a rear door for the Owl, who glanced up and down the street and took the other rear seat again. For once he put the hat on his head, and he looked out upon the end of his days. As the car came around behind the big church on Calle Claudio Coello, the two commandos in electricians' uniforms and a spotter watched it approach from the next corner. Jale had left the Austin parked where it would force the Dodge directly over the charge.

When the Dodge drew abreast of the Austin, the spotter on the team scratched his jaw. A commando threw a municipal circuit, and the second power failure tripped the battery and detonator under the street. The commandos' Goma-2 bombs and mines of the strangers went off at the same time. The spotter said the Owl's car popped out of the fire, dust, and smoke like a soup can. The car bounced off the roof of the five-story church, flipped, and disappeared.

Peru was three blocks away. Some part of the blast moved faster than the jolting noise and tremor. It threw him against the hand truck of a cigarette vendor. The force of it was beyond the senses and yet was entirely physical. Peru came to think of it as his sin, his complicity. All remnant of his Christian faith vanished in the instant of those murders.

From an intersection near the church a patrol cop yelled, "There's been a very heavy explosion here. Over."

"We felt it. Where are you, R-22?"

"Claudio Caello at Juan Bravo. We need people here. Now!"

"We're busy here with the business of the bull. The municipal police are trying to kill it with pistols, but they're just making it more aggressive. See if somebody can bring us heavy arms. This way . . ."

"Forget the bull!" another cop shouted. "What caused the explosion? Was it a gas leak?"

"R-22!" interjected a third cop with an air of command. "Can you tell us if the president's car that went by there suffered any damage?"

"Five or six cars have been damaged, from what I can see. Ambulances are as close as they can get. Water's spilling up out of the street. It's like a geyser! Traffic's all balled up. We're going on foot."

"Has anything happened to the president of the government?" the senior cop yelled. "Yes or no? His car must have been in the vicinity. Central Office is trying to locate the president's car to make sure everything is okay."

"The bull just hit a pedestrian."

"Well, get a matador!" yelled another cop still in his car. "Whatever that was, it's blown up the whole street."

"Can *anyone* find out if anything happened to the president's car?" cried the one of senior rank.

"Send over more armed police to move back the crowds," said the one still in his car. "It smells like gas and there's danger of another explosion. This is not good."

"*Go over . . . go over . . .* to the president's house on Hermanos Bécquer and find out if the president's car is in front of the door! That's an order—any of you, whoever's close."

R-22 was now back in his car and breathless: "They're telling us that a car got a direct hit and is on the roof of the church. The firemen are just coming down. Car had three occupants."

A moment later R-22 said, "I have just seen them carry out the president of the government on a stretcher. But he is still alive! *He is alive!* There's a mob of reporters and cameramen—"

"*Don't* give out any information until the superior chief says something."

Again the frantic cop in command: "Colonel Sanchez Alcalde and Colonel Davila both are requesting, concretely, that they be informed with exactness . . . if he is a cadaver, yes or no."

"Cadaver, cadaver."

"No, no, *you* can't say that. The commanding officer must tell us! You must inform him that he must call and speak to the director in order to be able for us to inform His Excellency, the chief of state!"

The rear of the cathedral where the Dodge had crashed was a seriously damaged pile of rocks, and inside, walls were cracked and crosses had fallen from the force of the blast. At the state funeral Carrero Blanco's mourners were enraged that they could only pay their respects to a closed coffin. The undertakers were not miracle makers. Jeers greeted the archbishop of Madrid, a moderate, when he appeared to officiate the Mass. "*Muerte a las comunistas!*"

On Christmas Eve, four *gudariak* in black clothes, white masks, and black hoods met Spanish and foreign reporters across the border near the town of Oloron-Ste.-Marie, just outside the French Basque Country. The journalists had been transported to the site blindfolded, and they returned to Spain the same way. Peru was chosen to help answer their questions. He was rewarded because he was articulate and more educated than most of the nine. The Spaniards never connected the riddled bull with the assassination.

Relations between France and Spain were as ruptured as the water mains that filled up the crater. The day of the funeral *Le Monde* clamored in Paris: "The Spanish Government Stupefied by Perfectly Prepared Assassination. An Act Without Precedence." *Libération*, the French daily founded by Jean-Paul Sartre, piled on: "Proof That Fascism Not Invincible in the Enchained Peninsula."

Already songs were being written, recorded, and broadcast by pirate radio stations throughout the Basque Country. The one that got the most airplay was titled "Whoops He Goes."

FIVE

MAY 1993

Not quite twenty years after the killing of Carrero Blanco, in the old quarter of Quito, Ecuador, Luke Burgoa pared chunks of avocado into a yellow potato soup seasoned with floating parts of cattle hooves. His French companion watched with fascination and disdain. Luke cleaned the blade of his pocketknife with a paper napkin, raised a handful of popcorn from a bowl, and dropped it in his *caldo de patas,* soup of feet. Then proceeded with his spoon.

Pascal Seguines, the Frenchman, wore aviator sunshades and a gadget-laden diver's watch. His chinos were bloused at the ankles military-style, above his air-pump basketball shoes. Sleeves rolled to the elbows, just so. His chin rested in one hand. He said, "Boil it for days, it's still crusted filth."

Luke raised his spoon. "Want some?" he said.

They spoke English at Pascal's insistence. Luke's reading of French was passable, but he couldn't make his lips and tongue negotiate those sounds well at all, and to Pascal the Spanish and Quechua about them was babble. Neither man was conditioned to sit in crowded public places with his back to the door. They hunkered side by side with their knees cramped under the table and gazed at the dingy street. Brown schoolgirls with white socks and blue uniform skirts were the street's only grace. Buses packed like cans of tuna careened around a corner, then passed from view with roars of rusted-out mufflers and billows of soot. A little boy leaped from the door of one bus and landed sure of foot. He roved the sidewalk, peering left, then as another bus passed slowly with its doors open he jumped again and landed on the steps. An agile kid.

Pascal was employed at the French embassy by the country's intelligence agency, Direction Générale de la Sécurité Extérieure, the DGSE.

The only things he really liked about his assignment in Ecuador were the pisco sours. He indulged them most nights and put lines on dollies in their hotel's disco. Many were shopping for a resident visa in America, but they didn't know what to do with a Frenchman. Except take him to bed, maybe. He was a handsome guy.

Pascal said, "So you're going off to meet the great man?" Gil de Ordeñana was an acclaimed Ecuadoran novelist, but French and US interest in him concerned arms control, not his fiction.

"Sure, just to meet him. I doubt anything will come of it."

The bill for the soup and soft drinks was two thousand sucres—a dollar and fifty cents. They left the café and ambled through the quarter, giants at six feet two. "I've been to his *estancia,*" Pascal said.

Luke stopped and cupped his hands to light a cigarette. Below his eyes an Indian woman with a blue shawl and fedora pressed her palms together in front of her throat and implored his riches. "How was it?" he said, walking on.

"It was an embassy thing for some academic bigwigs who were on their way out to the Galápagos. The place is oh so *criollo*. They've got the first eucalyptus trees planted in the country, half a kilometer of them, two rows straight to the door. The foreman rides his Appaloosa through the orchards and asparagus and rose fields. There are rooms where Simón Bolívar and Baron Von Humboldt once rested their weary heads. And, on the outer walls, those little broken beer bottles set up to puncture tainted climbing hands. Monkeys, perhaps."

Luke squinted. "You're right. It's time your French bosses got you out of here."

At the end of the block, the soiled white walls parted and revealed an astonishment of green. Tenement shacks were dug in far up the scarp. The sky in the Andes was always changing. It brushed them now with the softest rain, just as quickly returned to sun. A small man weaved along bent far over, with two cylinders of welding gas on his back. He bore the weight with lengths of rope attached to a rubber strap across his forehead—a harness called a *mecapal*. His ankle buckled and his foot slipped off the curb. Strapped to his load, he staggered and reeled, in danger of going legs up like a capsized turtle. "Whoa, stop," said Luke, jogging a few steps. "Let me help," he said, setting the load aright. The man gasped his thanks and then wearied on with his life and burden.

Luke was not invited to the novelist's *estancia* in the southern highlands. The rendezvous carried him east across the mountains in a decrepit DC-3. Luke had a fear of flying, and also had little use for the roughnecks and tool pushers of the earth's oil patches. One of them poked Luke on the shoulder and asked him if he was an engineer with ARCO. *"Yo soy europeo,"* said Luke, gazing at the cloud. *"No hablo inglés."*

"Well, rooty toot toot."

The plane cleared the mountains and came down hard in light rain outside the town of Coca. Set beside the pipe yard of a tool company founded by Howard Hughes that still bore his name, the terminal was a cinder-block tin-roofed shed attended by a lone, bored soldier. A brown helmet sat on his head like a lampshade, which might have been funny except for the careless swing of an AK-47 propped against his hip.

The airport bus consisted of a covered truck bed with rough wood benches. Coca proved to be a mess of whores and mud. The driver slowed down and honked through a crowd gathered around a drunken street fight. It was ten o'clock in the morning.

Luke got off at the river dock, where an Indian boatman waited as promised. "Domingo," he introduced himself. He wore shorts and a plastic poncho and rubber boots. The *cayuca* was a hollowed-out tree fitted with a Mercury outboard and a roof of thatched cane. Furls of dense fog clung to the river. The Napo's rank among the Amazon's tributaries was well down in the teens, but in the rainy season it was a vast, brown, moving lake. Periodically, the Indian closed the throttle and raised the prop, navigating sand spoils and snags of flood-borne trees. Ospreys and herons passed overhead. Luke made a bed of life jackets, covered himself with his slicker, and went to sleep.

When he woke the Indian had killed the engine and steered close to shore. Domingo pointed at a tall red bank crowned with weedy brakes of immense bamboo. Its foliage swayed and fluttered. Luke eventually saw that an apparent fissure in the earthen bank was alive and moving, too. As the boat glided past, the line on shore peeled off and became an eruption of parrots: hundreds of them, squawking like crows. They had blue heads and shamrock wings.

"What were they doing?" said Luke.

"Comen tierra." Eating dirt.

"Why?"

"Who knows? Strengthens their eggshells? Maybe it tastes good."

Luke thanked him for the show. Domingo nodded and recranked the motor. "How much longer?" Luke asked him.

Another shrug. "*Más agua.*" More water.

Luke fidgeted for a time. Finally he stood and pissed over the side. The urine came out darker than the river. The Indian looked away and dwelled deeper in his poncho.

After two hours on the Napo they put in at another floating dock and negotiated a gangway consisting of a slack rope and a narrow warped board. A red macaw with clipped wings stepped back and forth on the porch of the cabaña, observing with chortles the snooze of a mud-caked pig. The hut contained a desk and chair and some radio equipment. Nobody was around.

Domingo gave him a pair of rubber boots and a knapsack in which to carry the dry ones. "*Ándamos,*" he said, gesturing at an arch and footpath hacked through the jungle. A path had been constructed with staves of hard black wood. They walked hundreds of yards through dripping shade and a pandemonium of whoops, screeches—songs of love and territory. They came to another bank, boarded a dugout canoe, and Domingo paddled them through narrow tea-colored channels. Roots of bromeliads dangled toward the water from tops of two-hundred-foot trees. Spider monkeys leaped and thrashed in the foliage. The Indian's paddle stirred barely a gurgle. Attendant were slow-floating Morpho butterflies which opened up wings that were black on the undersides, then peacock blue. They were big as prayer books.

The sun broke through as they crossed an oxbow lake. On the point of land ahead was a more elaborate set of *palapas*. A stout man with a bald head came out on the porch and watched their approach. This was no lavish *estancia* of one of the country's extolled magical realists: it was the jungle hideout of a man up to no good. He wore khakis and a style of white pleated cotton shirt that Luke associated with Latin American cops. The man's feet were broad and ugly, encased in sandals, but his moustache was neatly trimmed. His greeting and handshake on the dock had an air of condecension. He said, "I'm called Gil de Ordeñana."

"Luken Burgoa. It's an honor to meet you. I've read some of your novels."

"Have you!" Ordeñana said with pleasure. "In Spanish?"

"No, in English," Luke answered. "Sorry."

"Don't apologize," he said. "The best translators are in North America. I try to keep them busy. They're trying to make me rich."

Luke was not crazy about the man's writing, celebrated though it was—his novels contained the usual flatulent tyrants, sharks swimming upside down, and strong women whose changes of mood caused their hair to burst in flames. Luke gave up quickly on the one that was a single paragraph of seven hundred pages. Ordeñana motioned for Luke to precede him. Hung from the first cabaña's doorway was a varnished woodcarving. Luke's gaze fastened on the inscription: *EUSKADI.*

At the top of the steps Domingo parted with a word to the writer, a glance at Luke, and walked on with his paddle on his shoulder. Ordeñana showed Luke to wicker chairs set around a table cut from the trunk of a ceiba tree. Bundles of mail and pages of manuscript were scattered around a laptop computer and a printer. There were two stands of bookshelves, but the walls were otherwise bare except for two large maps. One detailed the countries of South America; the other portrayed the eastern Atlantic's Bay of Biscay and the seven provinces, French and Spanish, of Euskadi, the Basque Country. The dotted border of France and Spain zigzagged across the westernmost Pyrenees and divided the French and Spanish Basques. The seven provinces together had the shape of an English saddle.

Ordeñana poured them glasses of red wine. "We'll have lunch," he said. "I wouldn't bring you this far and starve you. How was your trip?"

"Fascinating. You're way off in here."

Ordeñana watched a pair of white and pale blue swallows skim the lake. "Good for concentration," he said. "Sieges of work."

"And appointments with people who'd never find their way back."

The writer eyed him kindly. "Domingo warns against doing business with you. He thinks you're sick. Your health."

"Tell him I've already exceeded his life expectancy."

The writer chuckled and raised his glass to Luke. "What do you think of my country?" he said.

"I like it," Luke said, looking out on the jungle. "People are nice. Too many of them are poor. And it's strange that you've been officially at war with Peru for half a century." Their conflict over a huge swath of mountains and rain forest had gone unnoticed by nations consumed by world war in Europe, Africa, Asia, and the Pacific.

Ordeñana smiled. "I'm fond of the North American expression, 'oil play.' Six hundred fifty workers account for forty percent of our economic production. They say the oil will last twenty or thirty years; we have to make them count. Schools, highways, hospitals. We have a demagogue for a president now, but our military could get rid of him, if it came to that. The last time Peru attacked us over the Disputed Territory, they were surprised to get their noses bloodied."

"I was in Quito," Luke said of the latest outbreak of violence and its truce. "Most places, people would be outside shooting guns in the air. That night, everybody was hanging on to a helium-filled balloon. Pleasant evening." He got laid that night by a girl who worked for the Interior Ministry and danced up to him on the street, and they were together for a few days. Nice girl, Esmeralda, but she was one of those visa seekers.

"There's hope here," Ordeñana said. "Tourists like us. They come to see the birds and the Galápagos. Go home saying, 'What a nice little country.' But we do have these neighbors." He carried his glass and pointed to a spot on the South American map. "You could cross into Colombia here, but you'd be killed or whisked off for ransom in an instant. Three towns just across the border—Puerto Asis and Peña Colorada and a third one called Wisky." He chuckled at the name.

"I've been to Wisky," Luke said. "You do have to stay alert."

Ordeñana hiked his eyebrows, impressed, and walked back to the table and poured more wine in his glass. "Peru is just as bad. Who rules it? That pipsqueak president or the Maoists who control the mountains and are getting the upper hand in Bolivia? They pay for their outrages with cocaine, and why not? Sell the devil his poison. And, hah, Paraguay! It's a toilet of lawless fanatics, a lot of them Muslims who cut the throats of Mennonites on sight."

Ordeñana's hand shook with enough anger that wine splashed the table. "And into this situation," he went on, "the two most sanctimonious nations on earth have inserted enough armaments to tilt the continent."

Hung to ripen from a hook was a bunch of the choice short bananas called *oritos*. Ordeñana set his glass down and plucked one. "Can you explain this?"

"I can tell you how it happened. I won't try to justify it."

Ordeñana peeled the banana, ate half of it, and flung it out the window. *"Dígame,"* he said.

"Eleven years ago," Luke said, "the Israelis went into Lebanon planning to eliminate Yasser Arafat and the Palestine Liberation Army. Turned out to be a terrific mistake, but you couldn't have convinced the Syrians at the time. The Israelis shot down their air force and routed their army. The Israelis couldn't use what they captured; it was all Soviet-made. So the Israelis traded us their loot for future credits and spare jet parts. We shipped it on to friendly regimes in Latin America. What the Israelis couldn't unload on us, they put directly on the market. Guns go where there's money. And there's plenty of money down here."

"You were a part of this," said Ordeñana.

Luke shook his head. "I speak Spanish. I was in the military."

Ordeñana sat back down and looked hard at Luke. "You're described as a rare man in your trade who might have some conscience."

"I wouldn't exactly call it my trade."

The writer studied Luke and said, "Certain individuals believe the situation I described is averse to their interests. But these individuals have found that legally, diplomatically, nothing will ever be done. Because it seems that some nations are expendable, and the train has already left the station. So with great reluctance, these individuals intervened in the marketplace. The merchandise was impounded in places of safekeeping. These are responsible people. They didn't create this problem. They're trying to solve it the only way they know how. I assure you, they have nothing to do with radical politics or traffic in cocaine."

Oil companies, Luke already knew. Only they would have the financial resources, the transport and storage capability, and the heavy equipment.

"Where would they—you—like these weapons to go?"

"Why, back to Washington and Tel Aviv! Moscow and Damascus! But we're under no illusions. Any shipments will have to cross an ocean. Proof of that will be required." He sighed and said, "The great bulk will arrive in other luckless places. Homelands all. God forgive us." The man was a pompous ass.

"Don Gil, if I may, do you know where your people came from?"

"Of course, province of Guipúzcoa."

"Nation of Euskadi."

"Baietz. Hemen euskaraz mintzatzen da." Yes, Basque is spoken here.

"I hope you haven't been misled. I don't know if I could even make the contacts. ETA's separatists are like most insurgents; the ones doing most of the damage don't know whom they get their orders from. They want to get even for what Franco did to their grandparents. Or they just don't believe they're Spaniards. Or maybe now they're all just criminals."

"Though I differ with some of their methods I believe their cause is just," Ordeñana said stiffly. "Tell me, where are you from?"

"Salt Lick, Texas," Luke said.

He made a face of disdain. "Don't patronize me," he said in Spanish, and then in Basque: "You're only as good as your ancestors."

Luke sang a line of a song. *"Nafarra, oi Nafarra, Euskadi lehena."*

Navarra, oh Navarra, the first Basque Country.

Ordeñana smiled. "Ah. Where in Navarra?"

"Some river valley east of Pamplona. El Río Salazar."

"Yes, yes, lovely. Have you seen it?"

"No. To me that's all just a bunch of stories."

The man snorted. "You say that to a writer?"

Luke sat back in his chair as Ordeñana told him the story of the father of Basque nationalism, Sabino Arana, a God-fearing racist fanatic who founded the Basque nationalist party in 1895 on the Saint's Day of Ignatius of Loyola, who was Basque. Arana designed the flag, composed a national anthem. "In 1902 he tried to send a telegraph to Theodore Roosevelt congratulating the United States for its liberation of Cuba. The telegraph agent took it to the police, and Arana was convicted of treason. He was only imprisoned six months, but the experience broke his health. He died at thirty-eight after writing a play about a woman who commits suicide rather than marry a Spaniard. His widow married a Spanish cop."

Ordeñana smiled. "Go on, laugh. It's funny. And tragic."

He told Luke about José Antonio Aguirre, a *fútbol* star and successful businessman who at thirty-two was elected president of the short-lived autonomous Basque republic in the 1930s. He walked the rubble of Guernica while it was still smoking from the Nazi bombs, and when the Basque military surrendered he fled for his life. After months of hiding, in Berlin of all places, Aguirre met a Panamanian diplomat in Belgium who helped him and his family escape to Sweden and then to Uruguay and Argentina, where people received him as a hero.

Ordeñana pulled a book off the shelf and opened it to a bookmarked page. "Aguirre taught history at your Colombia University and in 1942 published a best-selling book about his adventures. In the English edition he poured out his love for your country and people. 'Everything depends on you, this new man that you are, symbolic fusion of all races and lands, all who can hope are hoping, those who will fall for the Cause, those who suffer for the Cause, and those who trust in the holiest of Causes. You will do it, you who encompass all the old blood in your new heart. And on that day, the Tree of Guernica—a universal symbol—will again give shade to a land of freedom.'"

Ordeñana closed the book with a clap. "Truman and Eisenhower embraced Franco's regime so they could put naval and air bases in Spain. Aguirre had a heart attack in Paris in 1960 and died heart-broken at fifty-six. The last letter in the files of his government-in-exile was a request for eight hundred pairs of children's shoes. Basques have not benefitted very much from association with your country."

Luke was not here to argue with him. "Don Gil, I come from a place in Texas that has a pretty little river called the Pedernales. Lyndon Johnson had a ranch on it and loved that river and pronounced it *purdenales*. He wouldn't have known that Sabino Arana's prison was in a village in Euskadi called Pedernales. On our Gulf of Mexico coast are towns called Aransas Pass and Port Aransas. They got their names from people who honored the shrine to the Virgin at Arantzazu. Let's say there's a market to atone for the crimes of the Americans and Russians and Israelis. When would you have to know?"

Ordeñana studied him then after a moment shrugged. "Life on the equator is ambiguous. On the equator we're governed by nature, and as Darwin discovered, our nature is most unusual. Every day—as it has always been—there is exactly as much daylight as darkness. It makes us indifferent to urgencies of time."

SIX

OCTOBER 1993

On the family ranch in southwest Texas, Luke Burgoa bumped the mare's ribs with his boot and made a smooching sound with his lips. Seldom ridden and hardly ever worked, she snorted with surprise and broke into a ragged trot. It was a warm winter day. Luke wore jeans, an old fatigue shirt, and his elkskin boots. Trying to break the rust off, Luke kicked the horse again, a little harder this time, to get her into a lope; for both their sakes, he let her take it slow.

He had given $800 for her at an auction in Kerrville the year he came home for Pop's funeral. She was a near-white gray. The dapples paled and faded as her winter coat shed and the days warmed up; points of red began to appear, about half an inch apart, on surfaces that caught the straightest sun. So he named her Freckles. She had a nice rhythm to her lope, though today he had to yank her head up. She wanted the bit in her teeth and plunged her neck, trying to seize it. Her mouth was tender, out of practice with the steel.

When Pop died the ranch had passed entire to Luke's brother Simon. Luke was party to the inheritance law of primogeniture—all to the first-born of children born with the same parents, the Basque emphasis on sons. It was short on sentiment but long on continuity. In the minds of Navarrese landholders, broken estates led to empty stomachs, and in Texas their thinking kept the cul-de-sacs and Century 21 signs away. So Pop's will made Luke into the *segundón,* "younger son." Luke could live with his inheritance. He got his share in cash. The problem was the old country's expression. Luke was two years older than Simon, the sheep and goat rancher. But Pop knew his boys well. He knew which son wanted to stay home and run the ranch for the rest of his days.

Luke and his mare burst from shadow to sun in a creek-bottom pasture, scattering sheep and mohair goats. He thumped the horse's ribs a third time and smooched to her again. His focus narrowed on the tossing mane and long wedge of spotted neck; colors blurred, objects blended. They came up through a corridor of trees laden by mustang grape foliage. Wary of holes and branches, he kept her on the trail cut in swaths by pickup tires. The woods were columns of blue shade and dusty gold light. On the pasture's higher shelf, sheep, mohair goats, and short-haired Spanish goats raised their chins and stared. Leaving the road, Luke aimed Freckles in their direction. Throat bells rang. As the horse came among them, sheep bleated and ran into each other, and the goats bounded like gazelles. A large white dog rose from the grass and padded forward with a lion-like stare.

The Great Pyrenees were guard dogs bred against predations of wolves and eagles in the old country. As soon as new pups were weaned, Simon penned them with sheep or goats, whose protection needs differed. He neutered them and built little feed corrals for them all over the ranch. They lived with their adopted stock, identities happily confused.

Great Pyrenees had few battles with coyotes, which they outweighed by eighty pounds or so, but this one was irked and alarmed by the running horse and its rider. The dog wheeled on its hind legs and galloped barking alongside. Fleeing goats stayed close together. Luke grinned and drove the mare through them like the prow of a boat. Freckles missed a step and staggered. Luke put his weight down on the right stirrup and viewed the sundown through the neighbor's trees. Some days, he envied his brother. The mare plunged her neck to the left and made another grab at the bit. Caught leaning the wrong way, Luke left the saddle. He almost admired his headlong flight. He landed on his shoulder. That was easy, a thought began to form, but then his cheekbone hit the ground. It had no give at all.

When he sat up, he was surprised to find the reins in reach. The side of his face felt hot as flame. Then another skull entered the picture. A low grumbling came from the dog's throat. Luke extended his arm and offered the dog the back of his hand. It ignored the gesture. Behind the broad lowered head, the long tail swung back and forth. Goats began to gather. One perched on a rock the size of a medicine ball. Another took a seat, licked its genitals, and began to scratch its ear with a hind foot.

Goats, Luke thought, must be the only hooved animals that do that.

"They think they're dogs," he said. The Great Pyrenees ceased growling and sank into the posture of a sphinx. After a while it yawned. It shifted its weight to foreleg and ribs. The eyes narrowed. It began to pant.

"Vaquero," someone called. "Are you hurt?"

After this came laughter.

He picked them out in the darkening line of trees. Two mestizo fence-builders started up the slope toward him, followed by a boy with stony tribal features. He walked with his wrists draped across a wire-stretching tool called a come-along that he braced behind his neck and shoulders. He wore an odd brimless hat that was dyed indigo blue. He swung his shoulders and turned his head, watching a buzzard make a skidding low pass. The boy's hat was a coonskin cap.

He raised an arm and waved them off. "Thanks for your concern," he answered. "Now go back to work."

"We've done all we can today," said the oldest one.

"Then go get something to eat."

The older one said, "Tonight we're going to town. There's a dance."

"How will you get there?"

The older one shrugged. "God will direct us."

"Where are you from?" Luke asked.

"We came from Guanajuato," the elder replied.

Christ, that was seven hundred miles. "Where did you cross?"

"Piedras Negras," said the elder. "And then seven more days through a midget's forest of thorns. Then there was no work. I have done it five times in my life. The boy is a boy. He may never do it again. Your brother met us under a bridge in San Antonio. He brought us here."

"Your feet owe him favors."

"Pay us more," said the second one. "We'll be grateful."

"Forgive the mouth of my friend," said the elder. "He thinks he's a joker."

Luke got to his feet and remounted the horse. "You can trust my brother," he said, "but lots of folks in this country arrange it with the Immigration so they don't have to pay you what you're owed. They work you until what they want done is finished. Then they have you arrested. And people even meaner than that are out to get you."

"The average number of sons of bitches," the older one reflected, "is just about the same wherever you go."

"The boy," Luke said. "Does he ever talk?"

"To us, of course. To others, with great reluctance." The Mexican shrugged again. "A poor Indian."

"Tell him to get rid of that hat. They're not worn here. He's going to get you caught."

After cleaning up, Luke borrowed Simon's old pasture pickup and set out for San Antonio. His return from South America was new enough that the truck's hood seemed broad as a ship's deck, and Interstate 10 and its median and rights of way were like an ocean passage. Five-hundred-foot solid rock hill, they just dynamite right through it. The cloudless sky was enormous. Luke puffed on a joint and threw himself into a race with gleaming Peterbilts.

As he neared the city the savannah began its turn into suburbs with run-down shopping centers and theme parks crammed into the jaws of a mined-out rock quarry. He stopped at a Purina store and bought some sacks of feed for the Great Pyrenees and twenty stiff new coils of lariat, all they had on hand. With the sun going down Luke meandered around the city—mansions shaded by palms and live oaks bearded with Spanish moss, barrios with florid murals and aqua walls. Ever since Mexico's revolution, San Antonio had been full of rapscallions and gun merchants out for one last rousing mission, watering their lawns with sloshes of gin and tonic. Luke wondered if he was one of them.

Dusk had gathered when he parked and walked past the Alamo, where street preachers caterwauled. He walked along Commerce Street to the Esquire. The place consisted of a hundred-foot-long bar with a pressed-copper ceiling, deep tall-backed booths trolled by a trio of mariachis, and a small deck overlooking the Riverwalk. Luke chased shots of Casadores tequila with Sol beer and watched Mexican tailors and construction laborers who drank like the beer was medicine and wondered how they had lost their way. Secretaries with bronze eye shadow loosened buttons of pantsuits and preened about with oleander blooms behind their ears. Homesickness wafted like a scent.

From his jeans pocket he pulled out a velvet packet filled with rocks that he rolled between fingers and thumb like rosary beads. They were emeralds from Colombia. One of the Germans, a grandson of escaped Nazis, had offered the gifts to the pilot, copilot, and Luke for a delivery of unidentified crated cargo to a coastal strip near Asunción. The German was dressed like a prosperous rancher—pressed khakis and shined boots, a fresh shave. Luke started not to accept it, but he did.

Down there it was not entirely clear whether Luke worked for the Outfit or the marines. He had to turn over his passport and dog tags when he arrived. Luke was going to mind his own business and do his job. The men called him Captain of the Load.

"Load of what?" the routine went.

"Whatever the load is. Lock and load."

Luke got to be the cargo chief because he knew about packing things, keeping them balanced. The aircraft were Cessna 206s. One time he had to load some crates that had Israeli shipping instructions stenciled over British army markings from World War II. Unable to make them fit, he got the men to help break open the crates and load the contents however they could. Packed in grease, there were over a hundred STEN guns, British nine-millimeter submachine guns that the Zionists hijacked in their guerilla war to take over Palestine.

This off-the-books mission of the Americans was intended to protect expat oil workers and a pipeline in Caño Limón, near the Venezuelan border. The commanding officer was Jimbo Hopson. As a Marine colonel he had been deep in the soup of Vietnam and Cambodia, but it was up or out when that war ended, so he negotiated a lateral step to the Outfit. Luke and Jimbo got on well. They had similar tastes in music, and many nights they enjoyed Jimbo's Bose stereo and cache of Black Bush and Jack Daniels. Jimbo was a maniac, but the men didn't jack with him, and after a day or two, neither did the brass and spymasters sent down on occasion to shape them up. Out in the bush were leftist guerillas, right-wing militias, and army troops that the campesinos called *telefonos,* because they kept pressing them to inform on people by handing out mobile phones like candy. Luke had been involved in two nighttime firefights, and even when they found three bodies they were unsure which warring faction the shooters belonged to.

Some days in the air were a pleasure. To the east was a snow-capped cordillera and to the west were plains and vast ranches where the grass looked like ocean waves in the wind. They might spend a day just following a river, taking photographs, for the images could spot clues known only to the geologists and help the oil crews define the boundaries of the warlords and coca smugglers. Still, he could also see what the oil production was doing to the country. There were pools of sludge and drilling mud everywhere you looked, and in the dry season, to tamp down the dust, the *polvo,* the companies sent trucks out spraying the roads with crude. When the rains came again the runoff could go nowhere but creeks and gullies emptying into a river or waterfall a mile away.

Though it was dangerous for anyone to walk the bush at night, adventurous girls from a lost little town called Santa María filtered over the ridge in the evenings, dressed for the money they could scare up in a wan cantina built for the oilfield hands and their black-ops protectors. Few of the prostitutes were anything but sad, but Yamile caught Luke's eye the first time he saw her. She was one of those young women who liked to fling her hair when she laughed. She saw Luke watching, swiveled off the barstool, and sauntered across the floor, wearing a short thin dress and flip-flops. Down the back of her right leg was a tattoo of a blooming vine of morning glories.

That night and in the months that followed she became the Captain's Girl. He teased her about the tattoo, said she must think she'd never grow old. She kissed him and said, "Why would I think I will?" He occupied a compact iron billet with a bed and a toilet squeezed against a shower stall. Yamile brought leaves of coca and cornhusks in which to smoke them. The dopers among the men said it didn't work, consumed in that fashion, but she proved that was nonsense when the leaves were fresh. Shamans of the Indians, she said, called it "the bridge of smoke," pathway to the world of spirits. There were jaguars, *tigres,* in the bush, and that's what he called her, Tigresa. She was such a wisp of a thing. Luke never showed her the purple packet of emeralds, but he hoped that when the day came and he had to let her go, the Nazi booty and blood money might set her up in Cartagena, that beautiful city by the sea she longed for.

The Cessnas flew low at lumbering speed. Potshots snapped through the hull and left punctures that looked like flowers. The pilots patched them up and painted them, comparing their bouquets. In the air Luke armed himself with an M-16, a Glock semi-automatic, and a hunting knife. He wore a helmet, a shrapnel vest, and athletic pads on both elbows and both knees, for all seats had been removed for cargo space, and any bad weather sent them all sprawling.

He had thought it was just turbulence at first. The machine gun rounds came so fast he didn't register them for what they were. Then he thought Parker, the pilot, was taking evasive action. But the right wing kept dipping down and he wasn't pulling the nose up. Luke crawled to the cockpit. Parker was draped over the yoke and his boot was jammed on the rudder. Friedman, the copilot, was slumped against him like a little boy napping with a pal at school recess. They were both dead or soon to be. Luke knew just enough to get them pushed apart, kill the engines, and haul back on the yoke. He got them a little slow-down of the plunge but not much. As they came onto the tops of the trees he saw a Harpy eagle sitting up on the tallest one. The eagle had lifted one foot with something to eat, like someone eating a sandwich, and turned its wildly feathered white head to watch the quiet death plane sail past.

The first touch of the trees felt very soft. The rest of the way wasn't. The plane battered and broke up. Luke was flung up and down and somehow thrown free. He was the only one who survived.

He remembered little after that, though he hiked for a couple of days and, one officer told him, he shot and killed a *telefono* who came at him with a knife. Another officer said he shot an oilfield worker who was just trying to help him. His superiors tended to believe the second story, even when he showed them the knife scar in his hand. At Walter Reed the morphine dreams were paranoid, terrifying. Ever since, his urine had run bloody off and on in coffee-colored spurts. The docs shoved up inside his bladder and kidney with a periscope-flashlight sort of rig, reached no conclusions, and told him he ought to keep an eye on that.

Well, yeah, he supposed he would.

Then came the audience with the brigadier general. He ignored Luke's salute and growled, "At ease." The general left him standing while he leafed through pages of military and medical records.

"Have a seat, Marine," he finally said. On his desk was a little trophy with a bronzed golf ball and notation of a hole-in-one in Tucson. He eyed Luke with a grim chuckle. "One thing I don't mind here. Panama City, trying to smooth over the Noriega invasion, 'Operation Just Cause,' they put you in the ring for a four-round exhibition against Roberto Duran."

"Yes, sir."

"How was he?"

"Forty years old, overweight, but he had ninety-five wins and was doing the senior circuit. Nostalgia matches with Sugar Ray Leonard, Macho Camacho, Vinny Pazienza. Real fights, though. We didn't wear sparring helmets, and he was doing it for the honor of his violated nation, he made that clear. He was one scary dude."

"You were told to take a more or less gentle beating, try to make the third, and please the crowd before you lay down."

"Yes, sir."

"You knocked him out in the second because he head-butted you, and then put your foot on his chest."

Luke touched the scar under his chin and smiled. "You could tell he was hungover that night. I think I broke my hand."

"Started a riot, but that was one time you made the Corps proud."

"Thank you, sir."

The scowl returned. "But the rest of this. How far did you have to hike with those wounds?"

"I don't know, sir. I didn't have a tape measure."

The general barked, "Do you know how much you've cost the Veterans' Administration?"

"Just doing my job, sir."

The general breathed out loudly. "These good people have stabilized your health, which they weren't obliged to do. You don't qualify for a disability pension, and if you ever so much as *inquire* about one, some great big dogs are going to take chunks out of your ass. It would not be pretty. It would not make your momma and daddy proud."

"Don't pay it no mind, sir. Them folks dead."

For a second Luke thought the fellow was going to come across the desk at him. The general moved his golfing trophy aside and pushed the file across the desk. "Look at these and sign or initial where the lines are marked."

Under the cover sheet Luke found an honorable discharge and a resignation of his officer's commission. As far as the United States military was concerned, for more than two years Luke had just ceased to exist. He resigned his commission, drew his discharge papers and last pay from the file, and slid the rest of it back across the desk. "You're dismissed," the general said.

Luke stood, clasped his hands as if grasping a golf club, and swung them up, ending with his right hand in a roundabout salute. "Aye aye, sir. Semper Fi."

In the Esquire's booth he fingered the rocks through the purple velvet. Oh Yamile, *mi tigresa*. He thought he had spoken only to the barmaid, but now he noticed people were staring at him. Had he been saying things out loud? He put the packet of emeralds back in his pocket, thinking he'd better head back to the ranch.

"Yeah, folks," he said, "for a while there I was an ill-tempered son of a bitch."

Remembered in the family, with ambiguous inflection, as the adventurer, Luke's grandfather had died in the Spanish Civil War. They never knew what happened to Aingeru Burgoa, even on which side he fought, or if he fought at all. One day his beret arrived in a package with a note in Spanish saying only that he died in the siege of Bilbao.

Luke's *amona,* his grandmother, had lived alone for sixty years in a ranch house built by a man she called a Scotch-Irish pirate. She admired the hardwood floors and oiled them, while she still could, until they were black. Until her vision became so poor she enjoyed the rooftop belvedere. She liked to sit out on pleasant evenings with her caged canaries. Within the fences she hardly ever said a word of English. And often she would say, "Today I don't feel like speaking Spanish."

"All right, Amona, don't," her grandsons would reply. And off she'd go in Euskera, her litany of *tx*'s pronounced *ch,* trilling her *rr*'s with the solemnity of a graveyard drummer. She had tried her best to school her grandsons in the language, and with Luke's brother Simon she partially succeeded. Amona always told them Euskera was spoken in the Garden of Eden.

Simon and his wife Lydia and their daughter Andrea lived in what had been the bunkhouse, when the ranch had full-time hands. Meanwhile a room on the second floor of the big house was always reserved for Luke, a source of friction between the two brothers. Surrounded by duffel bags, piles of clothes, his stock saddle, two pack saddles, the new coils of lariat, stacks of mohair blankets, all manner of tack, Luke stood on the bed in search of a plan.

Out in the hall, he heard the slow stamp of her cane. He was awed by this woman who was in her nineties but could still climb a flight of stairs and remember where she had set out to go. He stepped off the bed to greet her. She wore a flannel nightgown and a black cardigan that hung to her knees. Age had taken the handsome wedge of face in her pictures and honed it to an axe. She weighed about ninety pounds. Her cataracts looked like wool.

"What are you doing?" she scolded him. "Testing our bedsprings? Are you a little boy? Luken, I can hear."

"I'm working, Amona," he said in English. "Pricing inventory. Be careful. The room's a wreck."

"You taunt me with that language," she grumbled. "Knowing it sounds to my ears like the boots of marching Germans. Your Christian name is Luken. A physician and saint who wrote Acts and the loveliest Gospel. What is this 'Luke'?"

"It's the world we live in now, Amona," he said softly.

"Your world. Mine is *baserri*. Our home."

She poked the stack of saddle pads and said, "Sit down, Luken. I want to talk about your father's decision."

"There's nothing to say," he answered. "I love this place but never wanted to run it. Besides, that was years ago."

"I couldn't blame you," she said. "This is marginal land, much abused. Hot and cold, but seldom enough rain. Much like Álava, in the old country." Luke smiled. She had never set foot in Álava or any other province of Spain.

"All my life," she went on, "I have been marooned. Your grandfather didn't have to go over there and get himself killed. Even then, in my resentment and grief, there were your father and you and your brother and the great-grandbaby who have crawled on my floors. *Gure etxekoak*, our family. But all my life I have been a refugee."

Here we go. He couldn't count the times she had told him his family's story. One of his Burgoa ancestors immigrated to Cuba as *segundón*, a younger son, and worked as a lowly cutter of sugar cane. Still he was a noble with full rights under Spanish law. Those Burgoas achieved a sisal and sugar plantation in Cuba. Still they never thought of themselves as noble Spaniards. They were Basques!

Then came a premature revolt against the Spaniards, who found out the Burgoas had been giving money to the Cuban rebels. Warned by Basque soldiers in the Spanish army, they left the island in the dark of night. They lost everything and started over in the north of Mexico and achieved a second fortune. First in cattle, then tanneries.

Amona's Larrañaga family had immigrated in the 1830s to Argentina. The men first found work in the meat-salting plants and then became vaqueros. But her grandfather saw that the future was in *frozen* meat. And in holds of ships, he figured out how to do it. "My father," she was saying now, "died believing his move to the north of Mexico was a terrible mistake, but how could he have known? Poor Papa. A *segundón* with money."

That's right. Blood and money. An ancestry of titled Spaniards born in the New World, when the claim was to their advantage. Thinking of that boy with the fence builders who wore the blue coonskin cap, Luke found it hard to believe that no Indians had ever married into those families.

"When I married your grandfather," Amona went on, "the Burgoas had built a cattle ranch that was sixty kilometers across. We were on the side of the revolutionary Madero. But assassins got Madero, and the revolution fell into the hands of hooligans." She quivered with outrage. "Pancho Villa. He was a rapist and killer and a bully with a smirk. The day he rode into our compound, he rounded up my family's thoroughbreds and shot each of them, one by one, before our eyes."

Luke spun the rowel of a spur. "So what do you pine for, Amona? The state of Coahuila? Nothing like that's happened to you in this country."

"No. But here we're isolated. We're reduced. We're vagabonds, and for us, language is everything. Language is memory. Here I've heard the death of our tongue in my own family. This country has swallowed and digested us, Luken. We're Jonah in the stomach of a whale."

He thumped the rowel again and listened to it ring.

"It happened for good in your generation," she said. "That woman your father married was filled with spite. She strangled the language in my loved ones' throats. If I had another lifetime, I couldn't forgive her."

He said sharply, "That's not how it happened, Amona. Pop didn't sing us any lullabies in Euskera. He ran from this ranch until I was twelve years old. How was I going to learn it? Mama's language was English. Every night, she'd come over here to dinner and listen to you and him shut her out. She didn't understand a word of it. No wonder she left us."

The old woman's hands clenched the cane. "You're the favored son, Luken. You always were. Your father did you a favor. There's a belief among our people. 'The minute you buy land somewhere else, you'll never see the old country again.'"

"It's not just language, Amona. Let me tell you a story. The marines commissioned me and trained me in intelligence. But I wasn't cut out for it. I was insubordinate in ways that drove them crazy."

"You were a mercenary," she explained. "*Sarigudari.*"

He gave her an amused look. "When I wasn't on some mission, I was constantly in training. In the dead of winter one year they sent me to a government reserve in the Sierra Nevadas. After a month we were taken way back in the forest and turned loose. They gave us a map, a compass, and water, but made sure we had no food. We had to grub whatever roots we could. We weren't armed to kill anything we could eat. We had four days to reach a base camp in the desert. If we didn't, or they caught us, we had to stay another two weeks.

"The officer in charge said, 'Stay away from the sheepherders. This land is leased for grazing by people they work for. They're Basques who don't speak English. They stay out here until they're crazy. People say they're *sheeped*. They shoot coyotes and eagles, and they'd just as soon shoot you.'"

Amona smiled and perked up.

"It took us two days to get down the mountain. When we came out of the trees, it was solid sagebrush and sheep. Wagons covered with tarps were parked in a dry riverbed. We could see the herders; they were sitting around a big fire. It was getting close to dark. I walked down the hill with my hands in the air, yelling in Spanish. '*Paisanos! No hablo vascuence. Pero PERO! Yo soy Vasco!*'"

She laughed and said, "Yours could be a voice from purgatory. They might have been French Basques. They could have shot you just for the Spanish."

"That's right, but they were Navarrese who believed in apparitions. They spoke Spanish as well as I do. Coming down the slope I ranted about the Spaniards in Cuba. I cursed the bones of Pancho Villa. I longed for the beauty of the Río Salazar. By the time I reached the riverbed, they were cheering. I told them about my *compañeros*; they waved us on down. They roasted a lamb for us, Amona, and passed around wineskins. We all got drunk, saying all kinds of things in three languages, and we taught them to sing a few lines of 'God Bless America.'"

"Stop. You have no shame."

"No, let me finish. A young herder tried to teach us 'We Are Basque Soldiers.'" Luke opened a window and sang the line that he remembered. *"Eusko gudariak gara Euskadi azkatzeko."* We are warriors freeing the Basque Country. Luke's outburst set off loud barking by Simon's dogs.

"We passed the wine and sang his song in honor and memory of the last prisoner executed by Franco. He was a boy from the south of Spain who *chose* to be a Basque, Amona. A military court sentenced him to the firing squad for killing two Guardia Civil. Franco was on his deathbed. The guy refused a blindfold. He raised a fist and started singing that song. 'We are Basque warriors ...' The firing squad's bullets didn't kill him at once. He raised his head, the shepherds swore, and sang it till he died."

She issued a flattered sigh. "Take me down to dinner, Luken."

"Glad to," he said, taking her arm. For thirty years the same Mexican-born cook had aged with Amona and become her best friend. The flooring creaked as Luke and his grandmother came down the stairs. "I'm through being mad at you," she said.

"Good. It took a while."

"You can always charm me, Luken. No one else bothers to try. But charm can be a crutch and barrier, you know. If you don't settle down somewhere you'll be the boyish man who stays unmarried too long. The poor old *mutilzahar* who never knows great love and raising children. Don't laugh at me. It could happen to you."

EIGHT

NOVEMBER 1993

From the lobby of a small hotel called La Devinière Luke watched rain pour off the roofs in St. Jean-de-Luz. Outside, youths on Mopeds weaved in and out of the slow-moving traffic. Over his plaid flannel shirt, corduroys, and boots, he wore a London Fog raincoat. Every time he squirmed or crossed his legs in the narrow chair he was reminded that in the coat's right pocket was a Glock 19.

The Basque name of St. Jean-de-Luz was Donibane Lohizun, but it was far removed from its village origins. In the summer, vacationers swarmed the streets of its restaurants and shops and beach, but these last two nights Luke had been the only guest in the hotel. The hotel had once been a town house of François Rabelais, the sixteenth-century author and monk. Hung on the wall of Luke's room was a likeness of the man and in French and English some of his famous one-liners.

"Science without conscience is the soul's perdition." "If the skies fall, one hopes to catch the larks." And his dying words: "I go to seek the Great Perhaps." One hopes to put that off for a while, thought Luke. Seated across the lobby was Madame. She sat reading, a cardigan pulled snug around her. Luke checked his watch once more then said goodnight to Madame, holding up his front door key like a lectured schoolboy. She retired early and did not like to be disturbed.

The rain had lightened to a sprinkle. With his collar turned up he walked past a few open cafés and window fronts of closed stores. Past the famous church he turned toward the tavern named Ajuria, field of heather. The bar was narrow, crowded, and loud with a jukebox and young voices speaking French and Basque. It had one bartender and only a couple of waitresses. Luke spotted a squared bottle with a black and white label. Jack Daniels, a sure sign of American visitation. One waitress wore a fedora and a black jersey and had a nice long back. As Luke moved past she turned around with a tray and two glasses of wine. She glanced at him, looked again, and dipped her chin in recognition. It was the girl he had sold the chinks, the trim-line chaps he offered on the trail ride. She was wearing them. A cold grab went the length of Luke's spine.

Peru Madariaga sat alone near the pool table in back, wearing a wool sport coat and knit shirt. Before him was a glass of red wine. *"Mulero,"* he greeted Luke in Spanish. "Good to see you."

"And you," said Luke. "Sweet town. Is it captured?"

Peru smiled and pushed out a chair. The pool players and bodyguards watched Luke with no sign of affection. One was burly and wore a leather jacket with a sheepskin collar that enclosed a thick tattooed neck. Jale, like Peru, was a veteran *gudari*. The other was a slender kid named Txili, pronounced like chili. He sported a hopeless blond beard and chalked his cue as if he might soon kiss it.

"Are they necessary?" said Luke.

Peru shrugged. "Don't take it personally."

"Okay. Two with you, you won't mind my one."

"You said you'd be alone."

"So did you," said Luke.

"Our situations are different."

"Like hell they are."

Peru leaned back and locked his fingers on his stomach. "Then I guess we wait for events to unfold."

"See that waitress with the leggings and the hat?"

Peru had a sip of his wine. "French girl. Down for the ski season."

"She was on the trail ride with us."

After a moment Peru said, "Good eye."

"Man, one expects precautions."

Luke took a cigarette out of his pack, put the filter between his lips, and searched his pockets for a match. The bodyguard Jale cruised close, produced a butane lighter, and punched up the flame. Luke drew back in protection of his eyebrows. "Thank you," he said.

"No problem," said the goon.

The waitress greeted Luke in English. "How are you?"

He beamed up at her. "Good. And you?"

"Do you remember?" she asked.

"Sure, and not just the chaps. Your face. Your francs."

She laughed and cocked a knee, showing them off. She still wore the peacock blue boots. He fingered the rawhide fringe. "You're a picture in them."

"What would you like to drink?"

"Jack Daniels whiskey. A little ice, no water. Please."

She nodded. "Bourbon."

"Just so you know, Jack Daniels is sour mash whiskey that tastes smokier than bourbon, and is not so sweet. But if I could say that word like you do, I'd call everything bourbon. Diapers. Tractors. Shares of wheat in Nebraska."

She didn't follow it but grinned and looked at Peru. "Another for you?"

Peru shook his head. Moving on, she placed her hand on Luke's shoulder. Peru sipped his wine and smiled. "Pretty faces are your weakness."

"My infrequent consolation."

Peru watched the girl amble to the bar. "In Basque *haragiki* means 'a piece of meat.' It can also mean 'sexually.' 'I'm fond of meat.' 'I'm horny.' The words are the same."

"Guess I'd hate to be a woman here."

"Women say it the same way."

"Okay, three cheers to language," said Luke. "Let's do some business, what do you say?"

"You complain then all but fall on your knees. Sing her a song."

Luke put out the cigarette. "Yeah, but she kept her eyes off you."

On the Péage, trucks bound for Spain growled past the last French exits in roiling shrouds of mist. Guido de Marentes, Luke's helper on the moving of the horses, had overstated his ability to handle a tractor-trailer rig. The haul from St. Nazaire had been a nightmare of clashing gears, crosswinds, chugging deadweight crawls, towns to be gotten through or around, and the defroster didn't work. So he drove with the window down and was cold and wet.

He saw road signs for half the village saints in heaven—Geours-de-Maremne, Vincent-de-Tyresse, Martin-de-Saignant. Still no St. Jean-de-Luz. And then when he skirted Bayonne-Biarritz and saw the orange sign for the public beach—the exit to St. Jean-de-Luz—the relief and exhaustion got the better of him. He downshifted, sped up, and passed a Volvo, then had to lurch for the exit. A horn blast, the trailer's tires hit a curb, and he thought he was going to turn it over.

He was up to here, he muttered, with the American. He thought about the girl he almost married back home in Oviedo. Maybe he still could.

He found the warehouse, logged the false name, and on the second try backed the refrigerated trailer to the covered dock. An old man with a gray crewcut helped him plug in the power then retired to his chair on the dock, where he cleaned his nails with a knife. Guido killed the engine at last. He was snoring when the American banged the door. "You don't know how glad I am to see you," said Luke, standing with his hands in the pockets of a raincoat. His hair was wet.

"My own heart leaps," Guido replied.

"Problems?" Luke said.

"No major ones. No fun either."

"Well, get your things, you're through. Job well done."

Guido looked around. The old Basque was gone. The youth reached in the cab for his canvas bag and searched the accumulated trash for anything personal and incriminating. Luke hurried him gently toward the street. Before they stepped out of the warehouse, he handed Guido an envelope that contained six thousand dollars. The youth quickly counted the bills and said, "Thank you, señor. Truly."

"It's been a pleasure knowing you, Guido."

"You as well. An adventure."

Luke walked him to the corner and pointed the way to the *centre ville.* "The hotels are mostly empty. Avoid the one called La Devinière, if you don't mind." Guido nodded, ignoring Luke's pronunciation.

"How tired are you?" Luke said.

"Very."

"Take a shower, get something to eat. Don't lie down. There's an opportunity in this town with your name on it. Tonight for certain. Tomorrow, who knows?"

Guido looked him over with amused curiosity.

"In the *centre ville,*" Luke said, "there's a short promenade, Place Louis the Sixteenth. You can't miss it. Past the church, turn left and look for a little tavern named Ajuria. Got it? Ajuria. You won't be sorry. Go straight to the bar."

Luke watched him head off in the rain. He lit a John Player cigarette, filled his lungs with it, and walked back inside with the satisfaction of a pimp.

Peru watched as Jale shoved Luke palms against the trailer and began to search him. "Can I help?" Luke said. "Right pocket of the overcoat."

"Anything more?" said Peru. He inspected the Glock handed over by Jale.

"A pocketknife. For the packages."

At the end of the frisk Luke moved around the goon and climbed on the dock. The doors of the trailer opened with a cool sweet odor. Boxes of waxed cardboard were stacked the height of a man, with a narrow walk space between. Luke held his breath and entered the trailer. He squeezed between the boxes, and at the fifth row back pulled one off against his hip. The box was a little over four feet long. He maneuvered it back to the dock and dropped it at Peru's feet. He pitched his raincoat aside, rolled up his sleeves, and opened the box. He plunged his hand in short loins, rib roasts, porterhouse steaks, and struck hardness and wax.

He pulled out the package with care, pressing the beef back with his hand. The sealing wax was the same hue of red. He opened the knife and sliced the wax down a seam. Inside were two parcels. Luke handed them to the kid with the blond beard. Most of the packages contained AK-47s, but this proved to be one of the Dragunov sniper rifles.

The Dragunov had an elegant stock and grip. Luke turned on the scope's illumined crosshairs and handed the rifle to Peru. He handled the sniper rifle briefly and passed it on to the boy named Txili, who murmured, *"Eder."* Pretty.

As the youth handed it on to the goon Peru said, "Now we eliminate you."

He laughed at Luke's expression. They all did.

Once the small talk was exhausted, which didn't take long, the guards spoke Basque and waited for their orders. Luke still had a long night ahead. He didn't look forward to delivering the untainted beef and tractor-trailer to men in Toulouse. "Let these guys unload," said Peru.

"All right," Luke said. Peru's bodyguards peered at the cold murk of the trailer. Barked at by the goon, the boy rolled out a dolly. Peru led Luke upstairs to the warehouse office, where he poured them glasses of Calvados. He opened a briefcase filled with neatly bundled francs. Luke inspected the contents quickly and closed it. He raised the glass at Peru and tasted the apple brandy. Fine stuff.

"Where did these weapons come from?" Peru asked.

"I can't say."

"You'd better."

Luke shook his head. "It's in your interest as well as mine."

"Then it's been a pleasure knowing you. You're free to go."

"But we talked about more."

Peru nodded. "Then you have to tell me where these came from."

Luke sighed. He mentioned the names of Americans and British oil corporations doing business in South America, but not their novelist broker and ETA sympathizer Gil Ordeñana. Without naming them he praised the exiled *gudariak* in Montevideo. The Spaniards had deported members of ETA to places like Ougadougou, capital of Burkina Faso, the onetime French African colony. But the guys in Montevideo had acquired new identities and started a popular restaurant. The president of Uruguay liked to eat there. The shipment of beef came from their ranches.

The Tupamaros were a pacified political movement now, but they had been an inspiration for the newborn ETA. Luke told Peru that old Tupamaro longshoremen had loaded the cargo in the refrigerated holds of a ship under Panamanian registry, which later docked in the French Atlantic port of St. Nazaire. Luke said he had a French friend who got the cargo declared a diplomatic shipment, waiving it past customs inspection. "Our middleman was the French Foreign Ministry."

Peru laughed and slid Luke's gun and pocketknife across the desk. "All right. Do these suppliers have Soviet thirty-millimeter grenade launchers?"

Luke hoped he concealed his flinch. "Plamya Flames?"

Peru nodded. The grenade launchers made by the Soviets were nasty things; in the hands of Syrians and Egyptians they gave the Israelis hell in the Yom Kippur War. The world was awash in Kalashnikovs and Dragunovs, but Luke didn't want any Plamya Flames on his conscience.

"We'd have to do it some other way," he mused. "And I think they cost about twenty thousand American dollars apiece."

Peru swirled his Calvados. "I'm going to provide you with some accommodations. I hope they suit you. Go there and let's see. Ask your suppliers. We'll be in touch."

NINE

All the way down the mountain, the priest invoked meditations of the saints. Ignatius of Loyola, Thérèse of Lisieux. Total concentration. A harmony of small things. As he approached the border station, his hands tightened on the wheel. He drew a breath and rolled down the window of the stolen Peugeot. With each crank the glass slipped two inches.

The border guard glanced at the defect, took the priest's passport, and greeted him curtly. The priest, whose name was Jokin, smiled wanly at the car's condition, the rent seat covers. The guard leaned closer and compared the priest's face to the photograph. Though the narrow sky over the pass was still bright with sun, it was near dark in the forest shadows. The guard moved a flashlight beam around the seats and floorboard and drilled the priest's eyes until he blinked and turned his head.

Don Jokin was dedicated. He had pointed out promising youths to ETA's recruiters. He had been an occasional *mezulari,* a courier, for them. But he found himself unprepared for this. It was taking far too long. He prayed in all his soul for silence in the trunk. One thump back there, his life was ruined. "Where are you going?" said the guard.

"Bayonne," he said. "I have business at the diocese."

The guard watched the approach of another vehicle. He closed the passport, tapped it on the window, and called him Father. "Welcome to France, Père."

Don Jokin ran through the gears slowly. His black shirt was damp with sweat; he leaned forward and peeled it away from the vinyl. The French were people of such detail, poise, and control. He admired them. He admired them with one nostril and despised them through the other.

Above the dusk, a slice of bright sun angled across summits of the western Pyrenees. A furl of mist had already formed. He followed the road into St. Jean-Pied-de-Port and passed a crowd of youths milling and flirting on the town *pelota* court. The road crossed a low bridge of the River Nive. Framed by stone walls and arched by a second bridge that had known the traffic of crusaders and pilgrims, the water shone like an inky blue mirror.

Making sure he wasn't followed, the priest crossed the river and arrived in the higher part of town called the *ville haute*. There were walls covered with Algerian ivy and tarp-covered cars in flagstone drives. The street changed into a winding farm lane. Don Jokin took the graveled turn and killed the lights twice, a signal. Chestnuts popped under the tires.

The safe house had two stories, narrow windows of dim light, and a steep snow roof. He parked beside a relic ox cart with iron-rimmed wheels of solid wood. As he emerged from the car, a collie padded out to meet him, and gave him a start. It lowered its head and ears and wrinkled its nose, drawing its lip back over long clenched teeth. But then he saw the rump and tail moving and realized the fearsome grimace was an overture, a smile. Someone spoke in Euskera. "Any trouble?"

Don Jokin swung around and gasped. The young man wore jeans, athletic shoes, a long-sleeved knit shirt, and a hooded black mask. "No," the priest answered. "Well, the car. It labored, getting over the pass."

The young man looked at the Peugeot and nodded. He had stolen it himself in Logroño. "Which one are you?" said the priest.

"Txili."

"Ah." Don Jokin knew the boy slightly. He was holding a Luger. The priest patted the dog's head and his pockets, searching for keys. They were still in the ignition. "Where are the other cars?" he asked. "I thought for a moment ... "

"In the barn. There have been helicopters."

Don Jokin started to unlock the trunk. Txili stayed his hand and held up another black hood. "Oh, of course," said the priest. He pulled the hood over his head and fought it, hating the canvas smell, snagging the eyeholes with his ears.

"Calm down," said Txili. "You did it. You're here."

Don Jokin nodded and pointed the keys at the trunk. "Wait," said Txili. "Turn around." The youth stuck the gun behind his back into his jeans and arranged the priest's hood so it looked like less of a sack. He tucked it inside the clerical collar.

The priest was amazed at this act and terrified, more than at the border. Txili motioned at the trunk. Lashed secure and flat inside was a folded roll of carpet. At the sound of the trunk opening the carpet rose up like a worm. Unnerved, the priest shoved at the thing with his hands. "No," said Txili, who didn't like the sound it made. "Hurry. Help me get him out."

They lifted the flopping weight and dumped it on the ground. Txili tore at the carpet lining until he came to a face. Don Jokin had picked up the car across the border in Burguete. Until now, the freight had been an abstraction. The man was middle-aged and balding. His hair and white shirt were filthy and sopping wet. His head lashed back and forth. "Get the gag off," said Txili. "He's choking."

The priest pinned the man and ripped duct tape away from his cheeks and jaws. His mouth expelled a sodden wad of gauze. He bucked and coughed and drooled. Txili put the muzzle of the gun against the man's temple and held it there. "Don't yell. It makes me nervous."

Content to breathe again, the captive lay as Don Jokin tore away the carpet lining. His arms and legs were bound with nylon ski rope. Txili handed the priest a pocketknife. The man said, "I thought I was going to die."

Txili played with the dog. "You still might."

Leaving the man's hands tied behind his back, they got him to his feet and walked him toward the house. He looked at Don Jokin and stared at the clerical collar. Txili gestured and led the way; brush and vines snagged their ankles. They came in through a kitchen, then Txili steered the man into the shadow behind a staircase. He tapped the wall with the gun. There was a sound of a bolt moving. The wall jiggled then slid aside on runners. Two more men in black hoods gazed up. "Watch your step," Txili told the captive, helping him down.

"Let him fall," said Jale. There was a stale odor of soiled feet. The expanded cellar had army bunks, a refrigerator, reading lamps, chairs, a table used for a desk, a curtained toilet, a fiberglass shower stall, and a chipped rock wall that opened into the dark mouth of a cave. Jale removed the captive's ropes and watched him rub feeling back into his hands. He gave a flashlight to Txili and shoved the man into a cavern passage. At once the air turned wet and cool. The rock felt clammy and smelled sour. There were hundreds of these caves in the Pyrenees and

Cantabrian cordillera. They came to a narrowing of the rock and had to stoop. Don Jokin heard the sound of a compressor, and then saw light.

The stalactites were bright orange and impressive. But what struck Don Jokin was the plant life. Everywhere a light was hung, lime green fur covered the rock. Watching them approach was another hooded man. He wore corduroys, hiking boots, and a khaki shirt with epaulets. In his lap was a short rifle with a long magazine. He was seated in a barber's chair.

He greeted the man in Spanish. "Alvaro Molina. I've been reading your guest editorial. You write pretty well."

The captive made a show of gallows contempt. "You're animals," said Molina. "Cowards. Take off the hoods."

Peru shrugged and peeled his off. He dropped it on the floor and ran a hand through thick dark hair. The rugby runner that Don Jokin once cheered was in his forties now. His eyes looked restless and vain. "All we wanted was an appointment," Peru said. "Those bodyguards of yours, how much do you pay them? It amazes me how all those old Guardia Civil can still find work. They're not very good at what they do."

"You're wasting your time," Molina said bravely. "There'll be no ransom. My instructions are locked in place."

"Ransom?" said Peru. "We don't have anything against your wife and children. It's business. You're behind on your taxes. And we expect you to pay."

"Your 'taxes' are nothing but extortion by a mob."

"Yes, you said that in your column." Peru pulled some folded newspaper pages from his shirt pocket and spread them on his lap. He swung the barber's chair toward the priest and other men. "Here's a man who studied at the Wharton school of business in the United States. He's doing well in Madrid. A few years ago, he sold his family firms to a Japanese consortium. He buys art, supports the opera, goes sailing in the Canaries. But he feels discomfort. It's hot in Madrid. He wants back in the thick of things, in industry, and he has an idea. He'll start a new company that builds better air conditioning systems for hospitals and office buildings. He'll sell air so cool the women come to work in sweaters.

"But does he build the plant in Madrid? No. He comes north to Vitoria, where the economy's depressed, and the labor's cheaper. On the floor of this plant, it's hot, crowded, and noisy. The workers sit all day at machines that stamp holes in pieces of aluminum and cut insulation. They step on a pedal, a punch or blade moves down, and they toss the piece in a bin. Imagine the tedium. Their minds wander. Molina has gone abroad and bought old used machines. Belts slip. Switches short-circuit. As the hand reaches for the aluminum, the blade drops *twice*. When the workers come to the washstand, they find severed nubs of fingers turning blue on a tray. They look like puckered lips. This is Molina's idea of a workplace safety plan."

"You're nothing but a communist. And that man is no priest."

Peru smiled. "He doubts you, Father. Maybe a verse?"

Don Jokin clawed one from his memory: "'Now you are laden with the judgment due the wicked; judgment and justice have taken hold of you.' Young Elihu ridicules Job."

"Would you like him to say your rites?" Peru asked.

"Shit on God," said Jale. "Let me kill him."

Peru raised the newspaper and continued. "He opened this plant in 1988. We let him get his feet on the ground and grow the company. At the end of four years, we sent him a tax statement—seventy million pesetas. We saw Molina's books, and we asked him for a contribution to help free our country. Not only does he refuse to pay, he insults us. He sends this column to *El País* in Madrid. Listen.

"'The Basques have an ancient culture. But this 'nation' that the terrorists rant about is a figment of their imagination. Euskadi is bunk! This 'nation' of Basques has never existed. It's nothing but a front for organized crime. These people are gangsters, and they must be treated as such. I am glad I heard from them. My answer is this. Never! Not one peseta!'"

Peru handed the paper to Txili. "That's a courageous dare."

"I don't have seventy million pesetas!" Molina cried.

"About our culture, some of the things you Spaniards hear are myth," Peru said. "That we can change the color of our eyes. That we have extra ribs. That we can command electric appliances to short out. But did you know, Molina, that Basques have more Type-O Rh-negative blood than any people on earth? It's the purest blood in all mankind. Eighty-five percent of humans, people like you, have Rh-positive blood. Unlike our red blood cells, yours contain a protein called the Rhesus factor. Your blood and your ancestry are linked to the Rhesus monkey!"

The chief barked a short laugh, and the others laughed with him. Peru rose from the barber's chair and walked toward darker reaches of the cave. The hooded *gudariak* shoved Molina along. Peru tapped stalactites with the flash guard of his rifle; they rang like chimes; he played a tune. "So you collect art, Molina. Who's your favorite painter?"

"Goya."

"Of course. You're a Spaniard. I like him, too."

The cavern room became a dark narrowing wedge. Peru put his hand on Molina's shoulder. He exchanged the gun for Txili's flashlight and moved the beam across the limestone wall. Painted on it was a series of horses done in profile. Thick necks, rounded bellies, slashes of mane, the strokes sure and sparing. From left to right the images faded. They looked like they could have been drawn by a single hand. "What do you make of them, Molina? The doodles of savages?"

"They're better than that," Molina said.

"Yes, they knew perspective, didn't they? It looks like they are running. Who were these painters? Were the painters priests? Who held the torches while they sketched? Our language, Molina, is the oldest in Europe. All that's really known, Spaniard, is that an island of ancient people was left floating in an Indo-European sea. These paintings have been dated with radioactive carbon. The darkest ones have been on this wall for at least ten thousand years. The faintest ones, here, go back twenty-five thousand years. Those painters, Molina, are forefathers of everybody in this cave but you."

"Am I in Spain?" Molina asked. It seemed to matter to him.

"No, you fuck," said Jale. "You're in an imaginary hole in Euskadi."

Peru took Molina by the arm, led him back to the barber's chair, and gestured for him to have a seat. One of the men handed the captive a notebook and pen. Peru jacked the chair higher. "You're going to pay that tax bill with interest and penalty. But first you're going to write another little essay that we'll mail to *El País* in Madrid. It had better be good."

They heard footsteps; another young man came out of the dark. He wore a plain black business suit, a black shirt, and a narrow white tie. No hood. His dark hair was oiled and combed straight back. The quality of the makeup stunned the priest. The new one's hands and face were gleaming black with a green cast—except for the eyes. The lids and lashes were painted red. In one hand he carried a straight razor, its blade gleaming in the light. With the other he held the telephone book of Madrid. Don Jokin crossed himself. Someone had been reading the Inquisition transcripts. The man was made up like Satan himself.

The face-painted *gudari* showed Molina the razor and gave the captive's cheek, jaw, and throat a slow delicate scrape. Then he closed the razor, stuck it in his pocket, and displayed the thick directory with a mime's exaggeration. Molina stared at the phone book and the man's garish face paint. "He's come to help you get started," said Peru. The mime gripped the book with both hands and swung the binding at Molina's shin. Molina yelped and leaped; Jale shoved him back in the chair. The man with the makeup measured another swing and took the other shin.

"The essay," Peru told Molina. "And then your taxes."

The phone book thunked again.

Ysolina waited for Peru in a higher opening of the cave. She sat on a rock and ran her fingers through the collie's ruff. She had enjoyed making the boy into the devil. Makeup was something she'd learned to do at the university when she thought her future might be in theater. But this was the last thing she'd ever do for them.

Across the valley, the ramparts of the old fort squared the town's overlook, gave it shoulders. People who didn't know the town thought its name was funny. Saint John, Foot of the Pass. The town pointed the way to the easiest pass across the mountains. On a hill overlooking the polished little town was an imposing gray stone fort called La Citadelle. During the Civil War many Basque parents sent their children into exile, and until the German war machine stormed across Europe, the Citadelle became a school for those Spanish Basque children. The French Basques called them reds, *komunistak,* the scum of Spain. Some spent the rest of their lives in the Soviet Union and South America. Others eventually came back to their parents, but by virtue of their Spanish Basque birth, they were traitors without rights or recourse under Franco's Law of Political Responsibilities. Ysolina's mother had taught at La Citadelle, a secret she kept from the man she married. Ysolina thought she must have had a lover, that it was her adventure of the wild and sweet.

The collie lurched to his feet and barked at sounds to their rear. "Hush," she murmured. "Who is that?" Peru ducked under a rock fold and stood on the ledge beside them. She looked up at him, smiled, and pulled his leg against her. On the trail ride and weeks that followed, when he had followed her back to Paris, it had been good between them again. But now the serrated edge and sky beyond the range taunted the woman. The lower Pyrenees were little more than a kilometer above the tides, but she had made them into the Himalayas.

"I'm not sure what good it does. Coming back so close."

There was an expectant tension in his silence.

"I want to keep going."

"All right," he said. "Tell me when."

"I meant freely. Is there news from Tangier?"

He was quiet too long. "None of it good."

"What's happened?"

"The Moroccans broke off the talks. They decided neither side is serious. And they have their own concerns. The jihadists are making ugly noises down there."

She was stunned and sickened by this news. "And now?"

"Life goes on."

She sat on a rock and squeezed her arms. The nights cooled off quickly. He leaned toward the collie and gripped its nose with both hands. The dog waited a moment, and then struggled playfully. "Why don't you go back to Paris? I'll catch up with you as soon as I can."

"We need to be together," she said.

"I know we do."

"We're losing the knack."

Out of the cave and in a bedroom of the safe house, Peru and Ysolina lay with their backs to each other. "I love you," she said once.

When he didn't reply she listened to his breathing and gave him the benefit of the doubt. He was probably asleep. She patted the mattress with her hand until the collie stepped up on the bed and curled against her. She soon was remembering the turtledoves, *usapalak,* thousands of them billowing, hurled in somersaults as they fought through shafts of air raised by the mountains. In her journal she had written: "They came in dipping, feinting, spooked by anything that moved, by glints of reflection and changes of color, by the ache and imperative of Africa's grain. Then two columns of us were up and running beneath them, boys and girls, cousins and schoolmates, calling out to them, trailing pennants of white cloth, herding them toward stands of trees. The birds shot forward, faster than before. We could barely hear ourselves, for all the wings. From a platform high in the foliage, a man stood up with the warrior's scream and flung white disks dipped in brown paint that whistled through the air. With a moan that rolled back over us, the doves swooped and flew so low, in such numbers, that younger children threw up their hands in fright and fell to the ground. The doves never saw the nets. The force of the capture shook the trees."

But not in this valley. Not anymore. The dawns of the turtledoves were greeted now by the common thunder of well-oiled shotguns.

Awake beside her, Peru expected to die someday for his actions and convictions. It was the trap he had made for himself, but in the meantime he loved his wife and did not want to lose her. He knew that if he did not offer change in their lives he soon would. In the mountains with the horses, he couldn't help but note the sparks of attraction between the American and Ysolina. Peru did not trust Luke Burgoa and liked him only a little. But he had a wife who was desperate to get back across the border, and she had not lost the Basque accent in her Spanish. Peru needed a driver, a circumspect tourist. An American that smooth and cocky could talk his way past the Spaniards. Let him get Ysolina over there. And then we'll kill him.

TEN

They had married in 1978, when Peru was twenty-three and Ysolina was twenty-one. They had fallen in love in Paris, where Peru was on the run from Spanish authorities and was bumming around in the odd soup of europop. When Ysolina first saw him he was wearing a tie-dye T-shirt. At the Sorbonne she blazed through a history degree and was admitted to graduate interdisciplinary studies. She knew of Peru's sympathies with ETA—even in bed it often seemed to her they talked of little else—but she didn't know the extent of his involvement. Or didn't want to know.

ETA's insurgent war on Spain had raged for a decade by then, and Franco was three years dead. The *gudariak* were unmoved by the young king Juan Carlos, who proclaimed a new start in democracy for the nation. Ysolina followed Peru back to the student tenements around Universidad de Deusto, the Jesuit school he had attended in Bilbao. She planned to start field research on her dissertation. She had grown up amid the rural beauty of Euskadi and the excitement and intoxication that young people found in Pamplona and San Sebastián. To her Bilbao was a foul, crowded city, the Hole, and she didn't like having junkies for neighbors.

So Peru found them an apartment in Mungia. It had been rebuilt well since the Civil War. Springfed creeks flowed through the town, and the force of an aquifer spouted fountains. Mungia was twenty kilometers from an attractive stretch of coves and beaches on the Bay of Biscay, a favorite of European surfers, and it sat among verdant farms and the rolling foothills of the Cantabrian cordillera. In giving her back the Basque Country's natural beauty Ysolina longed for, Peru drew her into the fight, and it ended up battled on ETA's terms.

Falangist technocrats resolved to make Spain energy independent by construction of thirty-seven nuclear power plants. The utility company Iberduero set out to build four of its plants on the Basque coast. Iberduero's owners and executives were Basque, which infuriated the *gudariak*. One plant near Mungia was to go up overlooking the ocean outside the town of Basordas Lemóniz. The summer Peru and Ysolina arrived in Mungia, upwards of 150,000 Basques took to the streets in protest. As a schoolgirl Ysolina had taken part in protest marches against the Franco regime, but for her this was a cause spurred by real passion.

Her parents had known a famous sculptor named Eduardo Txillada. He was a revered native son of San Sebastián. He lent his reputation and artistry to the movement by designing posters that became its symbol. In Euskera they read "No, no, no, not a nuclear power station." Just plain no. Ysolina became a leader and organizer of the protests. She knew the power of images of women walking out front, many carrying infants, as police and television helicopters hovered like dragonflies.

Ysolina was no naïf. On their first night of lovemaking she had seen the scar on Peru's right shoulder and known it had been no fix of a torn rotator cuff. He never had a job and had been disinherited by his family. He came and went at all hours of the day and night. Finally he leveled with her. He received a monthly stipend from ETA's leadership and took part in "actions," though he wouldn't say what they were.

The brazen killing of Carrero Blanco had electrified the radical left throughout Europe, but it almost killed ETA—and not just because of the massive retaliation by the Spanish police state. The political wing of ETA broke away from its military wing, and a domino tumble of new proclaimed executive committees ensued. But Peru rose from the chaos. ETA propagandists issued joint communiqués of alliance with the Palestinians' Fatah, the Kurdish Democratic Party, and the Irish Republican Army. ETA had close bonds with the IRA, but their cause was never about religion. The organization that Peru studied with the most intensity was Irgun Zvai Leumi, the Zionists led by Menachem Begin, who broke the will of the British occupiers in Palestine and enabled the creation of Israel. He got his hands on a Spanish translation of Begin's memoir *The Revolt* and made it his own creed.

He persuaded Ysolina that a non-violent dismantling of the Lemóniz nuclear power plant was ETA's cause as well. Guardia Civil walked the razor-wired perimeter of the construction site. One night a gunfight erupted; the Civil Guards shot a member of an ETA cell in Basordas Lemóniz, and he died of his wounds. The *gudari* had been a well-known plumber and popular father of two. He was always playing tradition's card game of *mus* in the taverns. When the explosions began, Ysolina challenged Peru.

"We call in warnings before any bomb goes off," Peru told her. "Ignoring them is calculated strategy of the Spaniards. We have to act. They're about to bring one of the reactors on line."

ETA's bombers tunneled under the security and razor wire, the same way they had gotten to Carrero Blanco. A Goma-2 device blew up parts of one reactor, killed two workers, and injured more. In June 1979 an international protest against nuclear energy was coordinated throughout Europe. Ysolina's close friend, Gladys del Estal, was another organizer from San Sebastián. In the Navarrese town of Tudela a sniper killed her during the march. Ysolina was outraged by the murder of her friend, but before she could gather her wits, a bomb killed another plant worker. She and Peru fought to a fuck that night, as they often did early in their marriage.

One night in January 1981, Peru told Ysolina he'd like to see some old friends at a small restaurant in Bilbao. Peru shrugged it off when the friends did not show up. They enjoyed paella and a bottle of wine. For her it was a romantic evening. Then as they were leaving the city, Peru pulled over her Saab in an unlit parking lot. Two men flung the back doors open. "Go!" Ysolina yelled at Peru, thinking they were under attack. One of the armed men was Jale, who shoved a terrified captive inside. José María Ryan was the chief nuclear engineer of the Lemóniz plant.

The captive was in her car for only a few kilometers, and she made sure he saw only the back of her head. That night for the first time Ysolina told Peru she wanted a divorce. Meanwhile ETA sent an ultimatum to Iberduero's president and board of directors: demolish the plant in one week or the engineer would be killed. Ysolina watched in anguish as public opinion turned on its head. Now 40,000 Basques took to the streets demanding Ryan's release. The deadline came and went. On February 10 Ysolina was in their Mungia apartment when one of her friends called and told her to turn on a TV station in Bilbao. On a country lane outside Guernica, Ryan had been found with a bullet in his head.

"I didn't do it!" Peru yelled as she hurled clothes in suitcases. "Their orders were to let him go!"

"It doesn't matter. I have to get back in France while I can. And I beg you to do the same."

"I'll find you in Paris at that little Greek joint in the Latin Quarter. I can't try to cross the border with you. It would be too much of a risk for you."

Construction at the Lemóniz plant would stagger along under pressure of the government. Another nuclear engineer was murdered before it was over. But those eleven days in February 1981 caused the abandonment of a nearly completed nuclear power plant into a razor-wired concrete ruin.

Peru had one more matter to dispose of before other *gudariak* smuggled him into France on an anchovy fishing boat. A Franco loyalist named Juan Barela had been the regime's chief of political intelligence in Bilbao. Now he lived in Zaragoza and directed one of the prisons filled with Basque political prisoners. Barela was known as the man who had introduced the soldering iron and welding torch to the Spaniards' secret interrogations. One afternoon in February Barela parked his car and ran through heavy rain to the front door of his home. As his wife opened the door to let him in, their little girl was playing jacks in the foyer. Barela was stamping water off his shoes when Peru fired a bullet in his brain, then ran off in the downpour.

They never got a look at the killer's face.

ELEVEN

JANUARY 1994

In Santa Monica, California, palms stirred in the breeze, a truck roll-
over had turned traffic into a parking lot, and in the studio of Frank O.
Gehry and Associates, a light-industry-looking place with great piles
of clutter and about fifty people on the payroll, the famous architect
was driving his guests up the walls. Twenty people from California, New
York, and Spain had been putting in twelve-hour days of meetings, Sunday through Saturday. The sun was going down now, the participants
were weary, and tempers were on edge.

The architects' office was a scene of broad drafting tables and scattered piles and bales of paper. The walls were packed with framed photos, testimonials, and magazine covers honoring Frank. His partner
Randy Jefferson could tell the Basques were losing patience with Frank,
a slight man of sixty-three who wore glasses and had thinning white
hair. Jefferson had been educated and trained as a design architect but
had learned his real gift was for coordination and management. He was
essential if the Bilbao project was to succeed because only he and Frank's
wife Berta knew where the star might be at any time. That was prob-
lematic because clocks in California ran nine hours earlier than those of
the clients in the Vizcaya province of Spain, conference calls across the
Atlantic were conducted daily, and faxes flew by the thousands.

Jefferson knew that Frank was trying to relieve the tension, but his
charm wasn't working. He was relating how when he was a little boy in
Ontario, Canada, he drew something at his Hebrew school, and the rabbi
pinned it on a wallboard and told his mother in Yiddish, "Your boy has
golden hands."

Members of the Bilbao team began to whisper and mutter in Eus-kera. The Americans found it mystifying that human tongues and palates could even make those noises. Jefferson heard one guest saying, *"Gero eta txarrago."* It just goes from bad to worse.

Another: *"Mutil toxoriburua dela uste dut."* He's like a feather-brained boy.

"Please," Jefferson nearly shouted. *"English.* We conduct our business in English. It's in the contracts. Otherwise it's chaos."

The contracts for the Guggenheim Bilbao had been signed in February 1992. The partners were the Gehry design firm, the Spanish executive construction architects IDOM, the Guggenheim Foundation in New York, and the client Consorcio Guggenheim Bilbao. The Consorcio was composed of Basque delegates to the national parliament and the govern-ment of Vizcaya province, the city of Bilbao, and a public-private urban renewal group called Bilbao Metropoli 30. The government of Vizcaya had pledged to pay for the museum through private donations and tax revenues drawn only from its Vizcayan constituents, with not one peseta required of the central government in Madrid.

When the project was announced, the Guggenheim Bilbao was hyped in the art and architecture worlds as the deal of the century, but it was already on the verge of collapse. The Consorcio's preliminary con-struction estimate had been $93.7 million. In no time the cost estimates shot to $150 million. The construction architect firm IDOM was a giant headquartered in Barcelona; almost as important as Gehry in the mix was IDOM's hiring of a Basque, César Caicoya, as the executive architect. Caicoya's task was to respect artistic vision—Gehry's *Guernica,* he often said—while trying to keep costs in line with the projections.

IDOM's experience was in building large industrial and infrastructure projects—aircraft factories, highway overpasses, and the like. Its executives almost passed up bidding on the museum's construction contract but de-cided the opportunity was too great for future business, if it got built. But the contracts made IDOM responsible for meeting the target cost, with stiff fees charged if there were cost overruns or delays. And if the gargantuan enterprise cratered, Gehry's attorneys had passed off liability on IDOM. The Spanish giant even had to pay the Gehry firm's legal fees for drawing up the contracts. The Spanish firm's executives believed that a reasonable timeline for such a building was seven years, but the contract stipulated the museum had to open in five. The extravagance of the undertaking had already drawn fire and backlash from Basque politicians, journalists, and pundits. Why was all that tax revenue not being spent on education and health services or channeled to Basque artists and architects? Instead, the griping went, it was being lavished on Americans.

Politicians with the PNV, the center-right Basque party descended from the nationalist heroes Sabino Arana, Miguel de Unamuno, and José Aguirre, had a majority in the Basques' regional parliament, but they feared that cost overruns could make the Museo Guggenheim Bilbao blow up in their faces.

Just one week ahead of the meeting in California, Gehry had agreed to appear at a press conference and reception in Bilbao to present the budget and the museum's schematic design. The Basques in the room were exhausted by the talk of reducing the footprint of the building by twenty percent and taking a hard look at every material in search of cheaper ones. The Guggenheim Bilbao contract was calculated in Spanish pesetas, and the exchange rate between pesetas and US dollars was 110 to one. The Americans were stunned by contract figures that rendered the original dollar cost estimate to *tens of thousands of millions* of an unstable currency? And the Basques wondered how they were supposed to budget a schematic design when Caicoya and other IDOM team leaders said at least a thousand detailed drawings would be required in order to advertise for bids with any degree of reliability. And Gehry had provided only thirty sketches.

Thomas Krens was not the sort of fellow who ordinarily brought to mind a cowboy, but in the world of art his wheeling and dealing got him called that. The director of the Guggenheim Foundation was a balding man in his forties who wore round steel-rimmed glasses. When hired, he had been an art history professor at a small liberal arts college in Massachusetts. Ignoring those who said he was in over his head, he fretted that so many of the foundation's treasures lay in storage due to simple lack of space. So he pushed for restoration of the museum built by Frank Lloyd Wright on Fifth Avenue in New York, construction of a larger branch in Soho, and expansion of one in Venice. He paid for it by issuing $54.9 million in bonds secured by a letter of credit from the Swiss Bank Corporation. That debt was twice the amount of the foundation's endowment.

Krens wanted to test his concept of museum management, "franchise the brand," in Europe, but he did not want to put another Guggenheim in a city already rich with architecture and art, such as Paris, Rome, or Madrid. A big fish in a small pond was what he had in mind, so homely Bilbao edged into contention.

About the size of Dublin or Liverpool, Bilbao was home to a million people, and its history went back to the fourteenth century, but Europeans disdained the place. One year when its boosters made a bid to host the Olympics, Bilbao finished fifty-sixth among the entrants. The port area that once roared with drunk and whoring sailors was dark and dangerous now. The shipyards had been forced out of business by competitors in Iron Curtain countries and Asia, and coal and iron in the Basque Country had almost been mined out. Bilbao's unemployment rate was 25 percent, and the city had the worst air quality in Western Europe.

But the group called Bilbao Metropoli 30 meant to change all that. The *jefes* bragged they could bring half a billion dollars to their grand strategy. It included a new subway system, railway station, airport, music hall, and a classy footbridge across the Río Nervión that ran through the city. Thomas Krens listened to his Basque suitors for two months before agreeing to visit Bilbao.

In May 1991 he had asked his friend Frank Gehry to come along with him and meet these people. Two years before that, Frank had won the Pritzker Architecture Prize, his profession's highest honor. Frank's usual attire was a pair of black jeans and a black T-shirt. Thomas joked that his friend was like Peter Falk's slovenly detective in the television series *Columbo*. Frank had never heard of Bilbao and asked one of his interns to compile some preliminary research for him. On his flight to Bilbao, Frank read in the youngster's report that every day the Río Nervión received fourteen metric tons of ammonia and eight metric tons of heavy metals. He said, "Yikes," and a woman across the aisle gave him a look.

Their hosts showed the Americans a house with a distinguished nineteenth-century exterior, in one of the nicest parts of the city, but it had been remodeled inside with lowered ceilings to accommodate an extra floor. Afterward they went to a luncheon at the gleaming Lopez de Haro Hotel. Frank was startled when someone rang a glass with his spoon, came to his feet, and said, "We're happy to have Mr. Gehry here, and we'd like to hear what he thinks about our project."

Frank hadn't expected to be put on the spot that way. He didn't want to rain on his friend Thomas's greenbacks parade, but they asked him and he told them that the building didn't lend itself to being a museum. The only way to make it a museum was to tear down the existing floors and build it inside the walls of the old building. That way it would be a fit in the neighborhood and it would save the old walls. But the walls would look like a fence. Another option was to tear down the nineteenth-century façade and build a new museum on the site. The new museum could be beautiful if it was done right, but it would change the whole neighborhood and its character. He told them that they should find another site.

Stone silence greeted his remarks. But the Spanish Basques were persistent. They took the Americans up on a hill called Artxanda that overlooked the city and asked where an art museum of the first class might sit. Frank pointed at a part of the city along the bend of the Río Nervión where two handsome bridges, the Puente de la Salve and the Puente de Deusto, angled toward each other. His hosts told him that city hall had an imposing presence across the river from there, but the six- and eight-story buildings were separated from the river by the ruins of a shipyard, a brickworks, and warehouses where bums built fires to stay warm on winter nights.

That night in his hotel room Frank sketched the amazing jumble he'd seen of collapsed walls and broken rusted beams. He conceptualized his buildings in fast ink loops and rectangles that might appear to be doodles to someone peeking over his shoulder; the imagined walls and spaces looked like they were flung together without pause in one stroke, for he could finish a sketch of an imagined building in a few seconds. He boasted of drafting one while having an MRI.

The Bilbao *jefes* responded the next day that his ideal spot would cost too much. The dirt under the ruin was valuable real estate. Frank put them and their city out of his mind as soon as he belted himself into his seat, downed a glass of pinot grigio, and swallowed a Restoril for a snooze through half the flight back across the Atlantic. At this point in his career he rejected ten projects for every one he accepted, and he really didn't give a shit, Loretta, if his suitors thought his manner of turning them down was arrogant and rude.

The *jefes* of Bilbao lusted for an art museum that would be their showcase of urban renewal, and they wanted a Guggenheim museum and Frank Gehry. So Thomas Krens flew back over. The *jefes* next suggested a 60,000 square-foot wine storage warehouse in Bilbao's old town, Indaxtu. Thomas looked at that place and could only visualize something vast and formless. He made a pitch for a museum that would redefine the city, offering as example the Opera House in Sydney, Australia. It was a seaside structure designed by the Danish architect Jørn Utzon to strike viewers with imagery of the great masted sailing ships that brought the British exiles and empire to the continent. Some people thought the opera house looked like a clothes line flapping in the wind, and the cost overruns almost sank the Dane's career, but Frank was nothing if not competitive. He said, "Well, that's a tall order, but why not?"

The *jefes* were talking to Krens about a deal that would give the Guggenheim Foundation a hundred million dollars to build the museum, fifty million for new acquisitions, an annual operating budget of twelve million, and a twenty-year contract that could be extended to seventy-five. The proposal was kicked over to the politicians in Vizcaya, and Thomas began to doubt that the Basque clients could back up their talk of all that capital. He went back over to Bilbao thinking it was time for a firm yes or no, and thought it would likely be the latter. His hosts astonished him with a sweetened offer to give the Foundation twenty million dollars, no taxes owed, just for the Guggenheim name, and he would chair the committee search for the design architect. The Guggenheim kept the twenty million if the deal fell through.

In a happy daze Thomas went jogging that afternoon and passed a fenced-off and crumbling ruin on a bend of the river between two bridges. A chill went through him. He stopped, looked around, and realized it was the same spot Frank had pointed out that day from the Artxanda hill.

In a twist of great luck someone at city hall turned up an unpaid tax account that said, due to the former owners' abandonments of the property, the city of Bilbao already owned the 34,000 square-foot tract that Frank and now Thomas thought was so perfect. When Thomas got back to New York he asked Frank to come back to Bilbao with him, and this time bring his wife Berta, who was fluent in Spanish.

Frank told most potential clients that he did not care to compete for projects. If someone wanted him, then they should agree on design, budget, and his commission, and get on with it. Frank was fueled by his celebrity, not just his genius. Modesty was not one of his virtues. He recalled his pleasure on hearing, not reading, his first notice in the *New York Times* while he was socializing with famous actors. The paper's music critic had called the Merriweather Post Pavilion in Columbia, Maryland, "an unqualified architectural and acoustical success." He said, "I had just come home from the opening and was having dinner at Ben Gazarra's house. Ben and his wife had a beach house, and we'd gone over there to spend Sunday afternoon with them. Esther Williams and Fernando Lamas were there, as were other dignitaries of the silver screen. Ben was saving the review because he was so proud of me, and he read it out loud. When he finished reading it, I swam in the pool with Esther and Fernando. I had arrived."

Indeed he had. But at the moment he had just lost three straight major competitions. Frank and the firm needed the work in Bilbao, and Thomas knew it. Thomas left Frank dangling for months on whether he would be invited to the competition. Krens and his committee were told to select and recruit three candidate firms, with a payment of ten thousand to submit a proposal. Frank and his colleagues holed up in Frankfurt and spent forty thousand working up thirty illustrations and the pitch. Frank O. Gehry and Associates won out over finalists from Vienna and Tokyo. Krens said, "At the end, Gehry won, as he provided the most unusual project, juxtaposing the rectangular buildings of Bilbao."

Then it got into the press that the Guggenheim had received twenty million dollars tax-free. Was that a retainer, a tip? If private investment did not come through, would Basque taxpayers be stuck paying for the *brand?* Had the Consorcio sold out to the Americans? And it began to be murmured in Europe's ugly and timeworn fashion that Frank Gehry was a Jew.

Born in Toronto, Frank was in his teens when his family moved to Los Angeles in hopes of improving his father's health. When his architectural career took off, he reflected on his interest in the images of fish in Japanese painting. "When I was a boy and we lived in Toronto, there was a Jewish marketplace on Kensington Avenue, just a few blocks from my grandparents' house. I'd go there with my grandmother to buy groceries, and I especially liked going on days when she would buy a carp. We would walk home with the carp in waxed paper filled with water, and when we got there she'd put it in the bathtub. My cousins, my sister, and I would play with the fish and watch it swim around. Then it would disappear, and we'd have gefilte fish for dinner. I didn't put two and two together at first."

Nearly sixty years later, with the design architect's vision inspired in part by the image of a swimming carp, he and his team and partners in Spain worked through the budget crisis that could have killed the Guggenheim Museum. Though the revised budget was still $27.5 million over the contract terms, Frank breezed into Bilbao and carried off the press conference with his usual mixture of quirks and charm. An American art critic who had never cared for Frank's work asked him in barbed fashion why a man of his stature had bothered with such a project in a backwater of Spain.

"Well, I like Bilbao," Frank said. "I like the industrial feeling and the surrounding of green, so even though it's a dirty, messy industrial city, it has this forgiveness." He remarked on his general philosophy of accepting some offers and rejecting others. "I love to find myself in a dangerous place."

But one facet of Bilbao's situation was understated to the Americans. The Consorcio's *jefes* explained the separatist insurgency to them as a minor scuffle, really. Eight hundred or so murders in a quarter century, why, what kind of war is that? New York City averaged that in just two years! But the Pritzker laureate who bragged of loving danger had no idea how much of it was about to come his way.

TWELVE

MARCH 1994

Sounds of cars and blasts of electric guitars and rainforest drums from the jam boxes of the West Africans carried from the road outside the safe house in the French Basque city of Bayonne. They were Gambians and Senegalese who worked in sawmills and fishmeal plants and lived in tenements squeezed into the city's confluence of two rivers, the Adour and the Nive. Luke often ate in their pungent cafes.

At Peru Madariaga's direction he lived in woods on the outskirts of Bayonne in a nondescript house with no close neighbors. He had a bed and a desk built from concrete blocks and an old warped door, a semi-efficient wood burning stove, an Apple laptop and a printer adapted to French wiring, a refrigerator, stove, enough dishes and pots and pans to get by, and a growing array of empty wine bottles and quarts of whiskey and gin.

Below the house were two large plowed fields and a hay meadow, and a white stone barn stood off amid a line of trees, where a small herd of dairy cattle wandered up bawling for grain in the evenings. While plowing on a tractor, the farmer had raised a hand once at Luke, and that was all. Books were a lot of weight to lug around, but Luke had brought some paperback novels he wouldn't mind reading many times, and he scouted used book stores in Bayonne, which along with the once-chic coastal resort of Biarritz made a fair-sized city around the rivers' confluence.

Like Africans Luke had a boom box, and he had enough tapes of rock and roll to keep him entertained. His taste ran to the Stones, the Band, Van Morrison, Taj Mahal, Otis Redding. Luke also brought with him some tapes of the breathy flute music of Andean Indians that he liked, and had learned about a Basque rocker named Ruper Ordorika, whose moody voice engaged him, though he understood just snatches of the

Basque lyrics. Some evenings, walking past the Africans' houses on his way to one of their cafés, he caught a scent of hashish, and he wished he could score some of that.

Sacked out now in a hammock, he picked up the cable that had been routed to him in a bus station locker in Bayonne. Jimbo Hopson, who had been his commanding officer in Colombia and Ecuador, was now his Outfit superior. Luke knew that only Jimbo could have gotten him this gig, and he tried to let him know he was grateful. Otherwise he might have been back in Texas running a 7-Eleven or adjusting insurance claims. The cable he read now had gone out from the US embassy in Madrid to Outfit headquarters with copies to the State Department, the DEA, the US embassy in Paris, consulates in Barcelona and Toulouse, and an ominous-sounding "European Political Collective."

The author was Roberto Escamilla, whose Cuban parents had been close to Batista and fled to Orange County, California, after a stopover in Miami. Escamilla would be Luke's case officer in Madrid if and when this mission took him into Spain. He called the separatists *etarras*. In Outfit cable-speak Escamilla offered a sampling of ETA atrocities that included an explosion in a Barcelona supermarket that killed twenty-one people, a prosecutor known for impositions of long prison sentences who was riddled by automatic fire in front of her home, and an intercepted letter from an imprisoned *etarra* that read: "I love to see the pained faces of the family in the funerals. Their tears are our smiles, and we are laughing with joy."

They sounded like a cold-hearted bunch all right. But Luke wondered if his country really had a dog in their fight. Under pressure from Spain's post-Franco government, the Americans had moved their air force squadrons to Italy. The United States now had just the Rota naval base in Spain, and its purpose was to support the Brits' hold on Gibraltar and to protect American interests in the Mediterranean. The Outfit was interested in ETA only to the extent it was believed to be connected to jihadists in North Africa, the Middle East, South Asia, and Latin America.

Luke took the Outfit's denial of official cover as a pointed signal that he was expendable. So he again called on his friend Pascal, whom the French DGSE had cut loose when he left Ecuador. The espionage world called a man of his talent a cobbler. He was an artist at producing counterfeit passports, visas, work permits, all kinds of false documents. He provided Luke with an alternate passport and visas identifying him as one Selden Hale. He had business cards and a portfolio of a phony company they made up over a bottle of Beaujolais. You never know when you might need to be someone else.

In the marines Jimbo had made too many enemies with his sharp words and unconventional ways, and he didn't want to go back to Bossier City. Jimbo was grateful that the Outfit picked him up, but his assignment to the embassy in Paris felt like he'd been thrown a sop. He despised the French, and his accent murdered the language, in their ears. He had supplied Luke with a Finnish-made Nokia 2010 phone that would connect them anywhere in Western Europe through the 2.6 Groupe Spécial Mobile network. The phone looked like a hard plastic Snickers. At the embassy Jimbo had a so-called "stew phone," an STU-III that looked like any other office phone except a key-shaped chip contained the algorithms that encrypted and made conversations secure. Luke had finished reading Escamilla's cable when the Nokia rang in his pocket. He tossed the papers aside and got the Nokia to his ear. With no greeting, which was his habit, Jimbo said, "I been thinking that the Napoleonic Code started with Napoleon. Means over here you're guilty until proven innocent. So if you fool around and get hauled into a French court as gun runner selling to separatists and terrorists on French soil, the State Department would have to explain that you've gone rogue. You could be parked in prison for a long time."

Luke swung his legs out of the hammock and sang, *"The last thing I needed the first thing this morning was to have you say that to me."*

They had similar tastes in music, and Jimbo chuckled at his twist on a song Willie Nelson made into a hit. "Where you been?" he said. "Tell me something!"

"Nothing new here, Colonel. Sorry."

"Goddamn it, Luke, let's get after those assholes!"

"Jimbo, you guys didn't have squat on these people until I got involved. Now I've done business with Peru Madariaga, their alleged military commander. All by my lonesome I've set up a sting in which he and a high profile Latin American leftist writer and some of the world's major oil companies are set up for a large fall. But I'm hanging out here naked as a jaybird."

"All right, but go easy on that last bit. I'm not sure people above our pay grades are gonna want to go there."

Luke seethed. The oil companies get off!

"So you're in constant touch with this guy Madariaga?"

"Not constant but regular. He's asking for arms that are worrisome."

"Yeah? What's that?"

"Plamya Flames."

There was a soft whistle. "Sucker wants to hurt somebody."

"What they're made for."

"Well, can you get the guy over on the Spanish side? That's where we want to take him down. Would Plamya Flames coax him there?"

"I told him I'd have to find another way of getting them to him."

"Why, son, we don't need your amateurs in South America. We can get Plamya Flames straight from the Israelis."

"No dice," Luke said. "I don't do business with the Mossad. I don't like those particular Israelis and neither do you."

"Okay. But let's figure out another way to do it. Why haven't you called Roberto Escamilla?"

"I expect I'll like him about as much as the Mossad."

"What do you mean? Escamilla's a standup guy. Everything I've heard."

"I don't know. I was just reading one of his cables. It's like a baloney sandwich without mustard or mayonnaise. And every time I've tried to call him someone answers the phone for a Flamenco dance company."

There was an unhappy silence. "Well, damn it, why didn't you let me know? I'll get the right number for you." Jimbo sighed and said, "I've got this weird dyslexia, not with words, but with numbers. I'll bet there's a name for that."

"Dyscalculia," said Luke.

Another pause. "You make that up?"

"No."

"How'd you know that?"

"Because I'm your favorite smartass. Gotta go feed my birds now. Ciao."

THIRTEEN

Luke's other communications, from Peru Madariaga, came or did not come to the road outside Bayonne. There was a short stake with a basket attached to it, an honest-to-god breadbasket. Six days a week a baguette wrapped in a trim paper sack was placed there, and he was to look each day for the note that might be enclosed. Luke supposed it was a good system as long as the baker was one of your guys.

A grove of palm trees stood among chestnut trees in a cemetery where he broke and scattered the bread for birds and critters of the night. Lord Wellington had chased Napoleon's army out of Spain in a prelude to Waterloo, but one April night in 1814 officers of the Brits' elite Coldstream Guards got surrounded and extinguished. Set in the wall of the graveyard was a marble slab.

Her Majesty
VICTORIA
Queen of Great Britain and Ireland,
Empress of India,
Accompanied By
Her Royal Highness the Princess Beatrice,
(Princess Henry of Battenburg)
Visited
The Guards' Cemeteries
March 20th
1889

"Captain Lionheart reporting, Your Highness," said Luke, breaking up the bread. A dog huffed behind him in the woods. He looked around and a collie sauntered forth with lowered head, grinning like an imbecile. Luke offered his hand and let the dog smell him. The collie inspected the weeds, raised a leg, and marked the graveyard's wall. A woman emerged from the tree shade in a long belted skirt and a loose blouse, sleeves pushed above silver bracelets on her arms.

"Am I intruding?" Ysolina said as he stared. "Should I go?"

"No, god no. I didn't think I'd ever see you again."

"Well, now you have. You remember Barkilu?"

"*Claro*. Does he always show his teeth like that?"

"With him it means he's being friendly."

"Your husband sent you here?"

"Don't ask so many questions. Come have lunch."

He walked behind her. Her hips seemed fuller in the dress—her gait took on an aimlessness and roll. The collie plunged after a magpie, disturbing the weeds. "Doing any riding?" she said.

"No, I may be done with that. Shoes and tires suit me fine."

"André loves your saddle," she said. "He has it sitting in his parlor on a wine cask. He says it's a sculpture."

"I ought to write the saddler in Poteet. His name's Bunny Flanagan. He works in a wheelchair, owing to an unfortunate draw in a rodeo one time." He smiled at her glance. "I'm missing all that a little."

"Pity," she replied. To Ysolina he didn't have much standing as an exile.

"How long has it been for you?" he asked. "Since Spain."

"Eleven years. Maybe someday I'll go back."

Parked along the road was a brown Land Rover. She let the dog in back, plucked some brambles out of his fur, and put on sunglasses. She wheeled the Rover hard, turning around, and banged the gearbox with a carelessness and jangle of bracelets that left his eyes on the sinews in her forearm. The collie thrashed around a bit. The side windows were painted with smears of his nose. On the shoulder, a black man in a yellow dashiki watched the traffic and waited to cross. "This used to be a Jewish quarter," she said. "They were refugees run out of Portugal and Spain. Marvelous chocolatiers. The whole town reeked of it."

Luke lit a cigarette. "During the Inquisition, Spain attacked the French Basques. The villages were thought to be thick with witches, and people feared the Spaniards would burn everybody. The Bayonne regiment turned them back. They were out of ammunition, so they tied hunting knives to their muskets, and ran screaming down the mountain called Larrún. And invented the term 'bayonet.'"

She cracked a window. "What do you know about witches?"

He rolled down his window and tossed the cigarette. "Not much. But I go to museums. I take an interest. The Museum of the Basques in Bayonne devotes a lot of attention to witches and Simón Bolívar and Ignatius of Loyola. But I didn't see one word or image about the Spanish Civil War, Franco, or the other side of the Pyrenees. It's curious."

"They try not to think about it."

Luke's gaze followed the lines of her neck and jaw. "Do you know," he said, "you have one of the world's great throats?"

The car swerved slightly. "Thank you," she said.

"You just made a dark day shine, Ysolina. Diamonds out of chalk."

She grinned. "I get it. You're one of those guys with the lines."

They crossed the bridge of the Adour River. He watched her legs, trim and loose beneath the skirt. "Do you live in Bayonne?" he asked.

"No. Most of the time in Paris."

"Are you in hiding?"

"Not from the French police. Maybe thoughts of you."

The battered and ivied walls around the old quarter had stood for a thousand years. They left the car and followed the collie through a park fashioned from the ramparts and moat. They passed a row of rusted steel-barred cylinders that resembled birdcages but were seven feet tall. "Those were punishment devices for women," she said. "For touching a man's genitals, they locked you in and gave you forty dunks in the river."

"Must have been some mean fellows that turned them in."

She laughed, called back the dog, and put him on a leash as they entered the old quarter. Barkilu leaned against the leash and sniffed the walls and sidewalk, raising his leg often. Metal doors of delivery stalls were posted with concert posters and sprayed with grafitti, most of it in Basque. *EXTRADIZARIK EZ*, no extradition.

"My husband likes you," she remarked.

"Glad to hear it. He offered to kill me. Do we talk about him?"

"He's why you're here."

"Reasons change, don't they? Bright one morning."

She offered him the leash, and the collie evaluated pulling the new hand. "Peru says you're courageous and foolhardy."

Luke snorted. "He's one to talk."

"Are you ever frightened?"

"Sure. All the time."

"Of what?"

"Root canals. Cancer. Your husband. Three o'clock in the morning."

She laughed again. "Three in the morning?"

"Then to dawn. Morbid beasts out there. Take my word for it."

She hiked her shoulders agreeably.

"What scares you?" he asked.

"*Estasis.* Nothing changing."

Someone was playing piano in a loft. A tune by Jellyroll Morton ushered them down the street. They turned a corner and approached the silver and gray cathedral. A little boy smoked a cigarette and shoved a toy sailboat across a fountain in the courtyard. The church's twin spires and lesser points bristled and gleamed. Luke asked, "Are you the reason Peru quit studying to be a priest?"

Nothing he knew or said seemed to rattle her. "No. He'd tell you it was the struggle for a free and independent Euskadi. Actually it was rugby. He broke a bone in his neck, and several weeks in traction altered his view of many things. Such as a life of enforced passivity."

"Are you ETA?"

She turned the sunglasses on him then sauntered on.

The café she chose had two small tables outside. The collie circled like a wolf and laid his chin on his paws. The waiter brought menus and glasses of wine. She took Luke's hand and entwined their fingers, not so gently. "Some rules. Your purpose here, whatever it is, whatever you're doing with Peru—it has nothing to do with me. If it does, or if it begins to, I'm gone. *Foosh.* Do you understand?"

She sat back, put the sunglasses aside, and tasted the wine.

"Order for me," he said, staring at the menu.

"Your face is red."

She uncrossed her legs and leaned over the table. She picked his pack of cigarettes out of his shirt pocket, withdrew one, and shoved it like a pencil above his left ear, arranging a lock of his hair. "Now you're ETA."

"How's that?"

"In the early days, when Franco was alive, that was the secret signal. That was how you knew. But then everybody knew, and the signal became fashion. You put on lipstick and pulled back your hair. Not just any cigarette, though. Any brand with white rings around the filter, then ones that had a star and crescent and the words Turkish State Monopoly. Warnings at school, no more cigarettes behind the ear. Naturally, the last ones to take it up were Spanish cops. Broad lapels, flashy ties, sideburns and hairspray, cheap gold chains. And the cigarette. It was funny."

The waiter returned. She ordered trout with ham and garlic, frog legs in pastry, pimientos vinaigrette, and a bottle of Spanish village white. The collie dozed. "Oh dear," she said. "You've stopped talking."

"I can't get enough of you, but you intimidate me."

"I don't know the limits. Maybe there aren't any." Pushing with her arms, she came out of her chair and kissed him. Her lips twisted and reached even as she pulled away. All kinds of alarms were going off in his head. When she sat back she looked perplexed as well. "That's not the kind of thing I do."

"I wish you'd do it again."

"My heart's coming through my shirt."

The waiter arrived with clean glasses and the wine. He opened the bottle and tossed the cork over his shoulder in the street. Luke took this to be a statement about Spanish village wines. Or maybe it was because they spoke Spanish. "Tell me who you are," Luke said. "How you live."

She shrugged. "My father was a nationalist officer during the Civil War and a businessman afterward—a petrol distributor." She smiled at Luke's expression of surprise. "Papa and I had all the usual trouble. Some dear times, too. They were about my age now when they had me. My mother died when I was sixteen. After that, the last place Papa wanted me was in a Spanish university. The campuses swarmed with Spanish security police. There were demonstrations in San Sebastián, Pamplona, and Bilbao all the time. We used to go to them dressed to the nines—high heels, miniskirts, running shoes in our purses. Papa knew what would happen if I stayed in Spain. So he sent me to Paris"—she laughed—"where I met and married Peru. What can parents do?"

"Bring you up and let you go."

She nodded. "My father died from heart failure four years ago. I couldn't go to him, and he'd gotten too weak to travel. But we were as close as we'd ever been. He went to great lengths to get his money out of Spain. Politics don't amount to much in a deathbed. His letters were anguished and loving. Not his darling girl!"

"What did he think of Franco?"

"You mean, was Papa a fascist? He was an officer in their army and was a party member of the Falange. But he hated the unbelievable dumbness that followed the war. They set out to extinguish our language, and almost did. And the Guardia Civil were foul people. You could get a jaw smashed for just looking at them. *El Glorioso,* they called Franco. Dear God. His crowd plundered Euskadi and Catalonia because they had been prosperous and fought him in the war. You have to understand, ETA began as heroes, because they rose up and fought back. When Franco died, Euskadi Sur ran out of champagne."

The way he watched her drew out more. "I have friends in Paris," she went on, "and a nice place to live. I have a standing offer of a cottage where I summer on André's farm. I keep my horse there. I own some valuable paintings by Marie Laurencin, a marvelous woman half a century ago. I have an edition of *Alice and Wonderland* that she illustrated in watercolor for Lewis Carroll. I'd like to write a biography of her some day. I'm a doctoral candidate at the Sorbonne, but I'm stalled on the project that's been approved by my supervising professors. The most important archives are in Spain, and I can't go there."

She shook her head. "Married to one rogue, and here I sit with another."

She raised her glass in a mock toast. "To higher learning."

"What's your research project?"

She brightened. "A Basque ancestor, a confessed witch."

"Really. Did she go to the stake? I'm sorry, I guess that was rude."

"It's all right. She did come close. Enara was a young and wealthy widow. The Inquisitors never knew quite what to do with her, but they didn't like her."

Luke poured more wine. "What did you call her?"

"Enara. Enara de Añibarro. Swallow of the Pasture."

Another gong went off in his head. *Swallow* was spy-speak for an enemy woman who used sex to gain information and expose and turn agents. A woman who could get you and other people killed.

"Pretty name," he said. "You like this woman?"

"I like her story."

"Well, was she or wasn't she? A witch."

"She said she attended black masses. She may have; I don't know. Another

95

question is whether she did what she confessed to doing at these *aquellares.*"

"What did she say she did?"

She shrugged those wonderful shoulders. "Made love to the Devil."

Luke's laugh sent wine up his nose. The waiter left a basket of bread and a platter of halved pimientos afloat in olive oil, garlic, slivered onions, capers, and paprika or cayenne. "Go on," said Luke, spooning peppers on their plates.

She ate in the European manner, fork in the left hand, tines turned down. "My views of witchcraft are colored by our times. The stereotype of the crones is partly accurate, *Macbeth* and all that. But children came into the cults as young as age nine. There were all these nymphets in gauze and anklets, dancing to flutes and drums. Sex, drugs, and rock and roll."

"What kind of drugs?" asked Luke.

"Excretions of toad. The witches kept them in their homes. They made little garments for them and force-fed them like geese." He laughed again and she touched his hand with her knife. "Toxins in toads found here are known to be hallucinogenic. Confessions made four hundred years ago read like the LSD and peyote memoirs of our time. They could assume the forms of animals and leak through cracks in walls. They could fly."

The waiter arrived with the trout and puff pastry. Ysolina arranged the plates so they could sample freely. The frog legs in the pastry were boned, with a filling that had the consistency of flan, an aroma of shallots, sherry, and cream.

"Some ancestor," Luke said. "What did the Devil look like?"

"Horrid, handsome, horns of a goat, the tail of a donkey—every village had one, and the descriptions varied. The constants were the black suit, dark skin, red eyes. Everyone agreed, though, that Lora, the Lord of Pamplona, was the most distinguished and striking."

"Where did they, um, do it?"

"Sometimes in her home. More often at the *aquellare*. When the music and dancing began." She colored and touched her ribs beneath her breast. "He liked her here. He made her lactate, and she'd never had children. Her ears popped. He sounded like a running horse. She saw vermilions and blues that have no place in nature. She always bled. His skin was ice cold. Nails like the talons of a hawk."

"You've seen her confessions?"

"I've seen her journals."

"The Spaniards say you're a bad girl, Ysolina. *Neskatzar.*"

"But I'm not, I'm really not," she insisted. "So you speak Basque."

"Hardly. I just remember some words of it. I can't make sense of reading it or follow a conversation. What happened to your witch ancestor?"

"She got pregnant in one of the secret prisons."

"Who was the father?"

"Her parish priest, a young man named Ander de Saratxo. She swore to the Inquisitors that during his several visits he got her pregnant. No one wanted to see that child born in an Inquisition prison. The Inquisitors were convinced Satan was the real father."

"An Inquisition soap opera! What happened to the padre?"

"He spent the rest of his life in a mission in New Spain, the part you now call New Mexico."

"What happened to her?"

"They finally let her go. She died soon after."

"How do you know all this?"

"Enara kept these tormented, flowing diaries that women in my family have handed down all this time. Four hundred years! They came to me from an aunt in San Sebastián. Isn't that fine?"

"Yes, it is."

"I don't know if I even want to write the dissertation. It would be a violation of a confidence. Don't you think?"

His shrug offered no opinion.

"I don't know my people's grandchildren, the nieces and nephews," she said. "I *have* to go back to Spain. Not just to chase something that happened in the very distant past. To ever be happy again." Her expression was both hopeful and sad. "Could you take me there? Would you? Luke?"

FOURTEEN

APRIL 1994

The king of Spain muttered an oath and tried once more to tie an acceptable Windsor knot. At fifty-five Juan Carlos liked to think he could manage the damn silk without his valet. Standing in front of a gold-framed mirror in Zarzuela Palace, he turned and almost called for him. The sudden movement sent a jag of pain through the leg he had twice broken skiing in the Pyrenees. Hissing curses, he hobbled backward and took a seat on the bed. He rested on his elbows a long while, but then he looked at his watch, sighed, and returned to the tie.

After England's Queen Elizabeth, King Juan Carlos of Spain was the most popular and respected monarch in Europe. But the king was always seeking ways to entertain himself and escape his advantaged prison of a life. One time he and Jordan's King Hussein had flown F-16s in tandem. Juan Carlos was a ham radio operator, conversing at night with strangers all over the world, and he tore off alone on winding farm roads on a BMW K1 motorcycle, taking risks that drove his security guards wild. They tried dogging him in a helicopter, but in a fury he ordered them to cut that out. If assassins wanted him, the chopper would just make him easier to find.

One of those jaunts had enhanced his image as the People's King. He came across another biker who had run out of gasoline and was stranded in open farmland. The king came back shortly with a can of fuel for the man. It was a public relations bonanza when the story wound up in the press, but in his excitement over the encounter the man told *El Mundo*'s reporter that the king's bike and helmet were matching candy apple red, and with those long legs and arms, he had looked so gawky, hunched over, racing along. In disgust Juan Carlos had to repaint the motorcycle and get another helmet. If he didn't, the ETA killers or any others would know what to look for.

The king's drivers included a road-racing champion and a former stunt man for movie productions. There were four teams of them, and they drove armored black Mercedes-Benzes with darkened windows; they could hit one hundred seventy kilometers an hour if they had to. The gates would open, and the identical Mercedes shot out, each zooming in different directions. The king not only dodged potential assassins in his armored Mercedes-Benzes—he fled the motorcycles of paparazzi.

The gossip papers in Paris, Rome, and Monte Carlo had him sleeping with every beautiful woman on the continent. One recent headline called him "Juan Carlos of a Thousand Conquests." And the tabloids in London! Now they had him shacked up in Lausanne with Princess Diana. Dear God, he thought, let them slaver on that one.

If not for uncommon turns of events Juan Carlos might have been just another disenfranchised noble who inherited a fortune and drifted from one drink and plaything to the next. The prince's father, Juan de Borbón, heir to the vacated throne, was exiled by the Civil War first to Rome and then to Estoril, Portugal. He detested Franco but they communicated from time to time, and he asked the Caudillo to allow his son to be educated in Spain, and Franco agreed to it. When Juan Carlos was sixteen, while a student in Madrid, one time when his protectors let him loose he grinned too openly at *tricornios* worn by some Guardia Civil—he thought the hats looked like black lard tins turned upside down and carried off on the wings of a bat. They let him know right away that Guardia Civil were not to be laughed at.

Juan Carlos met the girl who became his wife on a cruise of Greek islands when they were both sixteen. Her name was Sophia Schleswig-Holstein-Sonderburg-Glücksberg, and her title was Princess of Greece and Denmark. Blonde and pretty, a past Olympics competitor in a sailing event, she converted from the Greek Orthodox faith to Catholicism and adopted the Spanish spelling of her name, Sofía. At the invitation of Franco they established residence in the Palacio Zarzuela, a former hunting lodge of kings and princes, in foothills just north of Madrid. Close by was the much more lavish Palacio Real de El Pardo that the Caudillo claimed after the rebels won the Civil War.

Juan Carlos and Sofía were parents of two daughters and a son when Franco officially named him heir-apparent to the crown in 1969. Franco had been persuaded that a figurehead king would help ensure continued Falangist rule after his passing. Juan Carlos publicly swore loyalty to Franco's document of fascist principles, *El Movimiento Nacional,* with no apparent misgivings. Juan Carlos, who spoke six languages, traveled with him and appeared beside him in addresses to the rubber-stamp Cortes. They made an odd couple because Franco stood five-feet-four, and Juan Carlos was an entire foot taller.

All of Spain was under martial law then because of the violence in the Basque Country. After the killing of Carrero Blanco in 1973, the thirty-five-year-old crown prince feared for himself, for his family, for his nation. He was frightened more when he received copies of classified memos of Franco's Nationalist Police and a district attorney named Fernando Tejedor. His hands shook when he read those documents. ETA had made their bombs of Goma-2, the standard explosives in their attacks. But what of the anti-tank mine that had gone off at the same time? Several months before the murders, a shipment of identical mines had been delivered to the American air base of Torrejón, on the outskirts of Madrid, from Fort Bliss in El Paso, Texas.

The district attorney was killed by a head-on truck crash on a road outside Madrid. It was ruled an accident, but drivers who saw the wreck said it looked like a calculated murder. Not all of Franco's intelligence chiefs went down that road of conjecture. But some in the secret police were certain that US agents had gone into that tunnel with the *etarras* and planted and set off the mine that could shred a tank. In their theory, the Americans did not want a prolonged fascist regime in Spain to sully their notion of an ideal anti-Soviet Europe, and the just-concluded state visit of Secretary Kissinger was a cover for the attack.

When Franco died in November 1975, his casket rolled through Madrid's streets on the bed of an armored military vehicle, not the horses and wagon of royal tradition. Two days later the crown prince became King Juan Carlos I and head of the Spanish state, thought to be a powerless position. He and Queen Sofía chose to remain in the modest three-story Zarzuela Palace and rear their children there. They did that because he came to be portrayed as the People's King. He owed that to the crisis known as *el Tejerazo,* or 23-F.

The newborn constitutional monarchy had no constitution, and it was hard to get one written. Elections could not be held at once because the regime had outlawed political parties. A transition prime minister served briefly, and the second resigned in frustration. Juan Carlos pressured the Cortes to grant two amnesties to Basque political prisoners, but ETA only stepped up the killing. A leader of the far right asked the king to consider *"la vía de un hombre ajeno y políticamente bendecido,"* the road of someone different yet politically blessed. He went on to say that the king's longtime mentor and then executive assistant, General Alfonso Armada, was such a man.

On February 15, 1981, reports circulated that a member of ETA had been tortured to death in Madrid's notorious Carabanchel prison. A general strike ensued throughout the Basque country. On the morning of February 23 a lieutenant colonel in the Guardia Civil named Antonio Tejero Molina led two hundred men under his Valencia command into the Cortes and Cabinet offices. Lieutenant Colonel Tejero had a thick black mustache, and all the men wore *tricornios*. Tejero grabbed the microphone, pointed a .45 automatic at the assembly's president, and yelled, "Lie down, lie down!" Then he raised one palm in the fascist salute and started shooting at the ceiling, as did all the other Civil Guards who could crowd inside the chamber. The deputies and ministers hit the floor behind and under their desks. The air was thick with dust from the shattered plaster.

Tejero demanded a phone and called a lieutenant general named Jaime Milans del Bosch in Valencia. "My general, no news," he shouted. "All is in order, all is in order. *Viva España!*" And then hung up. The national radio network started playing military music. The rebel Civil Guards told the deputies they were to await news of installation of a military government. They rounded up leaders of the Socialist, Communist, and Christian Democrat parties and herded them off the floor at gunpoint. From a radio station in Castellón, General Milans del Bosch said, "In view of the happenings taking place in these moments in the capital and the consequent vacuum of power, it is my duty to guarantee order in the military region of my command until I receive corresponding instructions from His Majesty the King." Tanks, mobile anti-aircraft guns, water cannons, and troop carriers moved into the center of Valencia.

The furious monarch spent the morning calling senior commanders and established that of the nine military districts, only Valencia was in revolt. General Armada, the king's chief of staff, proposed that he, Armada, be declared prime minister. "You'll have to shoot me first," Juan Carlos snapped. That afternoon, Juan Carlos appeared on state television wearing his military uniform and medals. In somber tones the king said that he had issued orders to commanders of the armed forces to protect the constitution at all costs and that he meant to guarantee governance in accordance with civilian law. Then he ordered a cowed General Armada to negotiate surrender of the rebel Guardia Civil and bring the eighteen-hour crisis to a close.

After losing the greatest world empire since the Romans in the nineteenth century, Spain had survived a near-brush with one more calamity, and Juan Carlos received due credit for his firm and reassuring performance. He joked to Sofía that the coup was undone by photos that raced around the world of a mustachioed madman with a gun in one hand, the other raised in fascist salute. The intent was menace, but the image was farce. It was the *tricornio*. It was the hat!

Juan Carlos got the wretched knot tied and took off down the corridors of the royal palace with two aides skipping along and trying to get his attention. *Alcaldes* in the Basque Country had persuaded the king to grant an audience to the acclaimed American architect Frank Gehry. By the time he reached the reception room he had walked off the pain in his leg. He walked into a hall decorated with the heads of stags, boars, lions, leopards, and an African water buffalo. Accompanied by well-groomed Basque men, Gehry stood in a formless gray suit and brown shoes. The architect was nine years older than the king and nine inches shorter. Juan Carlos knew that Americans were uncomfortable bowing before royalty, and he was amused by their awkwardness when obliged to do so.

"Mr. Gehry," he began in fluent English, "it's a pleasure and honor to meet you. Welcome to my unremarkable house," he said with a wry glance at the conventional surroundings. "Your country has dispensed with so-called palaces and people with titles such as mine. Probably not a bad idea."

"I was born a Canadian. I admire royal heritage."

"I'm told you're the great artist of world architecture."

Frank tilted his head back and smiled. "Well, Your Majesty, my buildings have toilets and can't cave in or leak."

"Tell me about your glorious transformation of Bilbao."

"I wouldn't go so far as that, Your Majesty. The Museo Guggenheim Bilbao is now a big ugly construction site. But we expect it will be a very nice art museum, and a credit to the city. It would be only a dream if not for these gentlemen of the Consorcio, the Guggenheim Foundation, our partnering executive architecture firm IDOM, and IDOM's brilliant executive architect, César Caicoya."

Gehry looked like he wondered if he'd left anyone out.

"Oh, but it is glorious," said the king. "We Spaniards have both an admiration and wariness of great buildings. For instance Gaudí's Sagrada Família in Barcelona. Gaudí started building that in 1892. A hundred two years ago! Go there today and you hear tiny little hammers hard at work. *Tink, tink, tink.* They'll never finish it. It's like paying off the national debt. Assure me the Museo Guggenheim Bilbao won't be like that, Mister Gehry."

Frank chortled, "I'll paraphrase an American expression. If the Good Lord's willing and the Nervión River don't rise, the museum is going to open on schedule in 1997. By the way, I'm a big fan of Gaudí. When I was a young man I had a job as a draftsman in Paris. I loaded up the family and drove to Barcelona to take the Gaudí tour, all of it. My favorite was the apartment building with balconies that look like the heads and mouths of fish."

After a few more minutes of chat and sips of coffee Juan Carlos apologized for another pressing appointment and shook hands once more all around. "We hope you will join us for the Museo's grand opening, Your Majesty," said one of the Basque *jefes,* with another bow. Juan Carlos did not commit to that but decided he liked Gehry, and that hellhole Bilbao needed all the help it could get.

FIFTEEN

MAY 1994

Luke left the Hotel Madison and strode down St. Jean-de-Luz's cobblestone street all but whistling. The rented Toyota was gassed up and ready to go. The night before, lying on the ground with a flashlight, he had wired a rubberized envelope containing their real passports and other important documents to the frame. From a jetty he had hurled the Glock out into the bay, and he ran and backed over and crunched the Outfit's laptop, leaving it such wreckage that no one would think to retrieve the hard drive from the hotel Dumpster.

The streets were scrubbed by a prior day of rain and there was a fresh tang in the air. In the *centre ville* a few waiters were stirring in the cafés, unfolding tablecloths, taking down chairs. They would open for breakfast in another hour. To hear a mass said in Basque, you had to rise early. Except for the sunrise service on Sunday, French and Latin were now the tongues of faith.

The exterior of the Church of St. Jean-Baptiste had been plastered over in mediocre fashion, but its portal formed a hood over a nicely chiseled Christ and a world-class set of brass-trimmed wood doors. They opened with a croak worthy of five hundred years on the hinges. Luke stood by the font and gaped. The exterior offered no hint of the sanctuary, ablaze in gold and cerulean blue. A large and detailed replica of a whaling ship hung from the ceiling—a talisman of safe passage in another time. On three walls were balconies where fathers and sons once sat in lordly segregation, before the French ways and tongue prevailed. A few dozen people now sat in the lower pews.

Luke saw Ysolina near the back. She was wearing a white turtleneck and red jacket. Old men in open-collared shirts watched him with a mix of curiosity and suspicion. Ysolina touched the back of his hand when he sat down. "It's beautiful," he whispered, staring at the sanctuary and the whaler replica suspended from the ceiling.

"Yes. The prettiest one."

Ears around them seemed alert to their murmured Spanish.

"So John the Baptist was a whaler."

She put her hand to her mouth, suppressing a laugh.

"Tell me again," he said. "Who got married here?"

"Louis the Fourteenth to a Spanish princess, María Teresa. Ended a war. Ruined her life."

"Well, that's relative. Doom and gloom at Versailles."

She leaned against him and said, "She had a retinue of dwarves."

Someone shushed them. The priest voiced his sermon with clear enjoyment. In the resonant cathedral his Basque seemed to capture bits and pieces of all languages, yet like no tongue ever heard before. When the singing began, a chorus of old men threw back their heads and bayed like walruses. The outburst startled Luke and touched him. But the magnificent church overmatched its native congregation. In the French bureaucracy the Pays Basque no longer existed. St. Jean-de-Luz was officially a commune in the region of Pyrénées-Atlantiques. To the French these were useful rustics—good for food, lush real estate, and local color, an underclass of their own land.

Ysolina knelt with them when they prayed, but she didn't go down for communion. Afterward, a small woman with a headscarf, threadbare coat, and plain black shoes circulated among the pews with a collection plate. Luke dug in his jeans for his wallet and found nothing now but pesetas and dollars. He had thought he had no more use for the francs. When the woman reached their pew, he laid some Spanish notes on the plate. Her eyes came up angry.

Just then the Nokia went off in Luke's coat. He had used its alarm to let him make the mass and had forgotten to turn the damn thing off!

He whispered to Ysolina, *"Lo siento,"* and bustled outside, sweat broken at once. *"Cómo,"* he said, rattled, shoving through the door.

"How about 'yo'?" said Jimbo Hopson. "Or howdy?"

"Way to go, fella. I was in church with the wife of Peru Madariaga.

I'm in St. Jean-de-Luz, about ten miles from the Spanish border. I can't talk to you now."

"Golly. You banging this dolly?"

"She's no dolly, and that's none of your business."

"*All* your business down there is my business, pal."

"Jimbo—"

"Luke, you got to head this way. The Outfit wants face-time explanation of how it's going. And how you're spending all that money."

"Jimbo, that's crazy. Lose her now and they're gone for good. And this phone went off right *beside her*. This could blow the whole thing."

A long silence. "All right, Luke, I'll cover for you as long as I can. You go right on thinking that's my purpose in life. But people are losing their sunny dispositions. And you still haven't connected with Roberto Escamilla."

Luke hung up the phone and dropped it in his pocket as people came out of the church, among them Ysolina, her eyes flashing.

"I suppose you're going to tell me what that was all about."

"My brother asked me to come home and help run the ranch."

"Your brother in Texas calls people in the middle of the night?"

"He's a night owl, can't sleep. And he's like all Americans that don't travel; he doesn't know what the time zones are anywhere else. Do you want me to call him back and let you talk to him?"

There was a silence as she decided whether to call Luke's bluff.

"Let's reclaim your dog," he suggested. She had left the collie with his leash looped through handles of her luggage in the shadowed courtyard of the city hall, across the pedestrian avenue from the church. Luke hefted her largest piece of luggage, propped it on his shoulder, and carried the dog food sack. Ysolina carried the smaller bag, which contained her laptop and research notes, and hung on the collie's leash. Sunrise had turned the harbor turquoise; fishing and sailboats rocked against their moorings, flag chains ringing. "Thanks for showing me that," he said of the church and mass.

Under the jacket and pullover she wore jeans and brown walking boots. "We may have need of God's small favors."

He said, "Did you see the business with the Spanish money?"

"Did you hear my gasp?"

"She'd rather I'd given them nothing?"

"Never underestimate those mountains," she said. "French Basques have a saying. 'If they live in Spain, they're Spaniards.' They sympathize, some do. They hear about the police, the jails. But they live out whole lives and unless they're smugglers they maybe cross the border twice. It's dirty and bloody down there. They think history has spared them. They chose not to resist."

She gripped his arm and pulled him toward the dock and slips of pleasure boats. "Can I see that phone?"

He shrugged and handed it to her.

"Have you heard of location-based services?"

"I flunked technology."

"It's an arrangement between phone companies and government security agencies. In Europe a court order's required, but not in your country. Whoever called you doesn't have to hear what you say. They can track you whether you think you've got it turned off or not. They *always* know where you are."

When she handed it back Luke hurled the candy bar-shaped object over the sailboat masts to plunk in the bay. "That do?" he asked her. "You have my undivided attention."

The route Ysolina had chosen took them past hamlets called Ascain, Espellete, Itxassou, and St. Etienne-de-Baigorry. On the road they climbed a perfect tunnel that had been pruned in the roadside poplars. They followed a road that snaked upward through fields green with the first crops' shoots and lush pasture, sun diffusing as they climbed. Luke enjoyed the surges of response of the new car while Ysolina chewed polish off her thumbnail. "Here we are," she said.

She put on her sunglasses and for a second tightly gripped Luke's hand. The French border guard waved them across with barely a glance. On the other side of the checkpoint gates the Spaniard walked out with a black uniform and somber expression. Luke handed him the driver's licenses and visas and the forged passport identifying him as Selden Hale. Fitted with her photograph by ETA's cobblers, Ysolina's documents identified her as a French Canadian named Sybil Arceneaux.

"Papers for the car," said the guard. Luke gave him the rental packet. The Spaniard looked them over and said, "And health certificates for the dog." Luke handed them over. The collie sat up in back and panted serenely, casting glances side to side. The guard handed back the papers. "Welcome to Spain."

Luke watched the mirror as they passed through the little town. "Nothing to it," he said. "Talk to me. How's it feel?"

"Like eleven years, and the first three hundred meters. Unreal."

From the Spanish town of Valcarlos the road rose quickly and darkened with firs. She relaxed enough to pull up her knee and prop the boot heel in the seat. Ten miles of dark forest passed. The highway emerged from the trees on a mountainside, and a long, misty green valley stretched beyond. Luke almost believed in the ease of the crossing when a man walked out in black boots, camouflage pants, olive turtleneck, beret, and sunshades. He held up a black-gloved hand and waved them into the overlook. A second man was dressed the same way. Parked along the rail were gleaming black motorcycles, BMW K75s.

"Uh oh," said Luke. "Spoke too soon."

"*Sí.*"

"Don't speak Spanish to them," he reminded her. "Who are they?"

"Cuerpo Nacional de Policia. They have military authority."

The one who approached had dark good looks and a holstered Luger. He took his time with the passports. "You travel a great deal," he said to Luke.

"Yes. In my business."

"What kind of business?"

Luke started to reach for a valise with the phony brochure Pascal had made but the Spaniard gave his head a quick firm shake. "I was just going to show you our brochure," he said, putting his hands back on the steering wheel. "The company is Graffiti Gone, Incorporated."

"Say again?"

"Graffiti Gone. Our remediation works on brick, concrete, wood, metal, you name it. We apply a clear, non-toxic, unscented emulsification and let it dry. Then we wash it off. Then we apply another thin coat. It's revolutionary. New York City swears by us."

The Spaniard put his gloved palm on the roof of the car.

"Señora," he said. "Remove your glasses, please."

She didn't move. Luke repeated the command in English. She took off the shades and gave the man a smile. "She doesn't speak Spanish," said

Luke. "She does speak French."

Ysolina had spent the week absorbing everything she could about the nation of Canada. Capitals of provinces, distances between. The cop looked at the different names on the passports. "She's not your wife?"

"No. She's an author of cookbooks," Luke said. "I met her in Paris. Had worse nights." He gave the cop a smile and watched him put the passports and visas in his pocket. His heart began to sink.

"Unlatch the hood and trunk and get out of the car. Tell her to stay where she is, hands on the dashboard."

Luke relayed the order in English. She frowned as if puzzled and put her hands on the vinyl. The cop searched under the front seats, stooped and peered under the tire wells, and in the trunk raised the spare tire and tugged the carpet to see if it was loose. He made Luke open their bags, disordered them well, and he thrust his hand inside the dog food sack. "Where are you going?" he asked.

"Madrid. Maybe on down to Málaga. We're not sure." The second one now stood with his hands on his knees, his face two feet from the window of Ysolina's door. She met his gaze calmly.

The talker closed the hood and trunk and flipped through the passports and visas again. He stooped and peered at Ysolina; the other cop's pair of reflective shades were right beside her head. The one on the driver's side asked her in Spanish, "Where did you stay last night?"

Again she didn't take the bait. "Biarritz," Luke answered for her.

"Same hotel?" the cop asked him. Luke nodded. "Same room same bed?" Luke shrugged and nodded again. The cop frowned at her. "*Adúltera?*" he said. He was trying to make her react. She didn't bite.

"All right," said the cop on the driver's side, handing back their papers.

"Anything I need to know about?" said Luke.

"Be careful. This is the Basque Country. You'll know you're out of it when you stop seeing the bilingual signs."

"I thought all that was cooling down."

"Don't believe what you read in the papers. Good luck with your graffiti cleaning. And your companion."

"And good luck to you," said Luke. When the biker cops were safe behind them, he said, "Good work. You were very good."

She hissed, "Picked me up in Paris, did you? Pig!" His bit about her being a cookbook author had been an improvisation. "What would I have done if they'd known English and started asking me for titles to my books and *recipes?*"

"Hey, play the audience, whatever it takes to get the curtain down." He drove on, smiling. "Did you see those uniforms? Those motorcycles? I kind of liked those guys. I thought they were dashing."

"Dashing! They'd pull out your teeth with pliers."

SIXTEEN

Ysolina knew how close a call that was, and she could have chosen a crossing that wouldn't have been so scrutinized. But the Valcarlos route took them near a pass she wanted to see again. A few kilometers into Spain she directed him down a narrow and bumpy road. "Stop here," she said as they came on a long overlook toward the west. "Do you know the story of Roncesvalle?"

"A little. I know the *Song of Roland* is a French epic poem about Moors' massacre of Charlemagne's rear guard. I read it in college."

"That's not what happened. The attackers were Basques with arrows and stones, not Saracens on horses. The poet must have thought that was more dramatic. Charlemagne had sacked Pamplona and turned his riders loose for the usual rape and pillage. Roland was Charlemagne's favorite but commanded his rear guard. The ambush is supposed to have been Charlemagne's only defeat. Armies and mule trains and pilgrims trying to reach Santiago de Compostela have come across here for ages. And smugglers," she said. "You just smuggled me."

Luke stopped the car and they got out and gazed eastward. A lone ram grazed a ledge below them, sunlight glinting on its horns. A couple of miles away the angle of reflection made a small lake a teardrop of gold. The vistas unrolled in shades and triangles of green turning blue toward the horizon. She moved her breast against his arm and said, "Are you enjoying this yet?"

"Sure," he said. "As long as you keep on doing that."

They set off again, and the passing terrain set off a rush of emotions in Ysolina that took her breath away. She told him about memories of *fanoak*, favorite horse pastures, and higher up the limestone caves that were attended, children were always told, by *lamiak* who sat in the mouths of the caves grooming their hair with golden combs, wishing for human love, and they set off thunder and lightning and meteor showers as they leaped in agitation from mountain to mountain, cave to cave. "When a boy was smitten by a girl, he was supposed to look at her feet," she told him. "If she walked on the feet of a duck she was a *lamia* who could suck the life and soul right out of his throat. Between the second and third toes of my feet I was born with thin pale webbings of skin. You should have heard the shrieks of my cousins and schoolmates on seeing my feet! I'm still self-conscious wearing sandals or lying beside a beach or pool."

The road forked beside a small cemetery. He said, "Mind if I stop?"

"You're driving."

Needing to relieve his bladder, Luke got out with the dog and walked among discoid gravestones etched with the Basque crucifix of four wheeling figures. His grandmother said it was a symbol of luck and prosperity but ignorant persons called it a swastika. As Luke unbuttoned his fly Barkilu scared up a small covey of quail, the eruption just ten yards away. Luke composed himself and continued. The stream of urine came out pale and healthy, then like an inner dam had broken, it ran dark as coffee again. "Fuck," he said, staring at the leaves.

Through and above the trees, Luke saw a flat and bare hilltop. People up there were standing in a circle. Motionless, they gazed inward at a tall pole, from which billowed a long black pennant. He whistled back Barkilu and returned to the car. Ysolina was leaning against it. "What happened?" she said. "You were like a statue."

"Nothing." His hands shook as he tried to light a cigarette. "What are they doing up there? On the hill."

"Just a funeral, a burial."

"They have real cemeteries for that. Your dog and I just pissed in one."

"Why are you so rattled?"

"I don't know, maybe those cops that pull out your teeth with pliers. And something about this spot raised the hair on the back of my neck. Look at those people. No one moving, not a shoulder blade, not an elbow."

"They're just honoring a loved one."

She took the keys away from him, opened the trunk, and took off her jacket. She laid it on the bags, pushed up a shirtsleeve, and dug inside the sack of dog food. She pulled out a package wrapped with brown paper and tape. "I'm sorry," she said. "I should have told you."

"What is it?"

She took a pocketknife out of the coat and leaned against the fender, slicing carefully. "Enara's diaries."

Luke gaped. "That cop poked around in there."

"I would have explained. You hide rare books, in case somebody breaks in the trunk."

"Right, explain it in what language, smuggled antiquities, with my brain turned to jelly. Are you crazy? I thought we had a script."

"You're one to talk about script. But I am sorry."

She reached for his hand and pulled him near. Against the car, with their shoulders touching, she let him hold a volume, encased in badly cracked leather. "Be very gentle," she said. "The paper's almost dust."

The pages were thick but fragile. The slants of handwriting wobbled, with haphazard inking of the quill. He read aloud. *"Harrezkero hil aunitz igaro dita, eta ene oroitzpena oinaze askoren murriztua da.'* What does that mean?"

She said, "Long months have since elapsed, and my memory is feeble through much suffering."

"I think we'd better go." Back on the highway, they came out of the trees into a long valley. Back home Luke was accustomed to stacks of mown hay shaped like loaves of bread or rolls of shredded wheat. Here the haystacks were arranged in ten-foot cones, supported by a single pole. The expression "the stake" took on clarity in his mind it never quite had before. The flames would coil straight up, hottest at the center.

Luke tried to be patient, negotiating all the highway roundabouts. As they drove on he gazed at the horizon to the west and saw a gray furl enclosing the green mountains. "There's some kind of front coming in," he said, nodding at the nearest mountains. It looked like the peaks wore a muffler.

"It's the Everlasting Cloud," she said.

"The what?"

"That's what they call it, the Everlasting Cloud. It never comes closer, but never goes away."

"Weird climate, if you ask me."

In the folding green land ahead Ysolina began to see the russet roofs of Ezkaroze. Near the outskirts they encountered middle-aged couples out walking the hills for exercise. The houses were two-story, snow-roofed whitewashed blocks of stone with brown storm windows and balconies— pots of blooming geraniums, garlands of dried red peppers. A woman sewed on a bench and talked to another woman who idly wielded a broom. An old-timer ambled beside the curb with a cane, his back to the traffic. Between his cardigan and beret was a great white head. He acknowledged the car with an upward tip of his cane. Ysolina made a sound, and Luke gave her a look. "It's my hometown, *jaioterri,*" she said.

"Then we have to stop."

"No. There are both too many and too few people here. Some past schoolmate or shopkeeper could recognize me. We're going back up in the mountains," she said, directing him to a road that ran along a tributary stream called Río de Vellos. Soon there were no more villages. The horizon with its gray furl disappeared behind the nearest mountains, and a bright sun came back out. The river below them ran clear, broken by rapids. There were great tableaus of rock wrenched and rearranged in some ancient upheavals, and then they would come through stands of beech, birch, and black pine so dense and crowded against the road that for a few hundred yards it was almost dark as night.

She guided him down a lane through a thick stand of maple forest. The ruins of a castle emerged above the trees. "There it is," she said. *"La casa de infamia."* Luke gave her an uncertain glance.

"Enara's house. And my family's for a while."

"You *lived* in that?"

"A part of it was habitable." He parked beside a new wire fence; she reached over the seat and opened the door. The dog jumped out, bellied under the wire, and trotted off, nose to the ground. Ysolina touched a steel barb with her finger and searched the fence for a post sturdy enough to support her climb.

"Wait," he said. He shoved one strand down with his boot, pulled the other up, and directed her through the wire unsnagged. He followed with an ease that, given the length of his legs, made her blink. He grinned at her expression. "It's cultural. You had *lamiak.* I had barbed wire."

She took Luke's arm. "The church confiscated the property from Enara," she said, "but my great grandfather paid some bribes and bought it back. My mother inherited it, and we lived here till I was sixteen, when she died. After she was gone Papa couldn't stand it. He sold it to an Englishman. Now it's too far gone to save."

Later they lay on the ground outside the walls, nearly dozing. Barkilu walked up and poked a cold nose against her cheek. She rolled away and caught him by the ears, engaged him in a tussle. "Ooof. Get off me," said Luke when the dog stepped on him.

"I think maybe I'll call you Luken."

"Be all right. My *amona* would like it."

Ysolina smiled and sang a couple of lines from a song.

Nafarroa, oi Nafarroa, Euskadi lehena
zer egin de emetsa zure erregena

"That's nice. My grandmother used to sing it. What does it mean?"

"'Navarra, oh Navarra, the first Basque Country, what happened to the dream of your kings?'"

In the car again, she directed him onto an ever-bumpier lane that led them twisting into the mouth of the Cañon de Añisclo. They stopped and with the dog trotting ahead, she led him up a trail that left him cursing his loss of wind and leg strength. Then they came to the overlook and the ravine was a pair of matching white cliffs three hundred feet straight down to another stream of rapids breaking into a waterfall. A heron rose in slow elegant flight from the mist.

They lay again in the sunshine, Luke idly chewing a stem of grass. "What happened to your mother?" he asked. "You said she died."

"She drowned. We were on holiday, Mama and I were on our horses, Papa was fishing. It was not far from here, in western Aragón. The steep river canyons are very pretty, as dramatic as these. That day we were on the Río Alagón, at a point where the stream was broader and waters gentler, though the current was still strong. Mama and I had gone riding. We came to a stream that looked shallow enough to cross. Her horse walked off in a hole and rolled with her. He must have knocked her out. I jumped off and struggled out of my boots but . . . even in water that clear I couldn't find her fast enough. One minute I had been talking to her. The next she was gone."

He made a sad sound breathing. "So now you go off on a horse full speed down the Pyrenees."

"I don't cross rivers on them."

He rolled toward her, crossed his arms on the ground, and in time he kissed her. He let it be just the flesh of their lips. She touched his face and said, "I've been wanting to do that again."

"I've been hoping you would."

He spoke to the sky. *"Oi Nafarroa."*

She propped herself on an elbow, and with her fingers touched his mouth. Here and there, all around, lightly pressing. "I'm going to tell you a story. Just as my grandmother told me."

"Shoot."

"Antxiñen munduen asko lez . . . "

"I'm not gonna understand it."

"That's just how you begin childhood stories. Like 'Once upon a time.'"

"Oh."

"Like many in the world in the old days, a young man had a loving wife, and they were going to have twins, she could feel them moving in her stomach. But he couldn't make himself leave his mother's house. The wife knew his husband's mother hated her, but there was nothing she could do. Before the babies were born, he had to go far away, to a foreign land. The twins were a boy and a girl. But nothing could soften the old woman's heart. Seeing them, her hatred just increased. So she ordered her servant to take them up on a mountain and kill them. To prove he'd done it, he would cut off their hands and cut out her heart and bring them back."

"This a bedtime story?"

"Do you want to hear it?"

"Of course."

"They went off with the servant, and their dog followed. On the mountain he told them what he had to do. The young woman cried and begged him to let her children live. He felt sorry for them but feared for his own life. She pleaded with him to cut off her hands and say he lost the other two and the hag might believe it, so he cut them off, and then he killed the dog and cut its heart out. He put her babies in knapsacks and hung them around her neck."

Luke laughed, and she put her palm on his chest. "She wandered in the mountains for days. She came upon a river, and her babies cried out, 'Water. Water.' They were dying of thirst. She knelt at the bank so they could drink, but then the knapsacks tipped, and they fell in and drowned before her eyes. Because she had no hands."

He put his hands on his face, and she gave him a light punch. "She cried so much the river came over its banks. But then she looked across and there was a beautiful woman. The woman asked the mother, 'What are you doing here?' The terrible tale poured out of her, then the beautiful woman said, 'Put your right arm in the water.' She did, and when she pulled it out she had regained her hand. 'Now the other.' That hand and arm were whole again, too. She plunged both arms back in the river and pulled out her babies alive. It was the Virgin Mary. She gave the mother a wand and told her to carry her children up a mountain until she found a flat wide space. In the clearing she would draw a line with the wand, which she did, and their house appeared before them. They lived off their garden and trapped hares there for the next three years.

"One day some hunters chanced on the clearing. A storm was coming, and the mother made them supper and gave them room for the night. The next morning, one of the hunters rose before the others and rebuilt the fire. The boy of the house brought him a pitcher of water and a bowl so he could wash his hands and shave. Then his sister walked up and said, 'Papa, here's your towel.'"

Luke roughed the collie's coat. "Nice fable," he said.

She picked some litter off his shirt. "That's not the end. When the hunter recognized his wife and children, he took them back down the mountain to his home village. And that's where he had his mother burned at the stake in the middle of the square."

With a brief dab of tongue she tasted his neck, just under his ear. He grinned and, tilting his head, invited her to continue. She murmured, *"Ori alan ixen bazan . . . sartu deilla kalabazan . . . eta urten deyela . . . Ezkaroze'ko plazen."*

"And they all lived happily ever after," he supposed.

"No. 'If this was the way it happened, put yourself in a pumpkin and jump out in the plaza of Ezkaroze.'"

SEVENTEEN

The valley of the Río Salazar divided into fertile farms, hay fields, vineyards. There was a succession of villages, each one pristine. "All that grass," Luke marveled, looking at the terrain. "My grandmother used to say that she knew at least twenty words in Basque for 'pasture.'"

"Tell me about her," she said.

"She's ninety-five and blind. My grandfather was killed here in the Civil War. We don't know anything except he died at Bilbao. Amona kept that ranch running until Pop could take over. My mother ran off with an accountant and died of cancer. Then Pop had the big heart attack. Amona raised my brother and me and started running the ranch again. I gave her a lot of grief in my wild days. It's how I got to be a fighter."

She tilted her head askance. "A fighter?"

"A boxer," he said. *"Ukabilikari."*

"A professional?"

"No, no, an amateur. I wanted to go to the Olympics. It didn't happen."

Ysolina pulled her sunglasses down on her nose and eyed him with amusement. "So many things I don't know about you."

"Give us time."

"How is your grandmother?"

"I don't know," he said.

"You said this morning you talked to your brother. You didn't ask?"

When he didn't answer she punched his arm hard. "Don't lie to me. We can't lie to each other. Listen to me. I like being with you so much it makes me dizzy. But I've got this voice in my head saying, 'You make the same mistake. Over and over. Again and again.' I'm not going to let you hurt me."

"Hey, all right," he said, taken aback. "I won't lie to you. I sure don't want to hurt you. The man who called this morning was involved in my business with Peru. You told me 'if you ever get drawn into that, you're out of my life.' My relationship with that man is in the bottom of the bay in St. Jean-de-Luz. He's not a part of my life anymore. You are." He wasn't lying just now, but he was manipulating her, and he hated it. The lying came with the training. He wondered if anyone in the Outfit could stop.

"Tell me about the Basques over there. In your country."

"I've known more of them in South America," he said. "The younger sons came to the Americas with the Spanish empire because they were subjects of Spain, and they spoke the language. They were soldiers, priests, whalers, and some became vaqueros. The Basque identity where I come from is filtered through those countries, those cultures. People see and hear Basque names and words in Texas and think that's all just Mexican."

He went on, "It's different farther west. Out there they're mostly French Basques who arrived as sheepherders. Some stay on and you run into them as construction foremen, truck drivers, owners of small hotels. When I was in the military out west, one time I went looking for them. I passed through a town called Reno, Nevada. I saw a billboard advertising a Basque festival that same day. It turned out this festival was on a little parking lot between a freeway and a casino. They had the wood-chopping contests and the weightlifting. Aitor from Elko picks up a cylinder that weighs two hundred pounds and rolls it across his shoulders and the back of his neck. Then Aitor grunts and drops it, and they all applaud. There were college kids in white outfits with red sashes and red berets—a dance troupe from a college in Idaho. They were so scrubbed and wholesome, and the dances were pretty. But all the time eighteen-wheelers were roaring by on the freeway, and a neon message sign was zipping around the casino. *'Nevada's Premier Prime Rib, Nevada's Premier Prime Rib.'* I couldn't stay there. It made me sad."

In one of the villages they found a café that hadn't closed for siesta. The owner exchanged pleasantries with Ysolina in Euskera and showed them a table outside. She didn't give them menus. The patio was next to an impressive vegetable garden and beyond that was another set of white-washed houses with the red tile roofs and windows framed by the dried red peppers. The woman brought out red wine, sliced bread, and a hard white cheese and olives.

They were into another carafe when she brought out plates of the day
—lamb chops grilled medium rare and white asparagus with seasoned
homemade mayonnaise. "Those may be the best lamb chops I've ever
had," Luke said. Below them were an uncultivated field and a clear-
running stream. About a dozen large brown birds circled and swooped.
Luke said with surprise, "Those are eagles."

"You haven't seen them before?"

"Not in those numbers."

"They're Bonnelli's eagles," Ysolina said. "I think they're playing."

"Playing with your dog." The collie had raced out on the field and
was spinning about barking, which made them cruise lower.

"Barkilu, stop!" she called. "Come here."

"He's not bothering anybody. Somebody will let us know if he is."

"Why's he doing that?"

"He's a sheepdog, or once bred to be. Some dim part of his brain is
reminding him that used to be his job. Big birds carry off lambs."

A moment later he said, "Thank you, Ysolina."

"You're welcome. For what?"

He looked around and said, "For bringing me home."

When they arrived at the Plaza del Castillo in Pamplona the sun
was down, and the *paseo* had begun around gnarled tamarisk trees with
trunks painted white. At an outdoor bar they ordered wine and a succession of tapas, the Basque *pintxos*, and as the parade of young adults and
children began to thin out, the plaza was taken over by what Ysolina told
him was *sabaigain*, the widows' walk. They strolled with their heads close
together, talking and laughing, and then took their reserved tables on the
first rows of the cafés. Hung from balconies and clotheslines along the
upper stories of buildings were *ikurriñas*, the Basque flags, and fluttering
white pieces of paper with writing on them.

"What are those?" he asked.

"Names of political prisoners."

They left the plaza and she led him into a bar that was dark and thick
with cigarette smoke. The jukebox vibrated the floor with the bass and
drums of what Luke would have called heavy metal. Ysolina raised her
voice over the din and said it was called "radical rock." Centered over the

bar was a poster headed with the letters ETA. Below that was a snake wound around an axe, then the caption *"Bietan Jarral."* The bartender served draft beer from a tap in the shape of a hand grenade. "I'm getting the picture," Luke said. "But what does *'Bietan jarral'* mean?"

"ETA's slogan," she said. "'Keep Up On Both.' The axe means armed conflict—the snake, politics."

"I don't like it here. Can we go?"

Outside she reached for his hand. "I just wanted you to see one of those. They're called *herriko tavernas.* 'Popular bars.' The people in there are pathetic. That's not me. It never has been."

"I just wanted to get you back out where it's fun."

In contrast to the pretty but somnolent French Basque towns, Pamplona was rocking and rolling and, he thought, leaving the menace to the bruisers in the *herrika taverna.* A boy and girl were making out and shedding their shirts under a streetlight while onlookers cheered. A crowd gathered around a bare-chested youth, a fire-eater, who carried a torch, took a deep breath, filled his mouth with lighter fluid, clenched his teeth on a wick, and blew a five-foot spear of flame.

"I have an idea," Ysolina said. "Let's go take my dog for a short walk and then go to bed."

She came out of their bathroom in the small Hotel Eslava wearing her panties and her shirt unbuttoned. In a while he turned his mouth away from her lips and tongue and put his face in her hair. Her nipple rose up as soon as he touched it. She pressed hard against him, then freed her hands and started pulling at his shirttails and belt. Luke sat on the bed just looking at her. He watched the slope of her hip and back and shoulders as she reached to light a candle. After a moment he had to stand up and walk as the collie sidestepped out of the way.

"I'd better slow down," he said. "It's been a while."

"We'll get it right. But you have to come here."

She watched him delight himself. She twisted her head against a pillow and cried, "Where have you been?"

Later he lay on his back with his hands crossed under his head, still breathing heavily. "Are you all right?" she asked.

"Is that a serious question?"

She rolled and turned to the foot of the bed. She was on her stomach, one heel aloft. He raised his head and saw that she was taking things out of his jeans. He said, "What are you doing?"

"I'm after all your secrets."

His secret at the moment was the light scattering of freckles on her legs and a mole beneath the peak of a hiked shoulder blade. She looked back and lofted the purple velvet packet and the green rocks in her hand. "Are these emeralds?"

"Yes."

"Why?"

"Why do I carry them? Kind of like prayer beads, except I'm not religious. Sometimes prayers get answered anyway. You want them? They're yours."

EIGHTEEN

While the American roamed Euskadi Sur and lolled in the arms of his wife, Peru steeped in a whirlpool in a French Basque town named for its baths, Cambo-les-Bains. A beer sat on the floor beside the tub, and he smoked a cigar, tipping ashes over the side. Reading glasses were perched on his nose. The floors were marble tile, the walls cedar, and a sauna added to the smell. Above the churning water he scanned a thick bradded sheaf of pages, taking no great pains to keep them dry. Other bundled papers were pitched among towels and a robe on the floor.

He was thinking not about ETA strategy but the rugby games he had played in his hometown, Oñate. The bathhouse sat well down the slope of a white château with a slate roof gleaming in the sun. Txili and Jale paced and sunned themselves out on the deck. Their Kalashnikovs were slung on towel hooks just inside the door. The bluff overlooked the Nive, where in waders and shallow whitewater a fly fisherman could now be seen. To his rear the grounds of arbors, benches, hedges, and lawn melded into a cherry orchard. Peru and his bodyguards were using a retreat that belonged to an enamel and porcelain exporter whose son, a cyber thief whose hacking skill was useful to ETA, owed his health to *gudariak* protection in a French prison on the Ile de Ré. The prison had once been the departure point to Devil's Island.

"Txili," Peru called. The youth walked in with an inquiring look. Peru asked him to put ten more minutes on the whirlpool's timer and throw out his cigar. He had never been hard to work for.

The youth took the wet stub and asked, "Do you want another beer?" Peru shook his head. He tossed the sheaf of paper toward the others and sank to his chin and ears. Txili hung on a moment. He seemed to want to talk—if for no other reason, Jale was hopeless in that regard. Thin and

123

blue-eyed, Txili had a feathery beard and a gold-tipped front tooth. The *gudariak* had found him stealing cars and stripping parts in the more desperate barrios of Bilbao. At first Peru wondered why Txili was so eager to run small errands for them that carried enormous risk. But he had extraordinary thieving talent. It didn't matter to Peru how cool or reckless a shooter the boy might be—he wanted Txili with him full time. Txili became his protégé because he had no ideology, and the Civil War was as vague and distant to him as the Middle Ages. He was eight years old when Franco died, so he didn't get twisted up in all that. Txili was motivated by one thing alone. He was Basque and did not want to be ruled by Spaniards. To Peru he was the face of hope for the future. "How is it with your family?" Peru asked him from the tub.

"Not good," Txili replied.

Txili's father was going down from multiple sclerosis. "Have you talked to them?" Peru said.

"No. But I hear of them through a cousin."

"And?"

"He has these spasms of the muscles. The nurses that come to the house won't give him enough morphine. My mother lives to feed him and change his diapers and sheets. And hear him cry out. He's a tough old bastard. He won't die. And it's killing her."

The whirlpool's bubbles roiled. "We'll be there soon," Peru said. "You'll get to see them."

"Euskadi Sur? You mean it?"

"Sure. I think we've worn out our welcome with the French."

Jale had shaved his head and then thought better of it, so now had ceased to shave his beard. The dark stubble was an even length above and below his ears. He sat in undershirt and cutoff dungarees on the edge of the bathhouse deck, gazing at the fisherman in the river. Jale was a hairy man except he was bald. After the killing of Carrero Blanco, Jale had been arrested in a little town named Ciudad Encantada. The Spanish interrogations never broke him. Though never convicted of involvement in the assassination, he was in Soria prison for six years. He assumed they'd never let him out. On his right arm was a jail tattoo, among many others, that said *kaleitxi,* dead end street. But much to his surprise he walked out one day, a beneficiary of one of King Juan Carlos's amnesties. It didn't brighten his outlook toward Spaniards or their king. He had joined up with Peru again for the explosions and killing of that engineer of the Lemóniz nuclear plant. Jale made that decision and pulled the trigger. He was loyal to Peru but thought he was just as qualified to be the military commander. But all the prison ink left him too easily identified, a risk at border crossings, and he was uneducated. Peru had let him know he wasn't going to rise much higher in the organization than he already had.

Jale raised a pair of binoculars and brought the angler in focus. He had once worked maintenance for a rich man who was always going off to fish the trout with his short fly rods and the salmon with his long ones. The man would come out on a lawn much like this and fiddle with his gear and practice his casting. Through the filter of Jale's avid class resentment, the mannerisms of the sport struck him as womanly. All this knitting over itty-bitty flies, and the casting reminded him of a maid flopping out a sheet, trying to make it reach across a bed. He lowered the field glasses and yawned.

The angler, the *arrantzale,* fit the profile. Flop hat, sunshades, the creel and net and hip boots. Miguel Peralta was in his forties, dark-skinned. He was growing bald and had a well-groomed mustache. He worked the bank and the shallows below the houses and a cherry orchard, and he knew what he was doing. His backward cast stopped just behind his ear, hesitated as the line stretched out to the rear, then with a short soft flick of his wrist he brought the leader and fly sighing past his ear again. He leaned forward with the rod and billowed the line out gently, allowing the fly to drop lightly and float.

The rocks were slick. He crouched and picked his way carefully, fishing the eddies a few casts before he moved on. His rod plucked the fly out of the water with barely a drip. He laid the fly out, watched a moment, then with a rolling flip of the rod lifted the line and made the fly ascend and light again. Real mayflies spiraled in the air.

Peralta's eyes were on the cherry orchard when he felt the strike, and with a grunt of surprise he flicked the rod and set the hook. The fish had been lying up in a shelf of the undercut bank. The man smiled and reeled hard, trying to break the tippet. But the trout seemed to wish itself caught, so after a moment he enjoyed the tussle. When the fish wore out and turned over on its side, Peralta lifted it from the water to his net.

With a pair of forceps clipped to his jacket vest he freed the hook and let the trout go.

Three men were in the orchard. The one nearest the house rested on his elbows, picking through litter of a past harvest. Fifty meters farther down, the second one listened to the whine of a motorbike up on the road and sought just the right place in his shoulder for the rifle's butt. The other shooters were spaced out at the same distance farther down the fence line and a narrow graveled road. In the river they watched their team leader, the fly fisherman. Miguel Peralta lived with his wife and four kids in Móstoles, a suburb of Madrid. He was a retired army lieutenant colonel and a senior agent of the Guardia Civil's secret service.

On the bathhouse deck, Txili stood in the shade with his arms folded across a T-shirt that bore the likeness of Mariah Carey. Jale sat on the edge of the deck, banging his heels against a wood support. The angler now stood well back from the water, and something about his posture made Jale grab the binoculars. Beneath the sun hat his hand was cradled against his face, as if he were nursing a sore jaw. It was a walkie-talkie. The shooters in the cherry orchard heard Peralta say: *"Ahora. Hazlo."* Do it!

The first round hit very near Txili's crossed arms and the glamorous image of the singer. It blew out parts of him and spun him but the wall kept him on his feet. He looked at the sudden paint of blood and gristle on the wall, not yet connecting it with himself. Jale, in his haste to reach the AK-47s slung on the towel rack inside, jostled Txili out of his way. In the doorway the youth's head exploded, and the force of the bullet and the blood of his wounds sent him skidding across the marble tile. In a stupid reflex Peru groped in search of his towel.

After that the fire came in triangulated lanes, the center gun roving. The bullets came through the bathhouse wall with snaps and zings and a dust storm of shattered wood and plaster. Peru's instinct was to cower and sink lower in the tub, but chunks of its porcelain were falling in the water, and as adrenaline took hold the miracle came to him that he was not hit and Jale was out there, returning their fire. Peru rolled out of the tub and through the pops and sighs grabbed the other Kalashnikov and slid wetly on his belly toward the door. His bare foot touched something—Txili's shoe—and he jumped like it was a snake.

What he saw outside amazed him. Jale ran, weaved, tumbled, and rolled, shooting semiautomatic to conserve his rounds. He had placed and challenged the gunmen enough to rattle them. But divots of rich man's turf kicked up all around him. Peru laced the line of cherry trees with a burst of automatic and was surprised when several tracers took off in their drifting flight. The magic and terror of bullets was that they were invisible. Under the assumption that they would always be outnumbered, it was ETA's policy never to use tracers—they gave positions away.

Peru thought it must be one of the AK-47s that had come from the American with magazines loaded by his suppliers. In any case his position at the moment was no secret, and the green blurs made a pretty sight, especially to Jale. He hit the ground behind a stone bench and looked back with a shout and an upraised fist. The Cause.

"The riverbank!" he yelled. "Shoot the *arrantzale!*"

Peru picked out the man scrambling up and away from the bank. He ran slowly because of the waders. The burst of fire took him down but Peru saw from the tracers that his aim had drifted high; in the brush he lost the man. Peru realized they were the only ones shooting. On orders of Peralta, who was hit in the leg but able to hop along with an arm on the shoulders of one of his comrades, the assassins dissolved through the orchard toward cars in the lane.

A hush descended on the hillside of the chateaux. Above the grove Peru saw a halo of fluttering birds. It was old as time, vengeance and more vengeance. Peru flung the robe around his shoulders and started stuffing documents in the rucksack, trying not to look at anything else. The rich Frenchman with the hacker son in prison would have some serious explaining to do. Any moment would bring the first siren, but the roads were twisting and difficult.

Already Peru was wording the commendation that regular armies would have bestowed on Jale with a ceremony and medal. It would buy him quite a few more pesetas a month. For his dead comrade there would be communication with the family and arrangement for their pension. To his credit, Peru thought, Jale had the decency to stand outside and inquire. "Txili?" he asked.

"Don't come in here," was all Peru could say.

NINETEEN

MAY 1994

Most days in Pamplona Don Jokin wore a black long-sleeved shirt, full and pleated in the back, with French cuffs and the white Roman collar. He favored starched khakis and was known around campus for his brown and white Broadstreet wingtips. Don Jokin was the director of public relations for Universidad de Navarra, and this was an uncommon day. Following the private lunch of the chancellor, president, and King Juan Carlos, Don Jokin would escort His Majesty on a tour of the Instituto de Estudios Superiores de la Empresa, the university's graduate school of business. For this occasion he donned his black cassock with cape, the ferriola. The red piping and buttons identified him as Monsignor. Don Jokin had not warmed to it. An adage in the priesthood held that the title of Monsignor came with a bucket and a mop. But Pope John Paul II had approved the nomination by his bishop. It was a high mark of job approval on what amounted to a résumé in a holy corporation.

On meeting His Majesty, Don Jokin thought the man was taller than he looked on TV. Wearing a lightweight brown business suit, the king acknowledged the priest's bow, and waved aside the words of what an honor it was to be in his presence. He shook Don Jokin's hand with a firm grip. He thanked the chancellor and president for the excellent lunch, and said he would return after the tour to say goodbye.

The press had not been informed of the king's visit, and though the city was filling up with the riffraff drawn each year to San Fermín's running of the bulls, few students were on campus. Unless someone blinked and happened to recognize the monarch, the king was just a tall man wearing sunglasses, accompanied by a priest and five men, four of whom wore matching dark suits and sunglasses, carried pistols inside their jackets, and moved their heads with the jerkiness of fowls; the bodyguards were watching roofs and trees and shadows between buildings for movement.

Don Jokin's pitch was smooth. "Saint Josemaría Escrivá de Belaguer," he began, "founded our university in 1952 as 'a place where people acquire a high level of learning and a Christian outlook on life.' Saint Josemaría said, 'We want it to be a place which encourages deep thought and reflection, so that learning is soundly rooted in true principles, and shines its light along all the paths of knowledge.'"

"A quarter century, then, after he founded Opus Dei," said the king. "I see you're a Monsignor and a Jesuit."

"Ah, my raiment. You know the nuances of our Holy Church."

"Not as well as I should. But on a day like this, isn't that hot?"

Don Jokin was flustered by his tone of familiarity. "Oh, it does collect the sunlight," he acknowledged.

"I met Father Josemaría a few times when I was crown prince," Juan Carlos said. Don Jokin noted that the king declined to call him a saint. "I have read him quoted as having once said, 'I would rather a daughter of mine die without the last Sacraments than that they be administered by a Jesuit.'"

"Oh, I'd not heard that," said Don Jokin, threatened. "You know what sensationalists reporters and biographers can be."

"Yes. But it does seem odd that a priest would talk in terms of having a daughter." He offered that with a winning smile.

Don Jokin tried to steer the conversation back on course. "The principles of our founder are a gateway to the highest academic achievement. Year in and year out our institution is rated the best private university in Spain. We have satellite campuses in San Sebastián, Barcelona, and Madrid, and hope for one soon in New York City. Our library contains one point one million books. The *Economist* magazine in London ranks our MBA program the best in the world! The *New York Times* ranks us among the top fifty. Perhaps with some feet on that soil we can bring the Americans around." Don Jokin ended his rote pitch with a smile. "We are enormously proud of our university, Your Majesty."

The king nodded and mused, "Pride is one of the mortal sins."

"Yes, yes indeed," said Don Jokin, thrown off once more, but he set out to reassert himself. "You know, in his epistle to the Galatians Saint

Paul wrote: 'Now the works of the flesh are manifest, such as these: adultery, fornication, uncleanness, lasciviousness, idolatry, witchcraft, hatred, variance, emulations, wrath, strife, seditions, heresies, envyings, murders, drunkenness, revellings, and such like.'"

He left a pause and chuckled. "'And such like.' It reads like Saint Paul wondered if he'd forgotten a few. Our Holy Word comes to us in many tongues, many translations." Don Jokin's vanity wouldn't let him stop. "Latinate transcriptions added 'vainglory' as a definition of sinful pride. A monk in the fourth century, Evagrius Ponticus, rendered it in Greek as 'hubris,' or self-esteem. Pope Gregory the First and Dante refined the list to seven, rolling vainglory and pride into something called 'superbia.' Your Majesty, I assure you that my pride in this small university is anything but vainglorious and superb."

The king laughed. "All right. But tell me, are you worried?"

"Worried, Your Majesty? About what?"

"Murders. Sedition. ETA has set off four bombs on this campus over the years. I take it from your name you're Basque. Tell me, if you can. Why would these people blow up students and scholars in the capital of their ancient kingdom?"

"All one can do in the face of insanity is pray."

"That's a theological evasion."

Don Jokin glanced at a bodyguard, who cruised along, eyeing the roofs, appearing accustomed to this sort of royal dialogue. The priest tried to quicken the pace of their stroll toward the business buildings. "My outlook can only be my own, Your Majesty. I'm not speaking for the university. The Basque Country is still struggling to come to terms with the Civil War. A large majority of Basques in Navarra and Álava provinces supported the rebellion. But majorities in Guipúzcoa and Vizcaya did not. Brothers fired on brothers, cousins on cousins, a tragedy. The winners of civil wars rule over the losers with a heavy hand. It happens everywhere. In China, Russia, France, the United States."

"Yes."

"Some Basques blamed the Franco regime for everything wrong in their lives. They feared and imagined conspiracies. The offices of Opus Dei happened to be in the same building as the Caudillo's Interior Ministry. Some Basques believed he let Saint Josemaría build his university in Pamplona in gratitude for Navarra's support during the war. To ETA's madmen our university is a symbol of a future of Spain that is just not going their way. So they do immoral and cowardly and despicable things."

As Don Jokin went on with that prattle he knew he half-believed it himself.

The king said, "I've been reading a translation of a new biography of the Caudillo by an English historian. He writes that Franco wasn't a fascist 'but something much worse: he brought the African mentality of repression and coldness and treated the Spanish the same way he treated natives of Morocco.' What do you think of that, in terms of the Basque Country?"

"Oh, Your Majesty, I don't know politics. I'm not qualified to say."

Two weeks later, Don Jokin was still spooked but flattered by that conversation with the king. He leaned back in his office chair, crossed his hands behind his head, planted his brown and white wingtips on his desk, and seven stories below watched a farmer on a tractor plowing clean straight lines of pale yellow waxy soil. The farmland came right up to the edge of the attractive, nicely wooded campus. Jokin Beleak had grown up in Oñate and had been acquainted with the younger Peru Madariaga, a rugby star and member of the radical mountain climbing clubs that were loosely affiliated with the church, or some of its priests. On a mountainside amid people you could trust it was possible to talk openly about politics and insurrection. So Peru had taken as his nom de guerre the name of Aitzgorri, the forbidding mountain a few kilometers south of Oñate. In a way Don Jokin was not surprised that Peru had become such a violent man. After those rugby games he was agreeable in the taverns, but on the field he went after opponents in absolute fury.

Don Jokin's grandfather had sold off his family's small farm, sheep pastures, and apple orchard; his father had worked at a commercial dairy. Jokin was the firstborn son, so under the tradition of primogeniture all had come to him as . . . what, an ice cream truck? And so he opted for the priesthood, but not without regret. Even as he lay face down at his ordination in the Pontifical Major Roman Seminary at the Vatican, he wept over his earthly surrender, not just the joy of his eternal obligation and reward. He shed tears of loss for those girls in the Basque Country. Don Jokin's tenure as a parish priest in a village near Oñate had been brief, thank God. His aptitude for the business side of the faith had caught the eyes of superiors, and his appointment as a university publicist in Pamplona was a jewel of a job.

The phone rang on Don Jokin's desk. He picked it up without moving his feet and answered, *"Bueno."*

"Good morning, Monsignor."

Don Jokin's wingtips shot to the floor. The voice belonged to Bishop Renato Legarreta, the patron who had made him Monsignor. "Your Excellency, so good to hear from you," Don Jokin said. They exchanged pleasantries for a moment, and then he asked, "Pray, what can I do for you?"

"Is your afternoon flexible?"

"For you, always."

"I'd like you to come to my office at two o'clock."

"Certainly, Your Excellency. I'll be coming with the chancellor or the president, or both?" That was the usual protocol.

"No, I want you to come alone."

A cloud of gloom descended on Don Jokin. Had his relationship with ETA been exposed? Don Jokin's drive across the pass to St. Jean-Pied-de-Port with the kidnapped factory owner had been the only time ETA had used him in an action that was so dangerous, but they had their hooks in him now. Would he be in handcuffs and jail by sundown? He trudged toward the Cathedral of Pamplona, which contained three of the most colorful naves in Spain, but Inquisition tortures had occurred in that place.

The bishop was a round man in his early sixties, ruddy cheeks with just wisps of white hair on top of his head. "Monsignor," he greeted Don Jokin. "Please, have a seat." He smiled. "You might need to sit down."

The bishop was a smoker. He carried his cigarettes in a trim silver case, the kind favored by tarts and fops in old movies. He reached across the well-polished desk and offered one to Jokin, who used the bishop's butane lighter and wolfed his lungs full, he was so anxious. He almost burst out coughing.

The bishop, who was dressed as informally as Don Jokin, abruptly came out of his chair. "I have some news for you that's so exciting I'm excited. His Excellency the Archbishop phoned this morning, and he asked me to speak to you, since I know you better than he does."

In a fit of nerves Don Jokin flicked ash on the spotless floor.

"His Majesty Juan Carlos the First wants you to join his staff."

The bishop laughed at Don Jokin's expression. "I know, I know," he said. "His Majesty is known to be impulsive, but you made an impression

132

on him during his visit. He told the Archbishop he's given it much thought, and you're the man he wants. I might add, His Majesty has quite some budget."

"But, Your Excellency—"

"I know it's a shock, but what an opportunity! You've done a wonderful job here at the university, and of course you can live out your days doing just what you do now. But serving His Majesty and the Crown could launch you higher. You loved Rome, did you not? You could next find yourself a spokesman for the Vatican!"

"But what would I do for the king?" Don Jokin said.

"Zarzuela Palace, where His Majesty and Queen Sofía reside, is on the northern outskirts of the capital. You would live there in a comfortable, well-furnished apartment. The Royal Palace has a chapel, and you would officiate holiday masses, weddings, baptisms, but not for the surrounding community. Your position would be to counsel the king. You would craft press releases, draft speeches, that sort of thing."

"But I don't understand. I know almost nothing of official Madrid."

The bishop paced. "His Excellency the Archbishop explained it. First and foremost, His Majesty likes you. His attorneys have vetted you, of course."

Well, *not much,* Don Jokin thought.

"And here's the thing. His Majesty has to be politically neutral. But he believes Spain is poised to become again one of Europe's great economic nations *if* stability and security is assured. The gravest threat, he believes, is in the south. The government and security forces must find a way to stem and control the flood of Muslim immigrants from the Middle East and North Africa. Though they dine at Spain's table, many do not wish us well. They long for their lost caliphate Al-Andalus."

Don Jokin smoked and listened.

"His Majesty wants you because he believes you understand the north. The Catalans are driving the economy now, yet he hears radical separatist rhetoric coming out of Barcelona. And Galicia. He wants the Basque Country to be the centerpiece of new prosperity in the north. We see what tourist attractions that Pamplona and San Sebastián have become. And Bilbao has plans for a grand rebirth. You may have heard that the Americans are putting an art museum there that will be a wonder of the world.

"But the devil in the details, we all know, is ETA. His Majesty believes we are on the brink of the kind of peace negotiated by the Catholics and

Protestants in Northern Ireland. He longs to broker that peace. But he also believes that if peace cannot be negotiated, then ETA must be finished off for good. His Majesty wants to be a force in restoring España to its historic greatness. He wants that to be his legacy. And he believes you can advise him with prayerful insight and wisdom. Will you accept his offer, Monsignor, my good friend?"

Don Jokin glanced down at the cigarette quivering in his hand and took a deep breath. "Your Excellency, I believe any offer by His Majesty is better characterized as a command."

TWENTY

The digs in San Sebastián were quite a safe house. If it was safe. The rambling two-story house was on Avenida de la Infanta Beatriz, a two-block street on the west end of the city. Ysolina had swept through the rooms pulling dust covers off low beige sofas and chairs and a baby grand piano. Brightly colored trunks sat about as footrests and coffee tables, with an abundance of Persian rugs on the floors. The walls were gleaming white, ceiling beams were painted ebony, and the photos, woodcuts, and line drawings reeked of wealth.

On their second morning there Luke slipped outside with Barkilu, leaving her asleep, and prowled the grounds. The house had granite walls and peaked wings on each end and was roofed with terra cotta tiles. Half-covered with vines, it had the look of having gone native. Enclosed by a rock wall, the grounds were a jungle of lantanas, oleander, purple morning glories, and pomegranate shrubs with red blossoms dancing in the breeze. Tiled Moroccan patios and walking trails were overgrown by the excess. The collie didn't have to leave the property to get a treasure of new sniffs.

He put the leash on Barkilu and took him for a walk. The sky was full of gulls and the smell of ocean was strong. The houses were all big and the grounds were manicured. Luke thought he would have tried to make a safe house blend in a little more.

As he and the dog headed back they came across an old man wearing a black beret. He sat on a sidewalk bench under the intersection of Infanta Beatriz and Avenida de Brunet. The bench gave him a direct view of the house where for the moment Luke now lived. He started to say good morning to him but he appeared to be dozing in the sun. As Luke pulled the dog away the man raised his head, gave the sidewalk a sharp crack with his cane, yelled at them, and they had a conversation of sorts.

When they came back in the house Ysolina was drinking coffee and arranging fruit in a bowl as if she meant to paint a still life. Luke said, "What are *los gaztetxes?*"

She looked up and said, "Why do you ask?"

"I took Barkilu on a walk and had a strange chat with an old man in the neighborhood. He started off speaking Basque and I told him I just understood Spanish. He was all right with that but he got agitated. He kept pointing his cane at this house and saying it was a *gaztetxe.*"

"It means a squat."

"Say again?"

"A squat—a property where the ownership is abandoned or the titles are lost or murky, and young people move in and out, pay no rent, and get away with it. They're all over Europe. Barcelona has loads of them."

"He also said it's been a crack house full of hippies and bad-looking strangers. Maybe staying here is not a good idea."

"Come on, Luke. Look around you. If that were true we'd have found trash all over this place. Graffiti on the walls. That old man's a crank. This property belongs to my family. One of my aunts keeps it up and rents it out to people on holiday."

Theirs was a fragile kind of trust. They knew too little of each other, yet they plunged into a domestic routine and rhythm that Luke had never experienced. She bought a printer for her computer and he helped her set up an office in one of the bedrooms. He turned in the rented Toyota, and the American named Selden Hale paid $15,000 worth of pesetas for a black Lexus first owned by a Belgian. To reach archives she used it much more than he did. Luke knew this couldn't last, that they had to plan their next move. But the old quarter, Parte Vieja, was so damned seductive. At the other end of the bay, beneath the second promontory, Monte Urgull, it was a tight cluster of alley-sized cobblestone streets and *pintxos* bars, small shops, tobacconists, newsstands, open-air fruit and vegetable markets, and *txokos*—gastronomical societies of men who prided themselves as cooks. "They open them to women just one night a year," Ysolina said. "They say women stifle their talk."

One night they ducked into a lively spot called Bar Paco Bueno that specialized in fried prawns. Its owner was a thin bald man who wore glasses and was in his seventies. The walls were covered with mementos of Paco Bueno's heyday as a European fighter. Luke gathered from the framed clippings that "El León de Guipúzcoa" fought mostly in bullrings and *pelota* frontons in San Sebastián, Bilbao, Barcelona, and Madrid. A pair of his trunks were signed and framed on a wall. He saw Luke browsing the clips and carried their second round of drinks over to their table. He said, "You've got the nose of a boxer."

Luke smiled. "My last fight I was an amateur in the ring with a future two-time world champion. Thank you, Bobby Czyz, for deviating my septum. I can't smell a rose now."

Luke introduced himself and Ysolina, who asked the man to join them. Paco Bueno said, "I enjoyed it more when I was an amateur. I broke in the pros a couple of years after the Civil War. Franco's goons came around to threaten me when I started wearing a robe with an *ikurriña* sewn on the back. I didn't care. When you're young and strong you think you're invincible."

"It took courage to do that," Ysolina said.

He nodded his thanks and said, "I couldn't resist the regime any other way."

"And you were a champion," Luke said.

"Yes, light heavyweight and heavyweight, but only in Spain. I fought for ten years, 1940 to 1950. I was eleven and three in title fights but lost the two when I tried for a European title. I didn't have enough power in my punch."

The old man said, "You're young and may not recognize the names, but I got to know Marcel Cerdan and Édith Piaf pretty well."

"I've heard of them, of course," Ysolina said. "They were celebrities and their affair was notorious."

He nodded. "I also knew Marcel's wife. I was his sparring partner when he was training for his rematch with Jake LaMotta. Édith Piaf came around, to our pleasure, but not Marcel's trainers. People would see us on the town and think I was his brother." He gazed at the wall of mementos with a sad smile. "We looked alike and fought alike, though he was much better. Then his plane went down in the Azores. The French and Algerians wept. So did I."

After a moment he went on, "My last fight, they fed me to a hot young Algerian Jew. He took me out in a *fútbol* stadium in six. There was talk of me fighting Archie Moore in your country, but then Marcel's plane crashed, and after that, for what would I fight Archie Moore—brain damage?"

He asked Ysolina, "Are you Basque?"

She said she was.

"Then maybe you know the saying, *'Ameriketara galtza zaharrakin joan eta zaharragorekin etorri.'* 'To go to America with old pants and return with older pants.' I knew when I was done. I've enjoyed my health."

Most evenings Ysolina and Luke made dinner themselves. One afternoon found them at a fish market across the Zurriola bridge over the Río Urumea, which wound through the city. He pulled back from the pans of *kokotxa.* The triangular throats of hake or whiting floated in a repulsive-looking milky fluid. "But they're a delicacy," she said. "Look how much they cost."

"Right."

"It's all in how fresh they are," she said. "I know a way you'd like them. I coat them with beaten egg, drop a couple of garlic cloves in very hot oil, and fry them two minutes on each side. Salt them lightly and serve them with a spring salad."

"Oh, *fried* fish throats. That helps."

She put her hand in his arm as they walked on. *"Kokotxa* kept Spain out of the Second World War and helped the Americans and British defeat the Nazis."

He laughed. "What?"

"True story. Hitler and Franco met just once, in 1940. It was just across the French border in Hendaye. Hitler came down with his top ministers—Göring, Goebbels, all of those. Hitler pressured Franco to join the Axis, seize Gibraltar, and cut off the Mediterranean from the British and the Americans, if they had ideas of getting into the war. But Franco demanded Morocco and western Algeria after the war. Franco thought the Nazis were invincible, so he bargained for all he thought he might get. He told his people that he wanted the French Basque chefs to prepare the very best delicacy they had. It was stewed, served room temperature. The Germans could barely choke it down. On the way back to Berlin Hitler raged to his entourage that Franco and his crowd were 'Jesuit swine' and told Mussolini, 'I would rather have three or four teeth pulled than go through that again.'"

She laughed, "Sometimes on Basque menus you see *kokoktxa* called Guernica's Revenge."

Ysolina brought to their dinners sea bass, gilthead bream, crab, prawns, and one night scorpion fish to make a dish called *pastel krabarroka*. The fish were poison-finned predators of crustaceans in shallows and coral reefs. While she peeled carrots and cleaned leeks and made a fresh tomato sauce that with eggs and cream would cook into the terrine, he uneasily eyed the spiny fins and heads of the ugly red fish he was to clean and fillet. "Do they still have venom when they're dead?"

"Oh yes," she teased. "Be careful. If they puncture your hands they'll swell up and hurt for hours. And don't let any of the organs or roe stay on your hands when you're done. It's very dangerous, some say lethal, if you accidentally swallow it."

"Terrific," said Luke, rubbing his hands with enthusiasm for the task. She laughed at his clowning, and the labor-intensive pâté was worth the effort. Served cold with sherry-flavored mayonnaise and a white wine, her *pastel de krabarroka* was sweet, moist, and had a tang of flavor unlike any fish he'd tasted.

One night when they were cleaning up the kitchen, she was standing on her toes to put the wineglasses on a high shelf, and he remarked on the way her bottom filled out her Levis. She looked back at him and blew a strand of hair away from her eyes. "You're prejudiced, but thank you."

One thing led to another, and they soon had a fine time wearing nothing but their skins on a pile of laundry because it seemed too urgent to spend time and energy getting upstairs to their bed. Afterward her head rested in the crook of his shoulder. She was moving her fingers in the smear of their mingled juices on his thigh. "I like the way we smell," she said.

Moments later—he thought she had dozed—he was humming a song called "Jaded Lover." "What's that?" she murmured.

"Oh, just some song that came to mind."

"Sing it to me."

He tried to evade that. "But it's in English."

"That's all right. You know my English is good."

"That so? Why have we been speaking all Spanish?"

"Because I like your accent. Are you going to sing to me or not?"

Not quick enough to think of another, he sang a stanza of the song by a Colorado fellow named Chuck Pyle and made a hit by Austin's Jerry Jeff Walker.

> *The only kind of man that you ever wanted*
> *Was one that you knew you'd never hold very long*
> *Sitting there crying like I'm the first one to go*

"You make love to me and start humming that?"

"Come on. It's just a song."

Luke knew that if he did not check in with the Outfit soon, the people they sent to find him would not be bean counters. He took Barkilu for an afternoon walk and picked up a copy of *El Diario*. On the second page he read a story that in weeks past there had been a gunfight between Spanish agents and ETA fugitives in a French town, Cambo-les-Bains. One *etarra*, identified by Spanish police as Txili Iñiguez, twenty-four, had been killed. The Spaniards claimed that "the ETA military leader known as Aitzgorri" had been involved in the gunfight but had escaped, condition unknown.

Ysolina maintained her mask of nonchalance but she was terrified. At a tobacconist in the Old Quarter she had paid for a box of Cuban cigars. Inside it she found a package of materials that informed her of the hit on Peru and the killing of his bodyguard Txili. Peru, Jale, and other *gudariak* had come across the Pyrenees and the border into Aragón.

She took the car two mornings later and told Luke she was going to an archive in Pamplona, but she headed the other way to Lequeito, a fishing town with a gloomy cathedral near Guernica. The coast there was rocky, the weather had turned stormy, and she negotiated a highway that snaked through heavily wooded cliffs with surf crashing below, the ocean now gray and forbidding. All the fishing boats were berthed and anchored in the small bay. Her directions led away from the town and up a graveled road back into the forest. She stopped the car and dialed the number she'd been given. A gruff voice answered and she spoke the password, *"Pertsona zuriska."* Albino.

The man told her to come forward slowly. She dropped the phone on the seat and drove around another curve where two men walked out to meet her. The one on the left motioned for her to roll down the window. He said, "Pop the trunk."

They found nothing but a spare tire. "Step out," the man said, leering.

"No. You're not going to touch me, *alproja.*" She had called him a swine. He glared and called her *sorgina,* the witch, and told her to drive on.

This safe house was a dreary fisherman's wreck. Parts of boats were scattered around the grounds. The air inside was thick with cigarette smoke and unwashed feet and clothes. Seven men stared at her sharply as she came in. Ysolina recognized only Jale, who rocked back in a chair with a look of contempt. Peru walked in from another room.

She clutched her arms around him and squeezed hard. "Oh, it's good to see you," she murmured. He cradled the back of her head in his hand and kept her close, moving his hips as if they were dancing.

"Leave us alone, get out," he told the others. Some of them were playing cards, others watching *fútbol* on a fuzzy black and white TV. Peru poured glasses of a sour red wine and led her by the hand into a bedroom. He sprawled on the bed without taking off his hiking boots and crossed his hands behind his head.

"What happened?" she said.

He shrugged. "They came after me."

"I'm so sorry about Txili."

"A good kid," he said grimly. "Thief and want-to-be fighter."

"Is that all he was to you? He worshipped the ground you walk on."

"Cost him, didn't it?"

She turned away and downed a gulp of the wine. He sat up and pulled on her shoulder. "Come here," he said.

She resisted him at first but finally she lay back on the bed beside him and said, "What now?"

"Any suggestions?"

"Quit this, Peru. Go somewhere, become someone else. I know what you believe and why, but the ones with you now don't believe in anything. They're just thugs and criminals."

"You don't know them! And I couldn't quit if I wanted to. Don't you understand? They've got their sights on me personally. The Spaniards put it out in the news that the hit was intended to get 'the assassin of Carrero Blanco.' That man was evil and was fortunate to go out with a snap of the fingers like he did. I'm proud of what little I had to do with it that day. And as soon as the Moroccans canceled the peace talks, the Spaniards broke the ceasefire. If that's what they want, then we're going to answer on a scale that will make them remember the Owl."

"Oh, Peru."

"They're going to hunt me down whatever I do."

He pulled her close and tried to unbutton her shirt but she stopped him. "No, Peru. Please. It's over for us. You know it as well as I do."

"The American, isn't it? It's what I get for letting him bring you across."

"He's not your enemy, Peru. He's not. You and I haven't had a real marriage in ten years. I've tried as hard as I could to hold us together, and in your way I know you have, too. But I can't do it anymore."

He rolled away from her and put his boots on the floor. "I never thought of you as being cruel." She reached out to touch him, but he moved away. "All right, go back to him. Do you have a gun?"

"No, I never have. I've never wanted one."

"Does he?"

"I doubt it. He was very careful crossing the border."

"I'm sending two back with you. You don't know how dangerous things are right now."

"Oh, yes, Peru. I know."

"Ysolina, I think they'll give you amnesty. They're giving it to ones in prison that were involved in real actions. The only reason they want you is *me*. This is my bed and I've got to lie in it. But you have a life ahead of you. You can be a professor someplace. I never meant for this to be the ruin of you."

She drove away with a canvas bag containing two nine-millimeter Glocks and several boxes of cartridges. She didn't really cry until she passed back through Lequeito. The storm had relented enough that the fishwives were out with their brogans and buckets hoping to scare up some buyers of the prior day's catch. She pulled off in a narrow street of rough cobblestones. Her shoulders shook until she noticed a couple of boys staring at her. She smiled, gave them a wave, and they hurried on. In her other hand was the packet containing Luke's emeralds. She pulled off her wedding ring and put it in with them, then put his car in drive.

TWENTY-ONE

She found Luke lying on a sofa and reading a paperback in English that he'd found on the bookshelves. The sky had cleared and the afternoon was nearly gone when in a chipper voice she told him to put on good walking shoes and bring a light jacket. She wanted to go out for the evening, she said, and it would be breezy.

Holding hands like the lovers they were and the innocents they were not, they made their way up the Avenida de Satrustegui. She let the collie off the leash there and watched him scatter birds at the end of the beach called Ondarreta. Ysolina called him back from the beach after a while and they walked on along the shore beneath the steep and heavily wooded Monte Igueldo, which rose above the west end of the city and bay. They reached the *Peinte del Viento*, the Wind Comb, which was the work of San Sebastián's native son Eduardo Txillada Juantegui. For his large non-Basque following he went by Eduardo Chillada. When the tides were out the sculptor had laid down broad patios of stone with raised circular vents. Children stood on them now, and they were rewarded when waves struck with force that shot geysers of spray up from the vents as if they were blowholes of a whale. The kids screeched with delight.

Beyond the stone patios Txillada had somehow planted two massive iron sculptures in boulders, one of them several yards out into the bay. Luke could see in them gnarled pillars of a fortification the ocean had torn away, or the curled fingers of a beckoning hand, or figures in some mathematical equation, or remains of a blasted warship, or letters of an ancient alphabet. Whatever Txillada meant them to convey, Luke thought they deserved the praise that came their way, posed out there as the Atlantic smashed the boulders with explosions of foam and spray. He said, "I wonder how he made them look like they just grew out of the rock. I don't see a chip or seam."

"I don't know. He says he works in iron because its light is black. Isn't it wild how artists express themselves?"

"You know him?" Luke said.

"My parents did. I doubt he'd remember me. He'd be in his seventies now."

They backtracked and caught a funicular to the summit. There was an amusement park on the summit and the port's onetime lighthouse. Ysolina led them to a small bar with patio tables overlooking the bay. She gave his cheek two fond pats and brought glasses of Cañalva Tinto Fino and small plates of *pintxos*. She took the other chair and leaned over to stroke Barkilu's head. "I think he's your dog as much as mine now. Look how he's snuggled up against you."

"If that's true he doesn't have good sense either."

He finished the wine and set the glass aside. She touched a cleft in the web of flesh between forefinger and thumb of his left hand. "Why do you have that scar?"

"A guy stuck a knife through it one time."

"Where?"

"South America."

"What did you do?"

"I shot him with the other hand."

She said nothing, just stared at him.

The lobe-shaped Bahía de la Concha angled southeast into large parts of San Sebastián. Across the bay from where they sat on Monte Igueldo was the second heavily wooded promontory, Monte Urgull, and near below them was the unpopulated but imposing Isla de Santa Clara. The promontories and island had caused the tides to build two white sand beaches—Playa de la Ondorreata and the larger Playa de la Concha, sheltered by Monte Urgull and its summit ruins of a fortress castle and a statue of Christ. The island divided the waves and sent them washing in concentric patterns toward the two beaches. Ysolina said, "Look, it's like a part of someone's hair."

None of the buildings strung along the bay and its beaches were highrises. The ones on the shorefront stood shoulder to shoulder, rebuilt of blond stone in belle époque style. She told him that San Sebastián owed its look to Napoleon's attempt to make himself emperor of Europe, starting with Spain. He chose San Sebastián as his fortress, believing that with his cannons dug in the two mountains, the English leader titled the Duke of Wellington and his Portuguese and Spanish partisan allies could not possibly overrun the town. But the cannon fire from the ships overwhelmed the French artillery and as a terrible fire consumed the town the French soldiers fled. Some said the English and Portuguese invaders set it while plundering the town. Others claimed a freak windstorm set the town ablaze. Napoleon lost thousands of men in the rout and pressed on to the debacles of the Russian invasion and Waterloo. "The Basques rebuilt as fast as they could," she said. "Isn't it ironic they did it in the architectural style of the French?"

Luke said, "I see why you love it here. It's beautiful."

"It's my home, or where I want it to be."

He took a deep breath and said, "Ysolina, we need to talk."

"I thought we were."

"I know about the shootout," he said. "Not much detail, just that someone was killed, and Peru got away."

After a couple of deep breaths she cried, "You come in here and sweep me off my feet—"

His laugh shot her from her chair. "Wait," he said, reaching for her. "Please, wait. I'm sorry. Sit down. That's just so different from how I view myself."

"Who *are* you? A cop? A spy?"

At his silence she shook her head. "An American spy. I knew it, I knew it."

"Ysolina, I read about the shootout today in a Spanish newspaper! It's over between those Americans and me. I didn't know a thing about you until I saw you on that Arab horse. Since then it's been hard to think of anything else."

"So now I know."

"You know some of it."

She pressed her fingers against her temples like a migraine was coming on. "Is that the first time a woman's told you she's in love with you?"

"Is that what you said?"

"Are you going to make me say it again?"

"No. I feel the same way."

"Say it then."

He said it in Euskera. *"Nik maite zaitut."*

For once he said something just right. She took his hands in hers. "All right. I believe you. So what do we do? What do you do with me?"

"We could just keep going."

"Where?"

"Prague. Istanbul. Addis Ababa."

She gave him a wry look. "Addis Ababa?"

He shrugged. "Somebody told me it's a good place."

"I don't think I love you enough to go to Ethiopia." She told the dog to scoot and gestured at Luke to move his chair out from the table. She sat in his lap and put her arm around his shoulder, her fingers playing with curls of his hair. With nightfall the lights of the city sent dagger-shaped reflections reaching outward in the bay. Far out past the isle of Santa Clara, in the deep water Basques called Bizkaiako Golkoa, the night dropped jags of lightning, a passing summer storm.

TWENTY-TWO

The Guggenheim Bilbao roiled in crises of its own. The city's municipal authority, the Ayuntamiento, had to issue a permit stating that the design complied with fire and other city codes. Since Frank Gehry and his lieutenants had not finished the detailed designs, César Caicoya, the executive construction architect for IDOM, could offer documentation in only the wildest possible guess.

Frank had to anticipate storms off the Atlantic that subjected the Nervión River to mighty floods. Protection went beyond putting the interior's galleries high above the marks of the worst historic flooding. In a worst-case scenario, his museum could float and break up. The answer they arrived at was to set the foundation on 664 concrete piles driven fourteen meters deep in the bedrock. Within them were adjustable cables that could raise the entire museum in case of such a flood.

The foundation would not be finished for another year, but already the steel structure was going up. IDOM and its contractors and subcontractors were being asked to construct a building that undulated. Caicoya's team screened dozens of builders and selected five companies that might be capable of meeting the demands of the exteriors. Requests for bid documents went out to those companies. Only three responded, and all came in far over budget. And the parliamentary election hung over their heads.

Caicoya, Frank's partner Randy Jefferson, and their top assistants worked with the IDOM engineers and builders to bring down the pricing. Frank wanted to hang the metal sheathing, or cladding, on plywood. Caicoya said that would never hold up in Bilbao's climate. They changed the specs of the skeleton to steel. Frank wanted to use bronze valves for the plumbing; Caicoya argued that stainless steel valves held up just as well and cost less. They advertised for new bids with a two-week deadline, and if none came in, the whole project was sunk.

Sighs of relief were heard in California and Vizcaya when two companies submitted bids that met the target cost. Frank's firm and IDOM gave the principal exteriors business to a corporation called Balzoa. Headquartered in Bilbao, Balzoa had offices in Madrid, Warsaw, and Santiago, Chile. It had a record of successfully building skyscrapers, but it had never attempted anything like this.

Balzoa's difficulties triggered the next emergency. None of the building blocks in Frank's design, which he called "paquettes," were squares or rectangles. When it once more looked hopeless, the Gehry team adapted a software called CATIA that had been developed for French Mirage jet fighters. The software enabled them to show the executive architect and the contractors the building design in three dimensions, a crucial breakthrough, but the software was so confusing that a Spanish aerospace company had to be engaged to provide translations IDOM and Balzoa could use.

The meetings had moved from Santa Monica to Bilbao. After Randy Jefferson called the latest session back to order, Frank rolled his chair back, put his heels on the conference table, and opened a Bible in his lap. Frank was reminding them who was the alpha wolf.

"We were talking about the stone," said Caicoya.

"Yes, we were," said Frank, taking off his glasses and eyeing a smudge. He cleaned them with the tail of his black T-shirt. Then he put the Bible at the right distance and read, "I find this passage in Psalms interesting. 'Blessed is the man whose strength is in thee; in whose heart are the ways of them. Who passing through the valley of Baaka make it a well; the rain also filleth the pools."

The Spaniards eyed him with expressions of alarm.

He closed the Bible, set it aside, and brought his feet to the floor. "Anybody know why the Baaka Valley rings a bell today?"

Not a sound in the room but the exasperated breathing.

"Because in 1982 the Israelis invaded Lebanon and set off a war with the Syrians. The Israelis found it was easier to get into Lebanon than to get out. But the Syrians didn't know it at the time. The Israeli air force made the Battle of Baaka Valley a rout—they call it 'the Baaka Shoot.' It was over in two hours. They bombed a surface-to-air missile system out of existence, destroyed five hundred Syrian tanks, and in dogfights shot down seventy-two MiGs without losing a plane."

Frank raised a hand of subtle warning when Jefferson tried to interrupt.

CHAPTER 22

"What does this have to do with a museum in Bilbao? You guys," he said, addressing the IDOM contingent, "told us that an Italian company could get us the very best limestone at the very best price. But it turns out that's not Italian limestone. It's Lebanese limestone quarried in the Baaka Valley by an Israeli bunch doing business with a Lebanese partner, and they deal it to the Italians. The Baaka Valley looks like a pile of rocks to me, but the Lebanese see it as prime and historic farmland. Can we count on guaranteed supply from that quarry? And how are we going to explain the stone when some reporter gets on the story?"

Silence reigned for several seconds.

Frank smiled. "Well, I am the guy that solves problems and makes everybody happy. Forget the Italians and Israelis and Lebanese. They did business with us under false pretenses. That contract is unenforceable. And in Spain's province of Granada a company called Huéscar has a limestone quarry that went bankrupt some months ago. The rock is hard and clean, it's not going to change color, and the owners will re-open the quarry just for us. At a fraction of the price we were going to have to pay the Italians and Israelis and Lebanese. They see us as their way to get back on their feet again."

A couple of the Spaniards whooped, and others clapped their hands.

"Don't thank me," said Frank. "Thank my staff of youngsters who dug up the truth about that business in the Middle East, found the Huéscar quarry, and in great haste got the rock tested to our satisfaction." He nodded at Caicoya and the rest of the IDOM contingent. "You'll want to test it, too."

They nodded in turn.

Frank let the relieved murmur reign for a moment. From day one he had been worried about the metal. "This building," he said, "is going to respect Bilbao's history as a port, sailors on the Atlantic netting cod, harpooning Moby Dick, pirating the English, whatever. Bilbao was also a steel town, and that's why we want to use so much metal. We thought about cladding with leaded copper but scrapped that because César and his team said there's already too much lead in the river and soil. We decided on stainless steel because it was the cheapest. But we're building a museum with a bridge running over and through one end of the site. We've got to think about commuter traffic on those bridges, and stainless steel can blind you on a bright sunny day.

"Bilbao also gets a lot of rain, and when the weather is cloudy and gray, stainless steel just dies. It's gloom. Outside our studio in Santa Monica, I tacked a little square of titanium to a telephone pole. It rained one day, and I looked out and saw the square of titanium gleaming. Doesn't matter if it's cloudy and pouring down, that stuff is buttery and warm. It catches whatever light there is."

"We talked about titanium before," Caicoya said. "It costs too much."

"Yes, that's why we settled for stainless steel. But then our guys discovered that sheets of titanium can be cut twice as thinly as steel. That would help with the cost. NASA, for instance, uses titanium for parts of spacecraft that bang back into the atmosphere at seventeen thousand miles an hour. But the only stationary construction with it that we could find was some roofing in Japan. We had it tested, and it can hold up under rain driven by thousand-mile-an-hour winds, which don't occur, not on this planet. Salt water, acid—nothing penetrates or scars it. The Soviets used it on their MiG fighters and submarines. But thank god, the Soviet Union collapsed two years ago. Russia is a world leader in the mining of titanium, and Russia's economy is hurting. They just dumped thousands of tons of titanium on the market. It was costing fifteen dollars a pound. Now it costs four."

With that performance Frank transformed the Bilbao Guggenheim from a wobbly proposition into a fast-track enterprise. Within a week the Spanish limestone was on its way, screeching rock saws were running twenty-four hours a day, and they had bought all the titanium from the Russians they would need.

TWENTY-THREE

JUNE 1994

Since leaving St. Jean-de-Luz with Ysolina Luke had tried to have no phone conversations at all. But now there was trouble back home. Three times now while she was in the carrels of her archives he had left Barkilu in the house and used a public line at the phone company in town. This time it was eight o'clock in Texas when he called. Lydia Burgoa answered the call, greeted him in her usual friendly manner, and called her husband to the phone. "Simon, it's your brother," Lydia said.

"Yeah. How you?" Simon growled a moment later.

"I'm okay. How's Amona?"

"Well, she's out of the hospital. Sometimes she's out of her head."

Some bacteria that might have been trivial where it originated had gotten into a cut, maybe just a scrape, and in her bloodstream the infection wreaked havoc. Her blood pressure plummeted in the sepsis, her heart raced, her kidneys were stressed, and her fever jumped to 103. Simon and Lydia had put her in the pickup and raced through the ranch roads, dodging deer thick in the bar ditches, and got her to an emergency room in Kerrville. She was in there for a week on a constant drip of heavy-duty antibiotics. They almost lost her.

"What can I do?" said Luke.

"Well, you could get your ass back here and give us a hand. She's got to have someone with her all the time."

Luke sighed. "I can't do that, little brother, and you know it. Get her a round-the-clock nurse."

"You think they're just hanging in the trees out here? You know how much one costs?"

"Goddamn it, I'll wire you the money. Hire a nurse!"

"Why don't you do the hiring? I got a ranch to run, and it didn't rain a puddle of piss all spring."

He's under strain, Luke thought. Let it go.

But Simon bore on. "Where are you anyway? What are you doing with your life? I haven't had an answer to that in fifteen years."

"I call you, Simon, and I call her. I'm there when I'm there."

"Why can't we call *you?*"

Because the Outfit's trying to find me, you jerk, and it's easy to find you. They may be hearing this right now.

"Ever heard of television, Luke?" Simon continued. "Fellow sitting down with a beer after supper trying to relax? I was watching this program called *The Sentinel.* Guy was off in South America with the Special Forces, and when he comes back he's like Superman. Makes me think of you. Except, no it don't. You're a sorry excuse for a human being, as far as I'm concerned."

"Where's this getting us, Simon? Who's with Amona now?""

"Your niece Andrea, who needs to be doing her algebra."

"Go watch your TV and have another beer. I'm going to call Amona."

"Fine, real fine," said Simon, and banged the receiver down.

Luke muttered, "Asshole." Here's someone who doesn't like me, and I don't like him, so why do I let him punch my buttons? I should have just called her first.

Amona picked it up and voiced the Basque greeting, *"Kaixo."*

He was surprised by how strong her voice sounded. It had not been strong the day he called her at the Kerrville hospital. He started the drill of coaxing her back to Spanish. *"Cómo estás,* Amona?"

She said, *"Ondoxto,"* quite well in Basque. She liked to tease him with the language. There was pleasure in her voice now; her spirits had rebounded.

"We can't talk long. I don't want to wear you out."

"My great grandchild . . . oh, she is here with me." There was an embarrassed hitch in her delivery. She had forgotten the girl's name.

"Andrea," he reminded her. "I have to tell you something, Amona. I'm with a wondrous woman now. She took me to see the valley of the Río Salazar. It's beautiful."

"Wondrous. And she did? Oh, how fine. Tell me about it."

"Limestone chasms, clear-running mountain streams, and they come together in the Río Salazar. White walls, rust-colored tile roofs, windows decorated with frames of dried *pimientos*. Eagles playing in the updrafts— it felt like home to me, it really did."

"I'm so glad. And envious!" She paused. "You say you're 'with' this woman. Is she there? Can I speak to her?"

"No, she's away in her work. Another time I'll call when she's here."

"Is she married?"

Luke chuckled.

"Well," she said, "at your age, what else would I think?"

"People get divorced sometimes, Amona."

"Alderdi batetik maiteki mintzatuko natzaizu, baina bestetik zorrozki."

More teasing. "All right," he said. "What does that mean?"

"Oh, sometimes I give you a hard time, other times the loving gleams through. To fall in love, *maitemindu,* even I remember that. Do you know how many words we have that mean loving, in all its many ways?"

"No."

"About seventy."

Great, he thought. I'll pass that on to ETA.

"What's your lover's name?"

"How do you know she's my lover?"

"I don't have to see her. I hear it in your voice."

"Well, her name is Ysolina."

"Is she Basque? That's not a common Basque name."

"She was named for a grandmother who was Galician."

"Your Ysolina, she works at what?"

"She's a historian."

"A university professor?"

"Not yet. She's working on her doctorate about a Basque ancestor who lived on a headwater of the Río Salazar."

"Well, I'm glad you're in love with this woman. Don't fall out. *Maitegabetu.*"

He gnawed on a knuckle, afraid that he'd been drawing the Outfit a roadmap. "I'd better go, Amona. I'll call again soon. Tell Andrea that her uncle Luke says hello and good luck with her algebra. I love you."

"Take care of yourself, firstborn," she said. "And don't fall out of love with this woman, like you have before."

153

Luke didn't press Ysolina on how her research was going, and she didn't share much of it. She told him what archive was her destination of the day, took the car, and those destinations got farther and farther away. Pamplona and Logroño, and now she talked about the Archivo Histórico and Biblioteca Nacional in Madrid! Her obsession was like a death wish. One time when she had just returned, with the engine of the Lexus still ticking, he started out to calculate the miles she'd put on the odometer, but he turned on his heel and came back ashamed. Trust her, damn it, but *hurry up.*

Luke was taking a nap another afternoon when he heard an eruption of barking and the collie skidding down the stairs. He leapt awake and reached for the end table drawer and the gun Peru had sent him. Then he heard the thumping of Barkilu's tail against the walls of the foyer, and the tires crunching the gravel on the entrance.

He cleared his head, put on his shoes, and made his way down the stairs as she burst in the door. She was carrying her briefcase with a shoulder strap and set it on the floor with a thump. She was wearing jeans and a turtleneck, with her hair pulled back. She usually bent over to greet the dog first but this time she danced to him, put her arms around his neck, and kissed him. He said, "I take it you had a good day."

"I did," she said, playing with Barkilu. "I'm sorry I'm back so late."

"Late for what?"

"The party. Do you still want to go?"

His blank look drew one of exasperation. "You don't remember?"

"That's always possible."

"You've been saying you'd like to meet my aunts. Well, Tía Aloña is the one who keeps up this house and rents it out sometimes to people on holiday. She's helping host a party at a very fine restaurant near here. She's my most colorful aunt, the one closest to me, and the crowd will be full of interesting people. I told you about it.'"

He tilted his head acknowledging his lapses, but she was prone to occupy a separate reality. "I don't know how I forgot. You're the only person I talk to."

"Dress up a little more and come with me. You should see it before it gets dark. It's a very special place. You can talk to Eduardo Txillada, the sculptor, if you want. He's the official host."

Way too public, another gong went off in his mind. But it would just make things worse between them if he refused to go. "What's the occasion?"

"A reception for the architect Frank Gehry. Your countryman."

She had never told him about that party. With trepidation he showered and shaved and put on khakis, a clean white shirt, and a blue linen blazer he had picked up one afternoon at a shop off the Plaza Cervantes. He lay on the bed with his hands clasped behind his head, watching her ritual. Wearing a sleeveless blue dress with a fashionably short skirt, she sat with her legs crossed in front of a dressing table and mirror, touching up her fingernail polish and "putting on her eyes," as she described it. She dabbed her neck with a perfume he liked.

At her directions he turned left on Avenida de Satrustegui, which forked a sharp left away from the beach and Monte Igueldo's summit, where they had quarreled nights earlier. After some winding about they arrived on the other side of the promontory. Luke squinted and lowered a visor against the sun. "Am I Selden tonight or Luke?"

"Luken," she said. "I've told my aunt about you."

"Are they going to be speaking Spanish or Basque?"

"Spanish unless you give them reason to exclude you." She said, "I've been wondering. If the woman who raised you is so much a Basque, why didn't you learn more of the language?"

"When I began to speak we weren't living on the ranch. Pop made sure we knew Spanish as well as we knew English, but he let go of the Basque. And it's hard to make any sense of it if you're not born to it."

"Oh, pooh. All languages have their logic."

"Right. *Aitak bere burua hil du.* 'Father has killed himself.' Translation: 'Father has killed his head.'"

They bantered in that way as he drove, coming out on overlooks of the Cantabrian Sea. She told him to turn on a lane called Paseo Padre Orolaga and then on the right he saw the large entrance, Akelaré, and beneath that the name of the chef. He chuckled. "That means the witches' black mass, right?"

"Everyplace is haunted, my love."

The restaurant was a sprawling place, lots of angled beams and glass. "Holy smokes," he said. "Am I dressed all right?"

"You'll do," she said, taking his arm.

There was a wall-sized comic mural of the mustachioed chef. A cadre of lesser chefs all dressed in white with the towering hats, all lined up and smiling; a dining room of white tablecloths arranged for maximum views of the coastline, where a golden sunset was in progress.

A young woman approached them with a tray and glasses of wine, another with a choice of appetizers. He chose what Ysolina informed him was cuttlefish rolled in Rice Crispies, mustard, and herbs. Better than you'd think. Trying to be inconspicuous, he picked up one of the menus. "Gin tonic on a plate!" he read with delight. "What, you lap it like a dog? And wow, this is the mother lode. Hake and its *Kokoktxa* with Oyster Leaf and Mussel's Beans, Turbot with its *Kokotxa,* and Desalted Cod Box with its *Kokotxa.* Yum."

"Behave," she said cheerfully. She raised her hand and walked fast toward a tall woman in her mid-sixties who cried, "Ysolina." They kissed cheeks in the European way and embraced. Tía Aloña was horse-faced, with gray hair pulled back behind flat gold oversized earrings in the shape of the *lauburu,* the Basque cross. Wearing a loose, long, filmy dress, she was sexy in an Auntie Mame kind of way. Ysolina introduced her to Luke, whom she also favored with the two-cheek kiss. 'So," she said in her loud voice, "you are Luken, the one my niece raves about. You had better live up to your reputation, young man."

"Actually I'm trying to live it down."

She took his arm and said, "Come meet our host, Eduardo Txillida Juantegui." Luke tried to hold back but it didn't work. The sculptor had the classic Basque face—hair receded to the back of his head, dark eyebrows, pointed chin, and a long nose. He was dressed like Luke, with a sport coat and open collar. Tía Aloña presented Ysolina first. "Yes, of course," he said to her. "Some days I can't remember if I had breakfast, but I remember you. I knew your father and mother. So you've come back to us?"

"I hope so," she said, flustered by his unexpected recognition of her.

With her heavily ringed hand on the crook of Luke's left arm, Tía Aloña said, "And this is her *novio americano,* Luken."

"Ah, *Amerikar,*" Txillida said. "I've had exhibits and placed sculptures at the National Gallery in Washington, the Guggenheim in New York, the Symphony Hall in Dallas, the Museum of Fine Arts in Houston. I'm sorry, that makes me sound vain. But people in your country have been very kind to me."

"Glad to hear it. Ysolina took me to see the *Wind Combs.* They're amazing."

"Thank you. *Haizeen orrazia* is what I call them, the Basque name I gave them first. When I was a boy here I hated school, and the war against Franco was so frightening. I was in my early teens when it began. To get away from all that I'd run away down there for hours because I loved the place. Sand and sky and sea. I'd watch the waves and wonder what moves them? I still don't know. But the sea's been my master, and I've learned a great deal from it."

"How did you get the iron to rust that color so evenly?"

He smiled and nodded at the compliment. "I worked with a blacksmith, and we developed an alloy that brings out the color as it oxidizes."

"So it's true you once set up a forge in your studio."

"Yes," he said, beaming at the memory. "I was about thirty then, and my wife and I had small children. Dangerous as hell and it was hard to keep them out. In the summer it got very hot in there! Hotter than Texas."

"You must get tired of people asking you the same things."

"Not at all," he replied. "Artists who say they don't like being asked questions about their work are fools. What brings you to our country?"

"Ysolina," Luke said.

"The best of reasons," Txillada said with a smile. A woman came up to them and murmured to the artist, and the crowd was stirring. He said, "Our guest of honor has arrived. I have to try to remember what I'm supposed to say."

Txillada beckoned them to come along and introduced them to Frank Gehry and his wife Berta. "We have another American here," he said, presenting Luke. "His sweetheart is the daughter of two of my dear late friends."

"Excellent," said Gehry. After the introduction and handshake he asked Luke, "What brings you to the Basque Country?"

"Good fortune," he said. "The best of it's Ysolina."

"What kind of work do you do in the States?"

"I'm retired."

Gehry gazed at Luke. "You're young for that."

"It's another way of saying I keep getting fired."

The older man grinned. "Do you like Bilbao?"

"I've never been there."

"Well, we've got this museum underway, and we're hiring. Come see us. I'd like to have more Americans on the crews. If you can't do something for us already, maybe we can teach you."

Tía Aloña ushered the sculptor and the architect and his wife to the low stage arranged for them. Tía Aloña rang a wine glass with her spoon and called the crowd forward. In introduction Txillada offered quick praise for the architect's brave style of invention and said anticipation of his Guggenheim Bilbao was at fever pitch.

Gehry, who wore a black suit and a white mock turtleneck, nodded at the applause, as did his wife, who physically was much the more striking of the two. In a glimmering blouse and trousers, she had short dark hair with long jeweled earrings and a broad friendly smile. "My better half here speaks Spanish," he began. "I know just enough of the language to always have my essential translator at my side."

She delivered for him, and he went on, "It's such a pleasure to be with you in this gorgeous countryside and city, and to be introduced by one of our time's great artists. Txillada's sculptures are some of the most powerful I've ever seen. If the Guggenheim in Bilbao grows out of the mud pit it is right now, I hope you will honor our work with one of your sculptures."

"Thank you," Txillada said with a slight bow. "It would be an honor."

Gehry continued with pauses for his wife's translations. "Creating a building is like playing jazz music—you're improvising, working together, you do what you do, they do what they do. You've got all these people involved, pursuing different goals, and the architect has to try to anticipate all that could go wrong, as it always does. But buildings do get built. And when the clients are lucky, the architects have vision. Only on each building that vision is so elusive. And however grand a building might look, it had better work. You're no doubt familiar with the American architect Frank Lloyd Wright. He often told a story about getting a call from a client who complained that rain was coming through the roof and falling on her head. He advised her, 'Madam, move your chair.'"

Luke moved back out of the way and was enjoying Gehry's talk until he noticed a man staring at him and Ysolina. He had combed his thin black hair over his balding head in an unattractive way and supported himself with two hands on a cane. Luke moved his gaze then glanced again and the man's eyes stayed right with him. Luke had been on the wrong end of undeviating stares like that before. A cop.

Luke was shaken as they drove away from the reception but he said, "Nice party. I enjoyed that. Especially your Tía Aloña and Eduardo Txillada."

Then he saw Ysolina was trembling. "What's wrong?"

She held up an envelope. "Tía Aloña gave me this in a restroom."

"What is it?"

"Enara's death sentence. It has the stamp of a Spanish notary and is handwritten and signed by the Inquisitor. It says, 'You are a *negativo* bearing the witch marks of Satan and you will be burned at the stake on the plaza of Logroño on the fourteenth of November, 1610.'"

TWENTY-FOUR

L uke never snooped in her things, and he expected or at least hoped for the same from her. That morning, when she had gone with the car she had left her journal on the bed. He looked at it like it was something alive for a couple of minutes, then picked it up and opened it, believing she had left it there so he would. He went to the back pages first, a habit acquired somewhere, and didn't find what he expected. It was written in Spanish with a graceful hand and with few words crossed out or changed. It wasn't scholarly at all. He flipped to earlier entries and those had the weary and pressured style of graduate students, nota- tions for footnotes, declarations appended by multiple question marks of doubt. But the last entry was personal and emotional, with flights of fantasy. She styled the start of it, he learned later, as if it were a Basque legend. Maybe she was letting go of something. Maybe she thought it was just legend.

Near the canyon of Añisclo there lived a beautiful woman named Enara de Añibarro. They say that in the distant past she could be seen each day, flying southward to the seven mountains crushed into one called Aitzgorri. That as she crossed the heavens she left a trail of fire and combed her long blonde hair with a comb that made the most exquisite sound. *Keeer keeer.*

Or perhaps it was an eagle or hawk.

Enara was no lamia, no fallen ill-formed angel flying about Euskadi in search of love. She was a human who lived and breathed and suffered the outrages of the Spanish Inquisition. Her husband Austin was a wealthy man. Enara had not had a child with him yet, and it made her sad and anxious, because she was twenty-eight years old. Austin had used the es- tate he inherited and her dowry to monopolize the mule trains of freight and produce back and forth across the border. On the route back, they passed first through the villages of Zugarramurdi and Urdax, where a monastery had sat for at least five hundred years.

In the summer of 1609 Enara begged Austin to halt the trains for now. They were wealthy enough and they had again been trying to make her pregnant. She had miscarried two years before. And she had been told of horror and evil on the French side. The king had commissioned a judge from Bordeaux to investigate two feuding nobles' accusations of mass witchcraft in the province of Labourd. He arrived in Bayonne and at once burned an eighty-year-old priest and twenty-year-old cabinet maker at the stake. He wrote two books about his righteous adventure, boasting that he sent three dozen witches to the stake. He exaggerated greatly, but his reign of terror sent Basques flooding across the Pyrenees into the Spanish provinces. People were being burned to ashes and puddles.

The rocky trail favored by Austin passed so close to the monastery at Urdax that the hooves of the mules skidded and the monks heard the scraping of the panniers. They heard Austin and his muleteers calling the beasts by name. Inside the monastery, those sweetheart calls aroused an Abbot's suspicions of bestiality, a characteristic of witches, male and female. Also the Abbot alerted the Spanish Inquisition Tribunal at Logroño that a young woman had come over the mountains with one of Austin's mule trains. At confession she told an elderly parish priest that she had been a witch in the Navarrese village of Zugarramurdi, on the Spanish side of the border, ever since she was a child seduced, and she had taken part in black sabbaths in a Cave of Pleasure that a cold clear stream ran through. An orphan, she had moved back and forth between homes of relatives in Zugarramurdi and Ciboure, on the French coast of Labourd. She told the Abbot she had reconverted to Christianity, only now Satan's witches made themselves into animals at night and circled the farmstead raising a cacophony of howls, barks, and grunts, trying to reclaim her.

Four accused women, ages eighty to twenty, were taken from their homes and transported by mule-drawn wagon to the secret Inquisition dungeons at Logroño. It was a hard trek, and the witches were kept chained, out of fear they would fly away. Their husbands and children had no idea where they were. The Spanish Inquisition answered to no higher authority; a century before this, the joint kingdoms of Ferdinand of Aragón and Isabella of Castille had threatened to withhold defense of the Vatican against Saracen attacks if the Papacy did not bow to its clerics on how best to police the Church.

The Tribunal in Logroño, which answered only to a council called The Supreme in Madrid, consisted of a Theocrat of the Order of Alcántara, known as soldiers who fought and defeated Saracens in past centuries, as well as rival clerics, and a Lawyer or Licensed One who had been an Archbishop's secretary before his appointment to the Tribunal. The third seat was unfilled at first.

The Inquisitors declined to receive the judge from Bordeaux because he was not a priest and was French. That fall the Theocrat and his entourage made a visitation of the Basque Country and reported back to the Lawyer. The Theocrat was overjoyed by his discovery of the Devil's marks. "It is a fact that the Devil sets his mark on them, for I have seen it with my own eyes on the witches in Lesaca. The mark is a small one. On some it can barely be seen. It has really amazed me!"

Having the Theocrat close at hand, the Abbot at the monastery at Urdax complained that no one was inspecting the mule trains as they came across the border. Consequently the Abbot became the examiner. That summer, Austin started coughing violently on the road near Bayonne and Biarritz. He had pneumonic plague, in just three days he died, and his muleteers buried him by the road in haste, fearing his corpse could still infect them and others. The Abbot's inspection of the freight brought home to his widow by his muleteers produced an unauthorized Spanish translation of the Bible and some pamphlets written by a French Huguenot. The Abbot hated Huguenots as much as he hated witches. That seizure and the waif who had come over the mountains from Ciboure ensnared Enara.

By all accounts Enara was a beauty. Her priest named Ander went out to her estate first to console her for her loss and to encourage her to continue her husband's tithing, but they became friends. One day she watched him on his hands and knees, tilling her garden plot. She went out and knelt beside him, and in her bed that night she stopped calling him Father.

Gracia de Mayora, the homeless waif who made the first accusations of witchcraft in Navarra, was thirteen or fourteen. Constables in Zugarramurdi had arrested her for stealing and eating a pie cooling on a windowsill. The court turned her over to the Abbot and monks at the monastery at Urdax. The Abbot wanted to be rid of her; something about her was eerie, he was not running an orphanage, and he feared the turmoil she had caused in Zugarramurdi and four nearby villages. With the Abbott's blessing Father Ander took the girl into his custody. He brought her to Enara as a servant; he thought each of them might benefit from the other's company. Gracia lasted there just three months. Enara had wanted a child, but not this wretch of a girl. Gracia walked off down the mule trail after stealing some of Enara's jewelry and went back to Zugarramurdi.

The constables made Gracia once more the temporary ward of the monks at Urdax. The Abbot searched the girl's possessions one day when another monk had her sweeping out the hospice wards. Afterward the Abbot tossed the silver rings and bracelets on the girl's cot and demanded to know where she got them.

"From the queen!" she yelled at him.

"From the *queen?*" he cried. "What queen would that be?"

"The queen you're looking for! Queen of the black sabbaths in Zugarramurdi's caves. She sits beside the Devil holding his prick in her hand."

The Abbot slapped her so hard she flew across the cot, and he ordered monks to hold her in a room with a barred door until he could call back the Theocrat from Logroño. When the Theocrat arrived he joined the Abbot in pressuring the girl to admit to the evil things she had done under the influence of Enara de Añibarro.

Enara vanished from the family's castle near the ravines of the Río Vellos and was flung into a dungeon cell at Logroño.

There had been and would be no assertions of a coven in or near Ezkaroze. If she was presiding over black sabbaths at Zugarramurdi it was quite a long flight, for there were considerable mountains between their valleys. Enara was a rarity in the Inquisition's secret prisons because she could read and write. The Inquisitors gave her an authorized Bible in Spanish to read and due to her stature and nobility they allowed her to continue writing her journals. They planned to use the journals against her if she continued to claim she was innocent. She had been there a month when Ander found her, and he was allowed to see her. Ander had offered some pleasantries in Basque to the jailer who accompanied him, and it was clear the guard understood nothing. Ander then told her: "Enara, you are in very serious trouble."

"You come here to tell me that? You think I'm daft?"

"Shssh. Don't let them know you speak anything but Euskera."

"It's too late for that. They already know I speak Spanish."

"All right. But only speak Euskera to me. Kneel with me, please. We must pray together."

"Oh, for the love of God."

"Enara, that is not a good choice of words. Do this, so we can talk." They kneeled together and he murmured, "I'm here to help you."

"Yes, some help. That girl you brought me . . . "

"I know, I know. It's my fault. But we're going to discredit that girl. We're going to expose the liar." He looked about the cell and saw her writing table and chair, her plume and ink well, and her journals. He read a bit of them and gasped.

"Enara, you must not let them see this. I'll smuggle these out and bring you more tablets the next time I come. But you must be more guarded in what you write."

The next time he came, he said, "I think you have to confess."

"Confess? I've done nothing wrong but lie with you."

"When you confess you become a penitent, and in time they'll let you go."

"I don't know what to confess to. Tell me!"

"You begin by declaring your belief in Christ and the teachings of the Holy Mother Church."

"I don't believe in them, Ander. All I have now is wonder and doubt."

"Enara! These walls have ears, but you can hear through them, too. Listen to what others are saying. There are solitary witches and those who participate in the deeds of the covens. When you are questioning them, try to convince them you are one of the solitary ones. Not so harsh a charge."

"You want me to tell them I'm a witch of any kind."

"Outsmart them, Enara. You can do it. But they are powerful and ruthless."

"Oh, Father," she said as he turned to go, "one more thing. You are going to be a father."

He doubled over as if from a blow. "What?"

"You heard me. I'm pregnant."

"Is it mine?"

"Count the months. How long has Austin been dead? Or maybe like they say I've been doing it with Satan."

He put his forefinger to his lips. "Shhh! Do not say that!"

"Why? You told me to confess. That's what they believe of me."

The Theocrat took particular interest in the interrogations of Enara. He betrayed nothing when she informed him she was pregnant and the priest was the father. "I doubt that about Father Ander," he said, "but now we may be getting somewhere." The next time he came he asked: "Does the name Arrosa de Sastreana mean anything to you?"

"Yes," she said, startled. She had been with Enara when she miscarried.

"A midwife," he said.

"Yes. She lives in Ezkaroze."

"No more. She is here now, too. Was she part of the coven?"

"I know of no coven."

"She has confessed to being a witch, and like the girl Gracia de Mayora she accuses you of being the queen of the coven at Zugarramurdi. Two corroborating witnesses, even if they are witches, constitute an essential level of proof, Enara. And the midwife says something else. When you miscarried she cleaned you up and took the thing away. Your midwife says you miscarried a toad. She held it in her hands."

"Please. Have you no mercy?"

He leaned close to her. "Allow me to relate to you clauses twenty-four and twenty-five of the Positive Acts. 'The witches copulate with Satan in broad daylight as well as at the black sabbath, and they may sometimes conceive and give birth to toads.'"

Enara cried, "Why toads, my lord? Why not frogs?"

"These are powerful accusations. You can be sure that other witnesses will come forth. Especially if you and Satan were writhing like snakes for all the world to see. You are dancing very near the flames, Enara. I suggest you start praying."

Meanwhile the third seat on the Tribunal had been filled by an archbishop's former ambassador to the Vatican. The others disliked the Ambassador; they thought he was arrogant, but they put him in charge of the Tribunal's secret service that conducted most of the interrogations. All three Inquisitors came to Enara's torture, as required by Church law. They were seated, and without expression they saw Enara stripped nude. She was forced to stand with her hands tied to a rope slung over a beam. If she fell or slumped the torturer's assistant would pull her back up. The torturer bound her with eight ropes, one around each bicep, one beneath her breasts and behind her back, one around her abdomen just above her hips, and one around each of her thighs and calves. The tool of the garrotte was a slim iron bar. Starting with her right arm, he inserted it inside the rope and gave it a twist with great strength. She screamed each twist. "You are going to kill this baby! Come feel my stomach. Come feel! If you kill this baby you will all roast in Hell."

The Theocrat had developed an intense dislike of her, for the sharpness of her tongue, and perhaps he was repelled by what remained of her beauty. "She's obdurate. See the queen of the black sabbaths now. Still she holds God Almighty and us in contempt. Let this whore of Satan and mother of toads feel the Spider."

That instrument of torture was a three-pronged iron claw hung by chain from a wall. The prongs were filed very sharp and their bite could be adjusted. The torturer shoved and dragged her to it, and while the assistant held her upright, he started tightening them around her right breast.

"It's very simple," the Theocrat said. Neither of the other two had said a word. "It hurts now and bleeds, but that's nothing. When the Spider's grip is secure, he will grab you up through your armpits and clasp his hands behind your neck, then he will lurch backward and the blood and tissue of your breast will splatter the wall. Then if we've made no progress they will do the same with your other breast. You may bleed to death. In the best of it you will be terribly maimed."

"No!" she screamed. "Yes! I am a witch! I have taken Satan for a lover and done everything they say!"

In a room with rough tables and chairs the Theocrat took her confession, accompanied by two scribes from the secret service who were kept busy. The Theocrat wanted to know all the details. "Describe this Cave of Pleasure and what went on there."

"We recited our vow: 'I am a devil. From now on I shall be one with the Devil. I shall be a devil, and I shall have nothing to do with God.' Then we anointed ourselves with a green ointment made from the shit and puke of our toads."

"Your toads?"

"Yes, the ones we fed and kept dressed."

"Go on."

"We assembled in a meadow near a grotto near Zugarramurdi. Some walked there. I of course had to fly. We followed a stream into a cave that was like the nave of a cathedral. When the Devil arrived the witches lined up and kissed him on his left hand, on his chest near a certain point near his left nipple, then his private parts, and under his tail. He had a crude sense of humor. He entertained himself some by farting in their faces. After that the music and dancing began."

"What sort of music?"

"Flutes, drums, sometimes a fiddle."

"And then the intercourse began?"

"It did."

"Did you see men fornicating with men?"

"Yes. And women with women."

The Theocrat fell silent for a moment in his contempt. "Your lover, Satan, has been described as huge and dark-skinned as a Moor. An ugly creature with fierce glaring eyes. Fingers like hawk's talons, the tail of a donkey, the feet of a rooster."

"Someone's been lying to you."

"All right. Describe him to me. Some have said Your Lord of Pamplona is as much a goat as a man."

"Well, when he took off his boots his feet were cloven and hooved."

"Was he hairy? Were the hairs coarse?"

"On his back and shoulders and chest, he was hairy like many men. Not on his buttocks, though."

An angry silence. "What did he look like?"

"He's handsome. Cheeks dark from beard that he must razor every day. He has thick black eyebrows and long eyelashes, which draws attention to the fire in his eyes. They're bright red."

"You and the Devil had conversations?"

"After we'd lain together. Like all normal men and women."

He ignored the taunt. "Go on. Were his ears pointed?"

"Not that I noticed. They were covered by his hair. Unlike the hair on his body, it was straight and black and rather fine. It was one of the things I liked about him. He wore it long, to his shoulders, like the paintings of Christ."

The Theocrat shook his head in fury. "Does he have the horns of a goat?"

"No. He does have one long curved horn that grows out of the peak of his forehead. And at the point of it there's a pulsing light."

"Yes, yes, we've heard of that. He can control this light?"

"More or less."

"Your accusers have said you took his Evil Thing in your hand."

"How would they know? Everyone was in the frolic by then."

"Answer the question. Did you hold his Evil Thing in your hand?"

"Yes."

"So then it was firm when you and Satan copulated."

"Oh, it was readily firm. And there were other things we did beside that. The light in the point of his horn—it blazed and lit up the whole cave when I suckled his Thing in my mouth."

The Theocrat came to his feet. "You'll burn for that! You mock this Inquisition and the Holy Office and the Father and Son and Holy Ghost!"

Enara never consented to repent. As the Ritual of Public Penance neared, Father Ander pleaded with the Theocrat in tears. The Inquisitor shouted that Ander was going into the secret dungeon himself if he said one more word. At the start of the Ambassador's appointment to the Tribunal he had been as much a zealot as the other two. He made a visitation of the villages in the Basque Country that was more thorough than the one conducted by the Theocrat. But he observed that the only people incriminating anyone were those accused of witchcraft themselves.

The handling of the case by the Theocrat and Lawyer troubled the Ambassador enough that he voted against the verdict in the Tribunal's report of her trial to The Supreme. But the Inquisition's notion of a trial ensued. In the plaza of Logroño carpenters built a central stage surrounded by bleachers that would seat about a thousand people. One priest wrote that about thirty thousand people had come from Castilla, the Basque Country, Aragón, and there was a guest contingent of ranking French nobles. The Theocrat had ordered the carpenters to build one set of the bleachers against the tallest building on the plaza, so the Tribunal could make their appearance with royal power and solemnity. The Ritual of Public Penance began at two o'clock on a Saturday afternoon. Accompanied on both sides by Brothers of the Inquisition who held back assaults by the common crowd, the Delinquents were paraded barefoot from their dungeon, first those with minor offenses, then the Penitents wearing sack cloths of shame, then the Negative Ones, among them Enara, who had not repented. There were about fifty in all. Then through the same streets came low-ranking members of the Inquisition fraternity, then representatives of the Dominicans, Franciscans, Jesuits, and other orders in the region. Accompanied by musicians, then came a Franciscan monk carrying the holy emblem of the Inquisition, a Green Cross. And finally the Tribune, the Ambassador, the Lawyer or Licensed One, and the Theocrat of the Order of Alcántara.

The Ritual began with a sermon preached by a Franciscan who had been a member of the jury. The judgments and sentences went on the rest of the day and all through Sunday. The sentences of the Penitents ranged from ten to two hundred lashes and five years of hard labor in the galleys. Effigies of the accused who had died in prison would be burned at the stake along with the Negative Ones who would not repent. Charged on late notice with violating his celibate vows and consorting with witches, Father Ander was sentenced to life in exile in the Empire across the sea. Enara closed her eyes as his confession and sentence were being read.

The reading of crimes, confessions, and sentences went on for two and a half days. At night the Delinquents returned to their cells and were fed and given water. On Sunday night the Theocrat signed the notes of execution and had the first one delivered to Enara. A priest on the staff of the Tribunal sat with her all night, trying to persuade her. She had already confessed. Why could she not repent? Who can know what went through the woman's mind? By then Enara had to be deranged. It seemed she just wanted to be done with life and its consequences. Her abdomen was large with the baby when, on that Sunday morning in November 1610, she waddled out of her cell expecting to be burned to death before sundown.

But as it happened, the Ambassador had written a compelling dissent about all the witchcraft convictions to the Supreme, and Enara's husband Austin, the late monopolist of the mule trains and trade, had a relative on the Council of the Supreme—a distant relative, but near enough. During the night a fast-riding courier had arrived from Madrid with a notarized override from the Supreme of the Tribunal's death sentence and any further imprisonment and inconvenience of Enara de Añibarro. Instead of being prodded back through the streets of Logroño to her place of death by fire, she was ruled just a heretic and put out on the road to Pamplona barefoot, wearing the sackcloth garment of shame.

She made it back to Ezkaroze through the kindness of strangers. Ander de Saratxo was indeed banished to missions to the aborigines in North America. But Enara's case and release was a turning point in Euskadi. Though the Theocrat and the Lawyer wanted to press ahead with nearly five thousand accusations and cases, the arguments of the Ambassador prevailed in the Council of the Supreme. The other Inquisitors at Logroño died embittered before the decade was out, convinced that the Ambassador was Satan in disguise. Enara bled to death from complications of childbirth when she was thirty years old. Nothing is known of her infant, except that he or she survived.

TWENTY-FIVE

L uke sat on the bed long enough that the collie nosed around to see what was up. He stroked Barkilu's head, murmured a reassurance, and laced on his hiking shoes, which always excited the collie. Today Luke said, "Sorry, pal. There's a ball game in town, and they won't let you in."

With the hood of a light windbreaker pulled over his head, Luke walked fast through the parkland of the Palacio de Miramar and on along the Miraconcha boulevard and the green spaces of Paseo de la Concha, the Plaza de Cervantes, and the park Alderdi Ader, which framed the longer of San Sebastián's crescent-shaped beaches, Playa de la Concha. The sun had burned off light morning fog, and the swimmers and Frisbee-throwers were out in force. It was a twenty-minute walk to the entrance of the old quarter, which sat back between the end of the beach and the steep promontory of Monte Urgull. The promontory was separated from the bay by the old port, where the wood ships of the whale hunters once embarked; now pleasure crafts claimed the slips. The Guardia Civil had a station on the point that looked like a military installation. He had seen people in combat helmets moving inside it, but never on the streets.

Luke thought the station hung out over the water was just asking for attack. He wondered if he was guilty and could be incriminated by his thoughts.

Caged canaries were in full cry on the little balconies of upstairs apartments in the old quarter. Cats paced below them, jaws popping in reflex, trying to see a way to get to them. At the Pelotelaku Donostia he bought a ticket for seven hundred pesetas, about ten bucks. Inside the *fronton* the ricochet of balls echoed off the concrete walls. The teams of San Sebastián and Bilbao were warming up. They had grown up playing *pelota,* their national sport, with bare hands, gloves, and wooden paddles. The game was called jai alai in the States and Latin America, but few players and fans in Euskadi call it anything but *pelota,* ball. They bragged it was the fastest game in the world, and Luke had no reason to doubt it.

On a court that was about twice the length of a basketball gym, the scoring surfaces of play were a square on the front wall, a high ceiling, the back wall, a sidewall on the left side of the court, and the floor, all constructed of concrete dyed green in the mix. Scores were made when the ball bounced twice or landed on a red-painted hardwood floor that divided the court from the stands.

He found a seat about twenty rows up. This game was a doubles with two players in numbered gold jerseys from Bilbao and two in green from San Sebastián. They would play to forty points, which could take as long as a marathon tennis match. The players wore white trousers and traditional red sashes tied around the waist. Their helmets matched the colors of their jerseys and resembled those of bicyclists. With an interior leather glove and wrist wraps to secure them, the players wore *cestas,* scythe-shaped baskets about a yard in length, on their right hands. If any were born lefthanders, they had to change birth's orientations if they wanted to play this fastest form of an ancient game. The *cestas* were framed by ribbed arcs of chestnut wood and catch webs made from reeds grown only in the Pyrenees, or so it was claimed. They wore out fast, and pros such as these brought ten or more of them to a game. The balls were covered with goatskin or dog hide, made like a baseball but about three-fourths the size. They were as hard as rock and like the *cestas* they too wore out fast.

Walking between the wire and the bleachers were men with shoulder straps and baskets that contained tennis balls sliced halfway through. When spectators called out or gestured, these men tossed them the tennis balls. It was how they wagered. A bettor marked a piece of paper with a stub of pencil, filled the ball with pesetas, and tossed it back to the man on the floor.

The Bilbaínos were up 2-1 when a thin old man started up the aisle nearest Luke. His gaze fell on Luke, who raised a hand of greeting. It was the sculptor, Eduardo Txillada. Surprised and pleased that Txillada remembered him, Luke offered the empty seat beside him. Txillada excused himself over the knees of the spectators and shook hands with Luke as he took the seat. "We meet again," he said. "Do you like our *pelota?*"

"Yes, I like it. I've come here a few times."

CHAPTER 25

With a vertical leap the Donostian backcourt man caught a ball on a high bounce and with a slash downward and outward twist put such spin on the ball that it broke as sharply as a pitcher's curveball. Except a big-league curve might veer three feet across the strike zone. This one broke at least six feet, with the carom staying in the corner. The home crowd cheered, but their cries died as the Bilbaíno whacked it off the *frontis* to the ceiling and well back on the floor, and the Donostian frontcourt man was unable to put the point away.

"I'm a little surprised to see you here," said Luke.

"Why?"

"You have a public. I'd think you might be bothered by people."

Txillada smiled. "Fans of *pelota* don't necessarily appreciate sculpture. Much less recognize the sculptor."

The San Sebastián crowd cheered as a wicked return by their back-court man bounced twice before a Bibaíno could reach it, which tied the score at 2-2. "You were an athlete, weren't you?" said Luke.

"Long ago, but it was the time of my life," Txillada said. "I was the goalkeeper for San Sebastián's Real Sociedad in the national Liga de Pelota. I amazed myself with some of the saves I made. But one cruel day I tore up a knee so badly that it took three surgeries to keep me climbing stairs." He sighed. "One day that kind of youth is over. So I studied architecture at the University of Madrid while the Second World War tore up the rest of Europe."

"Architecture?" said Luke.

"Yes, I learned a lot, but it was not easy in those years of Franco's regime to go around Madrid with a Basque name. I didn't know what I was going to do with my life."

"But you figured it out."

Txillada smiled. "You never regain the fun you had when you were young."

The men with the tennis balls were busy on the floor. "I have a question," Luke said. "How does the gambling work?"

Txillada said, "They persuade themselves that this old way keeps the wagers honest and the game pure. When a point's made the scoreboard relays odds on the next shot. The man on the floor tosses you a ball that contains a piece of paper and a stub of pencil. You mark your bet on the slip of paper in the ball, put pesetas in, and toss it back."

"Well, I can manage that," said Luke. He raised his hand at a potbel-lied man with the shoulder strap and basket. The man took out a tennis ball, wrote something on the piece of paper, and lobbed the ball high. Luke made the grab that got some cheers from men and boys around. He grinned and pulled open the split in the ball. He took out the piece of paper and pencil stub, planning to bet on the home team.

The piece of paper read: *They know who you are.*

Luke was stunned, holding the paper in his hand. He tossed the ball back empty to the man, who caught it with a curt nod and moved on. Txillada must have seen the color drain from Luke's face. "Is something wrong?" he said.

Luke shook his head.

"May I see that?"

Luke handed him the slip of paper. Txillada frowned on reading it. "People communicated like this in the Franco years. I don't know what this means, but if I were you I would take it seriously."

Luke gave the sculptor's hand a grateful squeeze and stood up. *"Tengo que correr."* I have to run.

TWENTY-SIX

SUMMER SOLSTICE, 1994

"**H**ow's your day been?" asked Ysolina as she came through the foyer with her briefcase slung over her shoulder and greeted the dog.

"Good and bad."

She set the briefcase down. "Yes?"

"The good was reading the latest entry in your journal. I was moved."

"Oh, you found it," she said, rattled. "And liked it? Thank you. And the bad?"

He handed her the slip of paper. She looked at it and said, "Who gave you this? What does it mean?"

"I got it in a split tennis ball trying to make a bet at a *pelota* game today, while you were gone. Where were you?"

"In Pamplona. My research—"

He shook his head. "We weren't going to do that."

"What, Luke? What?"

"We weren't going to lie to each other. You weren't at the archives in Pamplona. You couldn't have gotten close to them. The crowds are huge this year for the bulls. The roads are closed. I saw that in the paper."

She leaned against the wall and put the back of her head against it.

"All right. I went to see Peru. We were just talking."

"Cooking up a little killing?"

She came off the wall and slapped him.

He nodded and held his hands out to the sides. "I don't care what you were doing. I mean I do. Any man would. But you went to see him in a car registered to the person who's on my forged passport and visa. I'm a fugitive, too, you know. And I put myself in this situation because of you."

"And now you're my guardian angel. Maybe you ought to flap your big white wings and just *go away*."

"Ysolina, we have to get out of here. This proves what I haven't been able to make you notice. It's about us carrying on like we don't have a care in the world. And this husband you went to see. Did you watch to see if anyone was following you? Do you get the picture?"

He had moved closer in saying this. She put the palm of her hand against his chest. "Can we talk about this over a drink?"

"Good idea."

Soon they were yelling at each other; the dog cringed.

"You've been using me," he lashed out.

"Is that right? I still don't know just how you showed up on that trail ride that day. Who's been using who?"

He sat on one of the barstools stirring whiskey with his forefinger. "Where are Peru and his gang?"

"'His gang.'" She laughed bitterly.

"What are they going to do?"

"I don't know. He won't say. He wants to protect me."

"Okay, let's level with each other. I'll go first. I was working non-official cover for an organization I call the Outfit. It means I've got no diplomatic immunity, whatever happens. I threw my associations with those Americans in the bay that morning in St. Jean-de-Luz. As far as my former friends are concerned I've gone over with ETA. Is that straightforward enough? I'm in a lot of trouble. Not because of you. I said that badly. Because I fell in love with you."

She drew a breath to steady her voice. "There were secret peace negotiations between the regime and ETA in Morocco. They seemed so promising. There had been a ceasefire for several months, and I hoped Peru might emerge as a kind of rebel turned peacemaker. What they're seeing in Northern Ireland."

"He didn't seem all that peaceable to me."

"Can I *finish?*"

"Go ahead. Sorry."

"The talks fell apart right when you and I met. I still hoped that scenario for Peru might work out, but that doesn't mean things were good between us. They haven't been for a long time. I was using you, yes, and so was Peru. He knew I needed to be here for my research and more. I'm glad you think I'm doing something genuine. The people who tried to kill Peru in France were a Spanish hit squad. The leader was an officer in the Guardia Civil's secret police. The others were mercenaries—an Australian former French Foreign Legionnaire, a member of the Apostólico Anticommunista de Argentina, and an Italian fascist."

He thought that if ETA already knew that, they had a pretty fair intelligence system, too. She shook her head and laughed. "Is that the most Spaniard thing you ever heard? Peru's all right but he's very angry. I don't know what he'll do. The last thing I did for ETA, and the first in many years, was a mistake. When Papa sent me to university in Paris I took drama but had no talent for acting. For a year or so I stayed involved in the program and learned how to do makeup. One night after the moving of the horses I made up a boy to look like the Basques' idea of Satan to scare a factory owner who owed them their so-called revolutionary taxes. It was a stupid thing to do. It made me party to a kidnapping and extortion."

"That's enough to get you locked up for a long time where I come from. And I bet the laws are harsher in Spain."

"Why are you making this so hard?" she said, tears spilling down her cheeks. Luke was no good at dealing with a woman in tears.

"Maybe I was naïve," she went on. "Grasping at straws. But I was *hopeful*—is that a sin? The Spaniards broke the ceasefire. They tried to kill Peru and did kill a boy Peru loved like a son. So all bets about a solution are off. He knows it's over between us. He knows I'm with you. If you'll calm down and just have me."

After a moment he pulled her into his arms. She beat his chest lightly with the side of a fist. "You're right, it's time to go. But where?"

"We could just keep moving, out-of-the-way villages, but that's no way to live. We need to be somewhere outside Spain. Somewhere you can write."

Her eyes glistened. "Do you mean that?"

"Of course I mean it. But how? The Outfit and Spanish intelligence are puppies out of the same litter. They gut each other all the time but when it's in their interests they communicate. They probably think we'll try to run by sea. They'll have alerts out at every crossing into France and Portugal."

She hung her chin on his collarbone. "I have an idea," she said, thinking of the trail-ride leader. "André Roumanille. He has a place near Pau.

He has this cottage away from the main house. Nobody's using it. I know because I talked to him this week, and he offered it again. He must have heard something in my voice. I trust him with my life."

"All right. But André's in France. How do we get there?"

"He can lead us across. He knows the trails blindfolded."

"That old man can lead us on a hike over the Pyrenees at night?"

"We wouldn't hike. He made his living as a smuggler when he was young. He'd bring saddle horses and a pack mule. We'd get out with more than just the clothes on our backs."

"What about Barkilu?"

"He'd be right with us. He thinks he's taking care of me."

"How soon can you arrange this?"

"I'll call André now. But tonight—just one more night here—can I show you one more thing?"

With the collie hanging his head out a rear window and enjoying the breeze, Luke negotiated the hellish traffic on the Carretera Rápida almost to the French border, then at Ysolina's direction he turned off at Irún on trunk roads. The roads twisted southward along the frontier then back north past to the villages of Vera, Lesaca, Yanci, Echalar, and Zugarramurdi—the valley of Las Cinco Villas. It was hard to imagine how those well-groomed hamlets had ignited a frenzy that wound up with two people out of five convicted of witchcraft.

Cars were parked along roadsides well before they reached Zugarramurdi. She told him to turn off on one of the lanes to a house. Luke steered around a Land Rover partly blocking the drive and asked, "How do you know we're welcome?"

"I've been coming here in my work and know them. He's a retired professor and she's a painter. I told them we might be here tonight." He parked beside a large garden, where she put the leash back on Barkilu and let him out of the back seat. Luke locked the car and she handed him a wineskin she had brought along. People streamed along the road, many in costumes, some of them fathers with children riding on their shoulders. He watched young people pass wearing black clothing and ghoulish white and red face paint. Some had rubber vampire fangs. Halloween.

Half a kilometer from the town, Sorgin Leiza is a system of out-croppings, caves, and subterranean streams. Ysolina said the celebration would be in the largest cave, Erreka Infernuko. A clear and fast-moving stream had carved a tunnel through a great slab of beige rock that looked like it had been yanked up and twisted. The keepers of the cave had planted iron handrails here and there. Lighting the way were burning torches planted in holders planted in the rock. Luke looked up from the meandering aquifer stream. "This is the Cave of Pleasure?"

"In the legend."

The party had begun. A large band of drummers sounded like samba groups Luke had heard in South America. There must have been a hundred of them, banging with their hands on all manner of drums, and costumed and face-painted dancers were whirling and leaping, showing off their moves. Parents were bringing kids up to pet the collie, who accepted them with patience and swishes of his tail. He licked a few of their hands and faces. A few thousand people had crowded inside the cave. The only light came from the torches on the walls. The centerpiece was a towering cone of logs, brush, whole trunks of trees. He unslung the wineskin, swallowed a couple of mouthfuls, and handed it to her. They made their way closer, keeping a short leash on the dog.

"What happens to the smoke?" said Luke.

"There are holes and crevices all through the limestone. They're like chimneys. The smoke finds them."

They watched as the drummers and dancers sashayed forward and put fire to the kindling. The crowd bellowed as small flames grew large. Soon the bonfire threw out enough heat that Barkilu pulled back on the leash. They could barely hear each other. "It's symbolic, right? They're burning witches at the stake?"

"It's a national fiesta—summer solstice and Day of the Witch."

He put his arm around her. "And your ancestor was queen of the *aquellare.*"

"So they said."

"Who was she really, Ysolina? Do you know?"

"I think she was a lonely widow who made a mistake and took a priest for a lover. When they put her in those cells and kept asking the same questions day after day she was defiant and went mad."

"Amazing thing," Luke said, "the imagination."

"Goya thought enough of the legend that one of his most famous paintings is a dance at the *aquellare*. Pairs of lovers will jump through the flames tonight. They think it brings them luck."

Luke said, "Let's skip that one. I'm not very nimble."

They made it back to the house in San Sebastián about one in the morning. They kissed and fumbled but came to the conclusion that they might enjoy the lovemaking more if they gave it another try when they woke up. And then they'd pack some things and in another night they'd rendezvous with André.

The cops discharged the battering ram and blew the front door off the hinges. Luke reached across her for the end table drawer where he kept the gun but she grabbed his arm. Barkilu had jumped awake at the crash and he went roaring down the stairs to defend them. Luke heard two gunshots and a yelp.

Ysolina was screaming. One of the cops, armored in SWAT team black, appeared in the moonlit doorway with a shotgun pointed at them and with his free hand tossed a flash grenade, then ducked back in the hall. The explosion blinded and deafened Luke for more time than they needed. They had him face down on the floor with a heavy knee in his back and were handcuffing him roughly. "You killed the dog," he was saying. "You didn't have to kill the dog." Then one of them yanked the hood over his head.

ELKARGUNEAK

JUNCTURES

TWENTY-SEVEN

JULY 1994

They had made him put on jail coveralls and dumped him hooded, barefoot, and handcuffed on the steel floor of a plane whose rattles and wobbles brought back memories of the C-130 shot down in Colombia. He was cold. He heard Ysolina sobbing. One of them barked at her to shut up. Luke knew what lay ahead. You get tangled up in your lies. He decided he could get through it best by sticking to the truth. Except the money. For that he had to lie.

Then the plane was landing, and his captors let him roll and thrash about. He cursed them heartily, and they kicked at him although they were belted into their seats. When the plane stopped they hustled him down a ramp. "Be strong, baby," he called, not knowing if she could hear him.

When the captors finally removed the hood it took a moment for his eyes to adjust to the glaring light. He was in a small room with peeling yellow paint inside the high-walled barracks at Colmenar Viejo on the northern outskirts of Madrid. The room contained a small table and four chairs. If he got any sleep it was going to be on a very dirty floor. The only amenity was a toilet without a door.

After Franco's death all intelligence operations in Spain had become the official purview of the Centro Nacional de Inteligencia, the CNI, but the Guardia Civil maintained jealous hold of its independent "Information Service" in the battle with ETA, the Catalan separatist organization Terre Lliure, the Free Galician People's Guerrilla Army, and the Popular Front in the Canary Islands. The officer in charge of Luke and Ysolina was Miguel Peralta, the Civil Guard lieutenant colonel who had been shot during the gunfight at Cambo-les-Bains. Peralta was out for revenge against anyone associated with ETA, but Aitzgorri was the one he wanted most.

Peralta walked with a cane and limp. He had on cheap dress pants, a long-sleeved permanent-press shirt, and scuffed brown shoes. He had a hapless comb-over of black hair on his head. He put the cane to the floor and stepped forward. "Let me introduce myself," he said. "I am your *comandante*."

"If I'm going to talk to you it has to be in English. And it has to be in the presence of a representative of the United States embassy."

Peralta smiled. "You entered our country with a false passport and visa. Your real name is Luken Burgoa. You are of Mexican heritage. You engaged in military activities in South America for several years. We will speak Spanish."

"I have trouble understanding the way you Spaniards speak your own language. You speak with a *lithp*. It distracts me. Makes me think of a cartoon character in my country. Daffy Duck."

Peralta took two steps forward and slapped Luke and then back-handed him. His watch slipped down with the first blow and it cut Luke on the cheek with the second. The *comandante* nodded at one of his goons, who held a pair of bolt-cutters. "Do you see those? You are going to answer our questions, and you are going to answer in Spanish. If you do not, my friend is going to cut off fingers at the little knuckle, then the large knuckle, one by one, until you realize who's in control here. You are not entitled to a lawyer or a representative from your embassy. Criminals are not pampered in our country. No one but us can see you. Do you understand?"

The goon raised the bolt-cutter and made a sound of *snip, snip, snip.*

Luke heard the door open behind him. Out walked a guy who was well over six feet tall and appeared to weigh about 220. He wore a ludicrous costume: black boxing shoes and trunks, bare chest, a black cape, a black mask over his eyes, and the Guardia Civil's black tricorn. "Whoa," Luke said. "Is that Superman or Zorro?"

In the Guardia Civil's counter-terror interrogations that agent had acquired a brutal reputation and the nickname Doctor Tricornio. Peralta looked at the big man and said, "The foreigner thinks we're amusing."

Doctor Tricornio made a show of binding his hands, fingers, and thumbs with cotton boxing wraps. "Where is Peru Madariaga?" Peralta began.

"I don't know. I was trying to find him. Then your team showed up."

"Have you been fucking his wife?"

"Who's fucking yours?"

Peralta sighed and shook his head. "You are not a serious person." He stepped aside and the goon who had wielded the bolt-cutters approached Luke with a large pillow. He reached across Luke and pulled the ends of the pillow tight and immobilized Luke's head and torso. Tricornio threw slow but very hard punches, intent on breaking ribs, damaging kidneys, rupturing the spleen. They used the pillow so he could take it longer.

Clear fluid dripped from Luke's nose when the pillow was removed. He raised his head at Peralta. "Ask me your questions. I'll tell you what I know. Give me a minute."

"That's better." Peralta waited for Luke's breathing to deepen. "When and where did you meet Peru Madariaga?"

"In the western Pyrenees, Béarn Province, France. September 1993. He and his wife were riding horses."

"You chanced on a horseback ride with this terrorist and his whore of a wife."

"I didn't just chance on them. I had intelligence they'd be there. She's not a whore. Gimp. Kiss my ass. Suck my dick."

The pillow holder stepped back in and the Doctor laid into Luke again. At last Peralta raised a hand. "You're making this harder than it has to be," he said. "Let's behave like professionals. I am an intelligence officer and servant of my king and España. You were once a Marine officer in service of your country. We have much in common. Where is Peru Madariaga?"

"I don't know."

"I don't believe you."

"I can't help that."

"Why did your superiors want to help rid my country of ETA's vermin?"

"They don't give a rat's ass about España. Sorry to break the news but it's true. They fear Islamic jihadists. They think there's a connection with ETA."

"They're right. There's a long history of those connections. Was this a solo mission for your country?"

"Yes."

"A bad idea on your part?"

"Could be."

"What were your orders?"

"Try to penetrate ETA and gain Madariaga's confidence, set him up to be captured or killed, and make sure Spaniards made the arrest or got credit for the killing."

"You brokered an illegal arms transaction with Madariaga. You were gunrunning to terrorists."

"It was an operation, a sting. The weapons were the bait."

"What was their point of origin?"

"Rainforest in Ecuador."

"Who supplied you with these weapons?"

"Oil companies."

That gave Peralta pause. "Oil companies?"

"What I said."

"Why would oil companies be engaged in gunrunning?"

"They thought the glut of them in South America endangered the business they're doing down there."

"Who made them available?"

"I can give you names but why would they tell me their real names? I didn't tell them mine. What's your real name? What's the name of the guy in the dumb hat?"

Peralta backhanded him again. "I'm losing my patience. We'll get back to their names. How did you transport the arms to France?"

"Shipped them out of a port in Uruguay in refrigerated bins of beef."

He tossed out the name of a bogus company in Buenos Aires called Embarcados Mundial SA. If the Spaniards ran that down they'd find themselves talking to the Outfit, annoying both parties.

"How did you get the arms into France?"

Luke shrugged. "St. Nazaire is a loose port."

"Where did you deliver these weapons to Madariaga?"

"A warehouse in St. Jean-de-Luz."

"Remember the name of it?"

"I could take you to it. I never saw a name."

"Was Madariaga pleased with the goods?"

"He had them carried off."

"Did he ask about Soviet-built weapons called Plamya Flames?"

That took Luke aback. A third party had to have told them that. "He mentioned them, yes."

"Did you bring them into France?"

"No. I told him I'd have to look into it. That was the last I saw of him."

"You're lying."

"I'm not."

Peralta stalked about, stabbing the floor with the cane. "During this time you developed an attraction for this woman Ysolina Madariaga."

"I liked to see her coming, yes."

"Do you know she is a propagandist for ETA?"

"You're wrong but I know you think that. She hadn't set foot in this country for eleven years. France has given her permanent resident status. Their university system has embraced her. She's an academic. She's consumed with writing a dissertation about an ancestor caught up in a witchcraft craze four hundred years ago. She needed to see archives in Spain."

"Is she a witch?"

"Are you?"

Peralta made a sound breathing through his nose. "So you gave her a ride to San Sebastián and lived with her."

"I thought she might lead me to Peru." Then the lie. "He'd stolen a lot of money from me, and I'd lost him."

Luke was aware that someone else had come in the room behind him. He stood jangling keys or coins in his pockets. Peralta said, "Why did you cut off contact with your superiors?"

"If I didn't, I knew I was going to lose her, too. My handler in Paris trusted me to know how to do the job. Your friends at the embassy can put you in touch. His name is James Hopson, retired colonel, US Marines."

Peralta poked him in the chest with his cane. "I don't believe you. That woman has turned you. You're ETA now, an enemy of my country. When you heard there had been an attempt to kill Madariaga you grabbed her and ran."

"Not true. We were already in Spain when your guys tried the hit on Madariaga. This woman is innocent. She's done nothing more than wish to come back and live in peace in her country."

"What happened to the money?"

"I told you. I spent everything I'd been given to set up that transaction. Then Madariaga ripped me off. I was lucky to get out of that warehouse alive. I'm as hot to find him as you are."

The man with the jangling keys or coins spoke up. "He's lying."

He walked into view wearing polished Italian loafers, pants starched to a crease, a cuff-linked white shirt unbuttoned at the throat, and a black blazer. He had dark hair, a well-trimmed beard, and a thin gold throat chain. "My name is Roberto Escamilla. I was your lead case officer until you betrayed our country."

Luke turned his head to Peralta. "Tell the California Cuban he ought to back up a step or two. I can spit a long way."

Escamilla shook his head. "He's lying about the money. He's got it stashed away somewhere. He's lying about everything. I don't care what you do to him. He's trash. Dump him in a landfill."

Luke didn't see Escamilla again, but for five nights and days Doctor Tricornio and other masked men beat him, hung him by his wrists, shoved his head in the toilet. The goon with the bolt-cutters clipped off Luke's little toe on his right foot, and as he howled the goon stuck it in a bucket of rubbing alcohol. He told them the names of large oil companies operating in South America. But they couldn't make Luke incriminate Ysolina or give up Gil de Ordeñana, the ETA exiles in Montevideo, Pascal Seguines, Guido de Marentes. He took care of them all.

The court orders allowing interrogation *incomunicado* at last expired. A judicial investigation would take over. Peralta, Doctor Tricornio, and the others left, and after some hours one of them rolled in tanks of acetylene and oxygen and a welding torch. The man wore a welding mask when he came in the room, but from the way he moved Luke knew it was the one who had used the bolt cutters. First the man strapped a medical whiplash collar on Luke. He pulled on thick gloves, produced a pair of vice grips, and showed Luke what looked like an insignia for a ring. It bore three letters—*ETA.*

The man lit the fuel and adjusted the torch, then holding the vice grips with heavy welding gloves, he dabbed the insignia in the flame until it was red hot. He put one gloved hand on Luke's shoulder in an almost consoling way, and branded him between his right cheekbone and jaw.

They had Ysolina in a room in the same prison. Peralta, Doctor Tricornio, and the others denied her sleep and water and lashed her shins and hands with bamboo. The worst of it began when Doctor Tricornio stripped her, tied her to a chair, and pulled a plastic bag over her head. His finger was deep in her. He crooned, "People say you just come and come and come, and then you're dead."

She struggled, trying to get away from the hand that violated her, then she panicked and started yelling, but that only sucked plastic in her mouth and sealed off more of her breathing. They watched her until she was frantic, dizzy, and asphyxiating, then pulled the bag off before she fainted or died. But she wouldn't tell them where she'd last seen Peru.

"All right, she's wasting my time," said Peralta. "I'm through with the bitch. You fellows have your fun."

Doctor Tricornio started pulling down his trunks. "You can't do this to me!" she screamed.

Peralta asked, "Why not?"

"Because I'm pregnant."

The *comandante* joined in the laughter. "She thinks we care."

TWENTY-EIGHT

AUGUST 1994

The bishop had understated Don Jokin's duties as the Zarzuela Palace priest. More than a hundred people were employed there, and he had to hear confessions. Don Jokin had always despised it. That Sunday he fretted behind the cloak and waited for what the next person had to say.

"Forgive me, Father, for I have sinned," a man said in Basque, which startled him. "It happens," the man said, changing to Spanish. "You know me, Don Jokin."

He wondered how he knew that voice. "Yes?"

"I'm Peru Madariaga."

Don Jokin gasped.

"I'm not here to confess my sins. I'm here to tell you what you're going to do. And if you don't, everything you've done for us is going to come out. The church will excommunicate you. You'll go to prison. Where it's fifty-fifty you'll die."

"How d-d-did you get in here?" Don Jokin stammered. He hadn't done that since he was a boy.

"It wasn't as hard as you think. Do you believe it's me? Do you want me to pull the cloak aside and show you my face?"

"No, no," said the priest.

"All right. This is what you're going to do. You're going to tell Juan Carlos that my wife Ysolina Madariaga has been tortured by the Guardia Civil and has been locked up without legal counsel, charges, or trial in the women's wing of Carabanchel Prison. We did get a doctor in to see her. Those agents of the Guardia Civil took turns raping her, knowing she was pregnant. She hasn't lost the baby yet, but any day she could, and what happens to the child if it's born in prison? Ysolina has done nothing illegal in this country. She came back here to finish research for a doctorate in history at the Sorbonne in Paris. For this she's been tortured and raped by Spaniards."

Don Jokin swallowed hard.

"I hope you've been listening. Because you're going to persuade the king that what happened to her is wrong. He has the leverage to get her released at once and allowed to go back to France. Have I made myself clear?"

"Yes, yes," Don Jokin managed to say.

"That's good. If you fail, I'll have you flayed naked in the street."

Juan Carlos appeared in the Zarzuela Palace office of Don Jokin with just a rap of his knuckles on the door facing. The priest's heart fluttered every time he did that. The king took a chair and leaned back, his hands clasped behind his head. "I've been thinking about our nation's calamities. Do you remember Manuel Fraga?"

"Vaguely," Don Jokin said.

"He was Franco's tourism minister. Remember when he liberalized censorship codes for the film industry? Billboards that read '*With Fraga you can even see the panties!*' And the Palomares hydrogen bombs. A B-52 of the Americans was refueling with a tanker over the Mediterranean. They collided, the tanker blew up, and the bomber broke apart. Some of the crew died, some made it out with parachutes. Three hydrogen bombs hit the ground near the village of Palomares on the coast of Andalucia, and explosives in two of them detonated. Not the big kabooms, but still. Nearly two square kilometers of plutonium contamination, lots of soil for Lyndon Johnson's people to scrape and cart off. And the fourth bomb was lost in the deep blue sea. While an American submarine searched for it, Manuel and the US ambassador went swimming on television to demonstrate how safe the water was. Manuel was our ambassador to Great Britain when Franco died. In the transition regime, he was the deputy prime minister. The situation couldn't have been more tense and volatile. Manuel came up with the helpful slogan *The Streets Are Mine!*"

Juan Carlos looked Don Jokin over and shook his head. "I wish you had a sense of humor."

"So do I, Your Majesty. So do I.'"

"Never mind. I need your input on something. In Bilbao, the American and Spanish architects and their Basque financiers believe this Guggenheim museum may succeed after all. You know how I hate to be harangued by my schedulers. The opening of the museum's still two years away, but the *jefes* are nagging me to commit to appearing at its opening. Do you think I should?"

"Well, Your Majesty, do you want to?"

The tall man flung his hands and laughed. "This is what they call an adviser! His job is to answer questions with more questions! Sure, I'd rather do that than go up there and make another speech about their ancient freedoms.*"

"Then you should go. Would your security aides be concerned?"

"Of course! They're always concerned!"

"There's been so much violence up there. It never seems to end."

The king gave him a closer look. "What's the matter, Don Jokin?"

The priest gripped the edges of his desk to keep them still. "Your Majesty, something scandalous has come to my attention and you should know about it."

"All right. Go ahead."

"A Basque woman now in Carabanchel Prison has been very badly treated by the Guardia Civil."

Juan Carlos groaned. "I have enough enemies in the Guardia Civil. Anything like that should be routed through the CNI and the courts."

"Your Majesty, this woman's late father was an officer in Franco's army and a member of the Falange. As a young girl she married a man who turned out to be a militant in ETA. She left him as soon as she found this out. In Paris she is a graduate student at the Sorbonne. She had been stymied in her research because crucial archives are in our country. She crossed the border last spring using a passport that was not hers. It was a serious mistake, no question."

He drew a breath and went on. "She was arrested in June by the Guardia Civil. They pressured her for information on the whereabouts of her estranged husband, Peru Madariaga. Information she does not have. These men tortured and raped her, knowing she is pregnant. No soul should be abused like that by officers in service of the Crown. Nor should her unborn child."

Juan Carlos sighed. "I know who Peru Madariaga is. We have briefings about ETA. You have proof of this?"

"My lord, I know it to be true." Another lie, this one not so minor.

"What's this woman's name?"

"Ysolina Madariaga."

"If she's broken with this foul man, why hasn't she divorced him?"

"Because her faith in the church is strong."

"You're playing on my conscience and asking me to intervene."

"I suppose that's the gist of it, Your Majesty."

"For God's sake."

TWENTY-NINE

OCTOBER 1994

I n a striped prison jump suit Luke had been bound over to the National Court in Madrid with no knowledge of where Ysolina was. At his hearing a laconic man in a disheveled suit introduced himself as his lawyer. "Oh?" said Luke, heartened for a moment. "Who hired you?"

"The court and prosecutors. I am appointed *de officio.*"

"Well, how are you going to defend me?"

"I can't talk to you. It's not allowed."

And the judge and prosecutor did all the talking at the hearing. Luke was charged with espionage, abetting terrorism, organized criminal activity, perjury, and entering the country with forged documents. Luke's lawyer didn't say a word.

The judge frowned at Luke's condition. "How did this man get that burn?"

The prosecutor said, "Your Honor, the *etarras* believed he intended to betray them, and they punished him in that horrid way."

"Anything else wrong with him?" said the judge.

"The *etarras* cut off one of his toes."

"Savages," the judge said. "See to it that this man receives medical treatment by a physician known to this court."

Then he told Luke, "Because of the severity of these accusations and provisions of the penal code, bail is denied."

Luke was put in solitary detention at Carabanchel, a hard-time place, constant bedlam and danger. The doctor examined Luke's burn and said it was healing all right, but added after changing the bandages on his foot that he was concerned about the wound. "You have to watch that. If you see any evidence of a black spot it's gangrene. You could lose that foot, your leg. Your life."

"How do I see the bottom of my foot? Can I get a mirror?"

"I'm sorry, it's not allowed. Shards have been used for suicides and attacks on other inmates. I'm leaving antibiotics with your guards. I'll be back."

Luke never saw the doctor again.

But one night he woke up soaked with sweat. His fever had broken, and some days later the hole in his foot closed over. The body's power of healing is a remarkable thing. He was moved into the general population but had no cellmate and was still denied contact with the outside. He was allowed an hour of exercise each day, took his meals with other inmates, and now that it was healed enough that one could see what it was, the brand drew attention, pro and con. A *gudari* named Piarres told him, "It may be three of four years before you're tried. That's average. Could be better for you because you're American, could be worse."

Weeks later in the food line he felt a nudge in the small of his back. "That's a thumb, not a knife. Keep moving. Don't look around. Just listen."

Luke did as he was told.

"You're coming out of here," the man said. "Going back across the water, unless you don't want that. And can figure out a way to keep from it."

Luke shuffled forward and kept his head down.

"These people aren't going to break you out. You're too hot. Not worth the trouble. But they want to see what you're made of."

The man added, "They cut the woman loose without charges."

Without charges? Luke wondered who and what she had to give up.

"These people are going to be with you every step of the way. They'll take care of you if you can do it. But that's all. It's up to you."

In ill-fitting clothes provided by the embassy, Luke moved through the Madrid Barajas International Airport with his right wrist cuffed to the left one of Roberto Escamilla. Travelers saw the handcuffs, dropped their eyes, and stepped aside. A couple of them gaped at the burn scar on his face. Madrid's station chief was dressed like he had been that night at Colmenar Viejo. He was not happy he had been given the job of returning Luke to the Outfit's citadel outside Washington. Escamilla taunted him. "I bet you wind up in a maximum security. You'll think Carabanchel was a *brasserie* on the Champs-Élysée."

Luke winced at how fast he was made to hobble along, and he knew they were nearing the departure gate. He saw a sign for restrooms and asked his handler for a pit stop. "Come on," he said when Escamilla resisted. "If I piss on myself you're going to be smelling it, too." Escamilla grumbled and led him to a john. Two guys were washing and drying their hands. Luke watched his urine come out coffee-colored. "Look what those sons of bitches did," he said.

The Orange County Cuban was tending to his own pecker and piss. Luke gave the handcuffs a tug. "I mean it. Look at this."

Escamilla lowered his head slightly. "You're breaking my heart."

As a fighter Luke never had any confidence in his left hook. His reflexes made him throw it straight and hard, like his jab. But he had better throw a real hook now. He took in a breath, pivoted, cut loose on Escamilla as he was pulling up his zipper, and caught him square between the eyes. Escamilla's loafers shot from under him on the tiles and he went down hard, taking Luke with him. That was all Luke needed, Escamilla knocked out by banging his head on the floor. "*Oiga!*" someone cried, throwing his paper towel aside and fleeing. Another man flung a toilet door open and ran out buckling his belt. Luke slapped Escamilla and glanced at the entryway. A young man turned a father and son away and gave Luke a curt nod.

Luke said, "Unlock the cuffs."

Escamilla said, "You're outa luck, asshole."

Luke wedged his forearm against Escamilla's throat and put all his weight down. "It's your life to lose. You've got about thirty seconds before you black out and your organs start to fail."

He glanced again at the entry and saw the young man position a yellow tripod indicating the rest room was being cleaned and closed. "All right, let up," Escamilla croaked. "But you are making a huge mistake."

With the unlocked end of the cuffs dangling from his wrist, Luke stood over Escamilla, who cowered and raised his arms. The Basque *gudari* whistled urgently through his teeth. Luke gave Escamilla a kick in the ribs and limped out of the john. He was joined by a small phalanx of guys, one of them hoisting an old boxing championship belt. Another carried a boom box and turned on a loud Spanish rap number. Still bearing marks of his beatings, Luke picked up on the charade and affected a boxer's strut. Startled people saw them coming and got right out of the way. As they hustled out into the midday heat a gray van pulled up by the curb. One of the commandos opened the back and shoved Luke in.

"Stay down," the *gudari* said.

"No problem," Luke replied.

THIRTY

The Italian-made power yacht set out from a dock of storage warehouses outside Santander. Since the escape from Carabanchel, Peru's men had treated him well, but they hadn't told him what they meant to do with him. The ninety-foot boat had been gleaming white when ETA seized it, but now it was christened *Agur*—Basque for *adios*—and painted gray so it would be harder to make out at sea. The boat whammed through whitecaps, and Luke tried to keep his gaze on the horizon. For a host of reasons he was queasy.

The inked-up one called Jale piloted the craft. Peru had nodded at Luke when he came aboard but his manner was cool. Luke didn't know the other two men on the boat. Luke could see few lights on the Bay of Biscay, and those on the towns ashore were fast getting lost in early evening fog. The air was damp and cool. He pulled a thick cotton hooded jacket out of his pack and put it on. The pack's contents were all he'd gotten out of Spain.

The Baglietto's engine rumbled like the Chevy 342 horsepower V-8s he remembered as a kid, but with a gurgle of water moving through. "Nice boat," Luke ventured, drawing no comment from Peru. Luke noticed that Jale had turned over the wheel to another, then he heard the click of a blade.

Peru backed him over the rail with the knifepoint just under his jaw. "You thought you'd get away with screwing my wife?"

"Peru, listen—"

"*Shut up.* Jale, now!"

The big guy came running. Peru tossed the knife aside, and with strong hands in his armpits and under his thighs they hoisted him up and over the rail. "Enjoy the water," Peru said. "It's nice and cool this time of year."

Luke didn't know how far out from shore they were, but it was a lot farther than he could swim. Then suddenly his feet were on the deck again, and they laughed a long time at his expense.

"Funny, real damn funny," said Luke.

Finally Peru got his breath. "The look on your face, oh man. Relax. I wouldn't have gone to all this trouble just to kill you. I would have had it done in Carabanchel. You really didn't do much time."

"Easy for you to say. But yes, I owe you."

Peru called to Jale, who still sniggered but had gone back to the wheel and was watching a screen. "Anything out there?"

"Nothing we can't slip through."

"Good."

Luke put his hands in his jacket pockets and braced his legs against the pitch and roll as Peru stood beside of him.

"Why did you help me?" Luke said.

"Tangle of reasons. I like the way you handle yourself. I'm confident you've broken with the people that sent you over here, and they're after you now. So you may be shy of options. And we're taking an action that involves Americans. They're rich and arrogant, or rich and naïve, or rich and ignorant, it doesn't matter. They're sticking their noses in our business and daring us to do something about it—not a wise thing to do. We can use you. And pay you for your trouble."

After a while Luke said, "There's only one American on earth that I really have a problem with. And I got that out of my system in that airport *baño.*"

"The one that did that to your face."

"He didn't do it. But he encouraged it."

"All right then. Work with us and you can help make sure the rich Americans don't get hurt."

When Luke said nothing Peru went on, "The Spaniards didn't just burn you. Disfigure you. They were trying to suck the soul right out of you."

"Maybe they did."

More jolts of the waves passed. "You don't just have money," Luke said. "You have connections. People in many walks of life."

"I suppose that's so."

"Can you set me up with a plastic surgeon? One that asks no questions?"

"You want some doctor that can get rid of that thing."

"I don't have to be rid of it. Just need it fudged, lasered, whatever they'd do to make it look like an ordinary scar. So the letters are gone."

Peru nodded. "We might be able to help."

"Where are you taking me now?"

"We're going to put you ashore in Biarritz. If you want to reach the train station you just start walking south. It's a long walk. When you get to the airport you're getting close. Where you go then is up to you. But if you have any sense you're going to go take care of that good woman."

Luke jerked with surprise. "Where is Ysolina?"

"She's in Paris." Peru added, "And pregnant."

"My God." Bobby Czyz's uppercut couldn't have rocked him more.

Peru's laugh was bitter. "I'm glad you have one. I know what you're thinking. But you're going to have to ask her."

At the dock in Biarritz Peru gave Luke a Nokia phone and an envelope containing francs and a slip of paper with a doctor's name and his phone number. "The phone's use is contracted to a Portuguese person who's dead," Peru said. "You don't want to be detained with it in your possession."

Luke raised the envelope and said, "Is this a gift or an advance?"

"Do we have a deal?"

"I guess we do. It doesn't make any sense for me to go back to the States."

"Then make of the money what you want. There's not a great deal of it."

They sped back out to sea. The Gare de Biarritz was indeed some distance away. A drunk gave Luke the only further directions he had. No taxis were running at three in the morning. A pair of cops slowed and gave him a look. It was all over if they turned on their lights. He kept walking and they left him alone. At last he found the station, clear across the city, where in a self-service booth he bought his second-class ticket to Paris. He found a bench on a half-lit boarding platform and fretted and dozed until sunrise. He bought a coffee and pastry, and at the train's first announcement claimed a seat with his branded cheek turned outward to the glass. The coast fell away and the sunshine glinted and blurred as the train entered the pine plantations of the Landes. A young girl on the train kept staring at his face. He escaped her in changing trains in Dax, buried the scar in a pillow, and slept hard for the first time in months.

It was half past noon when the train arrived that Sunday in Gare Montparnasse. With the pack slung over his shoulder, he followed the signs and ignored the moving walkway in the long corridor to the Montparnasse-Bienvenüe Métro station. He bought a ticket and on the platform of his line he was once more taken by the white and blue tiles and panels of art on the curved walls of the Métro stations. He boarded the car and found a seat. An old fellow with knots for a nose leaned across unclaimed seats, staring at red lettering on the window glass that said they were reserved for *"mutilés de guerre,"* wounded war veterans.

The British vet of World War II harrumphed loudly and said, "Well! There must not have been too terribly many of those!"

Luke smiled as the old-timer's wife clucked at his clowning and moved him along. It wasn't fair; the French lost a quarter of a million men trying to stop Hitler's Wehrmacht. French Generals who thought they could send the Germans fleeing in six weeks got that done to them.

Three stops later Luke ascended from the tunnels on the Boulevard St. Germain-de-Prés. He looked up and down the broad street and crossed with the light at Rue Bonaparte. It was an unseasonably warm day. He took a seat on a bench along the street. Above him was an imposing statue of Georges Danton. A pigeon sat on a forefinger extended in some rhetoric of the revolution that claimed Danton's life.

Luke studied Peru's sketchily drawn map, then took out the phone, and had started to call the numbers Peru had given him when a woman sat down beside him on the bench. She was toothless and dressed in a thin dress and flip-flop sandals, as if she were forty years younger than the lizard-skinned crone she was. An affluent-looking family ambled by speaking a language he didn't recognize. Two girls who looked like not quite pubescent twin sisters were gaping at the spectacle of what years could do. The old woman took offense and with a venomous spew of French yanked up her skirt, showing them skinny leathery thighs and the naked thatch of her crotch. The adults grabbed the shocked girls and hustled them along.

He elected not to make this call in the presence of a crazy person. He stopped in a sidewalk café and ordered a Kronenburg lager and a hot dog, which came baked in a crisp baguette with a dipping bowl of tasty mustard. He thought Paris hot dogs were the best in the world. At a traffic light, in a Mercedes convertible sat a young bearded man who wore the Arabs' traditional white robe called a thawb. He was playing "Sticky Fingers" loud.

> *Graceless lady, you know who I am*
> *You know I can't let you*
> *just slide through my hands*

Luke had an ugly branded scar on his face, tears were spilling down his cheeks, and he was eating a hot dog on the boulevard St. Germain—no wonder the waiter and other diners maintained a distance.

It would be cowardly, he decided, to call Ysolina without trying to see her first. He wandered until he found her nearby street, Rue Jacob. Her apartment sat back from a courtyard in a horseshoe-shaped three-story building that had been divided into apartments. A small lobby offered a buzzer and speaker system for callers. Ysolina answered in French with polite reserve. He said, *"Cómo estás, querida?"*

He couldn't read the seconds of silence.

"Come up," she said, and pushed the buzzer that granted him access.

She was barefoot and dressed in jeans and a sleeveless pullover. She gasped on seeing him—raised her hand toward the burn. "Never mind, never you mind," Luke said. He held her so tight, trying to feel the being within her, but maybe it was too early for that. He let go of her and she dabbed a finger at tears in her eyes. She wore no makeup and looked as fine to him as she ever had. Her stomach was slightly swollen. She said, "I didn't think I'd ever see you again."

"Thinking you might may have kept me alive."

She pushed him away. "I don't know about this."

"What do you mean? What did I do? Tell me."

"I didn't say you *did* anything. Just . . . things have changed."

"I know. You're pregnant."

She backed off further. "Are there fucking billboard signs?"

He blurted, "I don't know how else to say this. Is it mine?"

"That's the very worst thing a man can say to a woman."

"I know. But it kind of matters."

"Yes, it does," she said. "She is our daughter. Don't ever call her 'it' again. Now what?"

"I sit down." Her place was small but had Persian rugs and walls crowded with paintings. "Are you sure you want to have this baby?" he said.

"That's the second worst thing a man can say."

"I didn't think I'd do this very well. So you're sure the baby is a girl?"

"Yes. I could see her on the scan. When you're my age you find out. You find out everything you can. I'm in my fourth month. Her name is Enara."

"Like your ancestor. It's a beautiful name. And just right."

She sat on the sofa but not near him and said, "I've been so scared. Of losing her. Nightmares about Guardia Civil. And I hate throwing up. Some things I used to love, like asparagus"—she shuddered. "Now I'm a demon for pickled beets."

She extended her hand to his cheek, which he turned away. "Don't," she said. "I'm not going to hurt you." She touched the burn then abruptly clasped her hands between her knees. "I can't believe they did that to you."

"What did they do to you?"

"I thought they were killing her. At one point I thought I felt her die."

She had a small balcony that looked out on well-kept beds of shrubs and flowers and the dome of a church. "It used to be a convent," she told him.

"Well, you've got a great place." He looked closer at the paintings on her wall. The artist's pinks and blues were translucent, so he assumed they were done in pastels or watercolor. Three women were in the foreground, one wearing a sporty black hat, her arm flung high as if in dancing, another kneeling with a garland of flowers in her hair and holding the hand of a barefoot woman in full-skirted blue, that last one the real beauty of the three. A possibility of something erotic going on at their rear. He wondered how the painter manipulated those shades of pink and blue and white, and saw the inscription "Marie Laurencin 1929."

"This is the painter you collect and would like to write about?"

"Yes. It's called *Three Creole Women*," Ysolina said, on her feet and standing closer. "The original, an oil, is in the Boston Museum of Fine Art."

"It's an oil? How did she do that?"

"Light touch and knowing her colors, I guess. There's a reason why her work's hung in galleries with Picasso and Monet."

They began to reconnect in this way, at a remove from thoughts of Miguel Peralta, Doctor Tricornio, and Carabanchel Prison. He sat down and she coaxed his hand against her. "Feel her, Papa."

"She's moving?"

"She's been a little tadpole. But now I can feel her more, I don't know, it's hard to describe. Like a butterfly fluttering its wings."

Her remark brought up a morpho, opening sapphire and black wings as big as a prayerbook, slowly afloat in the air above that walkway of wood staves in the Amazon, just a year and a half ago.

THIRTY-ONE

Cold weather in Paris was like a glum wet cat that jumped in your lap. The produce and fish and flowers markets were driven indoors or heated under enclosures of plastic, and Ysolina's apartment seemed to shrink around the two of them. One day Luke said, "You said you have friends here. Where are they?"

"I'm not seeing them now. They don't know I'm pregnant; I don't want to answer questions. And you take up enough room as it is."

He sat on the sofa. "I have a friend here I very much need to see. He's been gone but now he's back and lives close by. Is it all right if I ask him over?" She hesitated. "I could just meet him in a café or go to his place."

"No. Call him. Use my phone."

"I trust him with my life. He doesn't like to speak Spanish, and he can't stand my French. So we speak English."

"I don't mind."

When he buzzed Pascal up and opened the door, they shared the male embrace. As Pascal was removing his wool scarf and jacket Luke noted his start of recognition on seeing Ysolina. He grinned broadly, crossed the room, and raised her hand to his lips. Luke said, "You two know each other?"

"We've met," Ysolina said. "Please sit down, Pascal. Can I get you something to drink?"

He told Luke, "I subjected her to a couple of short pathetic woos in a café a few months ago. She spurned me."

Ysolina laughed. "I did not spurn you. I told you I was married."

"That's one way to do it."

Pascal turned his grin on Luke. "Well, lives move fast, don't they?" He chose a wineglass, poured it half full from an open bottle of chilled

Brouilly, and raised a toast to them. Pascal leaned close to the scar and said, "Good god, man. ETA did that to you?"

"No," Ysolina answered for him. "Spaniard cops did."

"I hope they never get hold of me."

Luke said, "I need your help again, pal. I have no identification. I need all of it. A brand new me. Work and resident visas in Spain and France. And sure and secure access to my funds, now more than ever."

Pascal looked again at Ysolina.

Luke said, "She knows. They worked her over, too."

"Well, it's not going to be easy, as long as you look like that."

"I'll have a plastic surgeon. It's just going to be a scar."

"When is this surgery going to happen?"

"Right away, I hope."

"Okay. I can get started, but we'll have to wait for the surgery to heal for the photo IDs. Can you grow a beard?"

"I could in college. I got rid of it when I was home at shearing time. Mohair houses vermin that can jump."

"A beard will help. Put up with the itching. It passes." He tugged at a lock of gray just above Luke's hairline, then fondly raised Luke's chin. "And let your hair grow out. That's what we'll do with you. Make you an old American hippie."

The plastic surgeon's clinic was in the nineteenth arrondissement on the Avenue Jean-Jourès. The doctor was French but spoke fluent Spanish. He began by saying that all charges would be taken care of. Luke was surprised but nodded like he wasn't. Neither one of them wanted to talk about how the burn and scar occurred. It was evident. "That's a third degree burn, and a bad scar," the doctor said. "You understand there will still be a scar?"

"Yes. I just don't want this one."

The surgeon smiled. "I see you're an American. Are you going to be in Paris for a while?"

"Plan to be, yes."

"I ask just so we understand each other. Getting you what you want is going to take some time. It's good because the burn has healed well, but the letters are actually growing outward, because a protein called collagen keeps seeping in them. There are some superficial things we could try, but they would just take up time. You'll need surgery involving a skin graft from either a buttock or inner thigh."

Luke responded with a wincing chuckle. "Sounds like it wouldn't hurt as much coming off my ass."

He was sitting on an examination table with his shirt off. The doctor said, "After the surgery the side of your face will be swollen and you'll keep it bandaged for about a week. Every day you must remove the dressing and clean the wound. I'll give you a sheet with indications of possible infection. I'll remove the sutures in ten days. Then you'll start using a gel and nighttime strips that keep the scarring from the graft in control. You have to be very careful for about six months, the rest of your life really, to protect the site from the sun. Get used to sunscreen, if you're not already. After about six or eight weeks you'll come in for a laser treatment that abrades the scarring further. You'll look like you had some accident but the letters will be gone."

"Perfect. Will wild hairs from the cheek of my ass grow out of the cheek of my face?"

The doctor laughed. "Probably not, but that's why we have razors. Any more questions or things I need to know?"

"I don't do well with morphine," said Luke. "Dilaudid treats me better."

"I see you've had some use for it," the surgeon said, looking at his hand and torso. He shook hands briskly and said his nurse would make the arrangements. Riding away on the Métro, Luke reflected, *one more thing I owe Peru.*

The surgery, swelling, discoloration, healing, and the process called dermabrasion went off without complications. Luke's beard came out quite gray. When his hair grew long enough Ysolina applied a rubber band to his start on a ponytail. Pascal told him to give the beard another couple of weeks, and then he shot the photograph and finished his cobbler's work with Luke. As long as Ysolina was in France she had no need of that. Luke was now Jamie Shelton, a horse breeder and trainer from Oklahoma. She pronounced it *zhahmee*, which he thought was sexy. Luke thought he knew enough about the horse business that he could bullshit a cop. The surgery was what he needed. Now he could move freely, and often both he and she needed some space.

Ysolina's moods had improved, and her skin gleamed. When he complimented her on that, she told him, pleased, that it was because carrying a baby accelerated and enriched blood flow. When he arrived she had been reserved and edgy. Now some nights she was famished for him. Wanting him to have her from behind, she kneeled and propped her hands against large pillows and threw her head about with cries that must have titillated neighbors. Yet not all was good between them.

Rue Jacob was a prosperous and now quiet Left Bank street that angled through the sixth arrondissement between the Boulevard St. Germain and the Seine. Down the quiet street Ysolina showed him a building that was once Hotel d'York, where Benjamin Franklin and John Adams signed the Treaty of Paris that ended the war between the colonies and the English and effectively created the United States. On Sunday evenings when it was warm enough they walked down Rue Saint Benoit toward the storied haunts of St. Germain's past.

One of those Sundays, on the sidewalk in front of the boulevard's sixteenth-century church, a man who must have been six-five wheeled about on stilts as if they were running shoes. The stilts made him an eleven-foot giant. He chased people back some steps, then spun and went after others behind him. He had a beak nose and sharp chin, and he flung a red cape about, speaking so fast that Luke couldn't follow him, but he pointed a long index finger in rebuke at them. Ysolina murmured that he was saying, "Yes, to you I am a freak, but *you* are nature's disgrace, *you* are the doomed, because you presume to judge me!"

Luke was awed by the man's athleticism. Ysolina pulled his arm close and said, "Do you know who he is supposed to be?"

"No, who?"

"The red cape, the raiment. He's an Inquisitioner. He's like that judge who burned all those people at the stake in Labourd."

THIRTY-TWO

Luke didn't know how he fit in Ysolina's life, and she offered no explicit clues. It occurred to him that he might be jealous of his unborn child. Try that on at three in the morning. She went to see her doctor one day, and in the bedroom he found himself sitting at her dressing table and opening drawers. He saw the velvet packet and found the emeralds. The Spaniards had given back her goddamn jewels?

The blow-up had to happen, though Luke wouldn't have predicted the way it did. Ysolina said one day, "I have an American friend I'd love to see, and you'll like him. Everyone does." She said this man hosted a dinner party for fifty or sixty people every Sunday night, and had been doing that for years. The guests were friends he'd accumulated from all over the world, and strangers who'd been told about the parties and made reservations. Luke gave thought to Spanish police and informants who might be among those strangers but decided the outing would be good for both of them. She put on and styled about for him in a new red maternity dress with a plunging neckline and short skirt, bare legs and short heels. She was wearing an anklet. What beauties corded with muscle those sculpted legs were.

The weather was dry that night. They bundled up in coats, gloves, and wool scarves and rode the Métro far out north to the fourteenth arrondissement. She stopped before a green door on an ordinary sidewalk, keyed in the entry code, and led him to a small garden and apartment that her friend Haynes called his *atelier,* studio. It was packed with bookshelves and a crowd of chattering guests. In his sixties, Haynes taught a course in the Literature of Sex at the Sorbonne.

He called out on seeing Ysolina, they touched both cheeks in the French way, and he cried out again on helping her out of her coat and being shown she was pregnant. Then came a welter of French that Luke couldn't keep up with, and she introduced him as an American breeder and trainer of racehorses.

Damn, girl. I never said I knew about the *racehorse* business.

"I never go back to America anymore," their host said with a friendly handshake. "America comes to see me. You'll find almost everyone here speaks English. Plunge right in. A young woman from Transylvania, yes, Transylvania, has made us all a pasta with sherry tomato cream sauce for dinner tonight. Care for wine?"

"Yes, thank you," said Luke.

The host waved over one of the young men assigned the task. Luke picked a glass off his tray and so did Ysolina. Trusting his new look, Luke enjoyed the exotic mix of strangers. Ysolina was having an earnest conversation with an attractive young woman with short dark hair parted in the middle and pulled behind her ears. He drifted over and Ysolina introduced him to the woman, who wore a necklace with a cross. Sister Irena was an Ursuline nun who directed an anti-torture non-profit in Washington. "We were comparing our rapes," Ysolina said in English and a pretty loud voice. People glanced.

Luke put his hands in his pockets, looked at his shoes, and murmured his sympathies to the nun. Please, Ysolina, do not work yourself into a state in this crowd.

"I'm over what happened to me," Sister Irena said, taking note of the tension between them. "My life now is trying to help victims who suffered far more than me. What is your work, Mr. Shelton?"

Ysolina once more said merrily, "He breeds and trains racehorses."

"Do you? Have your horses ever run at the Fair Track in New Orleans?"

"Yes, the Louisiana Derby once, and lesser races. Great horse town, New Orleans."

"I entered the Order there. Sometimes we'd slip out of the convent and go to the track." She put her forefinger to her lips. "Don't tell anyone."

"Did your horse win the Derby?" said a young man who overheard the remark and made their trio a foursome. He wore pleated trousers and a black shirt with no collar that he'd buttoned at the throat. Bound to his head by a piece of soft black rope, his red-and-white-checked headdress framed a dark mustache and neat triangle of beard.

"No," said Luke. "He ran far back. I'm not a trainer anymore. I don't read horse brains too well, and I don't like to get out of bed real early."

CHAPTER 32

"Antwan Sadim," the young man introduced himself, with a gentle handshake and slight bow to the three of them. "I love to play the horses."

Luke tried to head that off. "Isn't gambling a sin in Islam?"

"You assume I'm Muslim."

"Honest mistake," said Luke, moving his glass with an air of apology.

Sadim smiled. "I am. The Koran says it's a sin, though many theologians believe the Prophet meant addictive betting. That's not me. I wager discreetly."

"What do you do for a living, Mr. Sadim?"

"Americans can't carry on a conversation without asking that. My family has a company that exports dates and frankincense. My home is in Muscat, Sultanate of Oman. Horse racing is very popular in the Emirates. Many great races in Dubai."

"Frankincense," said Luke. "What is that? I've long wondered. The wise men in the Bible came bearing gifts of gold and frankincense and myrrh. O Holy Night."

The man cocked his head, trying to read Luke. "It's a resin of olibanum trees that can grow out of cracks of rock. Our workers cut and peel bark in a process called striping. It has numerous health benefits. Oil of frankincense induces mental peace and relaxation. It makes one more introspective and relieves anxiety, anger, and stress. And it's used in cosmetics." He smiled at Ysolina and leaned toward her. "I can smell it in your scent." She blushed.

"What does it look like?" asked Sister Irena.

"Pieces of candied ginger," he said.

"Your headdress," said Luke. "Does it have religious significance?"

Sadim once more considered him with a patient smile. "No, the *guthra*'s purpose is to prevent sunstroke. It comes to us from the Bedouins. They like the red checked cloth." He touched the black rope that held it on his head. "When the sun's down and the tents are up they use these to hobble their camels. Tell me about your horses that run. Thoroughbreds?"

"Of course. We have this mare that's out of the line of Native Dancer, a gray horse that was the first TV star in racing. Won twenty-three and lost just one, the Kentucky Derby, by a nose. Breeding color to speed is said to be next to impossible, but I'm trying anyway. I dream of this big fine dappled gray colt. I'll name him Tiny Dancer, after the Elton John song."

Sadim blinked and Sister Irena laughed.

Luke drained the wineglass and said, "It's a fantasy, my gray colt."

"There's an American expression. You're putting me off."

"No, putting you on. The expression. But I'm serious. Maybe I'll come check out your horses in the Emirates. Do you have a card?"

On the Métro back to the apartment Ysolina slumped against him and giggled. "You are such a gifted liar. It's just effortless."

That was how it started.

At the apartment he poured himself a Jack Daniel's. "Are you going to tell me what happened in Madrid?"

"I was raped by the one you call Doctor Tricornio. And others."

He knocked down some more of the sour mash and bore on with it. "They let you have your computer and journals back?"

"They did."

"And even the emeralds. Who did you have to give up for all that?"

"I don't know who you are! Or what you're doing in my home."

"I can be gone tomorrow. Just tell me, who'd you give up?"

"No one. Not a soul."

"They burn ETA on my face and cut my toe off and spring you loose with all charges dropped? 'Our mistake, *señora*, here's your ticket, first class. *Buen viaje.*' You expect me to swallow that?"

She put her face in her hands. "You can swallow anything you want. Go away from me, please. They freed me because of an intervention."

"An intervention? By whom?"

"The king."

"Excuse me?"

"King Juan Carlos."

He gaped at her. The glass hung from his hand.

"A priest from Pamplona had been drawn into being a courier for ETA. He was hired as a publicist and speechwriter on the king's staff. The priest's forever compromised—do you understand? A man who made himself subject to blackmail. Peru told him he had to sell my story to the king. He must have sold it well. The Guardia Civil don't have to take orders from Juan Carlos, but they've learned not to cross him. They gathered up the materials and put me on a plane—yes, they did. But it wasn't first class. A stewardess hovered over me and said, 'Are you all right?' Oh sure, not to worry. I'm fine. I am so fine."

THIRTY-THREE

FEBRUARY 1995

"**S**coot," she said the next morning, jostling him for room on the sofa. He came up on his elbow, blinking and seeing it was light. "That was awful," she groaned, holding her head.

"It was my fault. I'm sorry."

She was wearing the loose cotton nightgown she slept in now. It was white with images of tumbling babies. She said, "I've been awake all night."

"So have I. Too much of it."

"We're not going to make it here. You take up too much space— physically, psychologically—it doesn't matter that I love you. It's been just my home for so long."

Luke's insides convulsed. He waited and said nothing.

"Remember I said I had a standing invitation to use a house on André's farm? Let's go there, please. I don't want to lose you. I don't want to drive you away."

Luke sat up, watching her closely. "Are you concerned about the baby? Living out in the country . . . "

"No. André's place is thirty or forty minutes from Pau, a beautiful and sophisticated city. There's no shortage of doctors and hospitals."

So they paid cash for a used four-door Peugeot and told André they were coming. They put her paintings in a storage vault, where he leafed through the edition of *Alice in Wonderland* illustrated by Marie Laurencin. Her Alice was a beautiful wisp of a thing, as were all women in her paintings, but for Luke her best take on the story was the Cheshire Cat. She made the cat's grin sly, funny, and dangerous.

Luke had a parting lunch with Pascal. Luke said, "I don't know what we're going to do about papers for Ysolina. And can you find out what's required for a baby?"

"Considering how it went last time, I think she'd need a change of appearance, not just a batch of phony papers. And smuggling an infant, is that wise?"

"I'm a pessimist that keeps hoping to be proved wrong."

They closed the apartment and set out for the onetime kingdom of Beárn. He let her drive them out of Paris, thinking his sanity and their health might not survive the Peripheríque. The countryside was wintry but no less astonishing to him in its looks. You could see farther and know more about the land and towns when most of the trees stood bare. She was uncomfortable if she sat in the car too long, and they took five days in what might have been covered in two. He disliked the long frequent tunnels and bullying habits of drivers of the Péages, so on secondary and scenic highways he got used to all the roundabouts. They spoke little the first day, but by the second they had decided that they didn't want their intermittent outbursts of hostility to continue.

They stopped for lunch one day in the prefecture of Périguex, and on their way back to the car, she spotted a shop with baby clothing that she said was worth a look. They came away with a small white shirt, a larger pink pant and shirt that the baby would grow into, and a wooden rattle shaped like a dumbbell. As she drove, with one hand Luke shook the rattle and tried to visualize the tiny plump hands that would grip and find pleasure in that.

"Peru and I've divorced," she remarked out of the blue. "We agreed it's time. Past time."

He didn't respond at first. "For it to be legal either one of you had to be French?"

"No. I have years of proven legal residence. A notary drafts a list of our agreed-upon split of assets—Peru has none, of course. Or none that he could claim. The only snag was my apartment, the real estate. I gave up the lease. For one this simple, no court appearance was required."

"I'd think any court record could be trouble for him."

"French judiciary is a black hole. Why are you so concerned about Peru?"

"Well, if it wasn't for him I'd be in a federal lockup in the United States with ETA branded on my face, not riding in this warm car with you."

Luke gazed up at the Château de Beynac, a castle set high on one of the Dordogne's limestone cliffs. The countryside reminded him of the ranch in Texas, though it clearly got more rain.

CHAPTER 33

"How about we get married?"

She let out a peal of laughter. "What kind of proposal is that? Enara doesn't need your name! She'll have mine. An unmarried mother, *mère célibataire,* can get an allowance from the state."

He looked away, wounded. "She might like to have a father."

She moved her hand and touched his thigh. "I'm sorry. I don't know what makes me such a self-centered bitch."

"Don't say that. I love you and want to spend the rest of my life with you. And help you raise her and see the day when she's as fine a woman as you are. It's what real people do. Besides, you're pregnant. You're supposed to act crazy."

She gave him a fond shove. "The marriage part's important to you?"

"I guess it is."

"Why?"

"I don't know, I like the way wedding rings look on men's hands. How movie actors wear them no matter what role they're playing. And I'd like her to be an American citizen; I think they have duality arrangements with the Spaniards and the French. Who knows if she'd ever want to even visit America. But I'd like her to be able to do it without immigration and visa hassles and stay as long as she wants."

"Divorce is easier in France than marriage," she said. "Getting married can be just a civil ceremony at the town hall, but we'd have to provide valid passports, long form birth certificates, medical certificates that screen us for AIDS or HIV, things like utility bills that show proof of our residence. *And* bring two witnesses, *and* present the court with notarized affidavits, one from your embassy or consulate, that we're not already married, *and* that the marriage would be recognized in your country."

"Oh." He looked at her and said, "How do you know all that?"

"I've been thinking about it, too."

She asked what Enara's US citizenship would require.

"I think just a birth certificate. And I'd have to get my identity back."

She leaned forward against the seat belt and whooped. "You are insane! You're asking me to marry some guy with a forged passport?"

"No. We have a few months to work on that." They dwelled on the road and scenery for a while.

"So are you going to give me an answer?" he said.

She looked at him in exasperation, and then turned on the Cheshire-cat smile. "All right, have it your way. We are married, you and I."

He looked at her warily. "That's great. But how do you figure?"

"The French call it *'en concubinage.'* We'd just sign a sworn *'attestation sur l'honneur'* that we live together, and have for a while."

"Wow. Now you're my wife *and* concubine?"

"Don't complain. It makes you eligible for French social security."

THIRTY-FOUR

In twilight two vans crept on roads cut through the Valdemingez municipal dump north of Madrid, following a man on foot. He wore a hardhat and reflective yellow vest. Jale drove the van in front and tried to keep from retching; the stench was overbearing. Peru looked about at all the birds. There were storks, gulls, kites, jackdaws, ravens, sand martins, partridges, hawks. The lavish supply of food had prompted some species to stop migrating. Foxes and feral dogs roamed the dump eager to eat them, if they were quick enough, and their eggs when they found the nests.

"In a few months Madrid will be closing it for a new suburb," Peru said. "Doing away with all this by using a new modern incinerator. What a furnace it would have to be, and they'll lose a great rookery, if you don't mind the smell."

"I do mind," said Jale. "I wish we could dump it on the Plaza Mayor."

"Deal with it. We won't be here long."

Sprawled or sitting up in the back of the vans were six men who were clothed but barefoot. Their hands were bound behind their backs with plastic cuffs, and their mouths were covered with strips of duct tape. The *gudariak* had captured them all: Miguel Peralta, the former army colonel who had led the hit on Peru for the Guardia Civil's Intelligence Service and interrogated and tortured Ysolina and Luke in Madrid; the big one known as Doctor Tricornio; the other Civil Guard known for his welding torch and soldering iron; and the mercenary snipers at Cambo-les-Bains—the Apostolic anticommunist from Argentina, the Italian fascist, and the Australian veteran of the French Foreign Legion. The mercenaries had been fools not to leave the country.

Earlier the guide had used a backhoe to claw out a trench as deep and wide as a tall man's height. After he led the van in, he climbed on a bulldozer. He turned it on with a billow of soot, but Peru motioned for him to kill the engine. If there was any noise, he wanted birdsongs. Jale and the other three *gudariak* hauled the men out of the van, ripped the tape off their mouths, and shoved them into a line in front of the trench. Agleam in the trench were chicken bones and shells of clams, shrimp, mussels.

"Perfect," said Peru. "Their souls can dine on paella."

The *gudariak* had brought pistols with silencers. One carried a small camera with a built-in wide-angle lens and flash, and Peru had a long-handled pair of pruning shears and a tricorn of the Guardia Civil. He lined them up side by side and put the hat on the head of the big one beside Peralta. After the *gudari* with the camera took the first photos, Peru addressed the one on Doctor Tricornio's left. "You're the one they call the Welder. You like to put brands on people and prune them like they're twigs of brush."

The man said nothing. Handing his pistol to Jale, Peru forced the pruning blades around the man's small toe and with a heave of exertion severed it. The man howled and fell back in the trench. Peru took the gun back from Jale, leaned over, and silenced him with two shots, one in the chest and one in the head.

One of the mercenaries started to quail and moan.

"Cowards, traitors!" Peralta yelled. "I wish to say—"

Peru fired a shot by his ear and shut him up. "This is a summary execution. You're not allowed to say anything. Prepare to meet your God." Peru stood in front of Doctor Tricornio and said, "This is for the rape of my wife," then shot him in the groin. The big man flopped in the trench spouting blood. Peru finished him with two more shots. The *gudariak* shoved Peralta and the mercenaries together for more photos, more flashes. The gunmen arranged themselves in front of the four and extended their arms and guns within a foot of the men's foreheads. "Look in our eyes and take the faces of your killers with you to eternity. *Gora Euskadi ta askakatua.*"

"*Viva Esp—*" Peralta tried to get out, but the handguns went off as one, and he and the mercenaries collapsed in the trench. The guns coughed again, and all was still, except for cries of jackdaws the humans had not scared off. The *gudari* who operated the dozer got down among them and shoved with his boot until all the faces were upturned. The photographer handed his gun to one of the other shooters and took more pictures.

"How do we know they're all dead?" Jale asked.

"They're dead enough," Peru said. "Shoot them some more if you want."

They walked back to the heated vans while their guide, who made his living in the dump, moved the dozer around behind the vile escarpment, and in a few minutes had them buried well with the surface smoothed off—deep enough that the foxes and feral dogs would be unlikely to dig them up. Then the *gudari* killed the dozer's engine and by flashlight led the vans out.

ndré Roumanille's house was a rambling two-story affair in need of paint and repairs. It faced away from the high country to its rear where they had run the horses and the mule. André was a widower of twenty years, Ysolina said, and had little contact with a son and daughter; they were estranged in some way, and both had moved far away. Accompanied by a border collie, the old man came down the steps wearing a plaid wool shirt, suspenders, and jeans stuffed in well-scarred boots. "Welcome, welcome, my friends," he said, kissing the cheeks of Ysolina, then holding her out in pleasure. She hadn't told him she was pregnant.

His eyebrows bunched with the quickest of frowns on seeing the scar on Luke's cheek, but with a show of cheer he gave the beard a tug. "Come look. I'll show you something." He had a fire ablaze in the living room and the smell of lamb stew coming from the kitchen. As Ysolina had said, Luke's saddle sat on wool blankets and a varnished wine cask in his parlor.

There was a large barn where he kept his tractor, two pickups when he wanted them out of the weather, a tack room, several horse stalls, stacks of baled hay, and sheds for shearing. Sheep grazed in the nearby pastures, round with thick wool. He told them to leave the car by the house for it would be stuck in mud when it snowed again. He said they could use the Dodge truck with the heater and four-wheel drive.

The cottage was like hundreds of others in the south of France— single-story blond stone with an auburn tile roof that peaked at the front. He had a wood fire going for them in a big tight stove. Their bedroom had an open fireplace, and a propane tank out back fueled a bathroom heater, water heater, and the kitchen stove.

After an appointment with a gynecologist one day, they took a walk in the center of Pau. Its streets opened to a view of mountains that were so close they looked like they could drop avalanches on the town. The main downtown street was called Avenue de Résistance. In a park they watched old men clicking iron balls in their hands and lobbing them at those of their opponents in their endless game of balls, *jeu de boules*.

Another day Ysolina was drinking tea and looking out the kitchen window. Horses had moved up close to the house. They went outside, Luke grabbed a halter out of André's tack room, and they walked out to call up her Arab mare. Ysolina voiced a high beckoning call, and the mare raised her head and pricked up her ears. She began to walk toward them. Ysolina hugged the head of her mare and wrapped her arms around her neck, pressing with her face and combing the mane with her fingers. The mare snuffled her own appreciation of the reunion. Her winter coat looked ragged.

"What do you call her?" Luke said.

"Masusta." She added with a smile, "It means 'blackberry.'"

He slipped the halter over her ears and led her toward the barn. "What are you going to do?" Ysolina asked.

"Put her in a stall, feed her lots of oats, groom her, exercise her, get to know her. Get her legged up for you."

"It's hard to imagine being able to ride again."

"You'll want to."

He spoke to the horse continually as he currycombed out the loose hair and tangles in her mane and tail. Before trying to ride her he worked her with a *longe* line, a long rope clipped to her halter. He got her trotting and loping in circles. The mountains were thick with snow but the weather below was often clear, with a depth of stars at night, and Luke was surprised by how much it warmed up most afternoons. Luke regained wind and muscle tone wielding an axe on firewood for André's house and their borrowed one. Riding Ysolina's black mare and using his Texas saddle at André's insistence, Luke helped the old man and a few day hands move the sheep and horses up country in the spring transhumance. There were no paying guests on this one, and the pace was slow.

Helping André allowed Luke to stay out of Ysolina's way. Her emotions were in flux between fear that she could still lose the baby and just wanting to get it over with. Her pregnancy became ever more private as the child flailed and twitched, her belly grew until it seemed like something she wanted to carry in her arms, and she was no longer so proud of her reflection in the mirror. Carrying a child humbled her. She often stood with one hand pressed against the small of her back.

Luke helped André doctor ewes and rode about with him in a puttering little Toyota pickup that had holes in the floorboard. "If you don't mind my asking, what exactly did you smuggle?" Luke said one of those days.

"Horses, mules. Horses and cigarettes were in most demand."

"Did you ever get shot at?"

"Nothing but a few bullets over our heads until the Spanish Civil War," he said. "We knew where the border guards camped. You could see the remains of their fires. We left them presents—cigarettes, cans of peaches. It wasn't personal for us or them. We were just making a living, and they were following the orders of someone who was plenty warm and sleeping in a bed."

"During the world war did you bring the fliers over the same trails?"

"No, not many of those fellows could have stayed on a horse or mule in rough country at night. Vichy is such an ordinary town. It gave us vichyssoise, and that's what the people there are like—potato soup. Someday that war won't be forgotten but will get dim enough in the past that Vichy can go back to being a sleepy little provincial town. The line between the Vichy and Occupied zones went west from the Swiss border, curved north above Vichy to the Loire River, and angled south to the hamlets in the old French Basque province of Labourd. There were plenty of collaborators with the Nazis and shame enough to go around. In the early days we just saw English fliers who'd been shot down—the real air war came later, when you Americans and the Canadians came into it. I've read that your country once had an underground railroad?"

"Yes, before our civil war it moved slaves from the south into free states in the north."

André nodded. "Ours was called the Line. On the French side, St. Jean-de-Luz is so fussied up today that you wouldn't think it could have been a hotbed of revolt. But we'd go in taverns there and find ourselves among communists, socialists, trade unionists, DeGaulle's Free French, exiled Spaniards. The actual railroad part of the movement ended in Bayonne. They were brought by brave women, many of them Belgians, who had convincing papers and passed them off as deaf mutes or husbands or brothers who weren't right in the head, if they were pressed. Why the

Nazis didn't burn the town and scrape it in the sea, I'll never know.

"I've heard there were about two thousand of us in all. My part of it was getting them across the lower mountains and handing them off to the Basques who got them to Galicians who moved them on to Portugal. If they were caught the Germans executed them as spies, because they were out of uniform. There was a Basque fellow with us named Dunixi. He picked up the fliers from the women in St. Jean-de-Luz, and we rested them on a farm for a day or two, then he led us over a mountain called Xoldocagagna—I'll never forget that name—then through a forest of ferns around a Gestapo station at St. Pée. The Germans used dogs to bark at people moving in the night and chew up the ones they caught. But their dogs kept dying from ground meat mixed with antifreeze. Hard on the foxes and raccoons and skunks, as well, but we had to do it. The border crossing we used was guarded by Austrian conscripts who weren't happy to be in German uniform. They were always falling asleep on sentry. We handed the fliers off to Basques on the other side, and they hurried them on to San Sebastián, the next stop along their way.

"One night the Germans started shooting, and Donixi was hit in the leg—we had to leave him. He convinced the Germans who arrested him that he was just another Basque smuggler. He always had a pack loaded with cigarettes and other lightweight things a foot smuggler would have. So a fellow went to see him at hospital and told him in Basque that we'd come the next afternoon to pick him up. And we did! The Germans could never make heads or tails of that language. The odds against any of those fliers or escaped prisoners of war making it to Portugal were so long. But they say about seven thousand got through."

"You miss all that," said Luke.

"Of course. The big war was the time of my life."

Luke didn't really want to witness Enara's birth, truth be told, and after Ysolina's water broke and the labor pains began, that suited her fine. When they brought her home from the hospital they thought in their addled, sleep-deprived states that they were not up to this. But infant Enara had become their ruler of the moment, and they heeded her commands. They bought a crib for her in Pau, but she wouldn't sleep on her back. She thrashed her little arms and legs, her face turned scarlet, and she howled in fury when they tried to persuade her. They feared crib death, so it went unused. She slept in the middle of their bed. She fretted and fought off sleep when a light was on.

For Luke the parental bond was not immediate. Just after the birth he was overwhelmed by the arrival from San Sebastián of Tía Aloña and Ysolina's cousin Jokiñe, who was studying to be a midwife. They helped in countless ways, but their constant presence for close to a month made him claustrophobic. Then after they left, it was the baby crying, the diapers, Ysolina nursing, and Luke feeling he was an interloper no matter what he did. The cottage's main room had a comfortable leather chair that could be tilted back into a recliner. In those first weeks, when Ysolina was taking her shift sleeping, he would be half-awake when Enara stirred and gripped the cloth of his shirt in her hands, and that was when he began to know what it meant to be a father. She had been born a furry little thing, short blond hairs all over her. Soon those were gone, and one night as he caressed her soft, bald head, he knew how much he'd miss it when hair that she would keep began to grow.

Tía Aloña came back after a few weeks, and at a distance one evening he watched André and her carrying on a conversation with obvious pleasure. She started spending her nights in his house, not in the cottage. Well, what do you know?

One day while Ysolina held Enara, Luke and André walked down to the corrals and barn. Luke clipped a rope on Mususta's halter and brought the mare to them. He had a firm grip on the rope, but the sight of the black mare nosing at what must have seemed a fragrant human worm, reaching and cooing in her mother's arms, produced a photo taken with an old box Kodak by André that they treasured the rest of their lives.

That winter Spain and its troubles in the Basque Country seemed far removed. As Ysolina's pounds fell off she began to warm to Luke again sexually, and one moonlit night she woke him with a nudge. Enara had turned over and was sleeping on her back. They watched this for a few nights and then Ysolina picked her up and laid her carefully in the crib. The baby awoke with a gasp and cry of alarm at the new surroundings, but her mother's hands and voice calmed her. They watched her more nights. Then one night Ysolina stepped over him in the recliner. She was naked under her slip, and they were lovers again.

He noted that during Enara's naps Ysolina only occasionally wrote in her journal.

"How's your paper going now?" he asked one day.

She looked around beaming. "Oh, I'm through with that. I wrote my professors that there's not enough to support a dissertation."

"*Through with it?* After all it put us through?"

She moved her head in acknowledgment. "I know enough to pass the story down to my family, in more detail than it was passed down to me. You've read it. Academics would call it historical fiction. I could expand it into a dry footnoted article for one of those unread journals that are peer-reviewed and edited to mush. But what's the point of that? I'm making a few notes for a Marie Laurencin biography."

He shook his head and wrapped his arms around her from behind.

"I never would have finished Enara's story if you hadn't come into my life," she said. "I feel so freed. How do you say in English? I quit!"

From the start she spoke to the baby in Basque, and Luke began to pick up more of it. A day came when they went into Pau for a routine appointment with Enara's pediatrician. Internet cafés had become the vogue. Luke had no use for them or curiosity either. He took the baby in her new stroller for a few blocks' walk. Then at the park where Ysolina said she would meet them, he pushed the carriage back and forth, seated on a bench as the baby burbled and he watched the old men with their underhand lobs and clicks of their *boules*. When Ysolina approached them, he looked up and was smiling until he saw her ashen expression.

"Come with me," she said.

She led the way back to the Internet café, took the baby out of the stroller, informed the owner that she had to bring Enara inside the café for a moment, and escorted Luke to a computer. She brought up the site she wanted, rose from the chair, and gestured for him to sit. They were black and white still photos: *Comandante* Miguel Peralta, Doctor Tricornio, the Welder who had branded Luke, and three others stood barefoot side by side, their arms and hands behind them, looking cold and certain of their doom. Peralta had a sneer on his face. Then a shot of the blood-splattered bodies, all their faces recognizable, in a ditch dug very deep in what appeared to be garbage. The new site did not mention

ETA. It just said, *"Hiltzaileak,"* assassins.

When they got back she asked Tía Aloña if she could keep Enara for an hour or so. "Of course," she said, troubled by the looks on their faces.

Ysolina roamed about the cottage with fists clenched in her hair. "What are we going to do?" she said.

"Calm down, for starters."

"Peru killed those men!"

"Are you surprised? Do you mourn them?"

She sat down in front of the woodstove with her hands gripped between her knees. "I'd feel better if I did."

"Here's what we're going to do. You're going to stay here and be a good mother to our child. I've got to go back into Spain."

"No. I'm going with you."

"You can't."

"I can. We can."

"How?"

"We'll take Enara."

"How would we get across the border?"

"André will take us."

"André?" Luke cried. "That old man—"

"That old man is smarter and braver than you'll ever be."

Luke took a deep breath. "I know that, but I've been over the kinds of trails he used that day I followed Peru. Do you remember I came off that mountain that day with one less mule? I'm not going across the Pyrenees on horses at night with you and an infant. André would tell you that's crazy."

"I know why I have to cross," she said. "Why do you?"

He couldn't tell her that he had to help take Peru down. That seemed the only way he could make peace with the Outfit, and his conscience wouldn't let him walk away from a bunch intent on killing Americans. Yet taking Peru down was the last thing he wanted to do. He answered vaguely. "I need my real identity back."

"And Euskadi Sur is where my heart is," she said. "Peru wants me to cut a deal while I still can."

"*Peru* wants you to cut a deal?"

"Yes, Luke, I have talked to Peru. Can you handle that? The Guardia

Civil were furious when the king forced them to let me go. But Juan Carlos is going to announce another round of amnesties. Peru knows this from the priest on the king's staff. He thinks I can claim one of those amnesties, but I can't get it done here. I have to be in Spain."

When the baby was asleep they lay with quilts and blankets piled on them and watched the fireplace embers. Luke finally said, "I can think of only one way."

"What?"

"Peru gives us a ride on his very fast boat. You're the one who's in touch with him. You have to ask."

After a while she said, "All right. I will." Moments later she spoke again. "I'll need a disguise. I learned how to do makeup when I was a drama student. I might gray my hair and make myself look much older. But I'd have to do that every day."

She had turned over trying to get to sleep when Luke said, "Redhead."

"What?"

"I've noticed something about men. I could be wrong but listen. If women are redheads, men react to the hair before they really see the face. Especially if there's a lot of hair. You could find a stylist in Pau who knows how to do that and tell you how to maintain it. Let your hair go and add a little more curl. And your shoulders are beauties, you know. And men get flustered when they encounter a woman with a baby. Disguise by combinations."

She turned back toward him and snuggled closer. "Who knows, it might work. But the weather will have to warm up a little before I break out the shoulders."

THIRTY-SIX

JUNE 1996

With Enara strapped in a car seat in the back of the Peugeot, Ysolina dropped Luke off at Pau's train station. He kissed the baby and his nouveau redhead and boarded the 8:53 to Paris. With a brief call Pascal had left word that the documents were ready. Luke wore khakis and a shirt and the linen blazer he had bought in San Sebastián. He reached Gare Montparnasse at midafternoon. At the apartment Pascal laughed on seeing him and turned him around. "A salt and pepper pony tail!" he exclaimed. "A derelict."

"We're all actors, Pascal."

His apartment was stylish and clean. The raised windows allowed in street noise and a little breeze as Luke admired Pascal's handiwork. With the photos Luke had sent, Pascal had made Ysolina a passport and other identifications of a citizen of Spain named Veronica Sandoval.

"What do you think?" Pascal said. "She looks good?"

"She always does to me."

"But is she changed enough?"

"Maybe. Depends on how hard somebody's looking. They're good though, Pascal. You're the best. And she's a pretty good actor, too."

That evening Luke walked with Pascal to a *brasserie* where they ordered a bottle of Merlot and the prix fixe. Luke said, "I need a pair of handcuffs and a gun."

Pascal rolled his eyes and shook his head. "I'd better make sure my coat pockets are empty, in case you get killed."

"Yeah, but other than that it's not your problem."

"Are you sure?"

Luke tapped the divot at the edge of his beard. "They gave me this the last time they had hold of me. Did I give you up?"

Pascal juked his head back and forth and forked the egg yolk on his *salade lyonnaise.* "You're right."

Luke said, "You really ought to find a legal way to utilize your talents."

Pascal laughed. "You're one to talk."

The handcuffs Pascal got him were a lever-locked Smith & Wesson model. The gun was a Ruger LC9, three-inch barrel, weighed just over a pound, seven nine-millimeter rounds in the magazine. Taking pains, he slathered DuraCoat on the disassembled gun. In the end you could make out *Ruger – Prescott – AZ* on the slide but the serial number had vanished. Luke was taking all precautions.

Later that day he found a shaded bench in the Luxembourg Gardens and called Jimbo Hopson on the stolen cell phone. The station chief picked up. Luke said, "Hey, Jimbo, it's me."

"Stay put. I'll call right you right back."

When the call from the stew-phone rang, Jimbo exploded. "You ass-hole! You almost got me sent *way out* in Mongolia! Any time I hear mention or think of you I hit the key that says Delete."

Luke groveled, coaxed, cajoled, implored. "Jimbo, please, listen to me. I'm here to give myself up, but only to you. You're the only one I trust. Only maybe they still want to take down Peru Madariaga. I've got him for you. For them. But you and I have to talk, and it has to be some-place where nobody else can see or hear us." Jimbo finally agreed to meet him on the Square de l'Abbe Migne, across from the Denfert Rochereau Métro station, at four o'clock.

Back in Pascal's apartment, Luke painted each of his finger and thumb prints with Gorilla Glue, let them dry, then gave them another coat. It felt creepy but his prints wouldn't show up on the gun. He hoped he didn't have to use it.

He slipped an envelope into the inside pocket of his blazer and put the handcuffs in a thick sock so they wouldn't rattle in his coat pocket. Denfert Rochereau was two stops south from the Luxembourg Métro station in Pascal's neighborhood. The car was crowded with people get-ting off work. Luke stayed on his feet, holding the rail above with his left hand, his right on the gun in case some pickpocket made a stab for whatever might be in there.

Their rendezvous was in Montparnasse. The 1920s and 1930s in that part of the city were known as *les Annés Folles,* the crazy years. The painter Marie Laurencin that Ysolina admired had a piece of that. Picasso's friend, the French poet Max Jacob, said he came there to learn how to sin disgracefully. The war and the Nazi occupation turned out the lights on the party. Montparnasse had rebounded and was still a classy part of town, but it was toned down. Luke wondered if those dancers of the Lindy Hop had known what was under their flying feet.

Luke watched Jimbo come up out of the Métro, look around, then start across the street. He stood a little less than six feet, was strong and wide, and had never looked quite right in a coat and tie. Age and pounds weighed on him now, and his gait had become more of a shuffle. He wasn't married, never had been, and it wasn't in his nature to enjoy what Paris offered. He grunted at Luke's hair and beard and shook hands, but cast a suspicious gaze at a squat one-story building painted black with no markings on the door. Signs on stanchions stated in multiple languages the hours of operation and forbade any use of camera flash. The black door was the entry to the Catacombs of Paris.

"Are you kidding me?" Jimbo said.

"Come on, you'll love it," said Luke.

"You got some nerve," Jimbo muttered as they descended a narrow stairwell cut through limestone and hustled through a macabre gallery. They encountered no more than a dozen people, all heading out. The air was damp, water gurgling and dripping. They walked a long narrow corridor of stone, with Luke talking all the way. On why he had to cut off contact after that call in St. Jean-de-Luz. The weeks in San Sebastián when he was hoping Ysolina would lead him to Peru. The bust by the Guardia Civil and Roberto Escamilla's collusion with their torturers. The hard-time Spanish prison. Most of it was true.

"You gave Escamilla a concussion and almost strangled him," Jimbo said.

"Can't do the fight don't come through the ropes. Madariaga got me out of Spain. Don't ask because I won't tell you how. Not now. In the course of all this he asked me to come in with him and ETA."

Jimbo glared at him. "And do what?"

"I'm not sure," said Luke. "But I know they're deep into the planning of it, a lot of people would get killed or hurt, and some would be Americans. And our station chief in Madrid and his Spanish pals don't have the brains to get close to them."

"How come Madariaga likes you so much?"

"I did what I told him I'd do. I delivered those guns from South America."

"Yeah, and thanks to you we lost track of them."

"On the other hand the Outfit took its own sweet time trying to get me out of that prison. He challenged me to shake loose of Escamilla, and his Basque friends would get me out if I did. I would have hurt Escamilla more if I'd had time."

Jimbo's eyes narrowed at a sign chiseled in the stone above the entrance to another tunnel. The sign read *Arrête! C'est ici l'empire de la Mort.* Stop! Here lies the empire of Death. "Man, you are fucking with me," Jimbo said.

"It was a limestone mine," Luke said. "The Romans were mining it two thousand years ago. The rock was used to build Notre Dame, the Louvre, half of what was then Paris. But the mining authority got scared the Left Bank was going to wind up the world's biggest sinkhole. They banned the mining and someone came up with the idea of digging up cemeteries and putting the land to better use. Every night for years black canvased wagons hauled bones down here. The French Revolution and the Terror dumped remains of six or seven million people in these tunnels."

They came upon a highlighted wall of bones that some artful soul had arranged like a layer cake—femurs the pastry, lines of skulls the icing. "This is a very strange country," Jimbo muttered. "So what do you want, Luke? You better start talking real to me."

"Just believe me. I'll stay in contact with you alone. I'll be in Spain, and Escamilla can't know anything about it. If the folks back home collar me, it's no skin off your back. But I have a favor to ask of you."

Jimbo stared at the bones and waited.

"Ysolina and I have a baby. A girl who's four months old."

Jimbo's eyebrows moved. "Yeah? Congratulations."

Luke removed the envelope from the inside pocket of his jacket. "Her name is Enara. This is her long-form birth certificate, holy writ in France. I want her to be a US citizen as well, if she wants to be. But Ysolina and I would have to appear at a US embassy or consulate to finalize it. That's impossible unless I make things right with the Outfit. And the only way I can do that is to follow through with ETA and Peru. You understand? If something happens to me, and it might, I want you to make sure she can grow up an American citizen. I know you can get that done."

"You take me for a chump."

"No. A friend."

Jimbo put the envelope in his coat pocket. "Okay, we go through all this crap in this *bone* yard so you can ask me that. Now you're gonna give me an approximate timeline for taking down Madariaga?"

"Not exactly," Luke said, relieving the weight on his coat pocket.

"You son of a bitch!" erupted Jimbo. "You came here with a gun."

"Of course. Knowing you would. Can I have yours, please?"

Jimbo breathed angrily and looked at the short-nosed Ruger. The only sound was the groundwater's dripping.

"Come on," said Luke. "You could have had me detained before I got to a Métro station. I can't chance that. I have to do this. Once you get over being mad, you'll understand. I've got to have time to be out of town and on my way. So give me your gun. Please."

Jimbo withdrew the blunt-nosed old-fashioned .38 from his armpit holster and handed it over butt first. Luke slipped it in the pocket of the blazer with his free hand, keeping the Ruger aimed at Jimbo's chest. "Thank you. Now the cell phone."

Jimbo surrendered that. Before he could draw his arm back Luke nabbed the wrist with one of the cuffs and clicked it shut. "I can't believe this," Jimbo said.

"You've spent worse nights. Now sit down with your back to the bones, there beside the cross."

Jimbo was enraged but did as he was told. Luke crouched and locked the other cuff around the foot of the cross. "I wouldn't fight it much," Luke said, grinning at the skulls. "You don't want to start an avalanche. I'm going to leave your things over here on the floor. Help will reach you in the morning. Good seeing you, Jimbo."

The station chief roared curses as Luke's figure moved off in the dark. The echoes spooked him quiet.

But then he heard footfalls and Luke came back out of the darkness. He sat down with his back to the bones but beyond the range of a furious elbow. "Forgive me, Jimbo. I can't ask you to trust me if I don't trust you. Hold still and let me get those off you. If we don't scoot we're both going to spend the night in here."

THIRTY-SEVEN

AUGUST 1996

Don Jokin had been on the king's staff for a year now. He had little opportunity to escape his quarters and office in Zarzuela Palace, and he longed for the freedom and light workload he enjoyed at the university in Pamplona. He comforted himself in solitary walks in the woods of Monte de El Pardo. Though Madrid's northern suburbs had enclosed El Pardo, fewer than four thousand people lived there; thanks to a buffer of woodlands, it still had the look and feel of a secluded Spanish village.

It was a warm weekday, and few people were out on the walking trails. Then a large man appeared beside him. His head was shaved, and masses of blue and green tattoos covered his arms below his shirt. He had a jewel earring. *"Anaia,"* the man said in Basque—brother. Strangers who spoke to Don Jokin usually called him Father.

"Buenas días," he answered, trying to signal he knew no Basque, and kept walking. To Don Jokin's horror the man walked with him and in a low, mean, patient voice recited a list of things he, Don Jokin, had done for ETA. If evidence of those actions were revealed to the king and the Spanish police, he would be ruined.

At some point during this terrifying lecture Don Jokin realized from the tattoos this was the profane one who had been in the cave outside St. Jean-Pied-de-Port. The man tugged at a jewel pin in his earlobe. "I saw you admiring this. Half a carat. I got it off a woman's wedding ring by cutting off her finger."

He reached in his pocket, brought out something in his hand, and with a metal snap it clicked out the blade of a knife. He aimed in the general direction of Don Jokin's vital organs. "I want you to tell me," the man had said, "if it's true that Juan Carlos will attend the opening of the Guggenheim Bilbao."

After a moment Jale said, "If you don't answer I'm going to kill you now. Nice thing about a knife is that it doesn't make noise. Drag you off the trail, somebody will find you when you start to smell. Hot days like this, it won't take long. I'll ask once more. Is he going to be there?"

"I don't know. I believe that might be a whole year away."

"I'll ask once more. Is he going to be there?"

Don Jokin said, "I believe he is, yes."

Judas! He had just become the most despised creature of his faith.

"Good. You'll live another day. We'll talk more as the time gets closer. Understand me. If any harm comes to me, you're a dead man. And if the king changes his mind about Bilbao, we'll presume you warned him, and you're just as dead."

Then he turned and with his hands in pockets walked the other way.

Don Jokin looked about, stepped off in the brush, and threw up. How could he ever have gotten mired in this? ETA was using him to shove Juan Carlos toward some catastrophic brink.

He attended mass at the small church in El Pardo as often as he could. He prayed without ceasing, but prayers were not enough to relieve his terror and guilt. So he sat in the confession stall and waited for the priest behind the cloak to say anything. The priest outwaited him. "Bless me, Father," intoned Don Jokin, "for I have sinned. It has been a year since my last confession."

The priest listened to vague and meandering explanations of the lies and deceptions he had inflicted on a superior he could not identify as the king. "I have been duplicitous in my relationships with others," Don Jokin tried harder. "For these and all the sins I have committed which I have forgotten, I am sorry."

The priest started to speak but Don Jokin blurted, "Sorry's not enough."

After a slight stammer the priest said, "You have not been diligent in the faith if it has been that long since your last confession. But you sound like an intelligent and educated man. Surely you know the lies you've described are minor venial sins. Duplicitous? What kind of duplicity? We all mislead others. It's good that your conscience bothers you, and that you came here with regret in your heart. But something more bedevils you. Your contrition is imperfect, and I can't bless you with penance, unless you tell me more specifics of what your sins are."

"I've endangered the lives of others," Don Jokin blurted.

A startled silence. "Well, if intentional, that would be mortal sin—the sin that offends God and destroys the life of grace in the soul."

"Yes, that's the one."

"What have you done, man?"

Don Jokin tried to think of how to articulate the monstrosity dwelling inside him to a faceless voice behind a curtain.

"I can't do this, Father. I'm sorry."

"Wait—" the priest began, but the sinner was gone.

THIRTY-EIGHT

P eru had not been on the gray boat that picked them up after dark at a slip on Oleron Island in France, then in rough waters delivered them to a private dock in Avilés estuary—both ports on the Bay of Biscay that were well removed from the Basque Country. Enara had fought the constraints on her and cried most of the time she wasn't asleep, and Jale, once more the pilot, had greeted Ysolina by calling her *sorgin,* witch. It was a long, miserable ride but Peru smuggled them into Spain. Now they were parked in an ETA safe house in Oñate, a handsome town in the green hills of Guipúzcoa province.

It was a walkup apartment outside the old quarter that afforded them a balcony with a view of the Cantabrian cordillera, and they had the whole second floor. Enara was a rambunctious seventeen months old. She crawled at great speed and laughed with glee at the noise she could make when she slapped the wood floor. She hadn't figured out the tricks of getting up, but if put on her feet with assistance she took off in a bowlegged ramble that reminded Luke of John Wayne's stride in the movies. He could see her catching on to the Basque and Spanish words her mother crooned at her. And he contributed some English. Enara liked pulling on Luke's beard, and the first word she said that he recognized was "Papa."

Oñate was where Peru had grown up, starred on rugby fields, climbed with the clubs of mountaineers that bred ETA, and was disinherited when Spanish police tore up his parents' home, looking for him or evidence of where he might be. Yet for them it was as safe a place as they could be. Spanish was spoken in consideration of those families whose Euskera had been lost in prior generations, but few people who weren't ethnic Basques would move here—it was a stronghold of the separatists. The red-bereted Basque police took pains to act friendly, and Luke had never seen a green and white Jeep of the Guardia Civil there. Still, he and Ysolina were marking time and had been since the day they arrived. Sometimes they took Enara out in her stroller to the Plaza de los Fueros, spooned her delights of ice cream, and enjoyed *pintxos* and wine, watching the twilight paseo.

But they couldn't do much of that. Ysolina ventured out singly to the markets for food and wine, for she spoke Basque. With the beard and ponytail Luke was confident he wouldn't be recognized. Sometimes he felt like they were under house arrest. When he went for solitary walks and people spoke to him he pointed to his right ear. He didn't want them reacting to an American Spanish accent so he played the role of being deaf.

He walked the campus of the former Universidad de Sancti Spiritus. Built in the mid-sixteenth century, the graceful buildings had been Euskadi's first university, but it closed for lack of funds in 1901; the buildings now housed an institute of sociology and law. One day he struck out and climbed the streets through the outskirts, reaching the ravine that houses the Sanctuary of Arantzazu. The scale of the place surprised him; the quarters of the Franciscan monks looked like college dormitories. The shepherd who claimed to have freed the Virgin from hawthorn brambles left a name to history: Rodrigo de Baltzategi. He reported the miracle thirty-three years before Columbus reached the Americas. Arantzazu became another destination of pilgrims. Someone had to welcome and care for these searchers, and with papal authority Arantzazu had been the charge of the Franciscans for five centuries.

Luke wanted to see the basilica doors of San Sebastián's sculptor and *pelota* fan, Eduardo Txillada. Instead of trying to salvage ruins of the original church, destroyed in the Civil War, several distinguished Spanish artists married the faith to avant-garde style. Luke walked down a staircase to reach Txillada's doors, and he smiled on seeing them. They fooled your eyes and even your touch. They had to be wood, for they were massive, but he made them look like iron. The benches inside were of plain wood with no cushions, but the enormous altarpiece was flabbergasting. The multi-colored sculpted wood mural presented scenes from Revelations and the myths of the Old Testament. Positioned high up in this statement of transcendence to heaven was a chalkstone gothic statue of the Virgin holding a cup in her right hand, an infant in the left. The slumping Christ on the cross was positioned lower right. All of it was bathed in the blue light of another artist's stained glass. Luke was the only person in the sanctuary. The calm it brought him was the closest he could come to praying that this might yet turn out right.

One day he was pacing the apartment, Enara propped against his shoulder, when the new Motorola phone went off. Jimbo Hopson had given him the phone, which was encrypted with 2G technology that was supposed to make it secure. As far as Luke knew, nobody but Peru and Jimbo knew how to call him. *"Bueno,"* he said as he handed Enara to Ysolina and got the thing to his ear.

"How you?" said Jimbo.

"Fine. And you?" Luke said with caution. The Paris station chief was still testy about that rendezvous in the catacombs.

Jimbo said, "Listen, you need to call home."

"What?" He thought it must be Amona.

"There was an accident. Your brother and his daughter were tooling around on one of those all-terrain rec vehicles. He flipped it, she was thrown free, but it landed on him. Your brother's dead."

Luke sat down, flummoxed.

"There's no other way than to just say it. I'm sorry."

"Thank you. We weren't close. He and I lost each other somewhere along the way. Still it's a shock."

Then Luke shook his head and said, "How do you know this?"

Jimbo chuckled. "The Outfit's trying to get a line on you, and I'm on the share list. The listeners have been all confused. There'd be Spanish and English and Basque, then teenager talk and then some other voices that came on and didn't make any sense at all. It took the Outfit a while to figure out they've been monitoring what must be the last party lines in America."

Luke shook his head. "My grandmother doesn't like telephones, and she wasn't going to pay anymore for their two lines than she had to."

"Well, sorry again. I'll let you go."

"Wait. When I use this phone, those listeners can't understand or trace it?"

"That's what the techies claim. If it helps, you're not important enough to have a listener on the Texas line all the time. Keep it short. And if anything changes in our stuff you by God better let me know."

Luke told Ysolina what had happened to his brother. She eyed him with concern. He didn't eat dinner, poured himself whiskeys, sat out on the balcony smoking again, and watched the town long into the night. Ysolina came out and put her hand on his shoulder. "You're going to call them, aren't you?" she said.

"Yes. I just can't tonight."

The next evening he called Lydia, Simon's wife. She cried, trying to get the story out, then abruptly quit. "You already know, don't you? However you know, I don't care. But you know."

"Yes, Lydia, I know. I'm so sorry. Is Andrea all right?"

"A little bunged up and devastated, but yeah, she's all right. Luke, I know you and Simon got crosswise a long time ago, and I never quite understood why, but you've always been nice to me."

He waited, fearful of what was coming next.

"Andrea and I can't keep this ranch going, what little help we've got, and your granny the way she is. We really need you to come back and help us get through this. I'll make it out in the will. You'll be a full part-ner. Andrea and I are fine where we are now. You can have the big house when your granny passes on."

"Lydia, I have my own family now. I can't tell you all the reasons why I can't do that. You'll have to hire a good foreman. Best as I can, I'll help find one."

"Well, it's almost over with," she said, crying again. "He wanted to be buried on the ranch, and day after tomorrow he will be. You wouldn't believe what I've had to go through just to get him declared dead by accident and put under where it suited him. God bless you, Luke," she said and hung up.

He then called Amona. They spoke Spanish, her voice stronger and steadier than his. After the commiserations he told her that Ysolina, his wife and mother of his child, wanted to talk to her. He handed off the phone and pressed his thumbs against his temples. They spoke Euskera for a long time. He didn't understand a word. Didn't try.

But one morning the sun came up bright again. Ysolina came in with posters in Basque announcing a festival. *Ikurriña* flags were hung above the streets, and a parade materialized and passed under their balcony. A man among them wore the shoulders and head of a laughing white-haired man that made him eight feet tall. The band's horn players and drummers stayed on beat but marched like a mob. Men danced with wives in the street. Enara hung her arms around Luke's leg, as she often did. He usually picked her up but now he took her hands and held her upright. With Ysolina clapping her hands and singing the band's tune in Basque, he danced with the little girl squealing and wriggling her hips in delight. Then the phone rang.

"Don't answer," Ysolina said, but he did.

It was Peru. "Do you know how to rappel?"

The question confused Luke. "Like on a cliff?"

"Yes, rappel. Like on ropes maneuvering on a cliff or wall."

"I used to know how. It's been a long time."

"The museum is going up fast now. They've put up the steel and concrete structure and a lot of the stone. They're hanging thin sheets of metal and have figured out it's easier to teach people who know how to rappel to hang the metal than to teach metal hangers how to rappel. You can give us a deep inside look at the place, from the top down. Will you do it?"

Luke felt like he was on a beach and a receding tide was sucking sand from under his bare feet. "All right. Tell me what to do."

"Get on a bus to Bilbao in the morning. Bring work boots and gloves if you have them. You'll be wearing a hardhat by the end of the week."

"Where will I live?"

"In an apartment."

"With Ysolina and the baby?"

"That's up to you."

THIRTY-NINE

SEPTEMBER 1996

The museum was going up in cores that Frank Gehry had named River, Neo, T1000, Cobra, Fox, Flower, Tower S17, Fish, Boot, Canopy, and Potemkin. Luke and three young Basques who had been Spanish soldiers were crimping and hanging titanium panels on the concave surfaces of Potemkin. Luke's household historian reported that Potemkin was a Polish-born Russian field marshal who directed the foreign policy of Catherine the Great and was her lover in the late eighteenth century. Or, Ysolina said, it could also be a façade covering up serious deficiencies.

Thanks for that one, *querida*. Gehry did not want the south side of the museum to overpower the conventional neighboring structures, and the museum's east end, abutting the angular crossing of the large bridge called the Puente de la Salve, could not blind drivers with reflections. So Gehry and the IDOM team had moved two entire towers downriver from the bridge. They would curve into the sky like stalks of windblown wheat.

Cranes swung about holding the roofless cages of the laborers, and the rock and glass saws buzzed and shrieked twenty-four hours a day. The construction site covered more than three hundred fifty acres, and the activity was synchronized mayhem. Landscaping crews were planting trees and paving sidewalks right up to the foundations, while other crews were trying to keep rain off workers struggling to keep the interiors on schedule. Dual rows of tall fencing topped with razor wire lined the perimeter, and heavily armed security guards roved around them.

Laurentzi Arista, the hustling young crew foreman who met with the climbers every morning, had once interned in the Santa Monica office of Frank Gehry's firm. He was responsible for the titanium cladding that would cover all the galleries. Laurentzi had taken a liking to Luke, whom he called by his alias Jamie. They often ate their lunches together. Laurentzi told stories and asked questions about America, and Luke learned more about the building than he could just observe.

The galleries' substructures were made of heavy steel modules three meters square and bolted together. Bolted over them were sections of galvanized steel tubing, each section connected by a universal joint that allowed adjustment in any direction. That layer was covered with thermal insulation and an asphalt-based membrane that expanded and sealed off L-shaped stainless steel connectors and any chance punctures that could leak water. This was the curving surface on which Luke and his fellow climbers rappelled up and down, day after day. The wages were excellent, for it was dangerous as hell.

The titanium panels were bent at the site and in many cases hand-trimmed to fit the curvature of the design. Titanium was alleged to be stronger than steel, but the segments, less than an eighth of an inch thick, were incredibly lightweight. They fluttered in the wind with the climbers trying to hang on.

In the mornings a crane operator raised Luke and the army vets on steel platforms that were heavy enough they didn't tip when one of them stepped or leaped off. The Spaniards in the climbing crews used two ropes and a harness that allowed them to descend and ascend in a virtual seated posture, knees toward the walls. But the marines had taught Luke single-rope rappel. He started out trying to do it that way. Right away he saw his technique was impossible, unless he wanted to try to hang on a titanium sheet with his teeth.

Another climber, a young veteran of the Spanish special forces, gave him a cam that would automatically catch the rope, like the mechanism of a car's safety belt. When he fed rope to each short incremental stop the cam locked in and kept him from falling. Bilbao was windy, though, and if he swung around too much, his loop of nylon rope could jump off the guiding L-shaped connecter, catch the sharp edge of the highest sheet they had hung that day, and he and the prized titanium would take a fall he wouldn't likely walk away from.

The younger climbers, all of them army vets, were always waiting for him with looks of impatience. When he caught up with them he bent and crimped an edge of sheet around the L-shaped connectors.

CHAPTER 39

Then with the hammer carried in the thigh loop of his jeans he tapped in nails that penetrated the titanium and stainless steel, and the membrane closed around them. Laurentzi talked about the magic of thermal conductivity, but it was just hard and dangerous labor as far as Luke was concerned.

One afternoon as he was taking a breather, he noticed a crowd of men on the ground, many of whom wore suits along with their hardhats. One man who wore a pale yellow padded jacket and a red hardhat seemed to be the center of them. When he stopped, they all stopped. When he moved they moved with him. They were like a school of fish.

When the sun was low, at last a boss on the ground blew a whistle, waved his arm in two circles, and the crane operator swung the steel crate over to carry them down. Once aboard, the macho young Spaniards planted their feet wide and crossed their arms on their chests, ignoring the wobbly ride. Luke sat and wrapped his arms around his knees. Hell with it, he was tired. He pulled the rubber band off his ponytail and shook the sweat-dampened hair out on his shoulders. The crate hit the ground with a bounce, and one of the youngsters gripped his shoulder and said, "Take it easy, *viejo.*" Old man.

Luke stored his climbing gear, hammer, and gloves in a small locker, gave his combination lock a twirl, and started the long trudge out through the gate and over the bridge's pedestrian walkway toward home, carrying his lunch pail and thermos. He knew this day was just getting started. "Hey, Shelton, wait," someone called.

He was so tired he almost didn't think to respond to his alias. Laurentzi approached with a couple of security types and the man with the red hardhat and yellow padded coat. The man was shorter than Luke, looked to be in his sixties, and wore bifocals with wire rims. It was the man he had heard speak at the chic restaurant outside San Sebastián.

"Jamie Shelton," said Laurentzi, "meet our design architect, Frank Gehry."

Luke moved the lunch pail to his left hand then looked at his right palm. It was awfully grimy. "Forget that," said Gehry, putting his hand forward. "I'm in the construction trade myself." He carried his head with a slight tilt, and a friendly or haughty grin accentuated his wedge of front teeth. Luke's beard and hair and scar ruled out any chance recognition on Gehry's part, Luke thought. He shook Gehry's hand and said, "It's an honor to meet you, sir."

"Call me Mr. Gehry, if you like, but I'm no sir. Laurentzi tells me you're the only American on the crews. The ones who are actually building things."

"I wasn't aware of that. I like working with Laurentzi and the young guys on my team. They keep me from doing double back flips off your walls. What a building you've got going here!"

"Glad you like it. Where did you learn your Spanish?"

"I grew up with it. And then the military."

Gehry nodded. "If it wasn't for my wife, who's fluent, there's no way this would have happened. Where are you from?"

"Oklahoma originally. I hardly ever get there anymore. The wages here are good. And working overseas I don't have to pay income taxes. I heard they were looking for workers who knew how to rappel. I overstated my ability."

"Don't let him fool you," Laurentzi said. "He takes pains."

Luke smiled. "Because I don't like to get hurt."

"There you go. Well, I'm glad you've joined the family and team, whatever we are. Good luck to you."

"And you, Mr. Gehry." Luke gripped the short plastic bill and tipped his hardhat to the architect. "This has been the experience of a lifetime."

FORTY

There safe house was in Bilbao's la Vieja, the old town. The district was populated by immigrant Maghrebis, who were no longer called Moors, and by gypsies, junkies, and hookers. Taxi drivers did not like to go or stop there at night. And the night after he met Frank Gehry Luke came home and Enara was gone. Ysolina didn't like this place at all. Luke had walked around smelling Enara's scents of piss and baby lotion, picked up toys that hadn't gone with her. But he didn't want to start another quarrel. Ysolina had made up her mind. Tía Aloña and her granddaughter Jokiñe would care for her, read to her every night, and Luke and Ysolina would see her every minute they possibly could. "Where is she?" he asked her. "San Sebastián?"

"No. The family has another home out in the countryside. It's quite removed, and it's beautiful. She'll be safe."

He showered, she made him a whiskey, and with a smile told him Peru had assigned him the alias "Pisu Arin."

"What does it mean?"

"Lightweight."

"Nice," he said.

The van pulled up in the street on time, at eight o'clock. A man wearing a ball cap and jacket with the collar turned up got out of the passenger side. He nodded at them, opened the rear doors, and gestured for them to hurry. The cargo part of the van had no windows. They sat on smelly carpet and with their hands braced against the van's quick turns. Two back seats were empty. She murmured in English, "Why did they put us back here?"

"So we won't know where we've been."

In time they were hustled into a ramshackle house. Luke was surprised that there were nine of them, not counting themselves and the two couriers. That was a lot of mouths to keep shut. Ysolina was the only woman. Luke recognized Jale from the boat rides. Animosity radiated between Jale and Ysolina. Others spoke and greeted her as "Nafar," for Navarrese, her ETA alias.

So she was one of them, or had been. Luke withheld a glance. Had Ysolina been lying to him all along?

"Pisu Arin is *amerikanu,*" Peru said. "He is Basque, he supports our cause, and he is one of us now. He is *gudari*. Raise your fists of welcome." They all did that, including Ysolina.

"We all know why we're here," Peru said. "The Americans and Basque *jefes* have taunted us by bringing this monstrosity to Bilbao. Thousands of millions of pesetas have been taken from Basque taxpayers that could have been spent on shelter for the poor and the schools of our children. Who knows why the rich Americans let themselves to be drawn into this folly? It doesn't matter. They're here, and the people who struggle to make a living under the yoke of the Spaniard occupiers didn't ask them to come."

There were grumbles of agreement. Peru looked at Luke and said, "We are going to blow this thing to ashes falling on the Nervión. Pisu Arin, do you have floor plans of this so-called museum?"

Luke was flabbergasted but tried to keep it from showing. "No, Aitzgorri, floor plans are not what I have access to. If I did, they would be computer files that none of us could open or read. But I can tell you what I've seen with my eyes. You've waited too late."

Peru raised his voice. "We blew Carrero Blanco's car over the roof of a five-story building. We blew up the Lemóniz nuclear power plant so many times the Spaniards just gave up and sealed it with razor wire."

"Yes, but a nuclear power plant is not a prospect many people are crazy about, especially since Chernobyl. A major art museum is different. I don't have blueprints but I know this about the supports holding up the Museo Guggenheim––"

"I'm not sure you know anything," said Jale. "You're trying to protect the Americans."

"Let him speak," snapped Peru. The big one glared.

"You put me on that jobsite," Luke argued, "and asked me to bring you my inside knowledge and opinion. Inside the loopy-looking thing you see going up in the sky is a steel and concrete structure you guys couldn't bring down unless you flew airplanes into it."

Boy, did those words come back to haunt him.

Peru swung his head to Ysolina. "Nafar, what do you think?"

"For many reasons I agree with Pisu Arin."

Jale sneered and cursed her. Peru jabbed a finger at him and once more ordered him to pipe down.

"The thing's got heavy security, and I don't think you could get inside it at night to plant your explosives," Luke said. "Tunnel under it, forget that. The foundation contains six hundred-odd concrete piles set fourteen meters deep in bedrock." Luke pressed on, "You could damage the exterior with hand-held rockets or something like that, but you've waited too long, and it's the wrong thing to do. You would be condemned all over the world. I don't know how many workers go through those gates every day, but there are hundreds. Or would you wait until they've hired docents and hung paintings on the walls? Across from the museum site are office buildings where hundreds of Bilbaínos work every day. You want to set their businesses and employees on fire? And explosions of that scale could also dunk the Puente de la Salve in the river. What's that going to do for ETA's support in Euskadi? There are statements you can make and actions you can take, but that's the wrong one."

Peru stared at Luke and may have decided to cool things off before the others killed him. "All right," Peru said. "We'll table that for now. Pisu Arin did what we asked him to do. All we were sure of until tonight was what we could see looking over those fences and flying a small plane over it. But Jale has an announcement that is going to make everyone happier."

The big man played it out and made them wait.

"Juan Carlos is coming to Bilbao for the museum's opening. And we're going to kill the son of a bitch."

The responses in Basque were sounds of jubilation. Luke glanced at Ysolina, who looked profoundly shocked. In a strained raised voice she said, "Assassinating the king of Spain is a very bad idea!"

These are maniacs! Luke was thinking. He raised his hand. Peru nodded with a look that said this had better be good.

"Let me just throw something out. Let's say Juan Carlos changes his mind about coming to Bilbao, or it turns out killing him is just too hard to do. You're expert kidnappers. It's how ETA first got its fame."

Peru's expression clouded more. "You're saying we *kidnap* the king?"

"Well, maybe if you could, but that's impossible, isn't it? Why don't you kidnap this American architect, Frank Gehry? He's an old man who thinks he's invincible. It would be easy to do. Unlike the king, who might or might not show up for the only chance you'd have at him, Gehry's around all the time. And he will be around even more as it gets closer to being finished. Snatching Gehry would bring down the wrath of the United States, but Spaniards would just be confused. Comes down to it, who does this guy think he is? How did he get to be the king of Bilbao? And the pressure of the Americans can work in your favor. Because the condition of Gehry's safe release would be the Spaniards' freeing all your political prisoners. It's the most daring and attention-grabbing thing you could do."

Their escorts let them out in front of the tenement without a word. When they were both inside and had glasses of brandy shaking in their hands, Luke said, "What do you think, *Nafar?*"

"Don't start," she said wearily. "They gave me that name nearly twenty years ago. Some day you were going to have to hear it."

"I already had. So had the Outfit in the United States."

"I guess I'm flattered. But Luken, I am not one of them."

She let him simmer for a moment and said, "Do you really want to kidnap Frank Gehry?"

"Shit, no! I just thought that might get their minds off killing the king. Does the big one with the shaved head and all the ink have the rank and know-how to pull off an assassination?"

"Jale," she said with contempt. "You may have noticed we despise each other. He used to be one of Peru's bodyguards. I was surprised to see him in that room. I guess he's gotten a promotion. And he seems to have a following."

She forced through his anger and fear, put her arms around him, and pressed her head against his chest. "You were good in there. I was impressed."

"What was your read of Peru tonight?" he said.

"I thought he was trying hard to hold things together."

"Maybe he doesn't want to do any of those things."

"Peru's not an idle man. I know he really wanted the peace that seemed so close in Tangier. I don't know what's going through his mind now. And I can't explain to myself or anyone else how I was ever married to him. For so long."

She looked up at him and said, "So what do we do?"

"We put our minds to it. We do all we can."

"Without getting ourselves killed."

"Well, yeah. There is that."

FORTY-ONE

SEPTEMBER 1997

Laurentzi laid off the rest of the climbers but asked Luke if he wanted to stay on through the museum's opening, a stroke of luck. Luke was to be his gopher, a runner of errands, attendant to last details. The ponytail was shorn now, the beard trimmed, and he had all the badges that got him past security. One day they were having lunch on the job site. Luke had put the sandwich wrapping away and had another sip of coffee from his thermos. "Gehry's a friendly fellow, isn't he?"

"Yes. In a way."

"Well, a man like that, it's almost like he's head of a country. The constant press of people around him. The security guards. No time to himself."

"He makes a game of losing them."

"Does his wife come with him?"

"I've never seen her here. I saw her when I interned for him. He's crazy about that woman. Nice to see, old folks that still have the fire."

"Seems like there would be a lonely side to his life, jumping between projects all over the world."

"He does it because he loves it. And he's disciplined. And because he is who he is, he gets to make up the rules."

"Wonder where they put him up when he's here."

Laurentzi looked at his watch. "He stays at a penthouse in a hotel close to here. We'd better get back to work."

It hadn't been hard to narrow the list of hotels with penthouses a short distance from the construction site, and ETA's intelligence network included plenty of bellhops. Ysolina had to go on a splurge of buying dresses, hose, high heels. Peru's people had gotten her a job on the staff of curators from the Guggenheim Foundation. Or rather they hired the person that Pascal Seguine's cobbling had created for her. She was attractive, efficient, poised under pressure, and spoke English with an accent, but well enough. She was fluent in French, Spanish, and Basque. And she knew her art.

The breakneck schedule had subjected Luke to seven-day weeks in the crush to beat their deadlines, but now that the climbing was over and his job was different, Ysolina's cousin Jokiñe picked them up every Sunday morning in an old Saab, and he saw how right Ysolina had been in making her call about their child. The two-story country house occupied by Tía Aloña, Jokiñe, and Enara sat amid apple orchards at a distance from Mondragón, a town with the world's largest number of worker-owned cooperatives, Ysolina told him. It was friendly terrain for Basques who might have something they wished to hide.

When he arrived on those Sundays there was a swirl of kisses and hugs. When they went up the stairs Enara insisted on climbing them herself, at her speed, but holding onto his hand. She fed herself with a spoon and cup, but both cup and spoon and any contents might go flying at any second. She scribbled and drew with crayons, eyeing her work proudly. When she sat in Luke's lap and he read to her, she would turn two or three pages ahead. He realized that she was mimicking his physical method of reading.

The women spoke both Basque and Spanish to her, and he added more English. She was already on her way to speaking three languages, and as she got older Ysolina would add French. The short sentences she uttered were no longer a jumble of baby patois. Then came the wailing of separation when the time came for the drive back to Bilbao. They could do nothing about that except reassure her, but Luke thought if she had to be raised for a while apart from him, he couldn't have hoped for more than those in that house in the apple orchards outside Mondragón.

Bilbao was always waiting for them, and one night so was Peru. He looked haggard and hadn't shaved in three or four days. He looked at the permanently soiled carpet and said in amazement, "Somebody took a car engine apart in here."

"Guess it was better than doing it out in the rain," said Luke.

Peru said, "Do you have a television?"

Ysolina blinked and said they did not.

"A radio?"

"Well, sure."

"Turn it on."

"Okay," said Luke.

"Louder."

Luke shrugged and found a station playing jazz. "If this place was bugged we'd already be arrested," he suggested. "Calm down."

Ysolina brought out kitchen chairs so they could sit close and hear him over the radio. "How goes the plan for this architect Gehry?" Peru said.

Luke looked at Ysolina and said, "I think we're ready to go. We know when he's here, we know where he stays, and he doesn't like to be hounded by security. I think the sooner the better, before his wife arrives."

Peru shook his head. "Has to be when the museum opens."

"That would make it a lot more difficult," said Luke. "Why?"

"It's not the only plan."

Luke turned the radio down a bit. "What's the other one?"

"Remember in St. Jean-de-Luz, I asked if you could get us Plamya Flames?"

"Sure. It was just talk. Wasn't it?"

"We have them. And there's going to be a hit on the king."

"Peru!" Ysolina shrilled.

"You can't do that," Luke erupted. "For one thing, not one of us sitting here would likely survive it. And if we did, we'd never get out of jail."

"I can't stop it!"

Multiple breaths went in and out. Luke said, "You're the military commander, and you can't stop it?"

"I didn't seek those grenade launchers. It *was* just talk! I was trying to decide if you were for real. I turned those weapons down. But they came to us anyway, and I don't control them."

"You don't control them?" said Ysolina.

"Don't talk to me like I'm your child," Peru snapped.

"Who offered them to you?" said Luke.

"Israelis. The Mossad."

Luke shook his head. "Wouldn't you know it. Who controls them now?"

"Jale."

"My God," said Ysolina.

"How did they pay for them?"

Peru shrugged. "Robberies, burglaries. Not ordered by me."

Luke's thoughts were blown up at the moment. "You're telling me this guy's running a rogue operation, and you can't pull him in?"

Peru angrily came to his feet. "I'm not sure I want to pull him in. I don't understand why you're both so concerned about the health of that man Juan Carlos. You do your part of the action, and I'll do mine. And if you don't, somebody's going to be throwing shovelfuls of dirt on both of you."

After he'd gone, Ysolina roamed about with red hair clenched in her fists. Luke gulped his second whiskey. "*Querida,* an English expression in my country comes to mind."

"What?"

"Fish or cut bait."

FORTY-TWO

OCTOBER 1997

Don Jokin sat behind his gleaming desk in Zarzuela Palace and smiled at an attractive woman who wore a flowered dress with a loose skirt and modest hint of cleavage. She was a redhead with her hair curled all about and she had a scattering of freckles on her face, neck, and chest. More on her bare arms. She wore slipper high heels and had come in with a small briefcase. She sat with her legs crossed and tossed the toe of her shoe up and down. He wondered if she was aware she was doing that.

He noted the plain gold band on her left hand and looked at his schedule for the day. "So, Señora Sandoval, I'm sorry I kept you waiting. I understand you're involved in planning for the opening of the Museo Guggenheim Bilbao, and we of course are anxious for that to be a huge success." He clasped his hands on the desk and said, "What can I do for you?"

"You can close the door. Please."

Don Jokin blinked and said, "Of course. Forgive me." He rose, shut the door, and came back to his chair, flustered.

"Thank you," she said. "I'm not Señora Sandoval. My name is Ysolina de Añibarro. Formerly Ysolina Madariaga. I owe you a huge debt of gratitude."

He fell back in his chair, dumbfounded. "Señora, your debt is to His Majesty Juan Carlos the First. I am just a public servant—"

She waved that off with a flip of her hand. "I know how and why I got out of that prison, Don Jokin. I also know that you drove a stolen car across the border into France with a kidnapped man named Alvaro Molina in the trunk. In a cave outside St. Jean-Pied-de-Port you watched my ex-husband Peru give him a very hard time for refusing to pay his revolutionary taxes and then bragging about it in the press. And you've been an ETA courier for years."

His hand twitched toward his phone, to his secretary, to security, and she saw it. She leaned toward him and crossed her arms on the leg, jiggling the shoe. "I'm not here to harm or threaten you. But you do need to be alarmed. A small group of men who call themselves ETA but have broken with my former husband are planning to kill King Juan Carlos in Bilbao on October the eighteenth. You may already be aware of that."

"Señora, please—"

She kept talking. "You at least have inklings of it because you've been bullied, badgered, and terrorized by a large man who has a shaved head, many tattoos, and a diamond earring. His name is Jale.'"

She observed another twitch of his hand. "We're too far into this conversation to call your nun secretary in here to end it. Here's how they intend to kill His Majesty. They're going to use thirty-millimeter grenade launchers made by the Soviet Union. They're called Plamya Flames." He again tried to speak, but she raised the palm of her hand. "These are not the kind of grenades we see thrown by hand in movies. It's more accurate to call them warheads. They kill anyone standing within four or five meters of the explosion. They kill with enough explosive to blast through a tank, they kill with tiny metal and plastic needles, and they kill with white phosphorous, which goes on burning even when it's inside flesh. So, Don Jokin, if you let yourself be pulled along in this, and are in the entourage of King Juan Carlos, be very careful how close to him you stand."

The priest leaned back in shock. "Woman, what do you want from me?"

"I want conscience and courage. You have to persuade King Juan Carlos that he can't go anywhere near the opening ceremony and festivities of the Museo Guggenheim Bilbao. Go to his security. Go to the Guardia Civil. What are they for?"

She reached for her briefcase and stood up with a dazzling smile. "I know in your heart you're a good man, Don Jokin."

Two days later Don Jokin twitched through a routine meeting with the king. When the other staff members left the king looked at him and said, "Stay a moment, Monsignor. Do you know Salvador Dalí?"

"Well, no, I mean . . . I believe he's deceased."

Juan Carlos waved that off, as was his style.

"No, do you like his work? His art?"

"Some of it," Don Jokin said carefully. "I believe it deserves the word fabulous. I hardly ever understand what he was getting at."

"Oh, I get the melting watch. Time is always dissolving on me. But listen. In his autobiography he wrote about the Civil War: 'I was definitely not a historic man. On the contrary I felt myself essentially anti-historic and apolitical. Either I was too much ahead of my time or much too far behind, but never contemporaneous with ping-pong-playing men. The disagreeable memory of having seen two Spaniards capable of indulging in that imbecile game filled me with shame. It was a dreadful omen: the ping-pong ball appeared to me as a little death's head—empty, without weight, and catastrophic in its frivolity—the real death's head, personifiying politics completely skinned. And in the menacing silence that surrounded the tock, tock, tock, tock of the light skull of the ping-pong ball bouncing back and forth across the table I sensed the approach of the great armed cannibalism of our history, that of our coming Civil War, and the mere memory of the sound of the ping-pong ball heard on the historic night of October 6th was enough to set my teeth on edge in anticipation.'"

He laid the book on Don Jokin's desk and took a cushioned leather chair. "Why can't you write me speeches that read like that?"

"Well, Your Majesty, there's a matter of talent. And the audiences . . ."

Juan Carlos shook his head. "Never mind. It amused me and I just thought I'd share it. You can go. I'm going to ride my motorcycle."

Don Jokin said, "Sir, could we have just another word?"

"All right. What?"

"I believe you need to reconsider your plan to attend the opening of the Museo Guggenheim in Bilbao."

"What? They're making it into a grand celebration of your Basque Country, which is ever so hard to please. Where's the draft of my speech?"

"Your Majesty, I have heard things about the Bilbao event that make me very concerned about your safety. And a large number of Basques believe this expenditure of tax revenue in Vizcaya amounts to American aggression."

"Who is telling you that? It's going to breathe life into that rotten city! It already has! Hundreds of jobs for contractors and laborers. Put that in my speech. Not the rotten city part."

"Your Majesty, I fear for your life if you go there."

Juan Carlos paused. "Why do you say that?"

"That young woman you had released from prison, the wife of Peru Madariaga, she came to see me and told me about an ETA plot."

"She's in Madrid? And came to see you? Tell me about her."

"Describe her? She's in her thirties. Red hair. Attractive. Sort of, I don't know . . . brassy."

"Bring her to me. I want to hear this from her. Assure her she won't be arrested."

"I don't know how to do that, Your Majesty. I don't know where or how to find her."

The king snorted. "Have you ever asked a woman for a telephone number? I don't guess you would. So she just drifted in with this threat."

"She was quite specific. She mentioned munitions."

"Monsignor, *someone* is always out to kill me. Listening to all those confessions, you fellows traffic in gossip and hearsay. That woman is not worth getting yourself in an uproar. Security will have that museum wrapped up tight, I assure you."

Don Jokin replied, "Your Majesty, if you insist on going through with this, then I . . . well, I shall have to decline to write your speech."

"Then I'll write it myself! Get out of my sight, priest."

Don Jokin walked in anguish through the woods of El Pardo, his blood pressure on a tear. He cried out when Jale appeared again. Jale moved in front of him and without a word stabbed him with the switchblade. He pulled it out and stabbed him again, this time holding the blade inside him and twisting. "You didn't think we would let you live, did you?" Jale knifed him again. "I like it this way. It's so personal."

He looked both ways and dragged the mortally wounded priest into the brush. He cut through his larynx so he couldn't cry out. He kicked some dirt and gravel over the blood on the trail and walked on.

The murder of a priest on the royal staff made print and television news all over Spain. Some reports noted that he was Basque and had grown up in a little town called Olazgutía, and some did not. A spokesman for the Guardia Civil, which had jurisdiction, said they had no suspects or leads, and provided a phone line for anyone who might have information leading to arrest of the killer.

A stricken Juan Carlos appeared in the garden behind the royal palace and made a brief and somber statement to the press. "Queen Sofía and I and all who work here are devastated by this senseless act. Monsignor Jokin had not been with us very long, but he challenged our thinking and warmed our hearts. The authorities will bring whoever did this terrible thing to account in our system of criminal justice. We pray for the Monsignor's soul, for his family, and for his colleagues of many years at Universidad Navarra, where we first encountered his intellect, integrity, and talent. For me, this tragedy is deeply personal and hard for me to comprehend and accept. Monsignor Jokin was not only my trusted policy adviser and writer of speeches and policy papers related to the Crown. He had become my very good friend."

The king took no questions.

Luke had to calm the distraught mother of their child. "Ysolina, you are not responsible for this. You're not. It did not happen because you went to see him and told him what you did."

"How can you be sure?"

"They were bound to kill him. You just happened to talk to him first."

"But what if . . . "

He grasped her shoulders and held her apart until she looked at him. "Ysolina, there's only a handful of them. That bunch we saw the other night are the best they've got. You can take Enara and try to slip back into France, but you're a fugitive, and Peru's not going to offer any more boat rides. You're safer here with me."

That day he made the call to Paris. "Jimbo, it's me."

"Hey. What's up?"

"Time to get a move on, Colonel."

"Let me call you back."

On the stew-phone he did that right away. "Talk to me, Luke."

"A breakoff gang of *etarras* is planning to assassinate King Juan Carlos at the opening of the Guggenheim art museum in Bilbao in two weeks."

"Whoa. They broke off from who or what?"

"The leadership of Peru Madariaga."

"All right. Go on."

"Ysolina had established a line of communication with the king through a Basque priest who drafted speeches and position papers for him. The priest was subject to blackmail and coercion because he had been an occasional courier for ETA before joining the king's staff. Yesterday she urged him to warn Juan Carlos about the plot and convince him to cancel the appearance in Bilbao. He wouldn't have had time to do that. Right after that meeting the priest was found stabbed to death."

"That sounds to me like a problem for the Spaniards."

"It sure is. The Spaniards will have to be cavalry to the rescue, but we're out in front of them no matter how good they are. These guys have an unknown number of Plamya Flames and no shyness about using them. Madariaga swears he turned the offer down and doesn't know how this other bunch got them. But they did."

"Did he say where they came from?"

"Israelis."

Hopson made a sound of disgust. "Son of a bitch. I know how they got their hands on them. Roberto Escamilla."

"What?"

"The Mossad. I saw it in a cable from him when he decided you were either dead or turned. He thought a sweet way to pull them into a trap was to give them what they wanted."

"Well, *somebody* with the Outfit has to go around him in getting the Spaniards horsed up."

"Why not go through highest channels to warn the king off?"

"They'd launch them at the museum in the middle of a huge crowd. The Outfit says it wants to take more than a scalp or two off ETA. Well, the worst of them are concentrated right here."

"Is Madariaga one of the scalps?"

"Could be. He's acting strange. I think he's trying to protect his authority and position."

"Your wife there, is she all right with him going down?"

"She's solid, Jimbo. She's the mother of a nineteen-month-old and wants to be rid of all this. She gets it, believe me."

"Okay. Tell me what you're throwing, Koufax."

FORTY-THREE

Frank Gehry had flown in for the Pritzker Prize ceremonies and the lavish rollout of the Bilbao museum from Abu Dhabi, where another Guggenheim with his name on it was already in the works. The flight's ban of booze had been lifted as soon as they cleared the Emirates' air space, but he was glad to get where he could ring up room service for a bottle of single malt scotch and a bucket of ice. The Pritzker was going to Sverre Fehn, a deserving Norwegian, but the whole affair amounted to a two-week victory lap for Frank. The king would "inaugurate" the Museo's opening, a major coup for the Consorcio. Frank's wife Berta was flying in from the States in two days.

He put on a fresh suit, shirt, and tie, and buffed his shoes, eyeing the time. A limo would pick him up and carry him to a private dinner with the same people who had tried, years ago now, to convince him he could make that squashed old building into a museum worthy of his name. And the Guggenheim's.

Frank finished his second scotch, walked out of the posh apartment, and called up the elevator. He didn't have time to think it odd that the doors opened one floor beneath the penthouse; the elevator was ordinarily reserved. A good-looking couple stepped in with nods of greeting. The man, who moved beside him on his left, wore a blue linen blazer, tan trousers, and a shirt unbuttoned at the collar. The woman was a pretty redhead and her scent was a pleasure. Gehry spoke to Luke, not recognizing him from the construction site, and turned his head for some chat with the woman when something blunt and hard pressed against his left rib cage.

"It's a nine millimeter pistol, Mr. Gehry," said Luke. "Listen closely. The elevator moves fast. Your plans have changed. When we get to the lobby, we're going to walk across it, just the three of us, out for the evening. The gun is never going to be more than a few inches from you."

Frank's jaw dropped and he cried, "What in the world?"

"You're being kidnapped, Mister Gehry."

"Kidnapped? Oh my God, Berta."

"No one's going to harm your wife, sir," said Ysolina.

"Here we go," said Luke. "Straight across the lobby, and no theatrics. We're going to put you in the back seat of a car, I'm going to tip the valet, and then we drive away. If you try to fight or run, this is going to end badly."

The woman had hold of Frank's right arm, as if he were a dear ailing elder. Luke opened the right rear door of the Toyota that Jimbo had gotten the Outfit to provide, pushed Gehry inside, gave some pesetas to the young man who'd delivered their car to the valet stand, and slid under the steering wheel as Ysolina got in the passenger seat. They buckled up quickly and pulled hard on the belts.

"No need to try and jump out, Mister Gehry. It's got child protection locks. And you're not big or strong enough to overpower me from behind. I suggest you fasten your seat belt."

After a moment Frank said, "I can't find it."

"Well, look."

He skirted the limo and its gaping driver and came to the end of the hotel drive, where the two vans of *gudariak* were waiting to pinch them in front and back. On both of the nearest side streets, he saw armored SWAT team vehicles with their lights off.

"Hold on, sir," said Luke. Instead of turning, he gunned straight across two lanes, banged across the median, and with a screech of tires tore off the other way.

They zigzagged up streets away from the river, Ysolina keeping him on track. At the top of one of Bilbao's hills, he stopped with the hotel and not-yet-lit-up museum in sight in the rear-view mirror.

As the Civil Guards and other CNI agents anticipated, the *etarras* had not come out with their hands up. Spits of blue and yellow flame shot back and forth in the night. A ferocious gunfight was going on but would not last long.

"What's that I'm hearing?" said Frank. He tried to look around, but the seat belt prevented him.

"Just some fireworks," said Luke, driving on.

They cleared the suburbs of Bilbao and he kept driving on small roads south toward Vitoria. The tires popped fallen chestnuts on the empty country roads, and the headlights fell on the reds and yellows of autumn foliage. The early frost had nipped the yellow blooms of gorse, but their brambles crowded up against the roadsides. Luke had to look for places where Frank could step off from the road when he needed to piss. Luke accompanied him and maintained a courteous distance.

"If the idea of this is ransom," Frank said, "I can get you bankloads of money. Just let me go."

"In time," Luke said. "Just be patient."

"I can tell from your accent you're an American—who are you with? The separatists?"

"I'm with you."

Ysolina had opened the trunk while they were off under the culvert. She had put a blanket and pillow in the trunk, and they were waiting in the back seat when Frank got back in the car. She asked him if he wanted another bottle of water, and he said he did. He fingered the blanket as Luke drove on and said, "Young woman."

Ysolina looked back at him and said, "Yes?"

"Why are you a part of this?"

"Because I had to be."

Luke took roundabouts and tried to avoid towns but they had to pass through a few. Frank muttered to himself and at one point said, "I never met Picasso."

Luke and Ysolina looked at each other and laughed.

"Who are you to laugh? I know lots of famous people."

"I'm sure you do," Luke said.

"We wanted his *Guernica* for the opening of the Bilbao Guggenheim," Frank said. "It made such sense. It's never been displayed in the Basque Country. But word came back from Madrid that it couldn't travel from that little museum where they've got it beside the Prado. That's crazy, it travels all the time. Politics, if you ask me."

"I know," said Ysolina.

"How would you know?"

She hiked her shoulders. "I just know."

"Ah, so you're some kind of artiste kidnapper."

"Make of me what you will, Mister Gehry. Can I ask you something?"

"Sure. I love conversation, and you're all the company I got."

Luke and Ysolina traded looks, amused by his spunk. "I've seen some of your sketches," she said, turning toward him. "They should be in galleries, if they're not already. Why did you choose architecture?"

"There's more money in it," he said, and snickered. "I appreciate the compliment. I do. When most architects were treating me like Joe Idiot, I gravitated toward painters, sculptors. Michelangelo made that marble Virgin Mary into one sweet-looking babe. People forget he was a great architect as well. Saint Peter's Basilica in the Vatican, that's Michelangelo's, and he took that on when he was past seventy years old."

She asked, "Do you know of a painter named Marie Laurencin?"

"Yeah, I've seen some of her stuff. Lovely color but a little airy for my taste. That one called *Spanish Dancers* comes to mind."

"*Danseuses Espagnoles,*" she pronounced the French.

"It's okay. But it doesn't belong in the Musée de l'Orangerie. Swell-looking babes, I'm a fool for that, but she's got a dog and a horse in there. It's too busy. I couldn't get a building out of that."

Ysolina looked at Luke. "That's enough. Let's get it over with."

Frank was quiet for a moment then realized it was a joke. "A comedian, too. Up yours, doll." He grumbled and groaned as the night wore on. He finally pitched into a sleep of exhaustion and despair. Ysolina dozed as well. The sun was just up as Luke drove into a town that still slept.

Frank stirred, looked about, and said, "Where are we?"

"Guernica," Luke said.

"This is Guernica? Christ it's ugly."

"There wasn't much left after the Germans got through with it. When the Franco regime allowed the town to be built back, it was done cheap and they didn't hire the world's best architects."

"Guys like that are builders, not architects." Luke stopped the car in what appeared to be the center of town. In a park was a fenced-in trunk of what had once been a large old tree. "That's an odd-looking thing," Frank said.

Luke released the child protection locks and said, "Mister Gehry, this never happened. I apologize for your fright and inconvenience."

"So do I, sir," said Ysolina.

Luke said, "You can raise a row or keep it to yourself—it's up to you. If you want to know why this did but did not happen, your friends with the Consorcio can put you in touch with the Spanish

263

intelligence agency, the CNI, and they'll steer you to the right US officials to ask."

He reached over the seats and handed Frank the Outfit's mobile phone. "You can call your wife or anyone else with this. You're free to go."

Frank stared at them and erupted, "Well, is there a fucking address?"

Luke laughed. "Tell them to pick you up at the sacred oak in Guernica."

FORTY-FOUR

The Bilbao ambush of ETA's commandos took out eight of them. Three were killed, three wounded too badly to continue shooting, and two gave up. Civilians in the range of all those bullets were terrified but somehow none of them were hurt. But that was not the end of it. They had never planned to put all their bets on the Plamya Flames. There would be a shooter.

After the firefight and all the screaming headlines, a man wearing a light jacket climbed the stairs of a decrepit office and apartment building across the Nervión from the museum. He rapped on a door and a man inside growled a demand. *"Erregezale,"* the man supplied the password. "Fond of the king" in Basque.

Jale turned the deadbolt, removed the chain lock, and frowned in surprise. "I forgot to bring you a pizza," Peru said with a smile. He showed Jale the palms of both hands and with a continuing air of command walked inside.

He looked at the threadbare furniture and the scoped Dragunov sniper rifle handy on the sofa. He walked to the window where Jale had built a foundation with concrete blocks to support the rifle and hold firm his aim. Peru said, "You carry those up the stairs?"

"They got here," Jale replied.

Peru looked out at the enormous silvery twists of the museum and the platform and podium where the king would be speaking. Across the museum from the river, out in front of it, was a large multi-colored sculpture of bedded flowers developed for the occasion by an American named Jeff Koons. It had the form of a dog sitting with its ears perked and was named *Puppy.*

"You like the flowered dog?" said Peru.

Jale grunted in disdain.

Peru said, "It's a long way over there but you're well-positioned, you have that scope, and you're a terrific shot. You can do it."

"I'm supposed to thank you?" Jale snarled. "First you disappear, and then the American and that bitch you're married to—"

Peru raised his hands again. "I know. They suckered us well."

"You're finished, I guess you know that."

"Of course. But you saved my life that day outside Cambo-les-Bains, and it occurred to me that I've never thanked you. So, thank you, Jale."

The big man started another sneer, then realized that through force of habit and years of being an inferior he had neglected to frisk Peru, and he had left his Glock on the dinette table. Jale lunged for his gun, but Peru had already drawn the silenced Luger. With deadly patience he shot Jale three times. He pulled from a trouser pocket the cloth he'd brought with him, wiped the gun down thoroughly, placed it beside the other one on the table, which was dusted with bread crumbs, and closed the door on that long chapter of his life.

ORBAINAK

SCARS

FORTY-FIVE

MAY 1998

As the movie ended and the screens on the plane went blank Luke tended the blankets of his sleeping companions and considered the many changes in their lives. Because of Ysolina's actions in Bilbao, she had been granted amnesty by the interior ministry of Prime Minister José María Aznar. Luke had regained his US identity and passport. With a classified nod and wink the Outfit had complimented him for his work in France and Spain and accepted his explanation that the *etarras* had robbed him of the dollars for the weapons at the warehouse in St. Jean-de-Luz. Higher-ups in the Outfit sent word they would get back to Luke if they could use his services again. It didn't bother him that they never did. A couple of the private security companies approached him. He told them he wasn't interested.

The three of them had lived together in the guest cottage of André Roumanille long enough to satisfy the residency requirements of the French. They pulled together their long-form birth certificates, months of utility receipts from her apartment on Rue Jacob for more evidence of her legal residency, and had blood tests and examinations performed by French doctors. Luke had to provide a notarized affidavit called *attestation tenant lieu de certificat de célibat de non-remarriage*. It certified he was not already married and their marriage would be recognized in the States. An official at the US consulate in Toulouse signed it.

To the simple ceremony at the city hall in Pau they each had to bring two witnesses. She enlisted her aunt Tía Aloña and cousin Jokiñe, and Luke asked André Roumanille. André and Tía Aloña were such an item that Luke thought they'd wind up living together if they ever could agree where it might be. Luke couldn't ask Pascal, who was now expatriated in Istanbul. So Luke asked Jimbo Hopson, who surprised him and said there was nothing he'd rather do than get out of Paris in the heat of summer for such an occasion in the Pyrenees. André and Jimbo had a rare old time, trading war stories. The brief wedding ceremony took place on July 4, 1998. Luke told Ysolina it guaranteed he would never forget their anniversary.

Then Luke, Ysolina, and Enara journeyed back to the consulate in Toulouse and jumped through the hoops to ensure that the child was recognized and embraced as a US citizen born in France. On her fourth birthday they set small flags of Spain, France, the United States, and an *ikurriña* amid the candles. Luke had found an honest way to start making a living. He caught on with an American company that offered horse vacations at extravagant prices in Europe and a few places beyond. A gelding and a mule, a western stock saddle, a packsaddle, riggings, and panniers, and Luke was good to go. The work was seasonal but the wages were splendid. The company even paid for a used pickup and trailer. His beat was the Pyrenees, mostly the Spanish side. He saw some wondrous country. And he had scored a couple of gigs as a backup guide and campfire cook in the Dordogne. His French was improving, though Ysolina said his accent was just murder. There was time to fix that. They were both only forty-one.

The pilot announced that they were beginning their descent to the Houston intercontinental airport. Luke woke Ysolina, who sat up with a yawn. She had found a hair stylist who gradually returned her hair to its natural color—brown and blond with some highlights of red, and now showing touches of gray. Luke's beard was gone, and only Enara missed it. Ysolina stirred Enara and searched in her bag for her hairbrush. Their child woke up cranky. Ysolina removed Enara's thumb from her mouth and set about brushing her hair. On the flight from Madrid Luke had worked hard on managing his fear of being on an airplane, but when the wheels jerked on landing Ysolina gripped his hand. For the first time in five years he was back on his native soil.

Because of Ysolina's tourist visa they endured slow-moving lines of customs and baggage inspection. They had a quick bite to eat in the airport. Enara's eyes were wide at the sights and sounds around her, and she took some interest in her first grilled-cheese sandwich. They caught a shuttle to the car rental and set out in the mid-sized Chevrolet. Traffic in Houston had always intimidated Luke, and on the enormous swaths of freeway his excess of caution had a couple of jerks leaning on their horns. Ysolina looked at all the stores, restaurants, mega-churches, and seas of car lots with amazement. Enara did the same in her back-seat safety contraption.

They reached Interstate 10 and cleared the suburbs eventually, bound west through the green coastal plain for San Antonio and points beyond. Because the girls wanted or needed to stop often, the trip to Salt Lick took over three hours. They were jet-lagged for sure, but still in a daze of ongoing motion. When Luke pulled off the country two-lane and stopped, after a moment he said it was customary for the person in the passenger seat to get out and open the gate, then close it after the vehicle passed through.

"Oh," said Ysolina. As he drove past she gave him a military salute.

The ranch looked good. It had been raining. The bluestem and grama stood tall, and the spring-fed creek ran over a paved crossing. Ysolina gazed about, and in Spanish Enara kept up a commentary on the horses, sheep, cattle, and *esos otros animales.* He told her they were mohair goats.

When they were out of the car Ysolina and Enara gaped at the big white house. Luke had been anxious to get his family across the Atlantic before Amona was gone. Wearing her black dress of mourning—a show of ritual grief she had sustained for sixty-two years—she came out on the porch to greet them, under the watchful care of the in-house health-care aide and new cook. Luke led them up and embraced her frailty. He made the introductions, they went inside, and soon Amona, Ysolina, and Enara were all chattering in Euskera.

Luke smiled, watching them and hearing their exotic language, and eased outside with Lydia Burgoa. She was not a pretty woman, but she was tall, rawboned, and assertive. She wore boots, jeans, and an old plaid shirt rolled up to her elbows. As they walked toward the barn she said, "I'm glad your wife speaks English."

Luke nodded. "Kind of a different accent."

"I understand her."

In the barn she introduced him to Ramón Gutierrez, a slim dark man with short black hair and a thin line of mustache. The foreman had been fixing something on a saddle. He shook hands with Luke in a polite shy way. Chat soon faltered, and Luke said he'd let him get back to work. The foreman smiled. "Taking my time," he said. "It's in the shade."

Lydia asked if he wanted to go for a ride and see his brother's grave.

"Of course," Luke said.

They got in an old open Jeep, which she bounced through a near pasture, banging gears. "The place looks good," Luke told her.

"Yeah, it was a good spring, but we never get enough rain." She stopped the Jeep and they stood before Simon's grave and simple marker, chiseled in the native limestone. There was a nice breeze.

Lydia said, "We buried him the old way, how he wanted. We hitched a team of horses to a wagon, saddled his favorite horse, tied her up behind the wagon, and we walked along behind, with one friend of his leading the harnessed team, another playing the fiddle. We put a clean new flag on his coffin and buried him with it. Your grandmother said she also wanted one of those Basque flags, I forget the name . . ."

"*Ikurriña,*" said Luke. He was surprised and moved that his brother wanted that. Luke thought Simon had gladly been melted in America's pot.

"State I was in," Lydia said, "I couldn't look for one here, if there ever was one, and you sure couldn't find it in Salt Lick or Comfort. San Antonio either, I bet. So I just told her one was on there, thinking she couldn't see it anyway. With help she made that walk, though we put her on the wagon seat going back to the house. Reckon she knew I lied?"

"She probably would have let you know."

They climbed back in the Jeep and headed for higher pastures. "Ramón has been a godsend," Lydia said. "I've never seen such a good hand."

"No family?"

"None he speaks of."

Ramón looked to be in his fifties. Luke said, "If he stays on with you, make sure he gets rewarded. Lots of landowners don't do that."

"I will."

Luke abruptly started laughing.

"What?" she said.

"I was just imagining Amona's reaction when she found out her ranch was going to be managed by a Mexican from Coahuila."

Lydia stomped the clutch and brake, and they sat and laughed a while. Afterward Lydia said, "You know that offer still stands."

"Oh, those two of mine back there, I don't think they could make the adjustment. Neither could I."

"Just keep us in mind."

"How's Andrea doing?" he asked about his niece.

"She's going great guns in Lubbock."

"Lubbock? What's she doing there?"

"Going to Texas Tech. You weren't around enough to get to know her much, but she kind of thought you hung the moon. Soon as such a thing occurred to her, she started saying she wanted to go to Texas Tech like her Uncle Luke did. She's got a pickup, an apartment, a part-time job at a Goodyear store, and a boyfriend I hope she don't bring home. But she's hitting those books, making her grades."

Luke was moved. "What's her major?"

"Range management. What else?"

FORTY-SIX

Six months later they were back in San Sebastián, in the same house where they'd known the first rush of their love affair and had been hauled handcuffed and hooded down the stairs. The neighbors were courteous now—word seemed to have gotten around—and after watching Luke's efforts to bring some order to the overgrown garden and grounds, a few came over to introduce themselves. The loss of Barkilu and how he died hurt them badly in that place, and they were in the market for a collie pup. Luke was wearing a T-shirt and a pair of khaki shorts, and at the moment his daughter sat on the floor applying blue polish to his toenails. He was glad he had clipped them recently. Ordinarily, his toes in his beach sandals wouldn't attract much attention.

Amona had not quite made it to a hundred, but what a brave life she had. Her second great granddaughter had hair the color of ripe wheat, down to her shoulder blades now, that in time would probably shade more toward brown, like her mother's. Luke thought Enara looked like Ysolina, who said she looked more like him. Ysolina had been invited to meet King Juan Carlos, but just the thought of it made her squirm. She was perched on a dining-room stool under one of her Marie Laurencin prints, which they had brought down from storage in Paris. She wore a tank top and shorts and sandals for the beach. Reading a newspaper, she said, "Papa, listen to this."

"War and famines and pestilence?"

"No, for once. New Year's Night, the Millennium, they're going to wrap fireworks all around the Eiffel Tower. They're expecting two or three million people. We have to go see that."

"I'm game. Cowgirl here can ride on my shoulders."

When the nail polish had dried they locked up the house and set off through the park of Palacio Miramar and the raised *paseo* along Playa de la Concha. Watching the bay's waves part for the two beaches, Luke thought again that San Sebastián was his favorite place in the world. Paris was the only one that came close.

He held Ysolina's hand and laughed and pointed at the entrance to the old quarter. "They've made the old station and jail of the Guardia Civil into an aquarium. Look, they've put up the sign."

They watched Enara skip ahead, making short work of a cone of pistachio gelato, her favorite. Then the obnoxious whine came at them like a hornet, but a big one. There weren't supposed to be any motorcycles on the footpath. The noise was coming up on them from the left, and he tried to pull Ysolina with him to the right. But she fought free and tried to lurch toward their daughter. One shot in the back of her head, no more than a couple of feet away. He saw the halo of blood, heard screams of their daughter, and then looked at the bike.

Both the driver and the shooter wore black-visored helmets. They looked like skinny punk kids. The shooter on back turned and stared at them, proud of avenging the treason. On his helmet was the ETA emblem Luke had seen in the radical rockers' bar in Pamplona, the snake coiled around an axe.

He cried out on seeing how bad it was and ran to catch Enara and keep her away. Then came a crush of people wanting to help, none of them knowing how. Then sirens and people asking him questions he couldn't answer. The EMS crew had appeared in what seemed an instant. The paramedics worked fast and did all they could. Wearing their red berets, Basque street cops started moving the gawkers back. One said something about *decencia*. Luke was glad the paramedics covered her. He looked past the strangers at his love's lightly freckled calves, her feet and ankles, and the two webbed toes on each foot that inspired teasing children to call her a *lamia*. How did she say it, *spirit beauties of the wild*.

A plainclothes cop, a detective, asked if anyone had been with her. The scarface with the blue toenails, Luke thought. He held Enara and sat on the steps down to the beach. "Oh, Mama," she wept. "Mama, please."

FORTY-SEVEN

MARCH 2004

Luke and Enara lived on the outskirts of Périguex, the town in the Dordogne, southwestern France, where he and Ysolina had stopped for lunch and bought the little wood toy for an infant not yet born. Neighbors and shopkeepers teased him that he was never going to pronounce the name of their town correctly, but when the hijacked passenger jets brought down the towers in New York, blasted the Pentagon, and crashed in Pennsylvania, the French folk in Périguex had laid bouquets of flowers at the front of the house and the barn of the American's horse stable.

Luke kept a dozen saddle horses, most of them paints and grays, a big black mule called Stagger Lee, and their new collie Gus. He ran his own small company now, boarding some horses in the cold months and in the warm ones guiding clients to partnering bed and breakfasts and the sights of a lovely country of canyons, white stone cliffs, broad pretty rivers, and caves where the ancients painted. He settled there because the terrain called back the Texas ranch where he grew up.

Tía Aloña and her granddaughter Jokiñe, now married and pregnant, had gathered all the clan they could at a villa on the slope of Monte Urgull. André Roumanille no longer drove much, but Tía Aloña had brought him to the affair. They had the party catered, at what must have been great expense, by the chefs at Akelaré. They hired the Basque songwriter and singer Ruper Ordorika, whom Luke had learned about when he was living in that run-down house outside Bayonne. Ordorika was a good electric guitar player and brought a fine band with him. Luke almost understood some of the Basque lyrics. Ordorika sang a handful of songs in English, among them Luke's request from the Stones, "Wild Horses."

At first Enara had lashed out and cried at having to go back, as she put it, to that place that killed her mother. Two youths from the Deusto barrio of Bilbao had been convicted of Ysolina's murder and sentenced to fifty years. At the party Enara rolled her eyes at the excess—a new trick she'd picked up from her onetime nanny and ongoing piano teacher Sybil—but she was a beautiful child, hair to her waist, and for the party she wore a new lavender dress with the shortest skirt she'd had since she was a baby, and she couldn't help but respond to these girls and boys who embraced her as kin. Their shrieks carried over the singing and guitars and drums of the band. Luke danced with her once, just them on the floor. Ordorika sang for them a Waylon Jennings waltz. The one about a song sung blue, helps me remember you.

Enara's birthday and party had been on February 23, 2004. Afterward they had stayed at the family's country place amid the apple orchards outside Mondragón. In their Volvo Luke had showed her St. Jean-de-Luz, the graveyard of the English Coldstream Guards outside Bayonne, and the canyons above Ezkaroze, before he yielded to her groans about scenery. The house had a television and satellite dish, which helped her keep the beast of boredom away.

One day he was sacked out on a bed reading when she came into the room with a haunted expression and said, "Papa."

Early that morning, March 11, three bombs had exploded in a train as it slowed to enter Atocha station in the heart of Madrid. Seconds later, four more devastated another train about five hundred yards away. One hundred ninety-one people died, sixteen hundred were injured, and the Spanish people gained a new watchword of terror, 11-M, the same way Americans were consumed by 9-11. The bombings took place on a Thursday, four days before a national election.

The People Party's prime minister, José María Aznar, expected an easy win over his Socialist opponent, José Luis Zapatero. But Aznar's approval ratings had suffered over his commitment of Spanish troops to the war in Iraq led by the United States. Though the Spanish army had only suffered eleven fatalities, the military's presence in Iraq had become a heated issue in the campaign. Choosing to ignore it, Aznar had run largely on a claim of decimating ETA.

Now his Minister of the Interior accused ETA of the 11-M atrocities with fury. Aznar called editors of the country's major newspapers, asking them to help stir public outrage, and in another call he told his opponent, Zapatero, that ETA's guilt was certain. Counter-terrorism agents had already planned to carry out high-profile raids against ETA on March 12, the last day of campaigning. A million people were in the streets of Madrid demanding arrests. The protest stretched miles in the rain, an unbroken stream of umbrellas. The US State Department lent its official voice to the clamor that ETA was to blame.

Luke no longer had access to classified intelligence, but Jimbo Hopson told him that in sorting through remains of the explosions, a police officer in Madrid found an athletic bag containing twenty-two pounds of Goma-2 explosives, nails and screws, and wires attached to a mobile phone. The politicos saw that as absolute proof ETA was the guilty party. But when a bomb squad defused the device, a chip in it led police to a Madrid phone and copy shop owned by a Moroccan man. More arrests of Moroccans followed. Spanish intelligence leaked reminders that soldiers had been ambushed and killed outside Baghdad. The killers had posed for photographs while standing over the Spaniards' bodies, photos that moved around the jihadist websites. A leak to the press accused the jihadists of paying for the bombs by selling hashish.

Spanish and American agents were embittered by allegations they had created a lie, a sham, to throw the election to Aznar. Some people would go to their graves convinced that it had been a joint operation of the Moroccans and ETA, and through luck and blunder the Basques had gotten away with it. But four days after the bombs in the train stations exploded, an unprecedented flood of voters swamped the polls—a seventy-seven percent turnout, many of them young people who had never voted before—and Aznar was booted out as prime minister. José Luis Zapatero condemned the war in Iraq in his first address as prime minister and said he was ordering the Spanish troops home.

Luke could not believe the explosions and the seething public anger were good for the psychological health of his daughter. He loaded the car with their clothes and her toys and favorite CD, Aesop Rock's *Bazooka Tooth*. But first he wanted to show her Bilbao and see for himself.

The grimy, smog-laden city he'd known was gone, at least the part of it along the Río Nervión. Propelled by Frank Gehry and the Guggenheim Foundation, the Consorcio of public-private leaders had pulled it off. Sleek office towers with well-groomed lawns stood nearby. Beneath a stylish pedestrian bridge the Nervión no longer stank. One-time slums had become some of the glitziest and priciest real estate in Europe. The ever-loyal *New York Times* saw in Gehry's building the famous photograph of Marilyn Monroe in high heels on a heating vent: "It is mobile, fluid, material, mercurial, fearless, radiant and as fragile as a newborn child. . . . . And when the impulse strikes, it likes to let its dress fly up in the air." He was praised for creating the architectural masterpiece of the century but chided in some quarters for letting his ego overpower the works of art inside. A young Basque woman wrote an influential op-ed scoffing at the notion that Americans had rescued Euskadi's largest city. The old quarter and other barrios were about as grim as Luke recalled.

It was a bright sunny day when Luke and Enara stood staring at the sculptor Koon's *Puppy,* which got a laugh from her. It had not been intended as a permanent exhibit, but it was so popular the landscape architects had to find a way to keep flowers in bloom year-round. Around back, on the side of the river, people walked under the sculpture of a vast long-legged spider. Luke and his daughter stared at the galleries of titanium, which gleamed silver then almost some shade of blue in a mirror of the scudding clouds. "Wow," Enara said.

"I built some of that," he told her.

"You built *that?*"

"Well, just a tiny piece of it. Your mother helped save it. And people inside it. And the king of Spain."

"She did?"

"She sure did. I'll tell you about it someday. Just keep that curled up with you when you're missing her. I know that's all the time." Her lower lip quivered. "What do you think of the museum?" he said, trying to head off her tears.

"I think," she said, pondering, "that it looks like a bunch of sardine cans and lids that somebody squashed all together."

Luke laughed. "I wish Mr. Gehry was standing here."

"Who?" she said, pleased with her quick recovery and his response.

"The architect, the man who imagined and designed it. Can't you see a great tall sailing ship? Or a huge silver whale?"

"No," she said in that tone of voice when she thought he was teasing her again. "I like it, though."

He paused with his hands in his pockets, reflecting. Jimbo Hopson had taken his retirement from the Outfit and was growing blueberries, of all things, near his Louisiana hometown, Bossier City. Pascal Seguines got out of the game before the game caught up with him and spoke highly of his new home, Istanbul. The Outfit sacked Roberto Escamilla. The California Cuban was now employed by a Washington think tank and could be seen and heard expounding on foreign policy and national security on cable news shows in the States, if you cared for those things. Luke had heard rumors that Peru was in Belfast, São Paulo, and the odd one, Penzance. They'd run him down someday. Or they wouldn't.

I haven't done much with my life, he thought, but I didn't kill a one of them, either side. Or maybe I did, the only one that counted. He blinked at something in his eyes and reached for his daughter's hand, as if she was a little girl again. "Come on, sugar. Let's go have a look."

This novel began as little more than a reading interest three decades ago. At the beginning all I knew of the Basques was about the running of the bulls in Pamplona, and as a youth I read Hemingway's *The Sun Also Rises.* I quickly learned that the mother lode of information about the Basques in English is the University of Nevada Press at Reno. Their titles led me to an American stylist, Robert Laxalt, and his lyrical memoir, *Sweet Promised Land,* and many novels about French Basques and descendants who came to the American West.

Then one day in the late 1980s I was shopping for dinner in an Austin, Texas, deli, and a young man working the counter suggested a cheese that he said came from the Basque Country. I told him of my interest in the Basques, and he said that his ancestors came from *el País Vasco,* the Spanish Basque country. He and I had lunch another day, and he told me about his family and their flight to Texas from the Mexican Revolution. I subsequently learned more from a bartender, my hair cutter, and a beautiful woman who was introduced to me as Basque. But in a real way this novel was spawned by a purchase of a wedge of sheep-milk cheese.

I could not have written this book without University of Nevada Press nonfiction titles that include the *Basque-English Dictionary* by Gorka Aulestia, *English-Basque Dictionary* by Aulestia and Linda White, *Basque Violence* by Joseba Zulaika, *Basque Politics* by William H. Douglas, *Amerikanuak* by Douglas and Jon Bilbao, *A Book of the Basques* by Rodney Gallop, *The Witches' Advocate: Basque Witchcraft and the Spanish Inquisition* by Gustav Hennigsen, *A View from the Witch's Cave: Folktales of the Pyrenees* edited and collected by Luis de Barandiarán Irizar and José Miguel de Barandiarán, and *The Basques: The Franco Years and Beyond* by Robert B. Clark, as well as Clark's *The Basque Insurgents: ETA, 1952-1980* (University of Wisconsin).

Other useful sources for me have been Mark Kurlansky's *The Basque History of the World* (Knopf Canada), *We Saw Spain Die: Foreign Correspondents in the Spanish Civil War* by Paul Preston (Skyhorse), *Voices Against Tyranny: Writing of the Spanish Civil War* edited by John Miller (Scribner), and *Guernica: The Crucible of World War II* by Gordon Thomas and Max Morgan Witts (Scarborough House).

After I started earnest work on the novel I chanced on a remarkable book about ETA's assassination of the ailing Franco's fascist heir apparent, *Operation Ogro: The Execution of Admiral Luis Carrero Blanco* by Julen Agirre (Quadrangle/New York Times.) I thought I knew the three major characters, but then I came to a grinding halt. I knew I hadn't given them enough strength of *story*. The Basque pages dwelled unexamined in a box in my mother's old cedar chest for the next fifteen years. On reopening that box and returning to the novel, I realized that the Basque Country had changed in a dramatic way since my wife and I journeyed through both Spanish and French provinces for several weeks in 1988. The chancy and dangerous construction of the Guggeheim Museum in Bilbao offered the added plot line I thought I needed. My primary sources for detailing that grandiose endeavor were three remarkably detailed publications compiled by the Harvard Graduate School of Design: "The Vision of a Guggenheim Museum in Bilbao," "Managing the Construction of the Museo Guggenheim Bilbao," and "An Evaluation of the Cladding Materials," by Katie Cacace, Marita Nikaki, and Anna Stefanidou.

This is a work of historical fiction loosely based on fact. It would be disingenuous to claim I plucked the characters of Spain's King Juan Carlos I and the acclaimed American architect Frank Gehry out of thin air. In *Time,* the *Guardian,* and many other publications I learned much about the bravura and political skill of the Spanish monarch. For Frank Gehry's background, flavor of speech, and public persona I studied the documentary *Sketches of Frank Gehry* filmed by his friend the director and actor Sydney Pollock, and *Conversations with Frank Gehry* by the arts critic Barbara Isenberg (Knopf).

For an understanding of the horrendous bombings of the Madrid train station on March 11, 2003, and its political aftermath, I am indebted to Lawrence Wright's August 2004 *New Yorker* article "The Terror Web." Other friends were especially important. Rick Pratt helped me develop the character of Luke Burgoa. Cecilia Ballí gave me insight into the character of Ysolina Madariaga. Jim Hawes and Howard Hart advised me on the tradecraft of espionage. The editor of my first novel, Scott Lubeck, long ago urged me to take on this one. My friends and writing peers Tom Zigal, David Wilkinson, and Christopher Cook gave me many frank readings and suggestions, as did my friend and agent David McCormick—my longtime best editor. An outside reader of TCU Press helped me sharpen and streamline the tale, and I'm grateful for the belief in the book of Dan Williams and the editing of Kathy Walton at TCU Press, the striking cover illustration of Preston Thomas of Cadence Design, the frontispiece map and graphics by my friend Jim Anderson, and the production of the Press's Melinda Esco and marketing of Rebecca Allen.

When my wife Dorothy Browne finally saw these pages, she exclaimed, "I've been to all these places!" Indeed she has, and this past summer we were able to share some of them with our daughter Lila, son-in-law Greg, and granddaughter Isabelle Wilson. For the first time I saw the Museo Guggenheim Bilbao I had been imagining from the ground up. It is an astonishment to behold, within and without, and it took the lead in the transformation of Bilbao. In 2011 ETA declared a "definitive end to armed activity," and though no further amnesties have been granted, and forced exiles have not been allowed to return, the peace has held. On March 17, 2017, ETA announced plans to forsake violence for good. On my family's voyage I found that San Sebastián remains my favorite city, and I treasure the Basque Country as much as I did way back when.

Austin, Texas
March 27, 2017

Jan Reid's highly praised books include his novel *Comanche Sundown*, his biography of Texas governor Ann Richards *Let the People In*, his memoir of Mexico *The Bullet Meant For Me*, and *The Improbable Rise of Redneck Rock*. Making his home in Austin, Reid has been a leading contributor to *Texas Monthly* for over forty years.